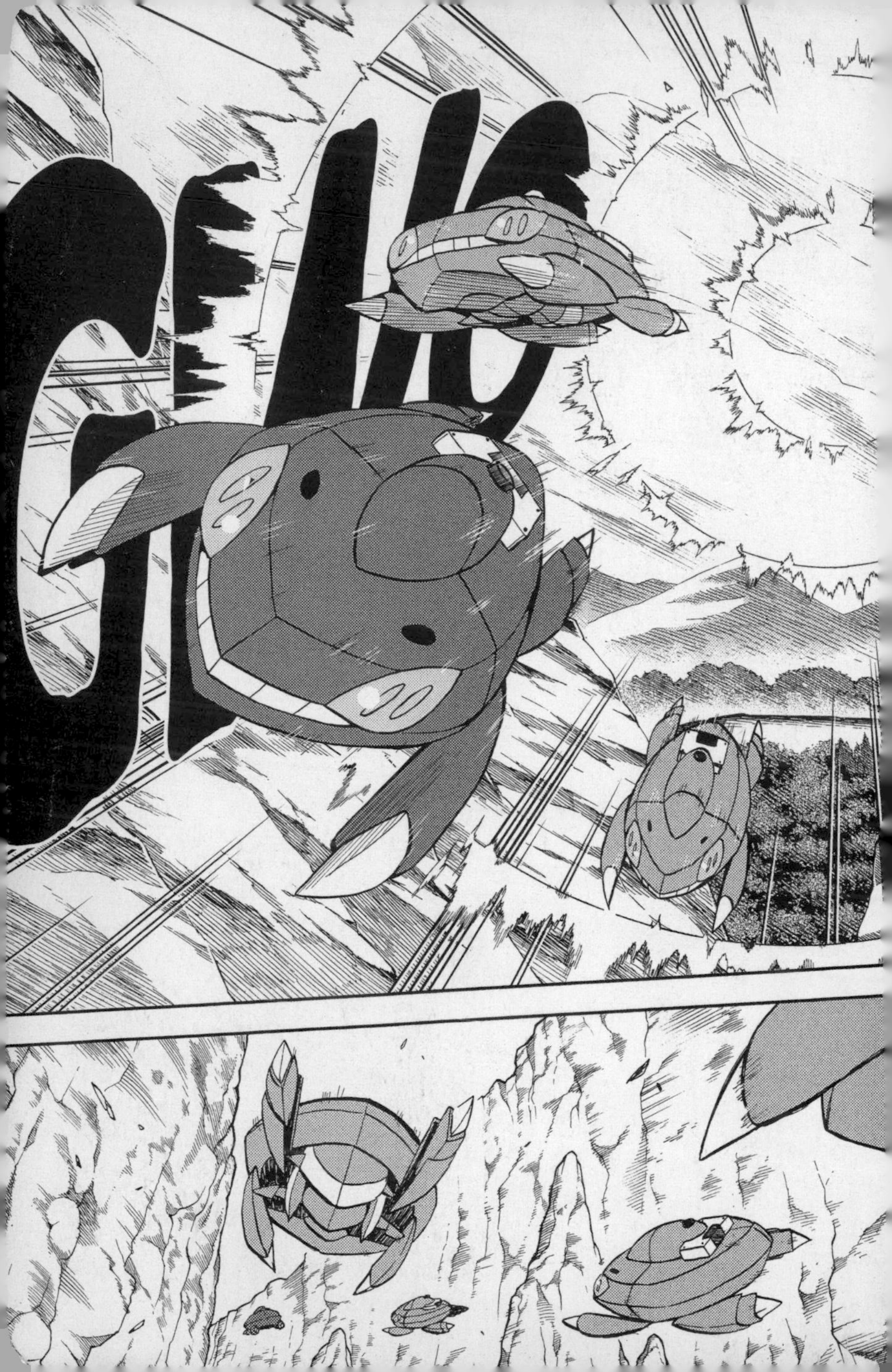

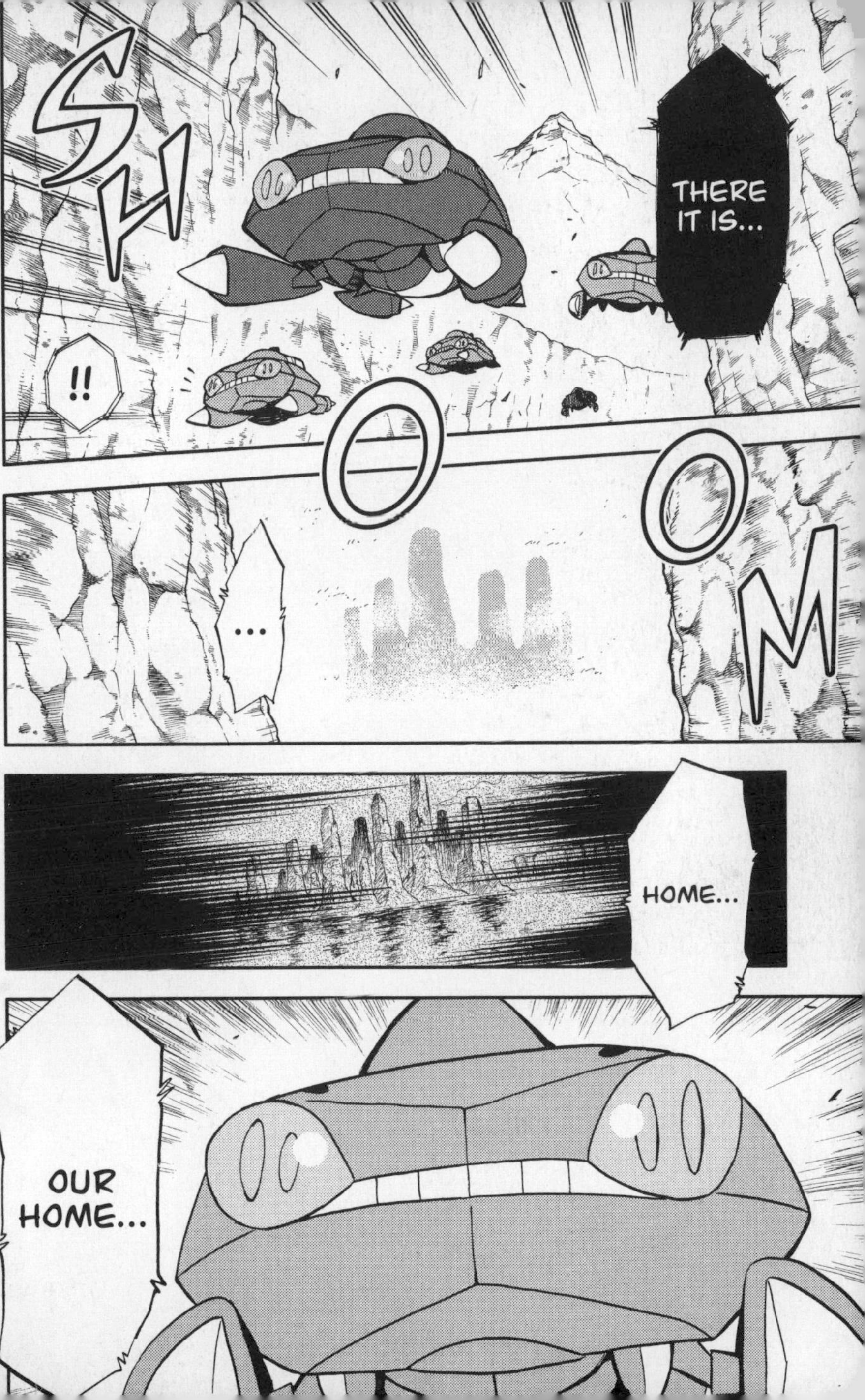
THERE IT IS...
SH
!!
OOOM
...
HOME...
OUR HOME...

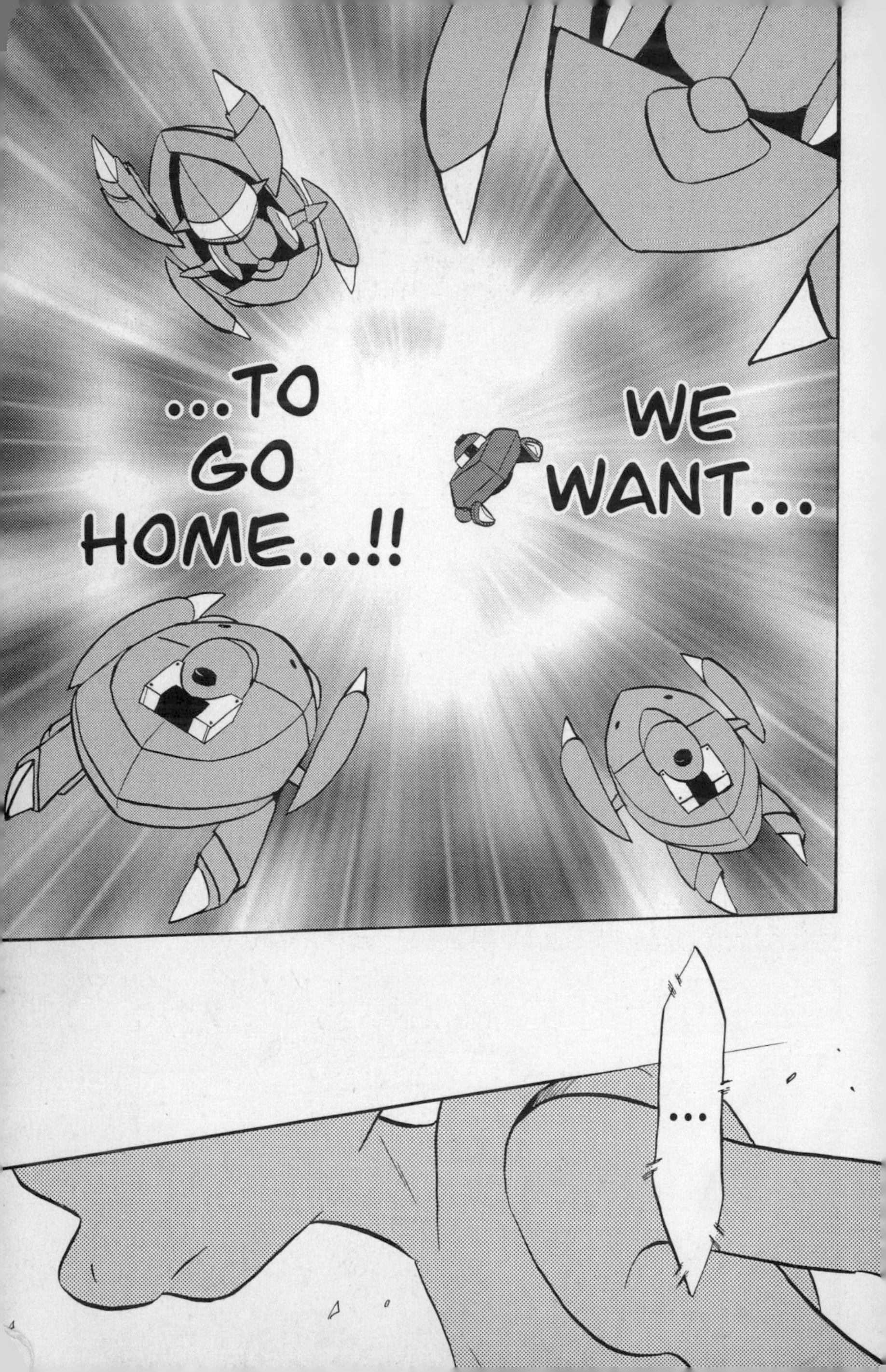
WE WANT...
...TO GO HOME...!!
...

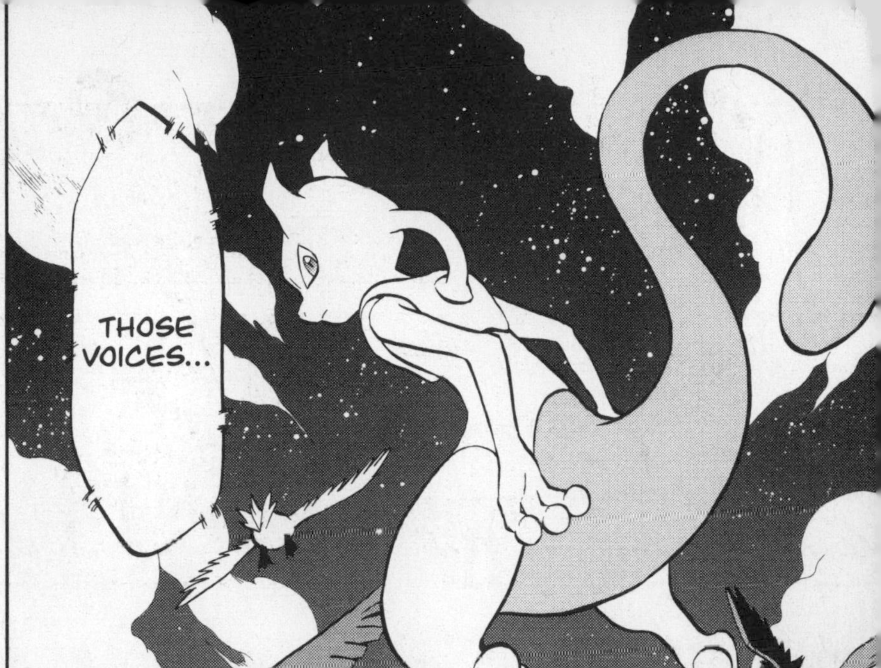
THOSE VOICES...
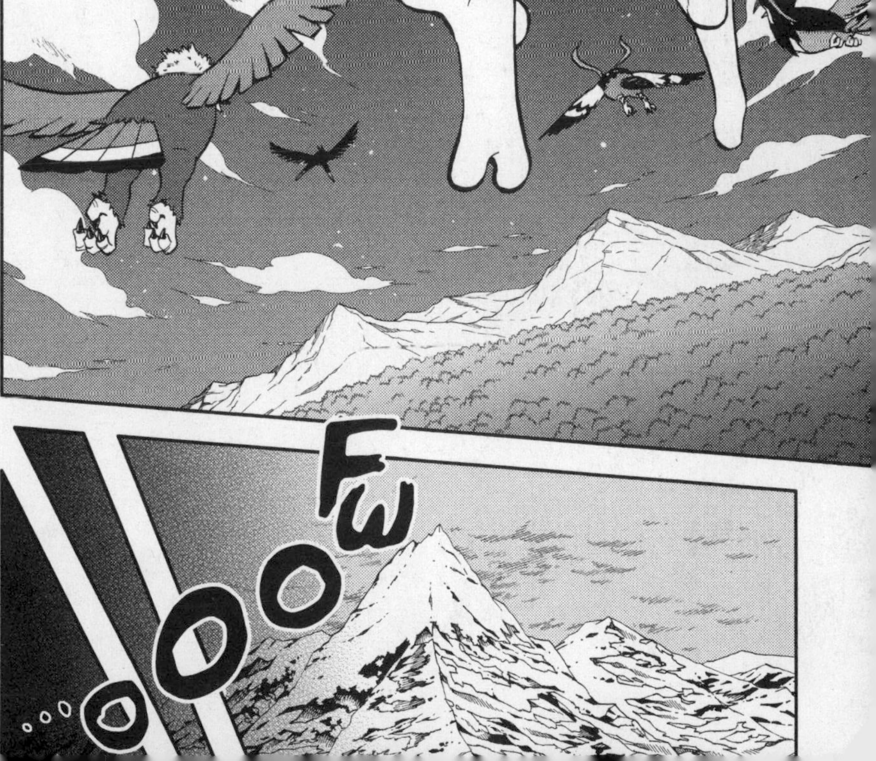
FWOOOO...

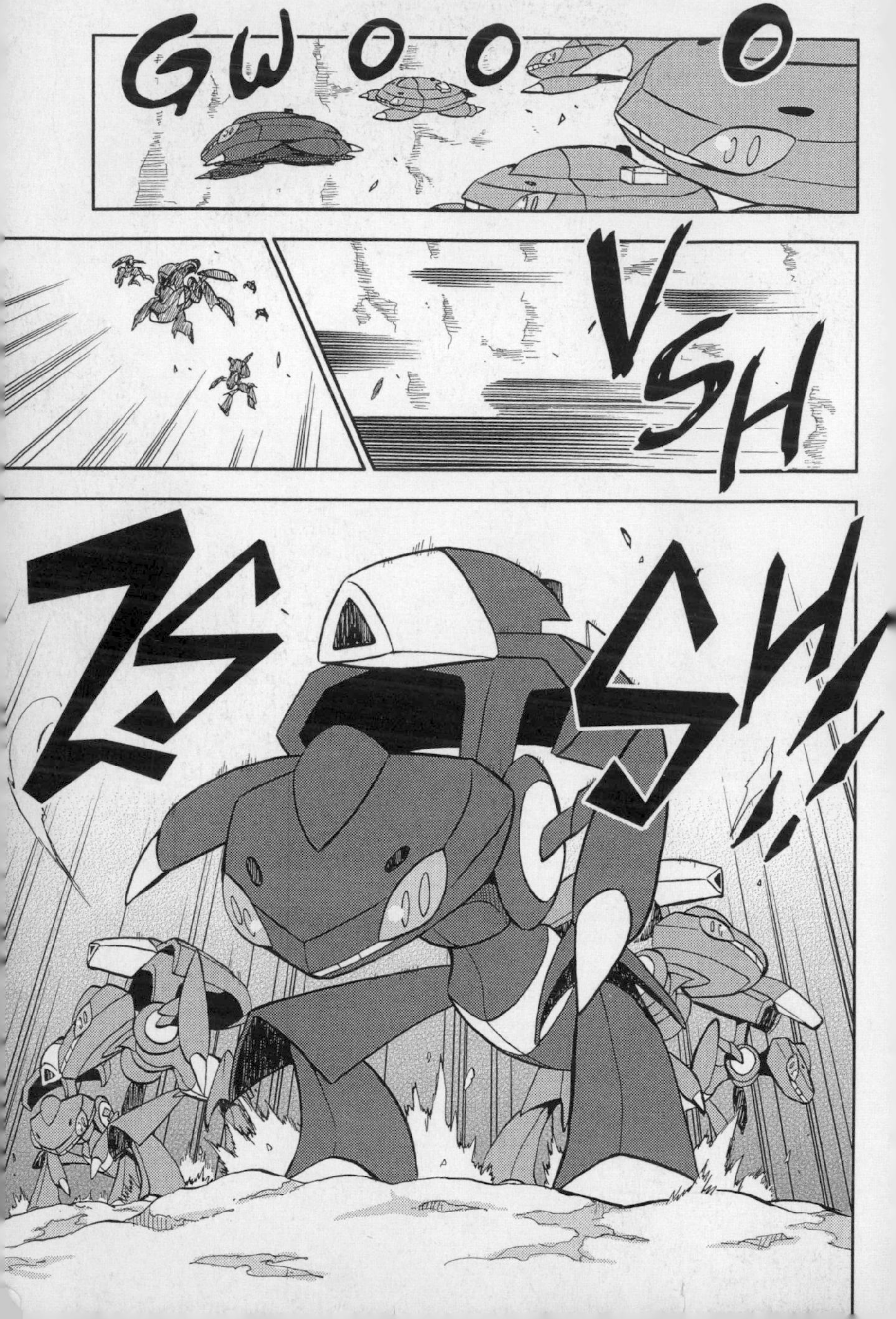
GWOOOO
VSH
ZSSH!!

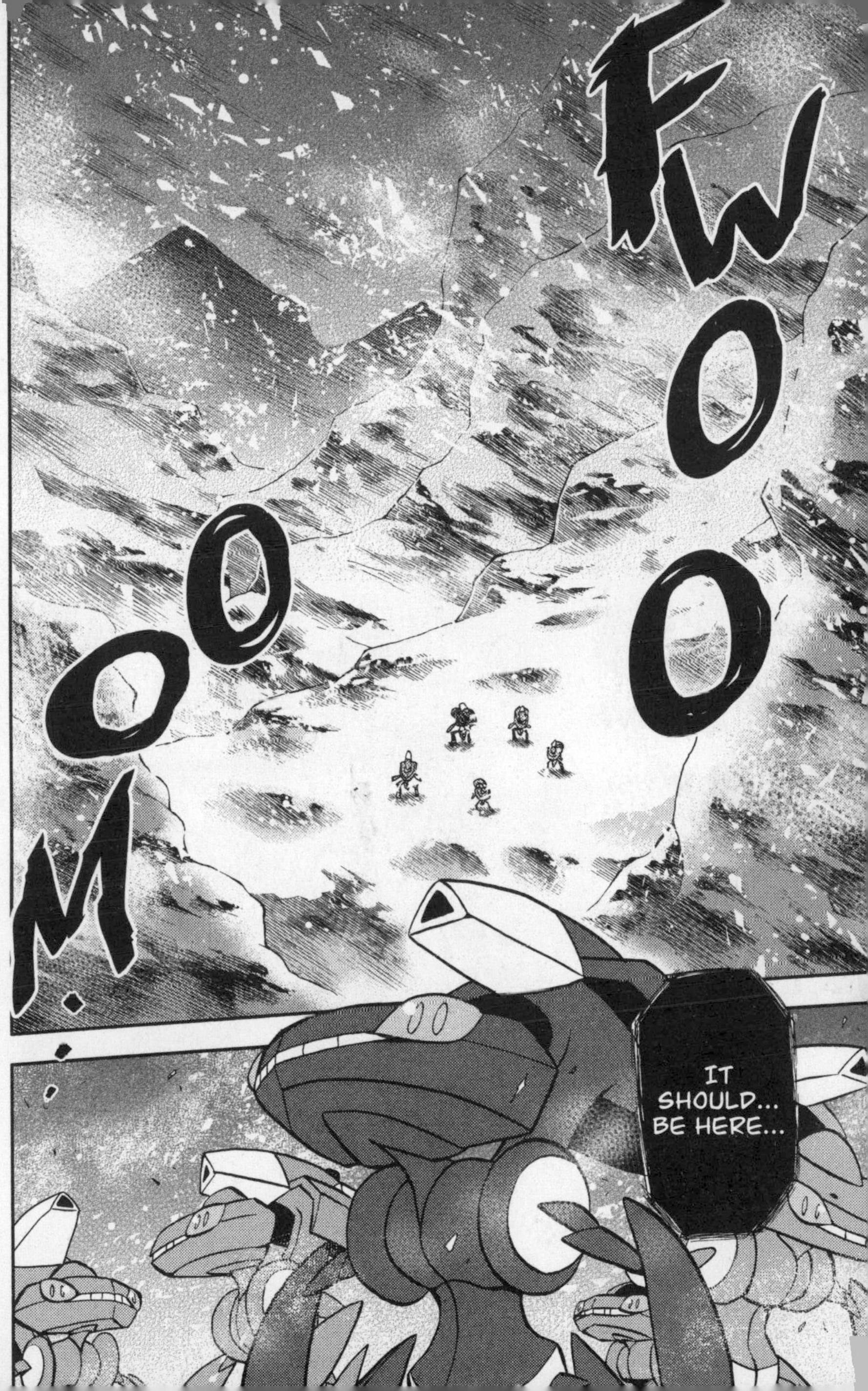
FWOOOOM
IT SHOULD... BE HERE...

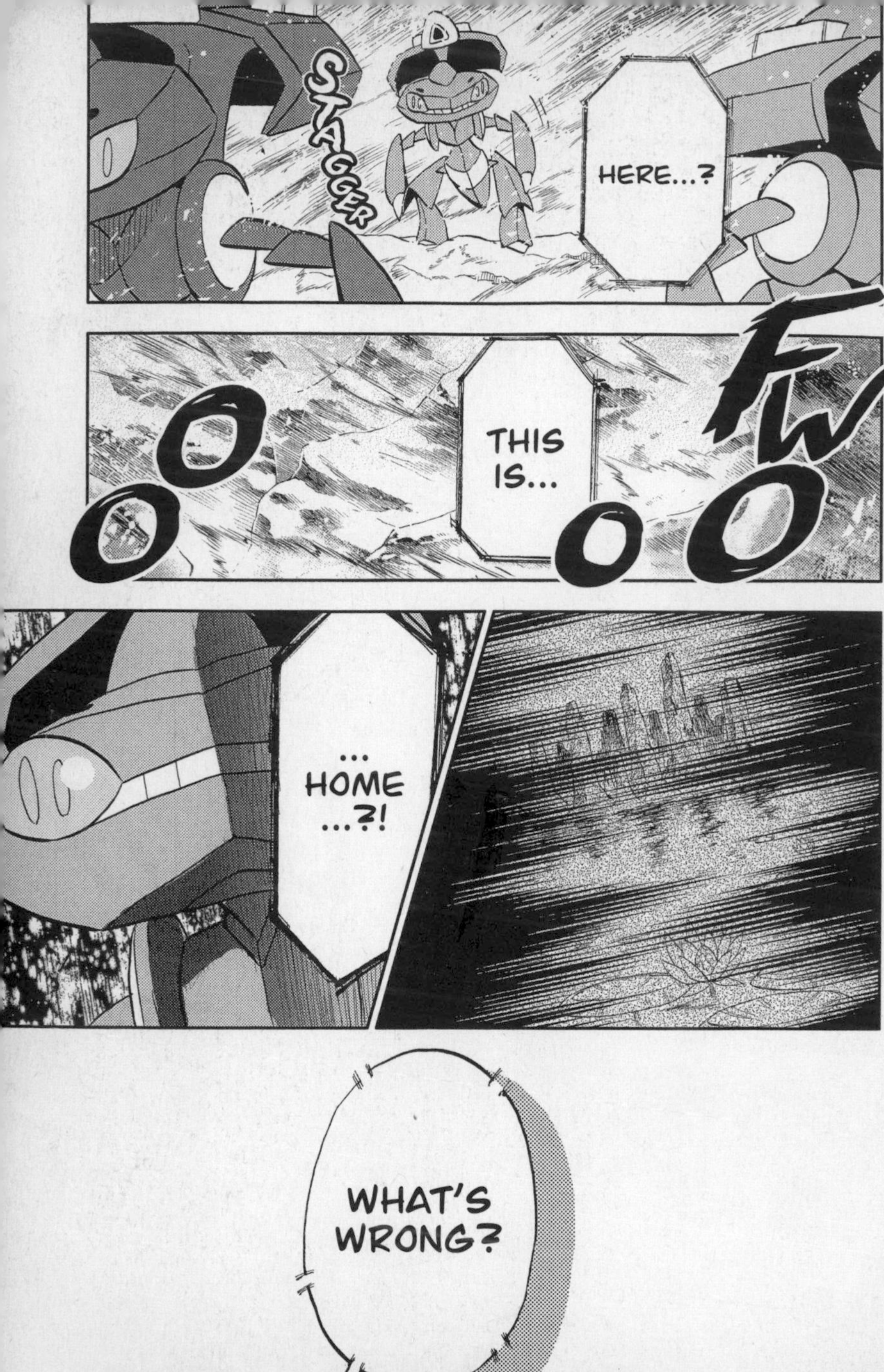
HERE...?
STAGGER
FWOOOO
THIS IS...
...HOME...?!
WHAT'S WRONG?

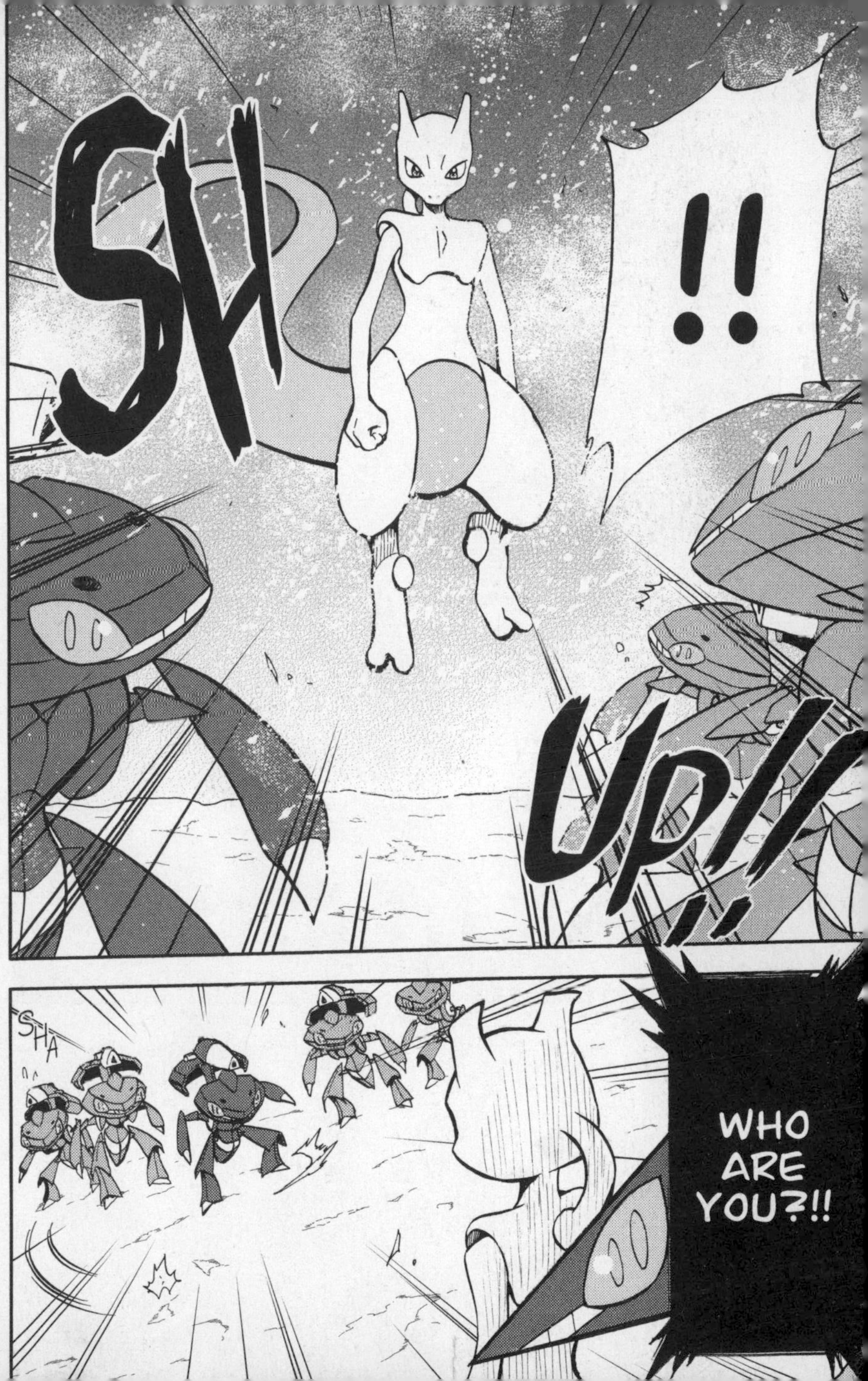
!!
SHUP!!
WHO ARE YOU?!!
SHA

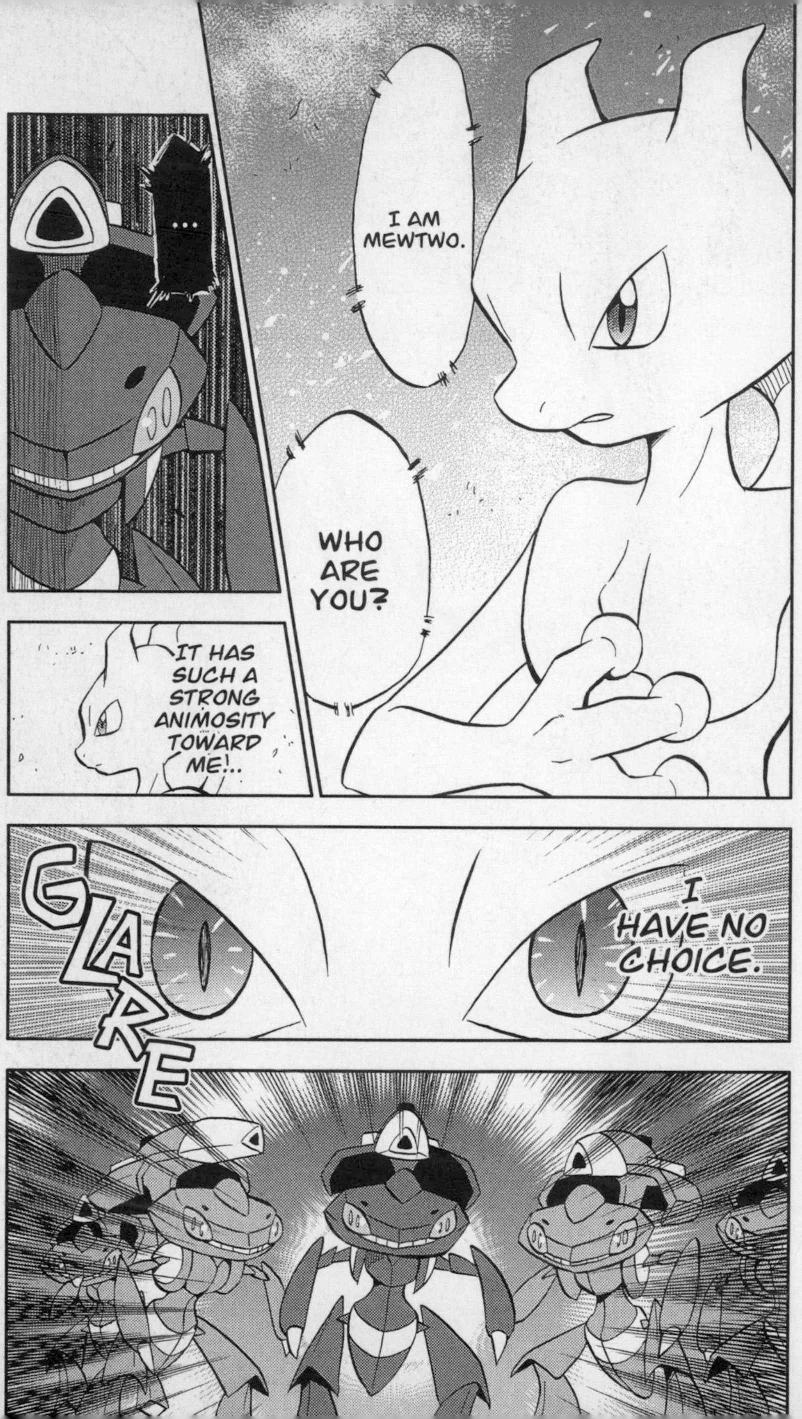
I AM MEWTWO.
WHO ARE YOU?
...
IT HAS SUCH A STRONG ANIMOSITY TOWARD ME!...
I HAVE NO CHOICE.
GLARE

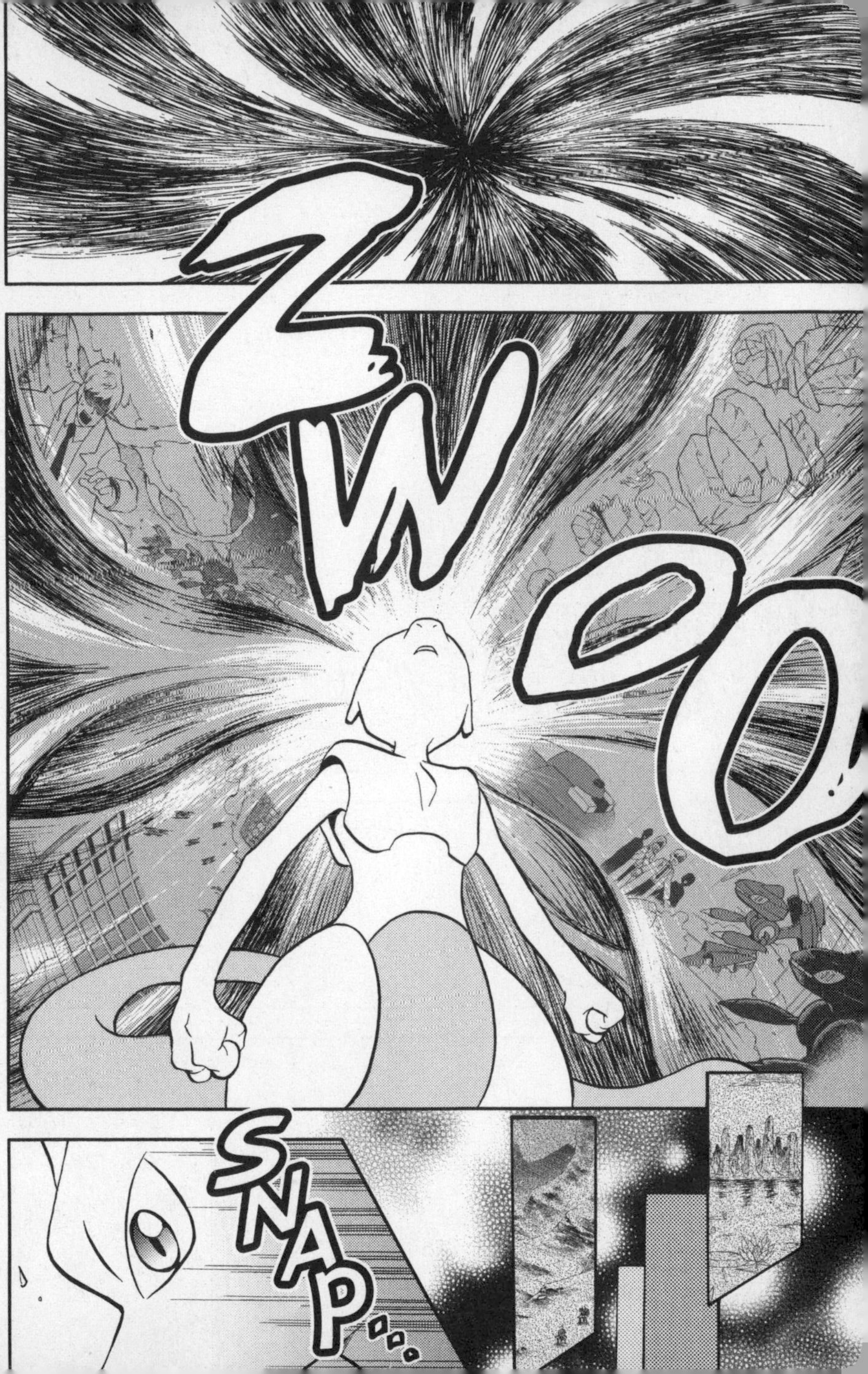
ZWOOO
SNAP...

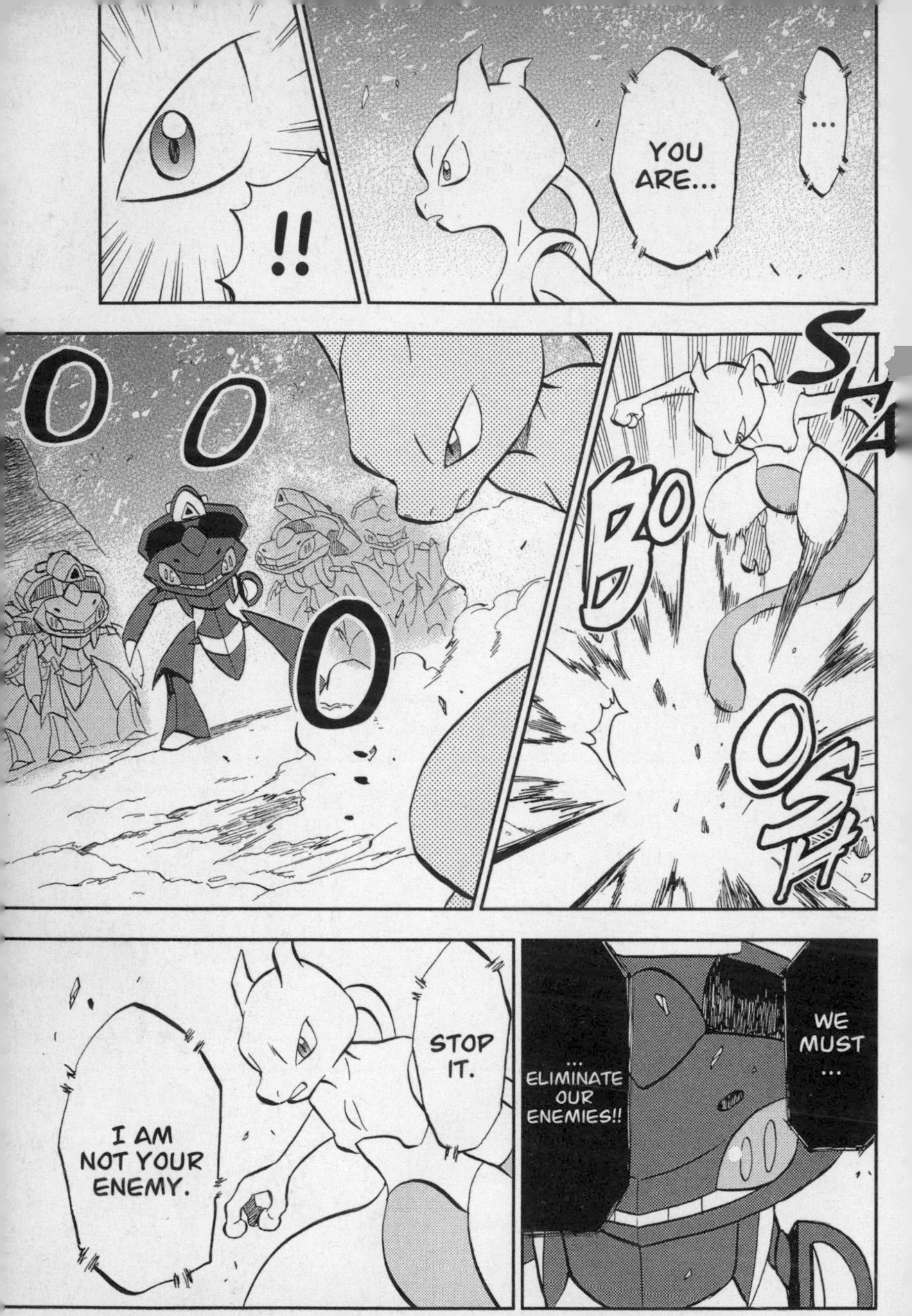
...
YOU ARE...
!!
SHA
BO
OOSH
OOO
WE MUST...
...ELIMINATE OUR ENEMIES!!
STOP IT.
I AM NOT YOUR ENEMY.

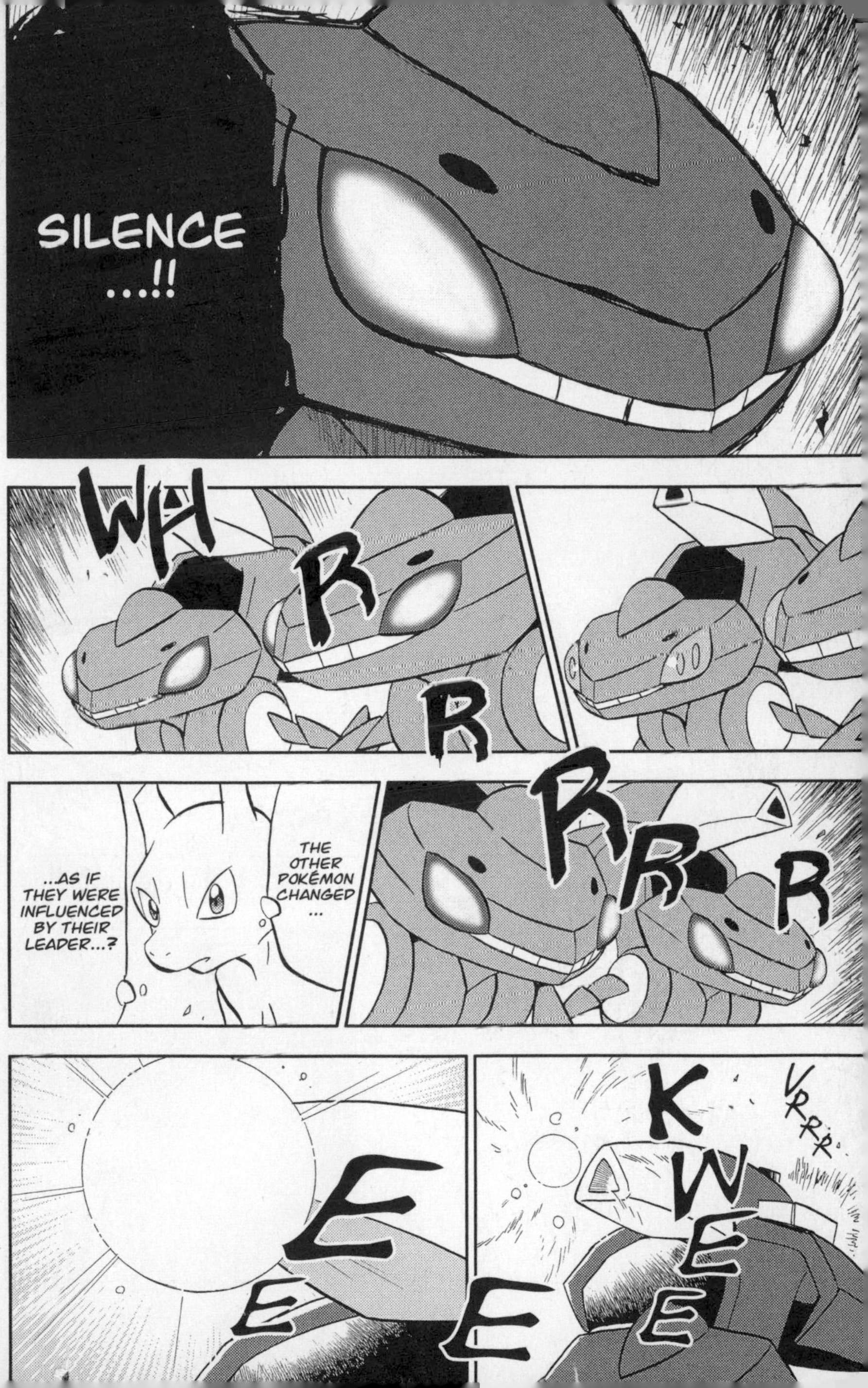
SILENCE ...!!
WAH
R
R
RRR
R
THE OTHER POKÉMON CHANGED ...
...AS IF THEY WERE INFLUENCED BY THEIR LEADER...?
KWEEE
VRRRR
EEE

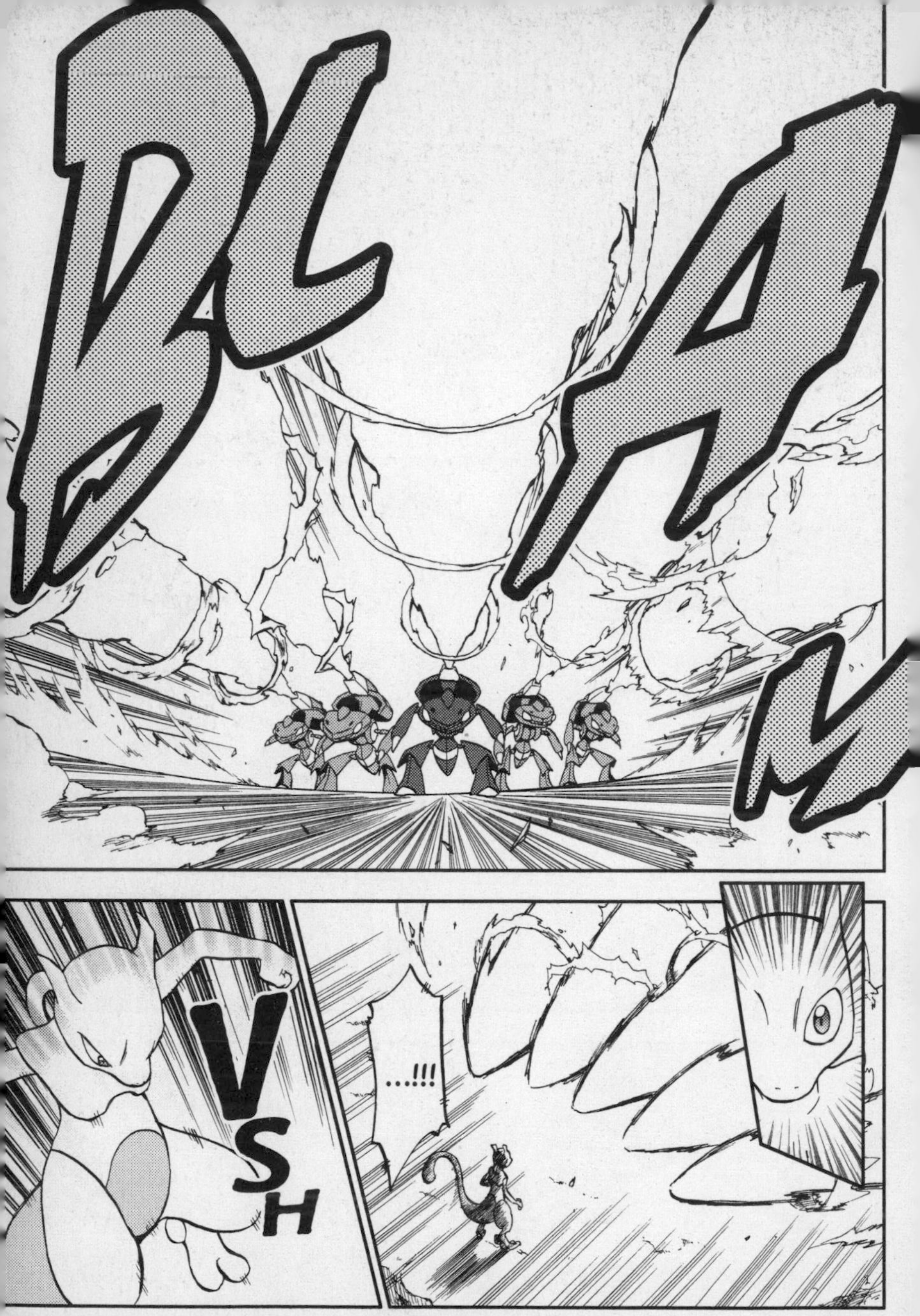
BLAM
...!!!
VSH

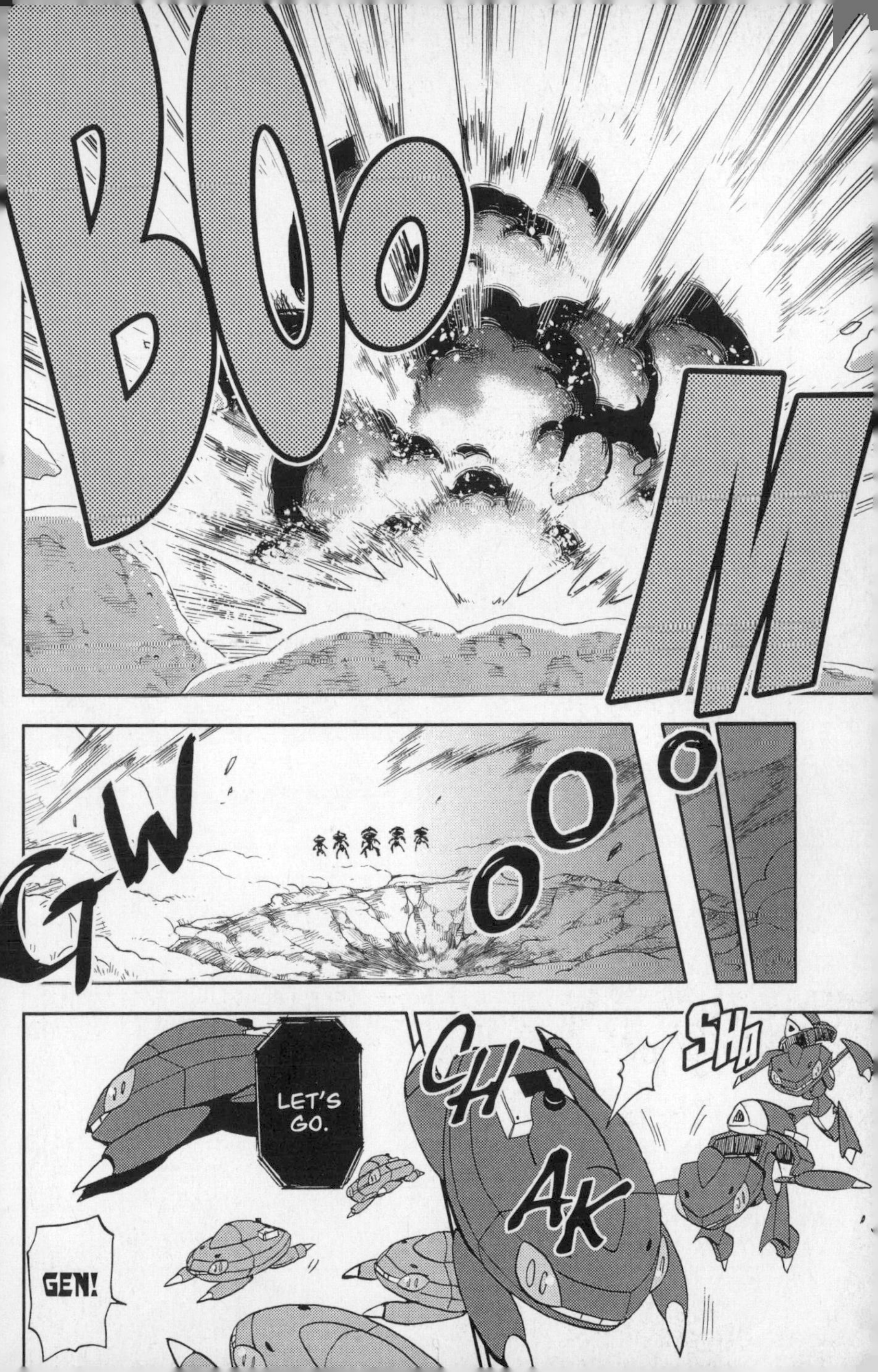
BOOOM
GWOOOO
SHA
CHAK
LET'S GO.
GEN!

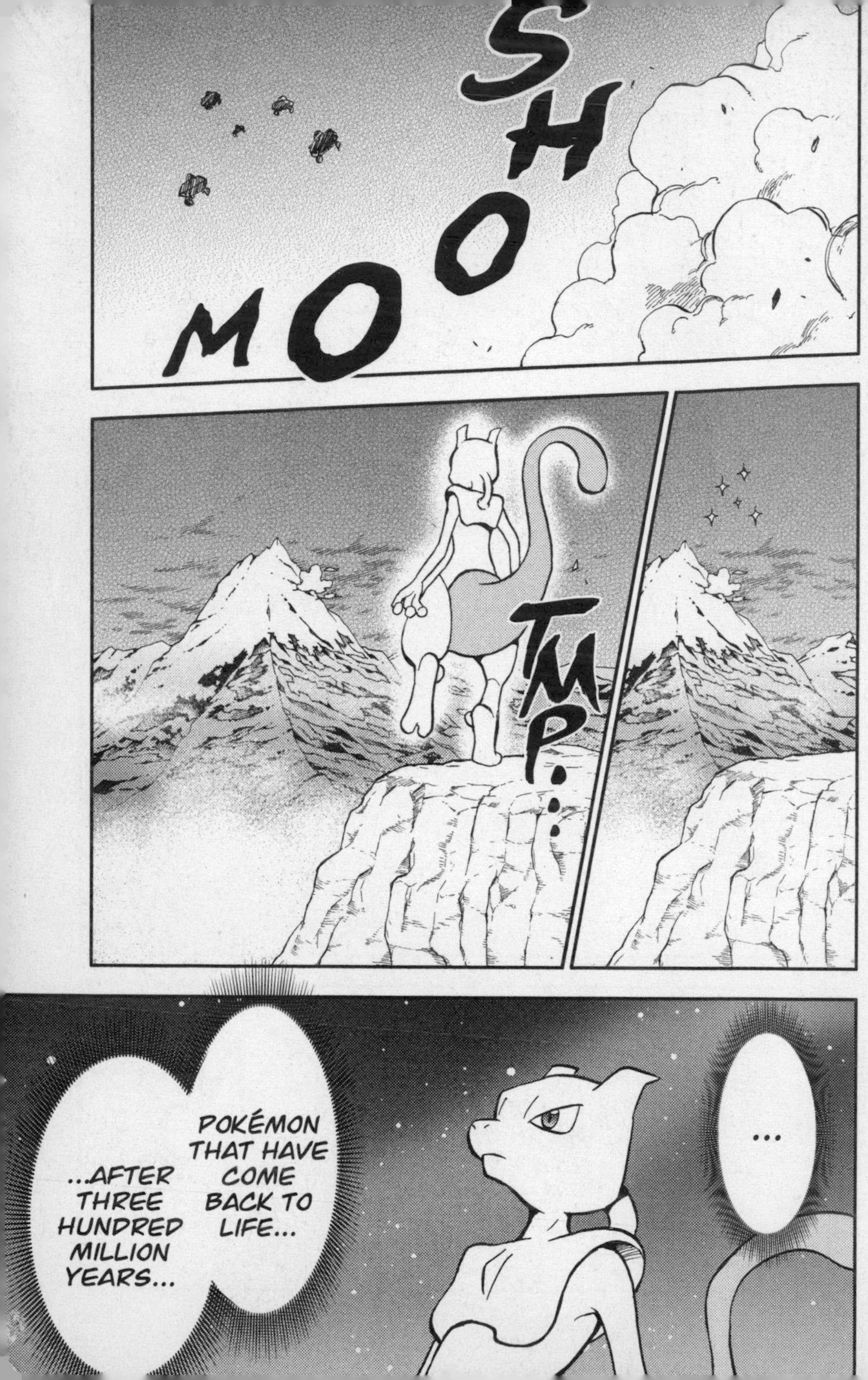
SHOOM
TMP...
...
POKÉMON THAT HAVE COME BACK TO LIFE...
...AFTER THREE HUNDRED MILLION YEARS...

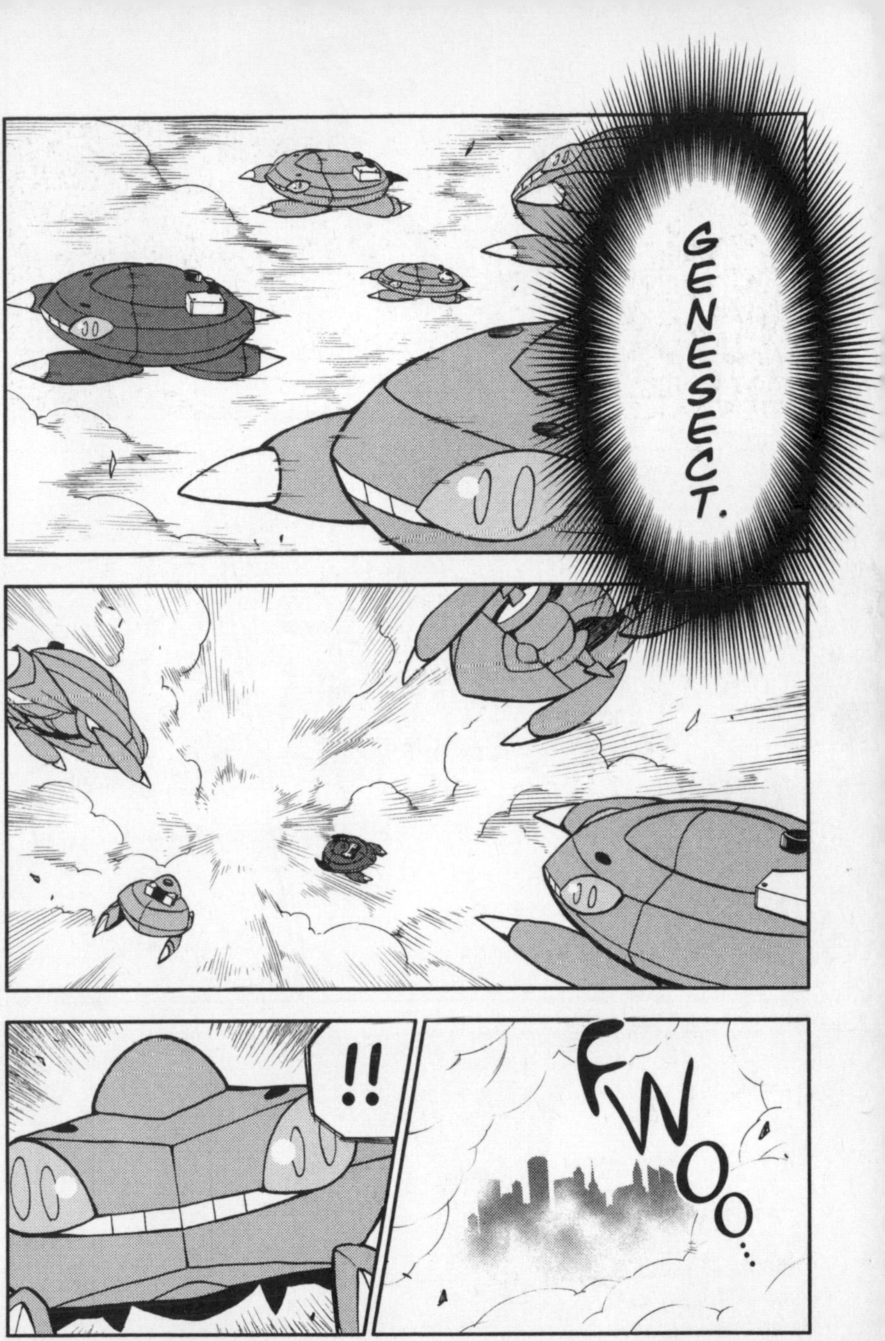
GENESECT.
FWOO...
!!

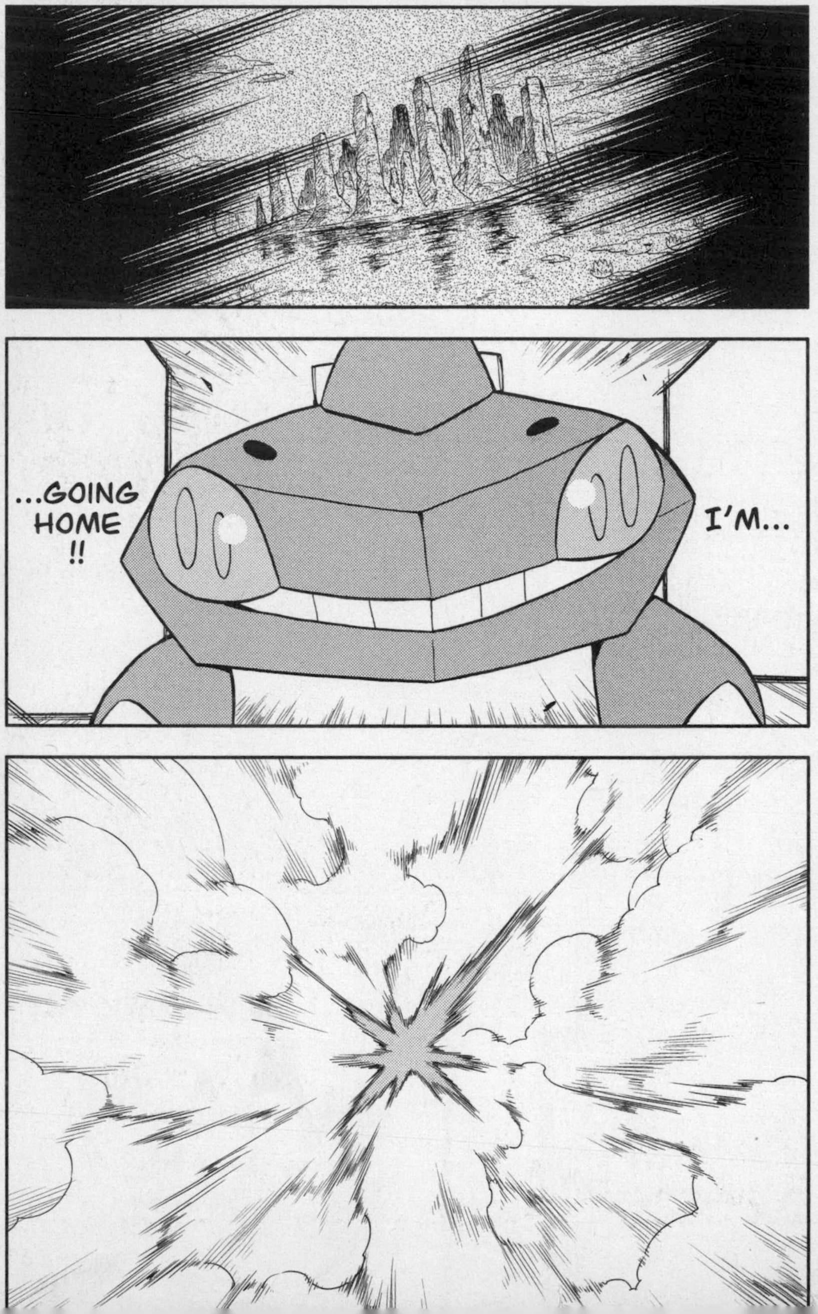
I'M...
...GOING HOME !!

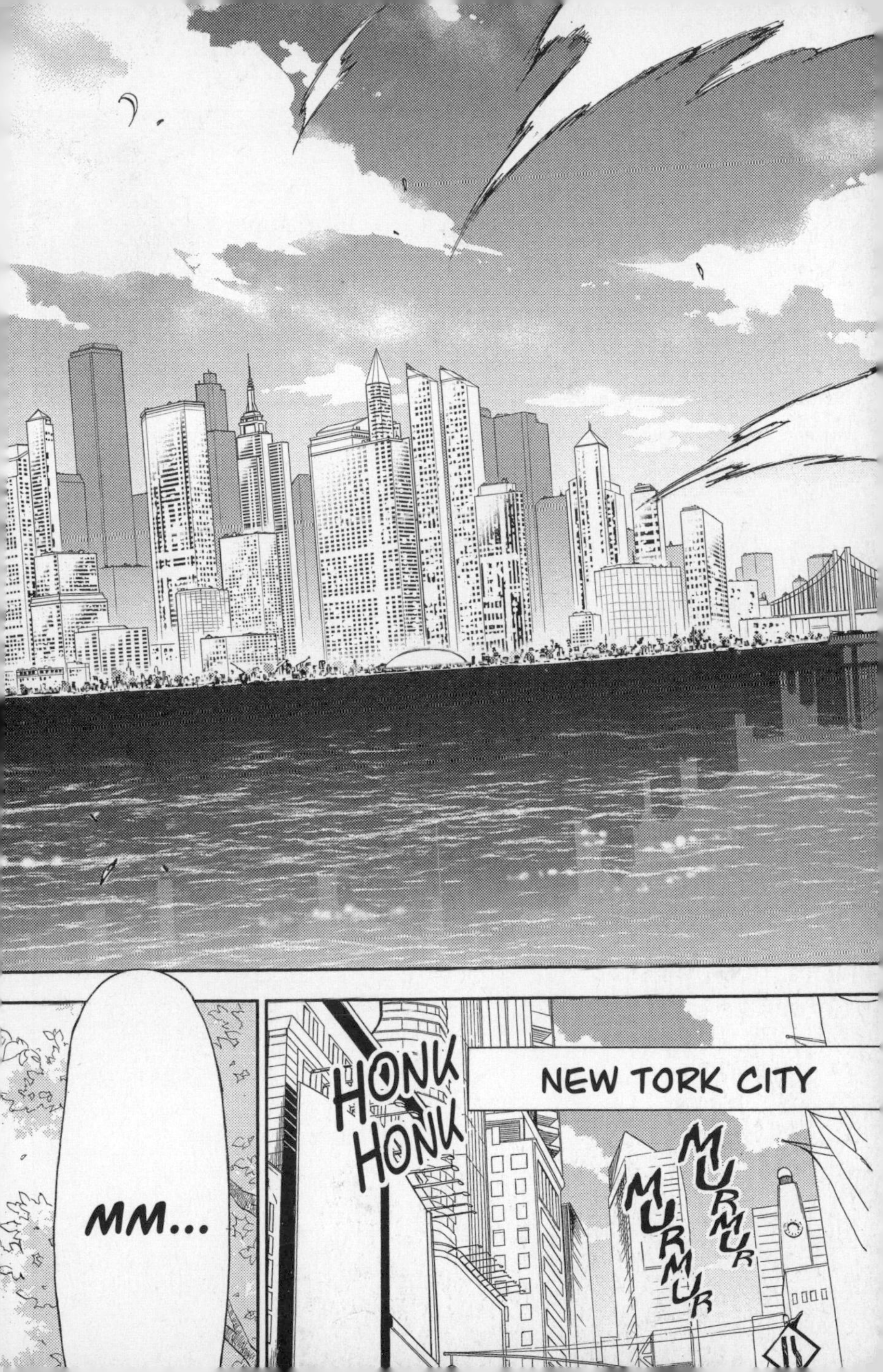
NEW TORK CITY
HONK HONK
MURMUR MURMUR
MM...

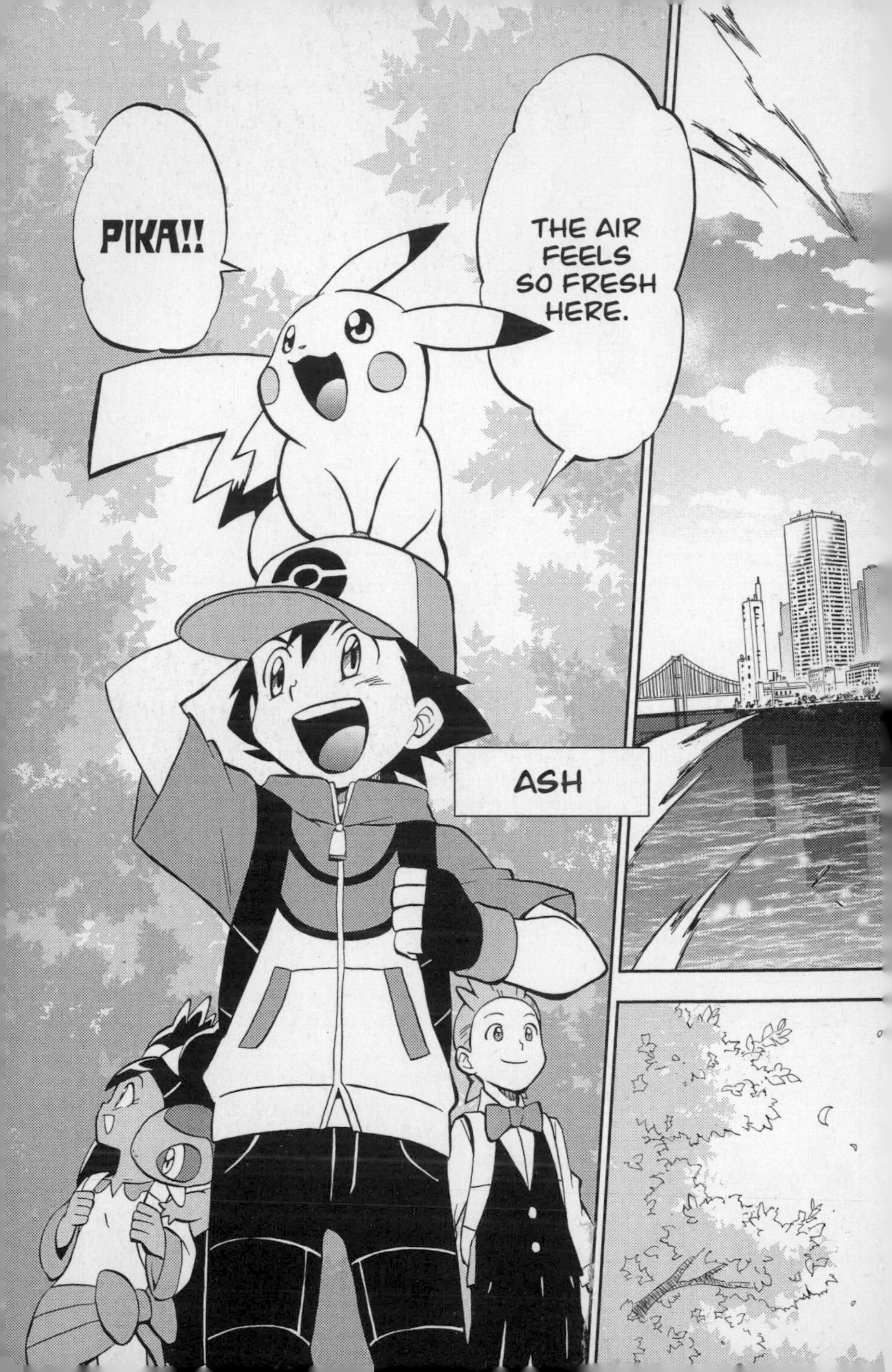
THE AIR FEELS SO FRESH HERE.
PIKA!!
ASH

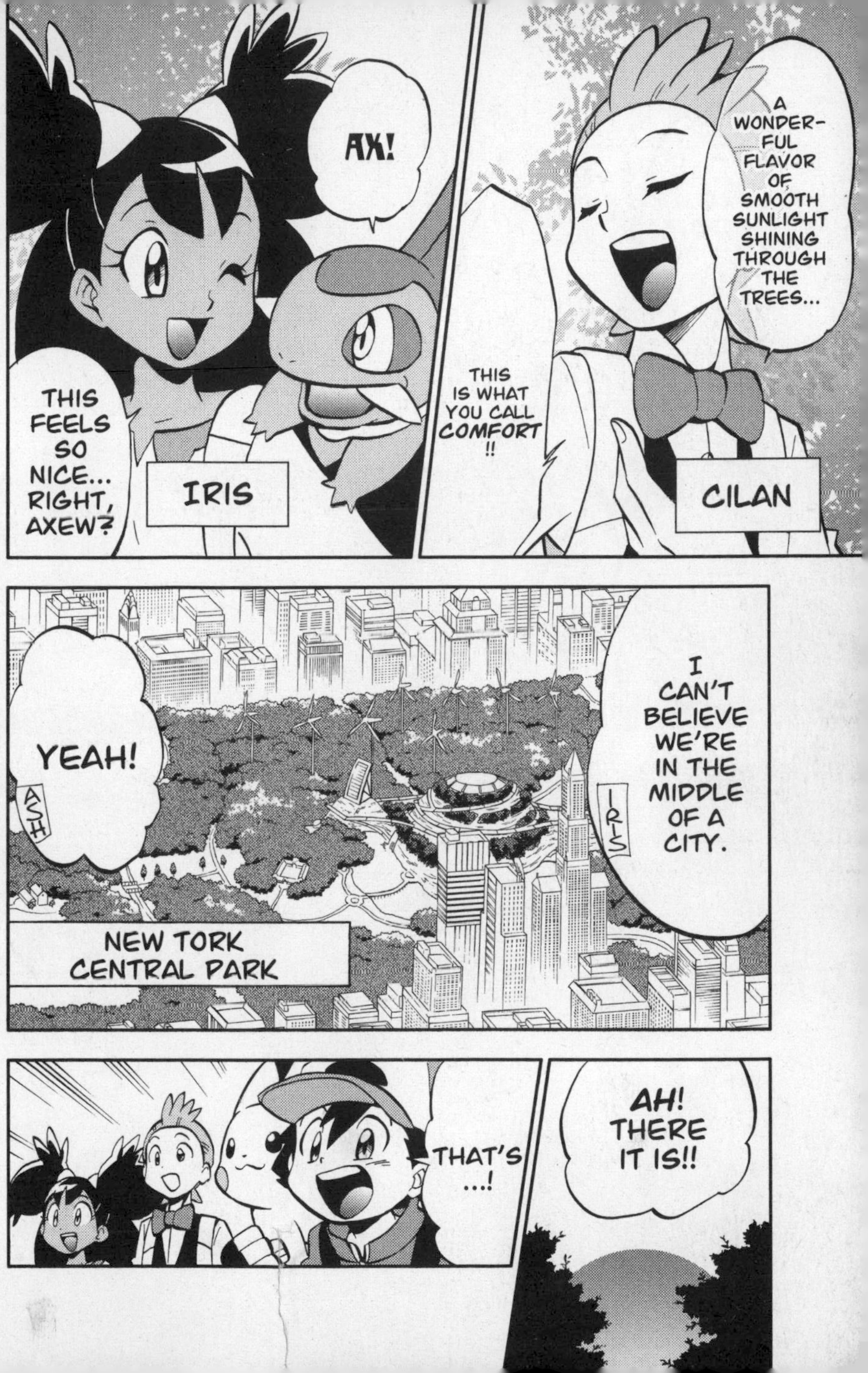
A WONDERFUL FLAVOR OF SMOOTH SUNLIGHT SHINING THROUGH THE TREES...
THIS IS WHAT YOU CALL COMFORT!!
CILAN
AX!
IRIS
THIS FEELS SO NICE... RIGHT, AXEW?
I CAN'T BELIEVE WE'RE IN THE MIDDLE OF A CITY.
IRIS
YEAH!
ASH
NEW TORK CENTRAL PARK
AH! THERE IT IS!!
THAT'S ...!

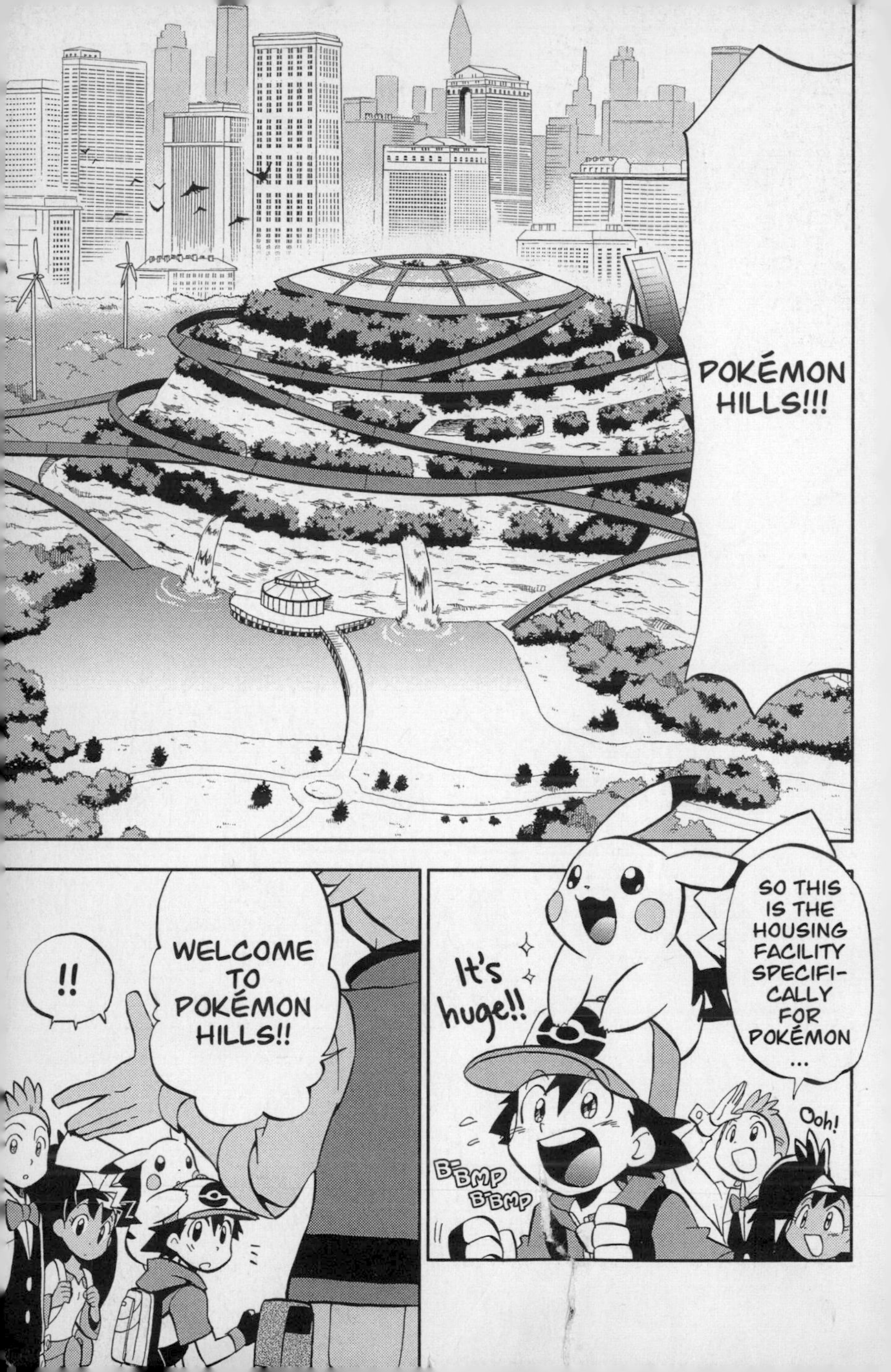
POKÉMON HILLS!!!
SO THIS IS THE HOUSING FACILITY SPECIFI- CALLY FOR POKÉMON ...
It's huge!!
Ooh!
B-BMP B-BMP
WELCOME TO POKÉMON HILLS!!
!!

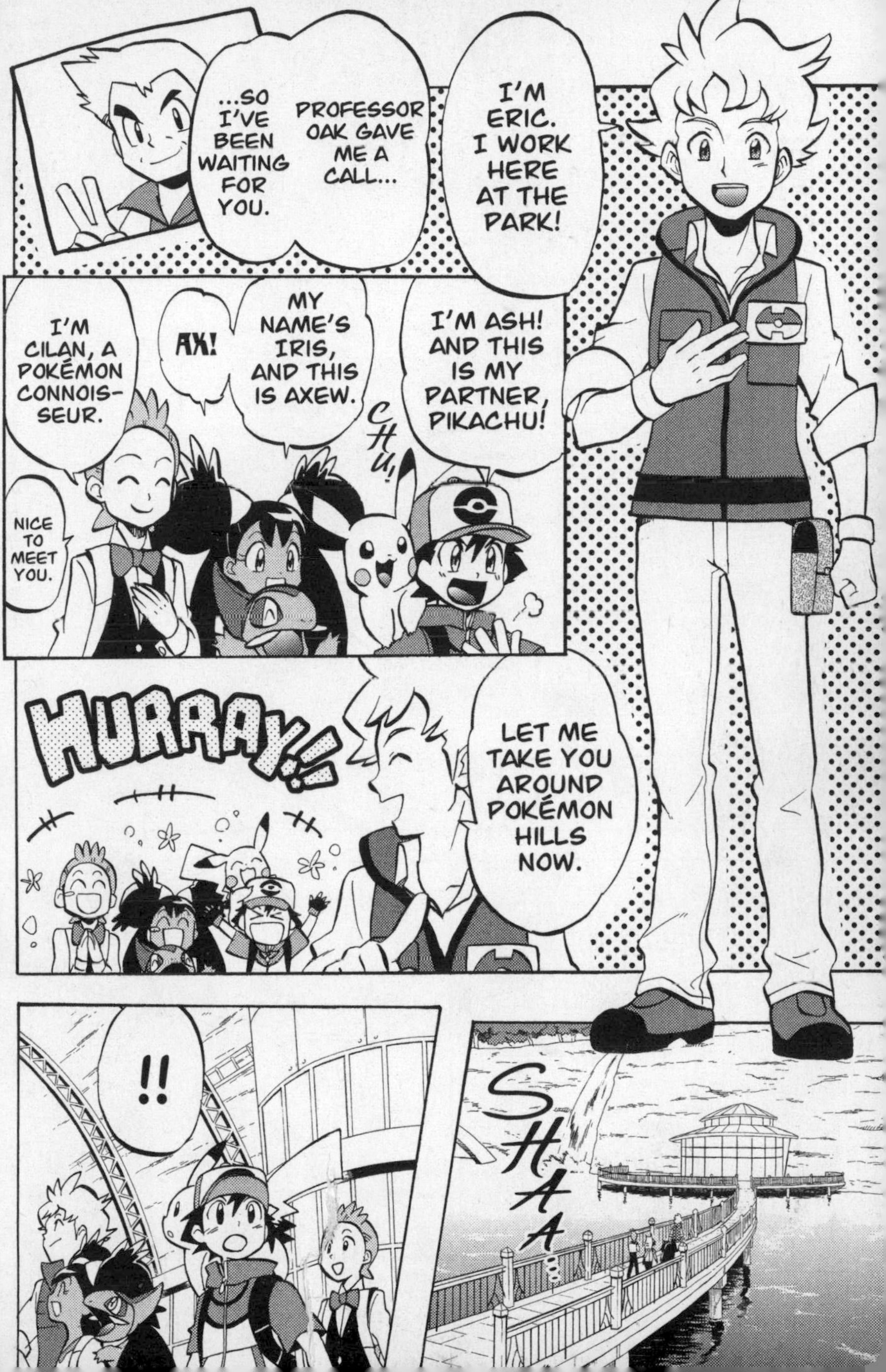
I'M ERIC. I WORK HERE AT THE PARK!
PROFESSOR OAK GAVE ME A CALL...
...SO I'VE BEEN WAITING FOR YOU.
I'M ASH! AND THIS IS MY PARTNER, PIKACHU!
CHU!
MY NAME'S IRIS, AND THIS IS AXEW.
AX!
I'M CILAN, A POKÉMON CONNOIS-SEUR.
NICE TO MEET YOU.
LET ME TAKE YOU AROUND POKÉMON HILLS NOW.
HURRAY!!
SHAA...
!!

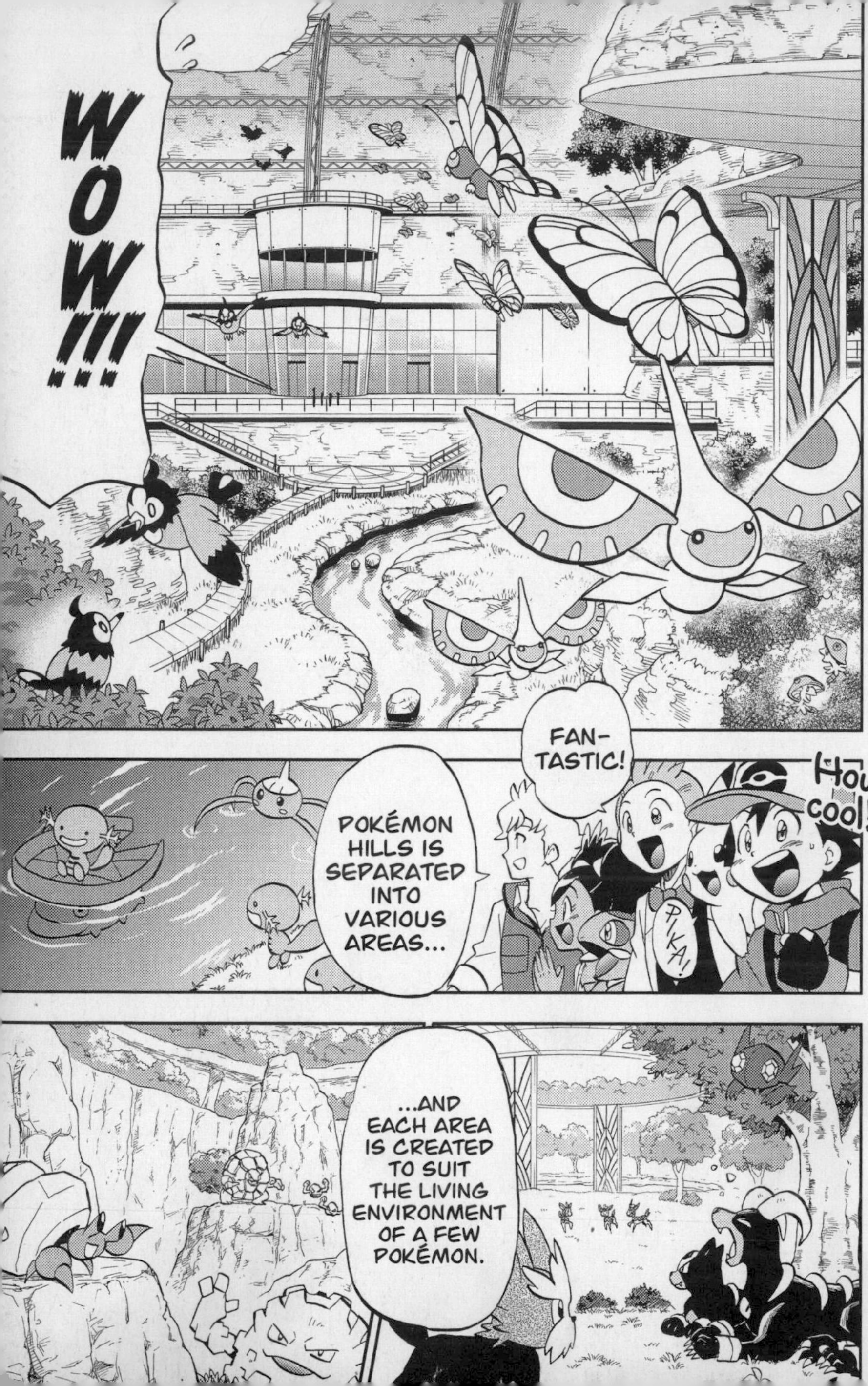
WOW!!!
How cool!
FAN-TASTIC!
PIKA!
POKÉMON HILLS IS SEPARATED INTO VARIOUS AREAS...
...AND EACH AREA IS CREATED TO SUIT THE LIVING ENVIRONMENT OF A FEW POKÉMON.

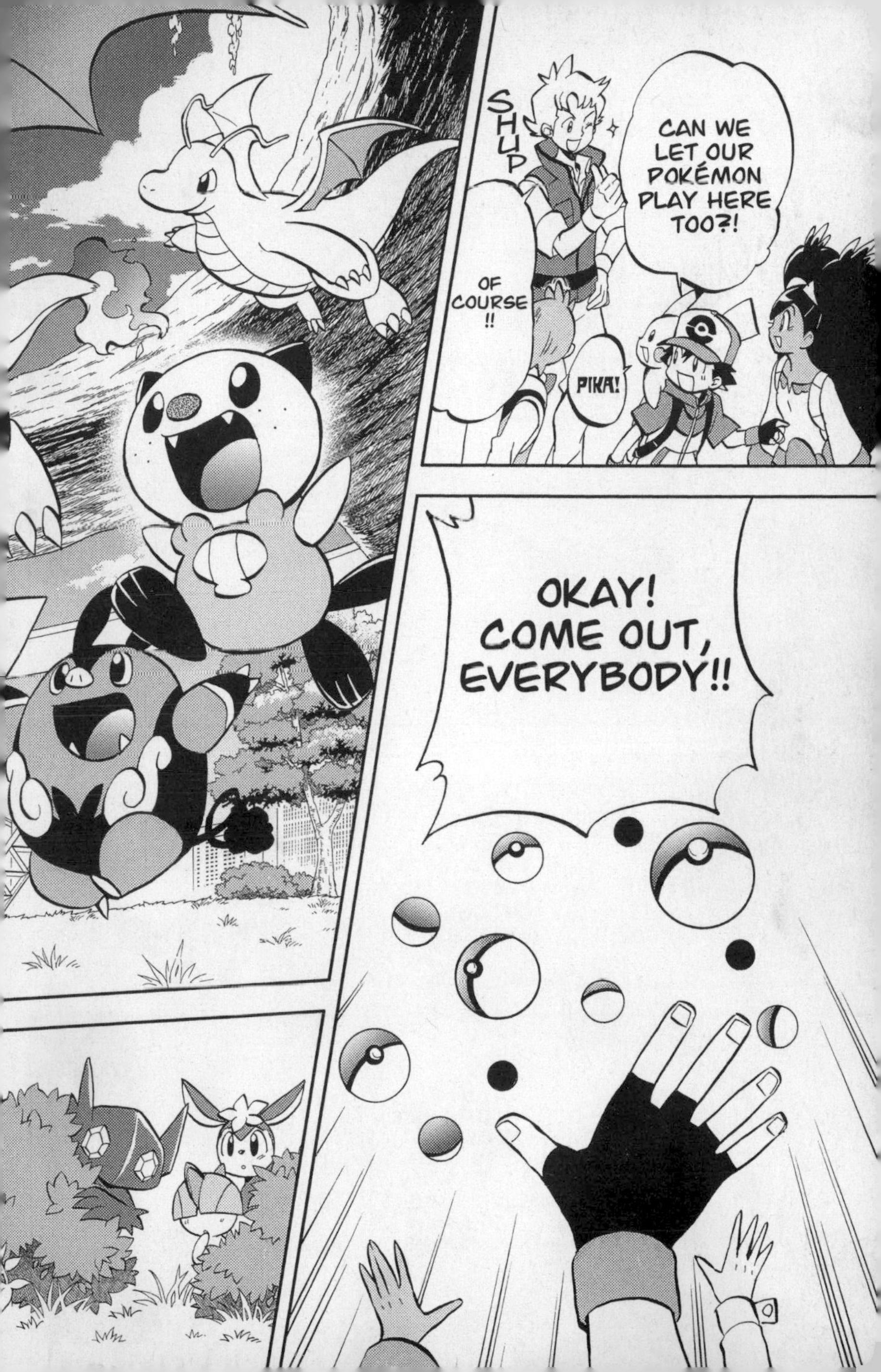
CAN WE LET OUR POKÉMON PLAY HERE TOO?!
SHUP
PIKA!
OF COURSE!!
OKAY! COME OUT, EVERYBODY!!

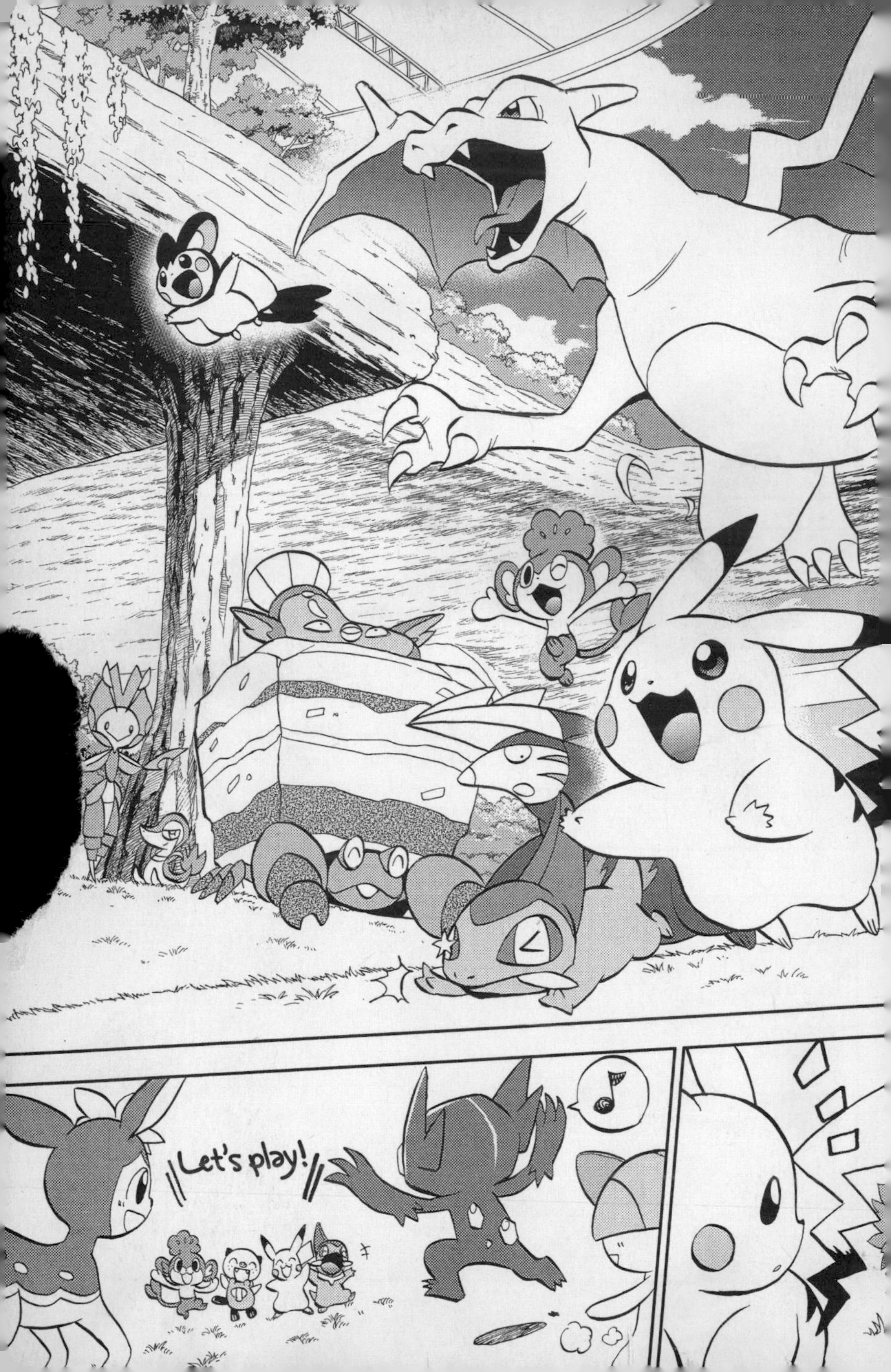

Let's play!

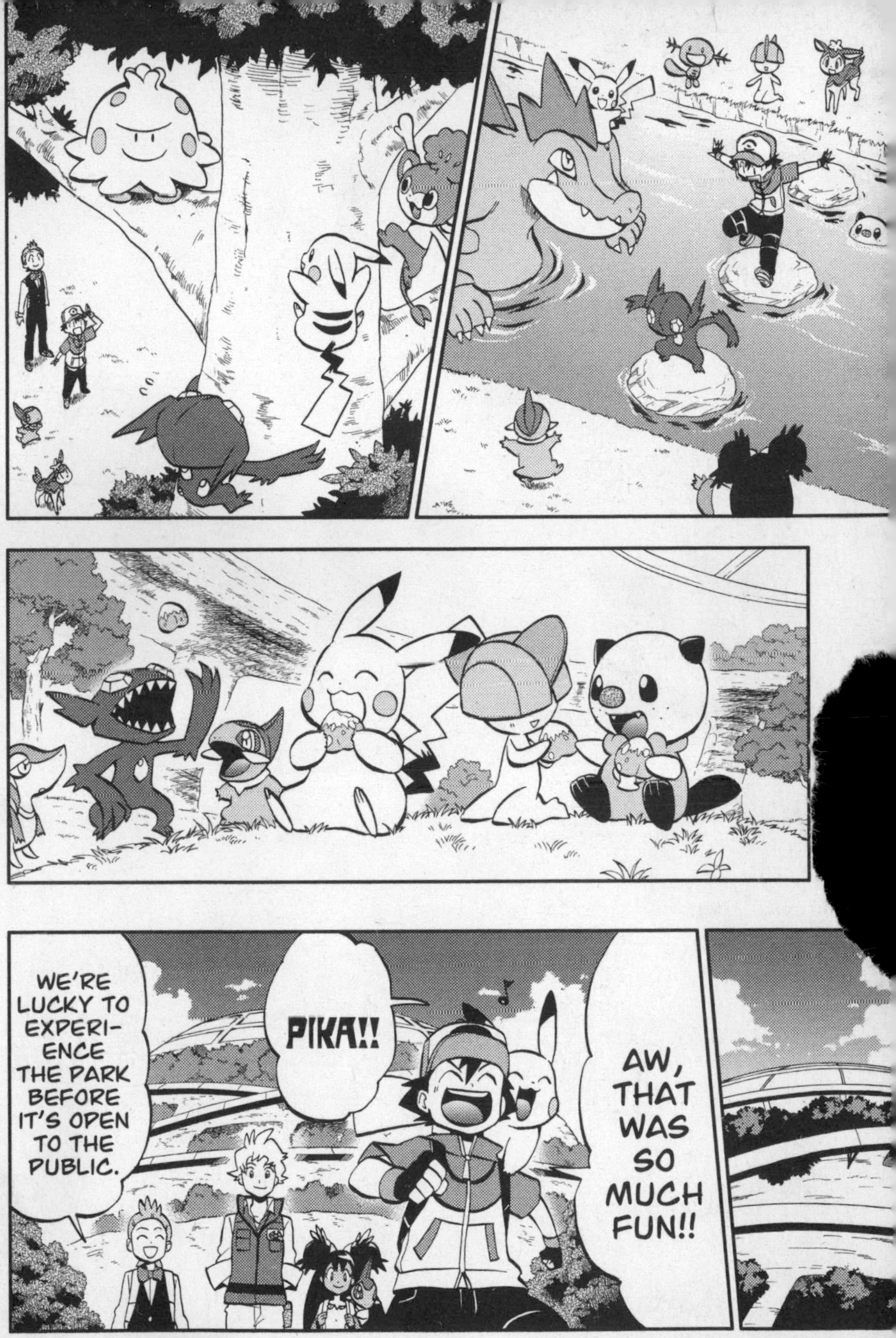
AW, THAT WAS SO MUCH FUN!!
PIKA!!
WE'RE LUCKY TO EXPERIENCE THE PARK BEFORE IT'S OPEN TO THE PUBLIC.

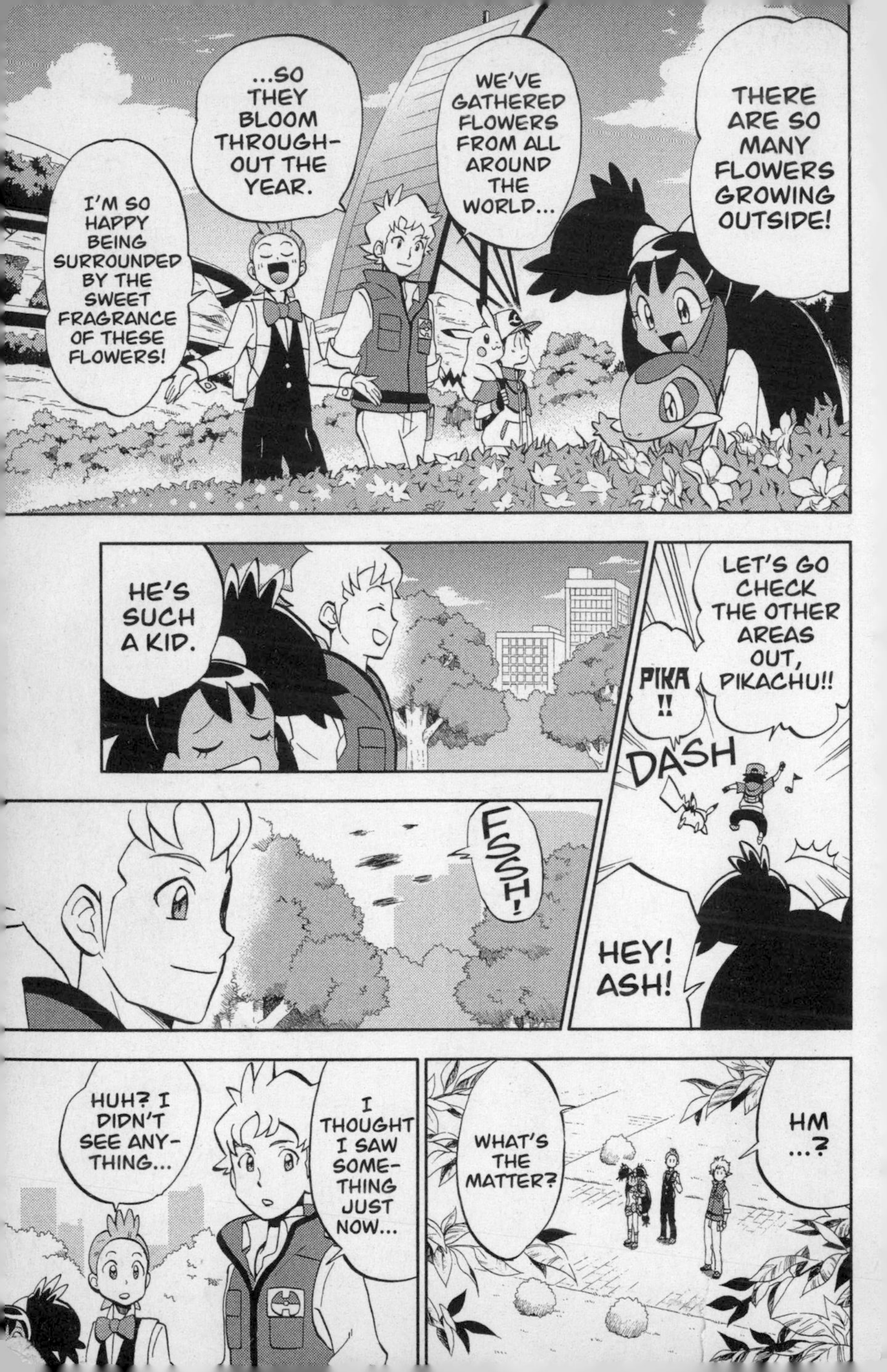
THERE ARE SO MANY FLOWERS GROWING OUTSIDE!
WE'VE GATHERED FLOWERS FROM ALL AROUND THE WORLD...
...SO THEY BLOOM THROUGH-OUT THE YEAR.
I'M SO HAPPY BEING SURROUNDED BY THE SWEET FRAGRANCE OF THESE FLOWERS!
LET'S GO CHECK THE OTHER AREAS OUT, PIKACHU!!
PIKA !!
DASH
HEY! ASH!
HE'S SUCH A KID.
FSSH!
HM ...?
WHAT'S THE MATTER?
I THOUGHT I SAW SOME-THING JUST NOW...
HUH? I DIDN'T SEE ANY-THING...

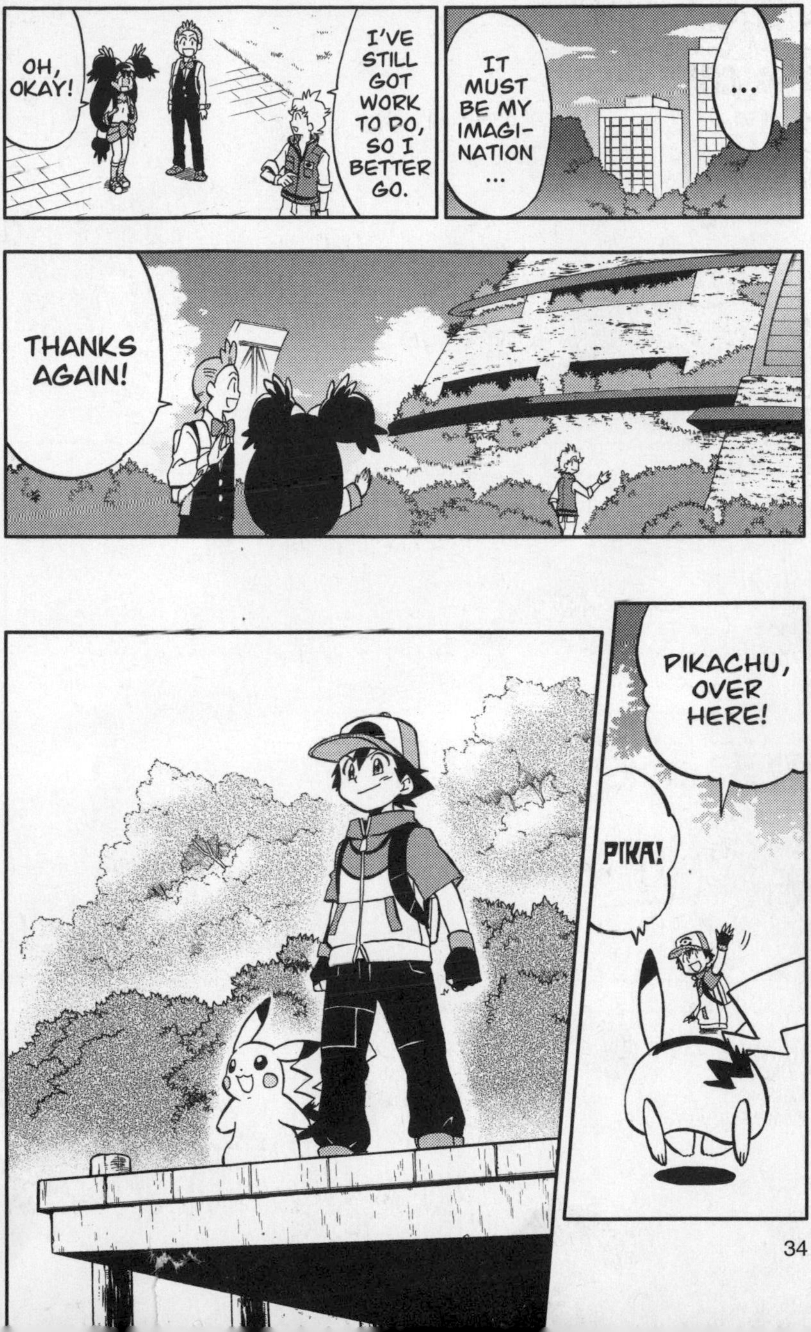
...
IT MUST BE MY IMAGINATION ...
I'VE STILL GOT WORK TO DO, SO I BETTER GO.
OH, OKAY!
THANKS AGAIN!
PIKACHU, OVER HERE!
PIKA!

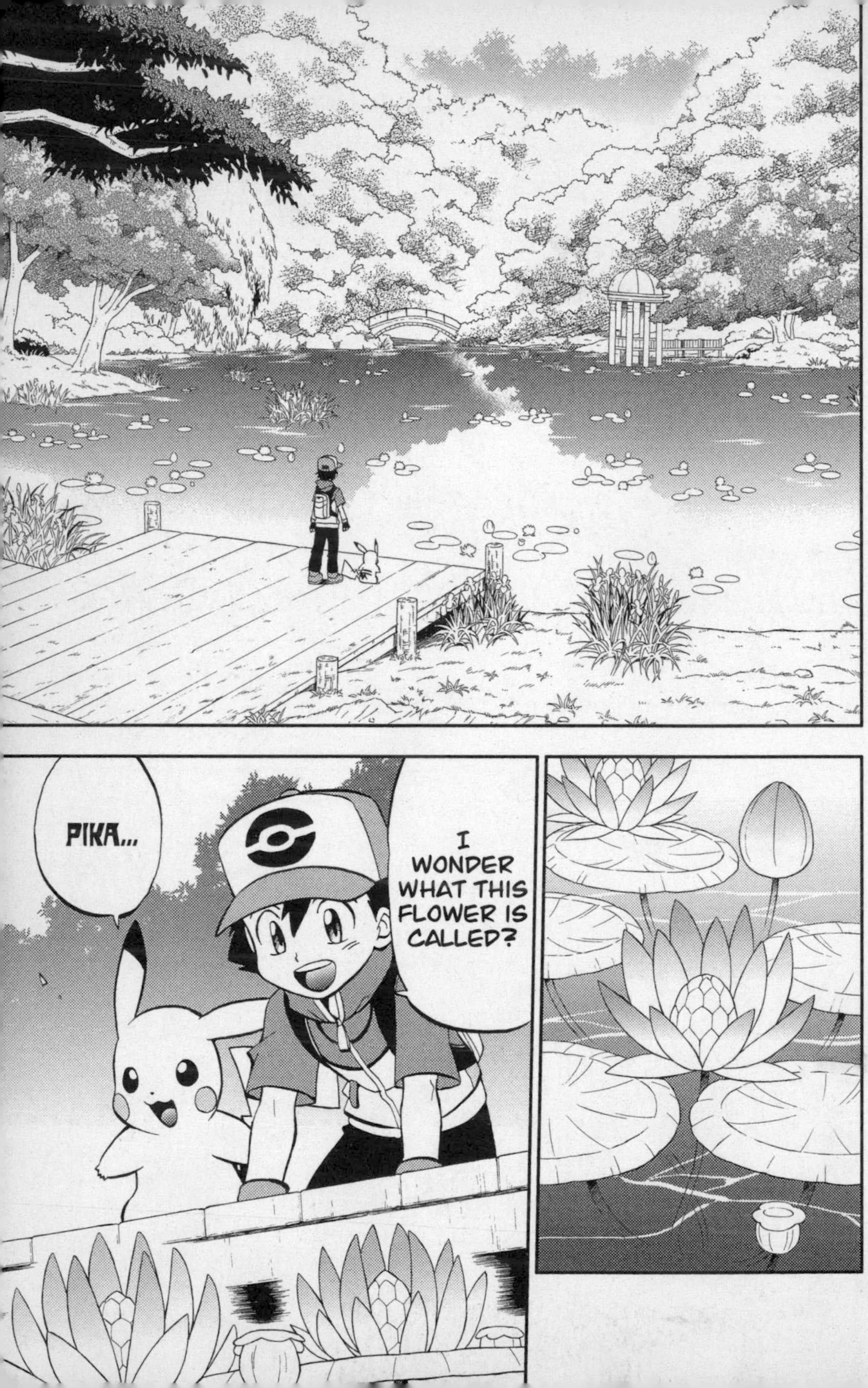
I WONDER WHAT THIS FLOWER IS CALLED?
PIKA...

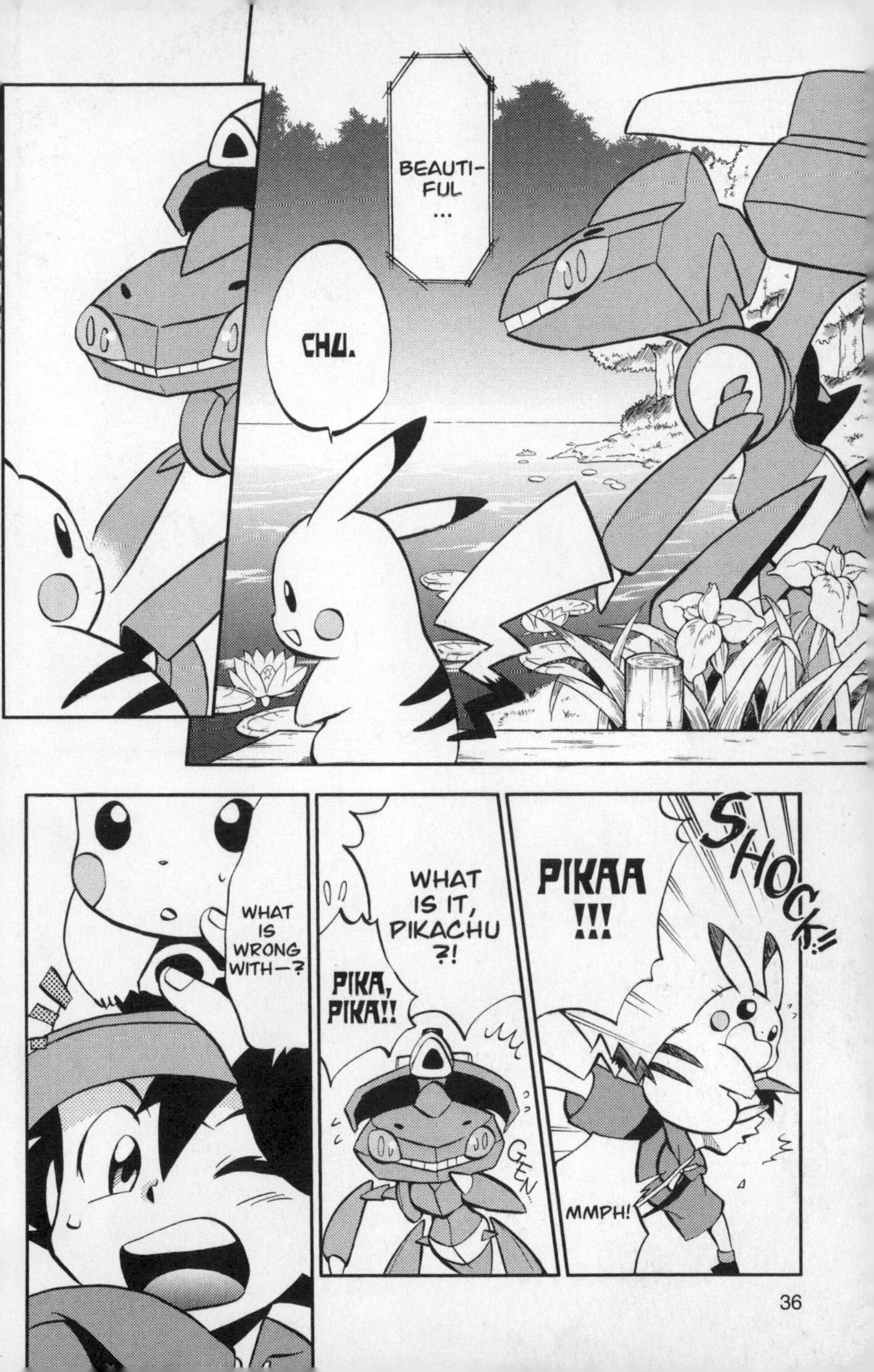
BEAUTI-FUL...
CHU.
SHOCK!!
PIKAA!!!
MMPH!
WHAT IS IT, PIKACHU?!
PIKA, PIKA!!
GEN...
WHAT IS WRONG WITH—?

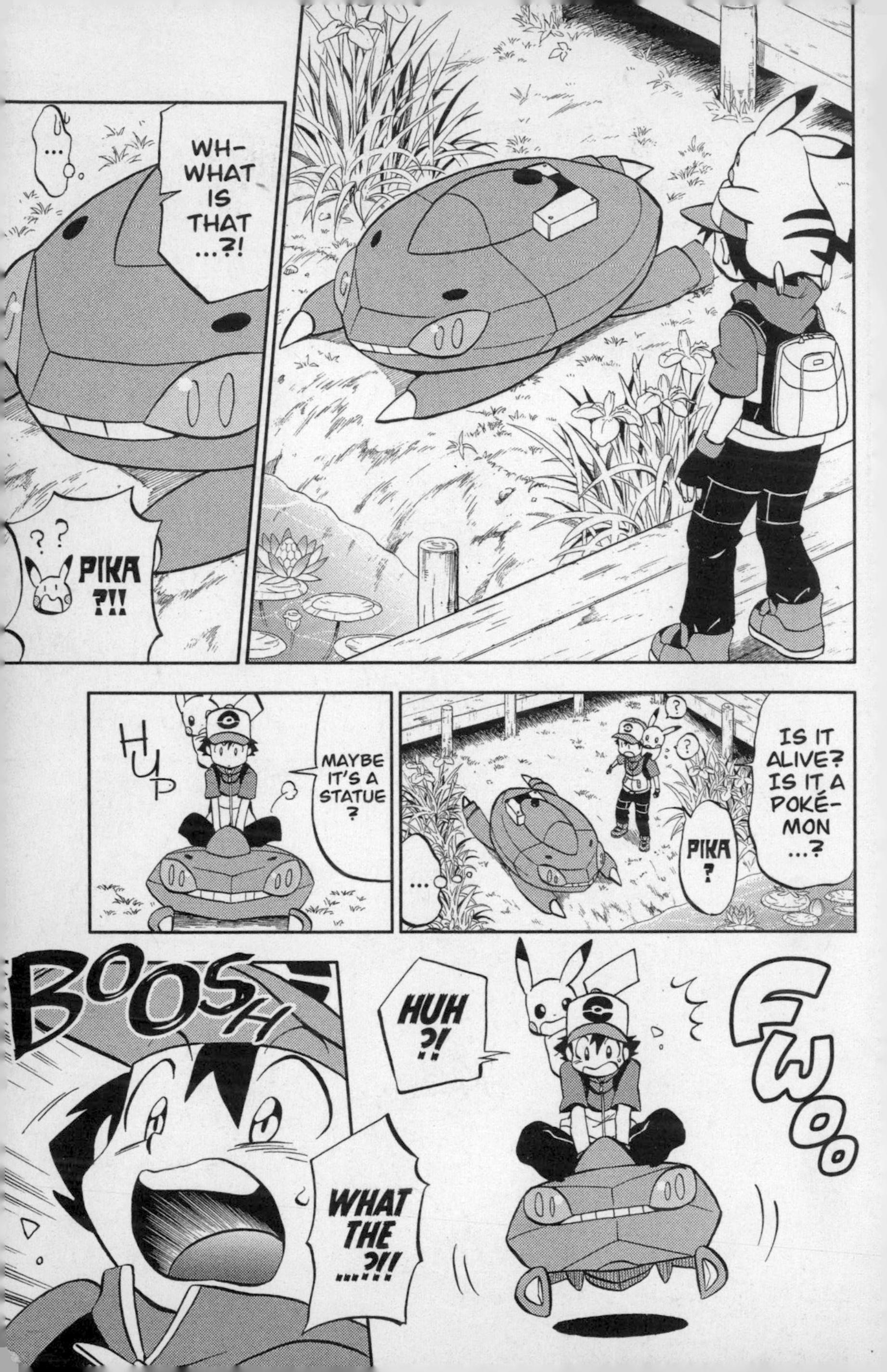
WH- WHAT IS THAT ...?!
...
? ? PIKA ?!!
IS IT ALIVE? IS IT A POKÉ-MON ...?
PIKA ?
...
MAYBE IT'S A STATUE ?
HUP
FWOO
HUH ?!
BOOSH
WHAT THE ...?!!

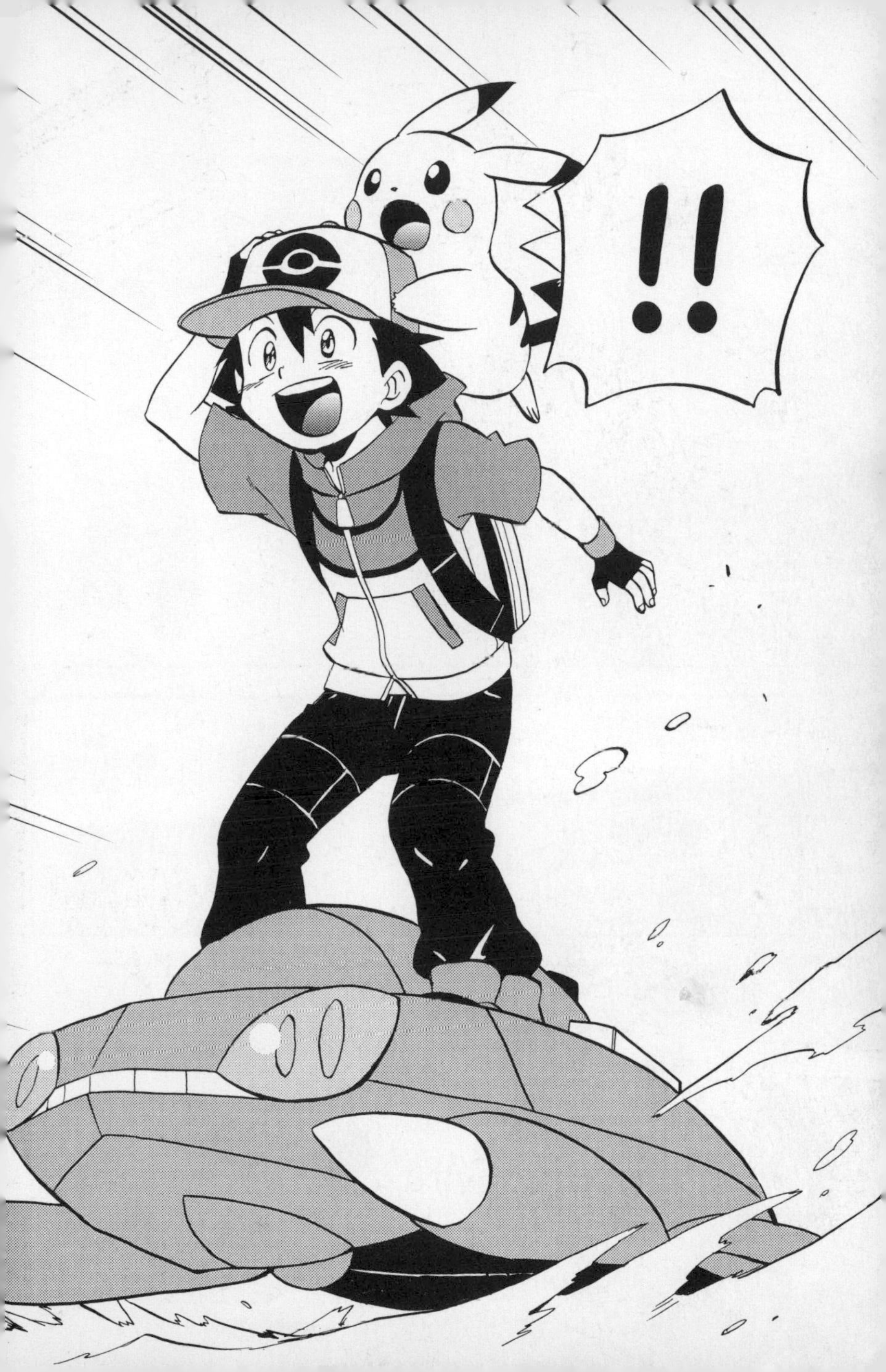
!!

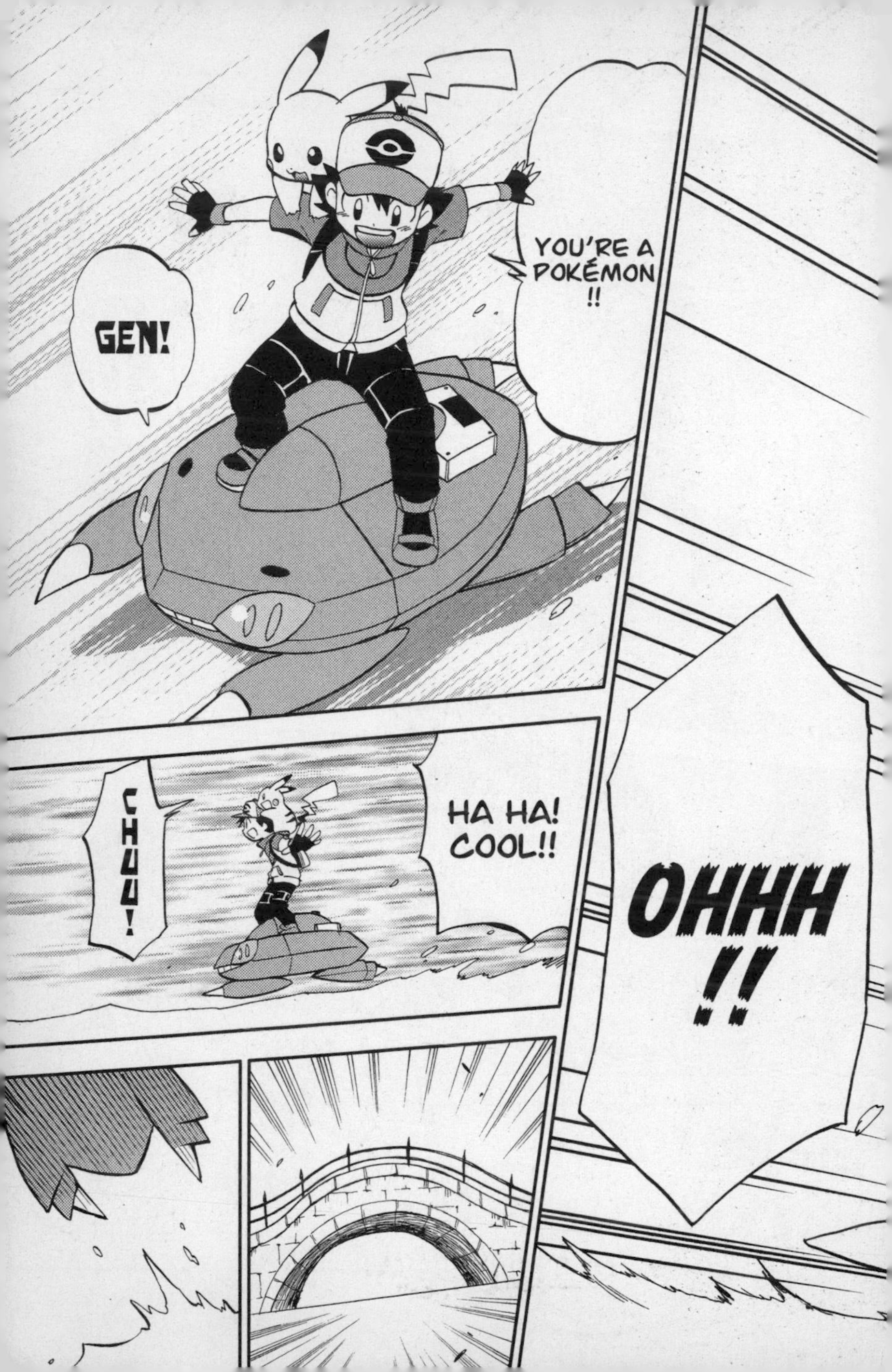
OHHH !!
YOU'RE A POKÉMON !!
GEN!
HA HA! COOL!!
CHUUU!

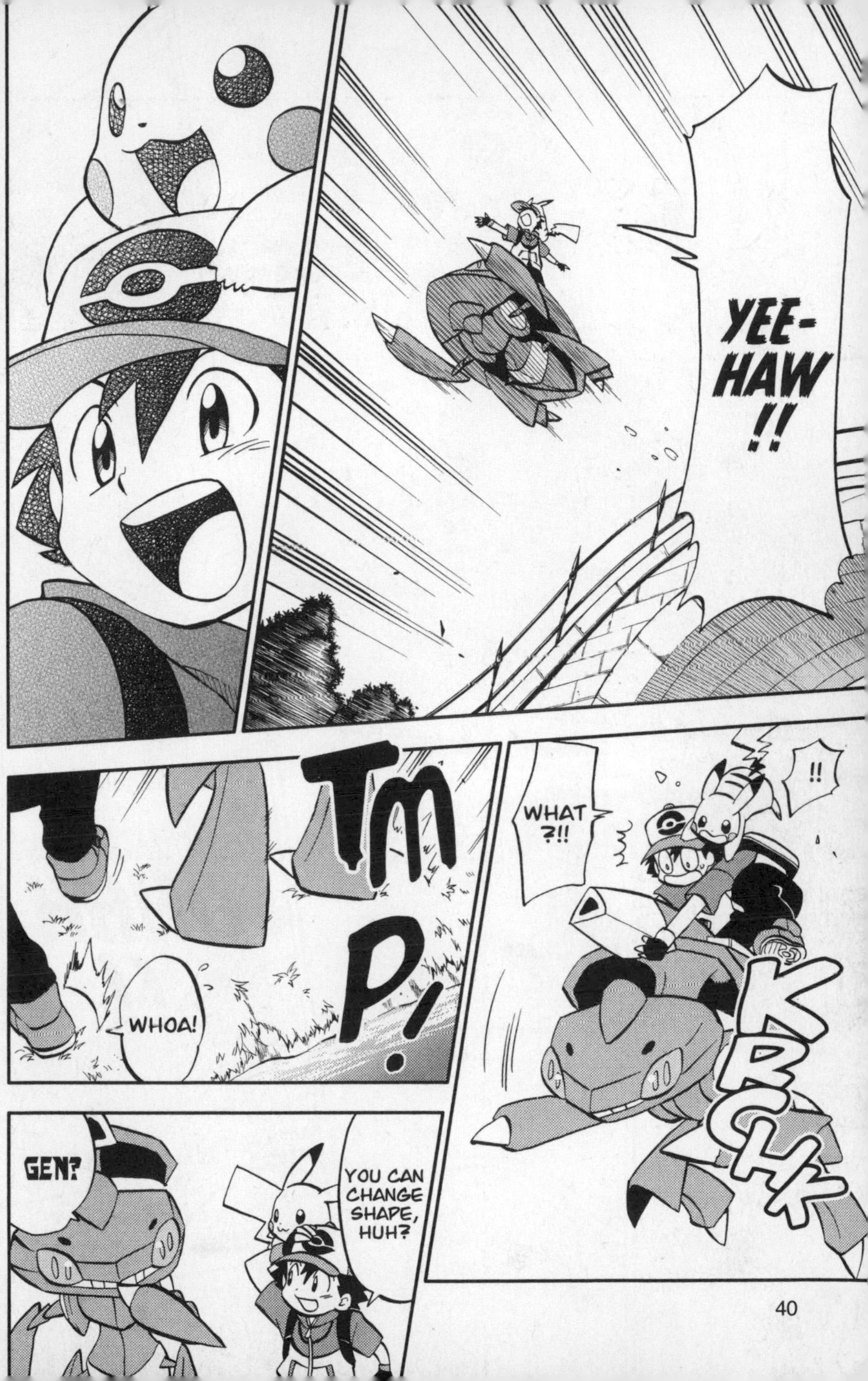
YEE-HAW!!
!!
WHAT?!!
KRCHK
TMP!
WHOA!
YOU CAN CHANGE SHAPE, HUH?
GEN?

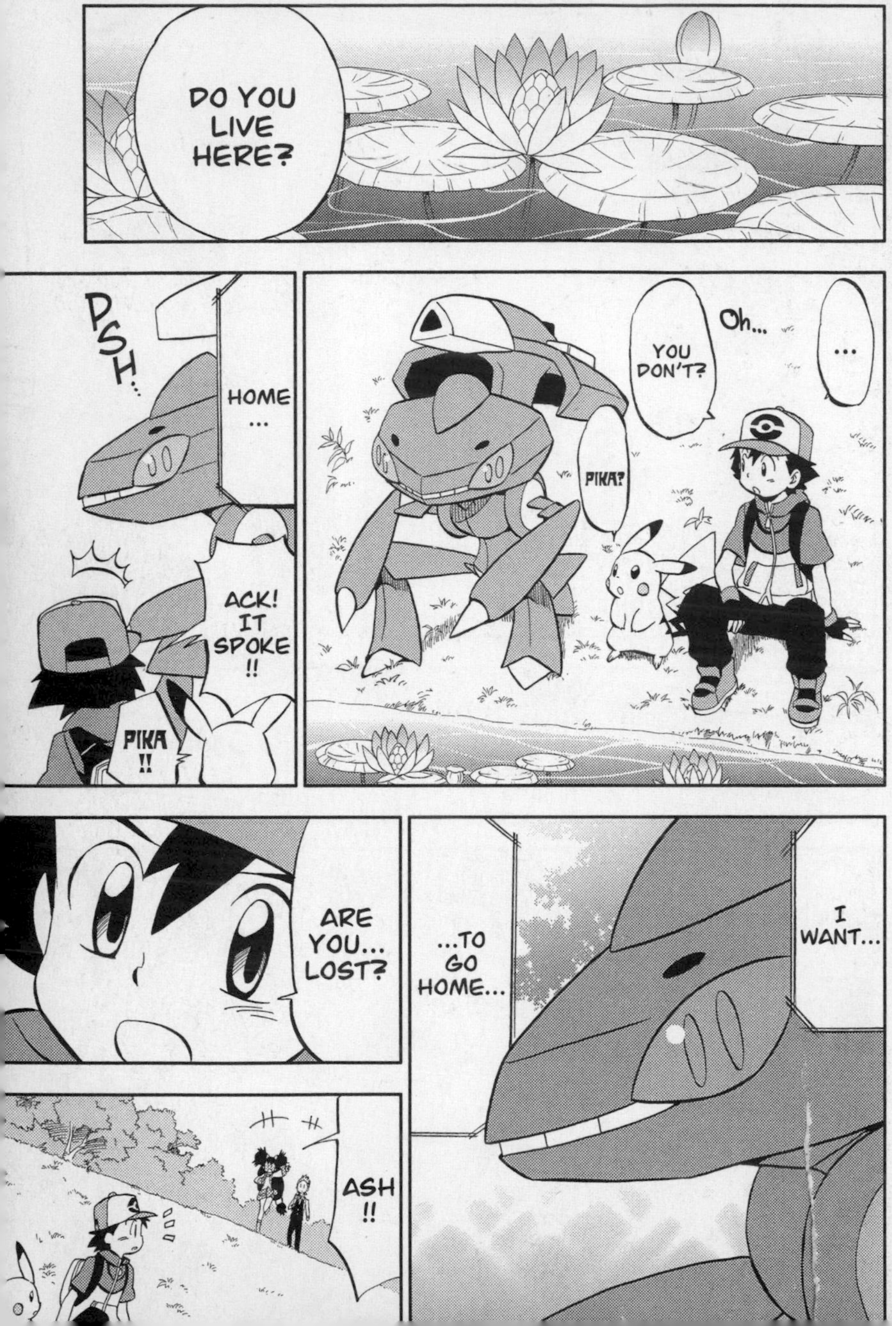
DO YOU LIVE HERE?
...
Oh...
YOU DON'T?
PIKA?
PSH...
HOME ...
ACK! IT SPOKE !!
PIKA !!
I WANT...
...TO GO HOME...
ARE YOU... LOST?
ASH !!

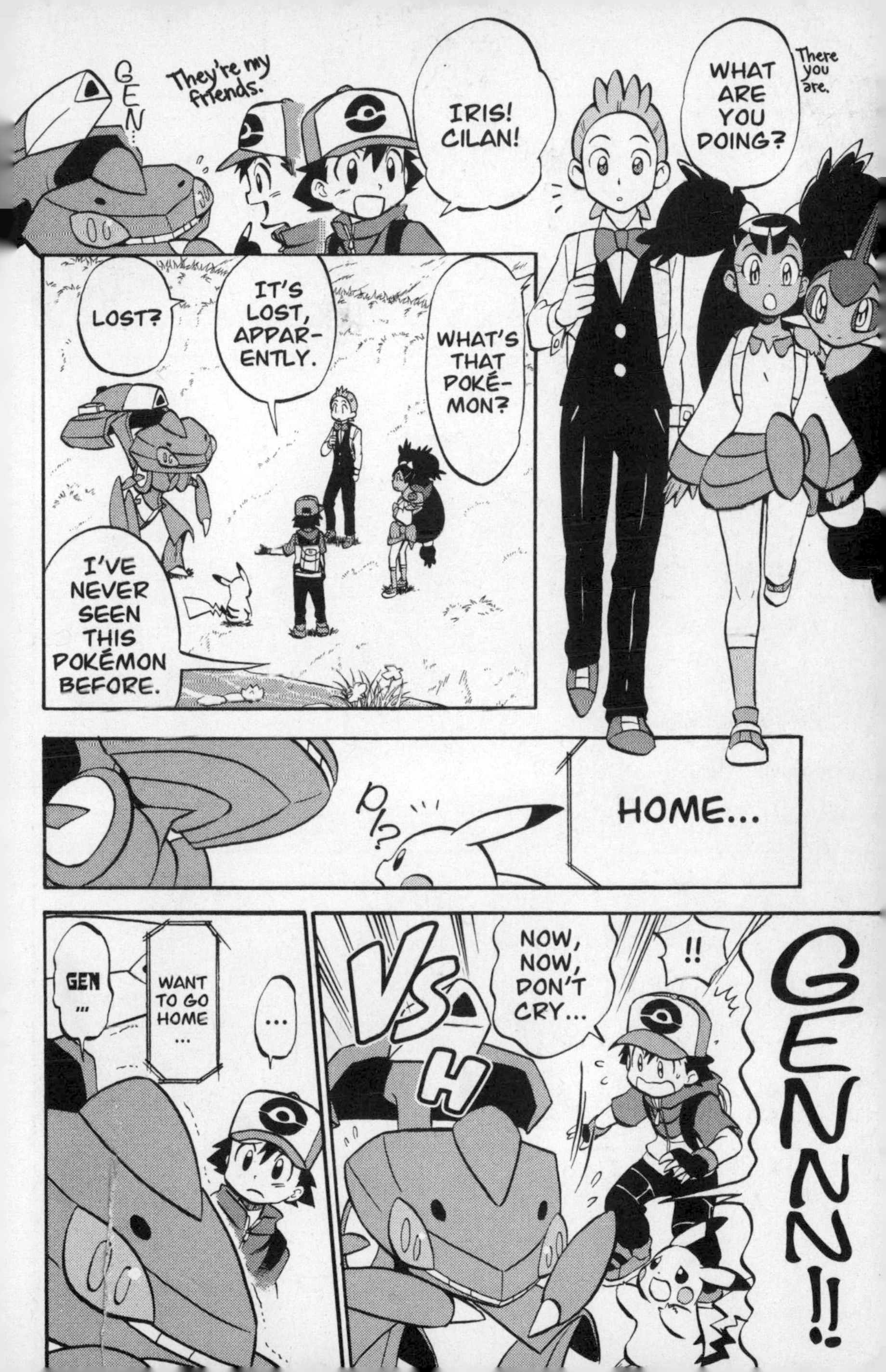
There you are.
WHAT ARE YOU DOING?
IRIS! CILAN!
They're my friends.
GEN...
WHAT'S THAT POKÉMON?
IT'S LOST, APPARENTLY.
LOST?
I'VE NEVER SEEN THIS POKÉMON BEFORE.
HOME...
Pi!?
GENNN!!
!!
NOW, NOW, DON'T CRY...
VSH
...
WANT TO GO HOME...
GEN...

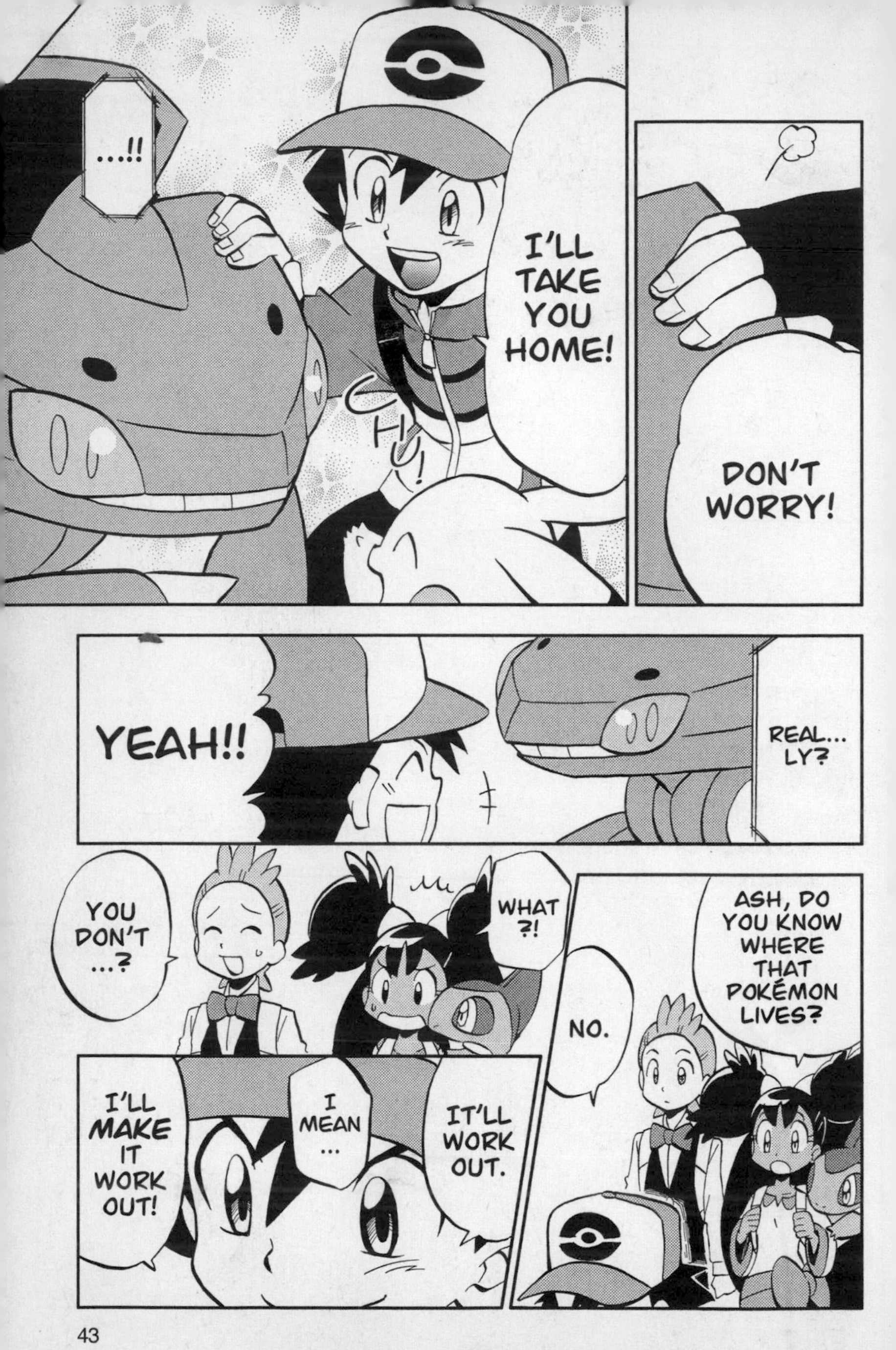
DON'T WORRY!
I'LL TAKE YOU HOME!
...!!
CHU!
REAL... LY?
YEAH!!
ASH, DO YOU KNOW WHERE THAT POKÉMON LIVES?
NO.
WHAT?!
YOU DON'T ...?
IT'LL WORK OUT.
I MEAN ...
I'LL MAKE IT WORK OUT!

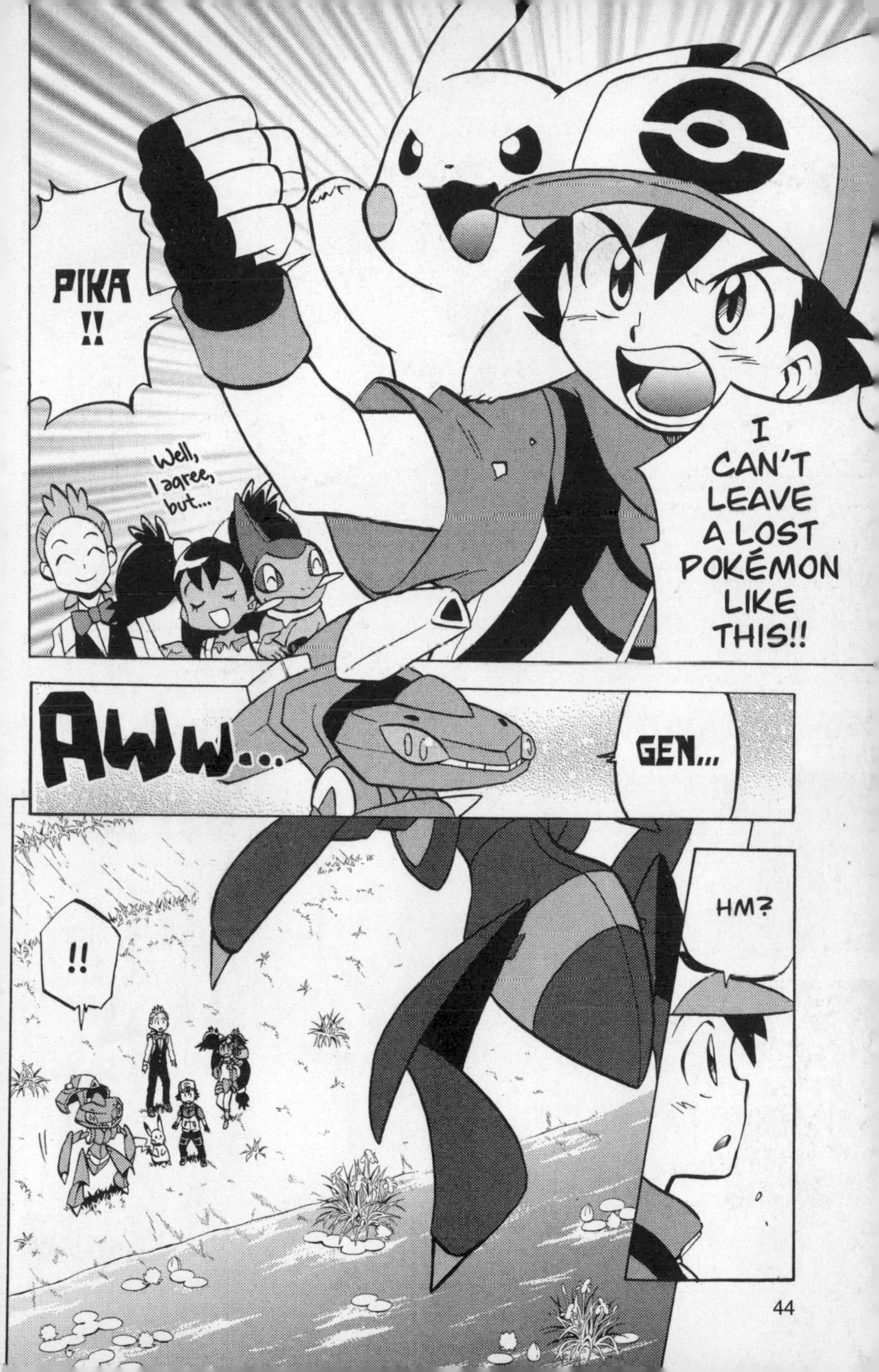
I CAN'T LEAVE A LOST POKÉMON LIKE THIS!!
PIKA!!
Well, I agree, but...
GEN...
AWW...
HM?
!!

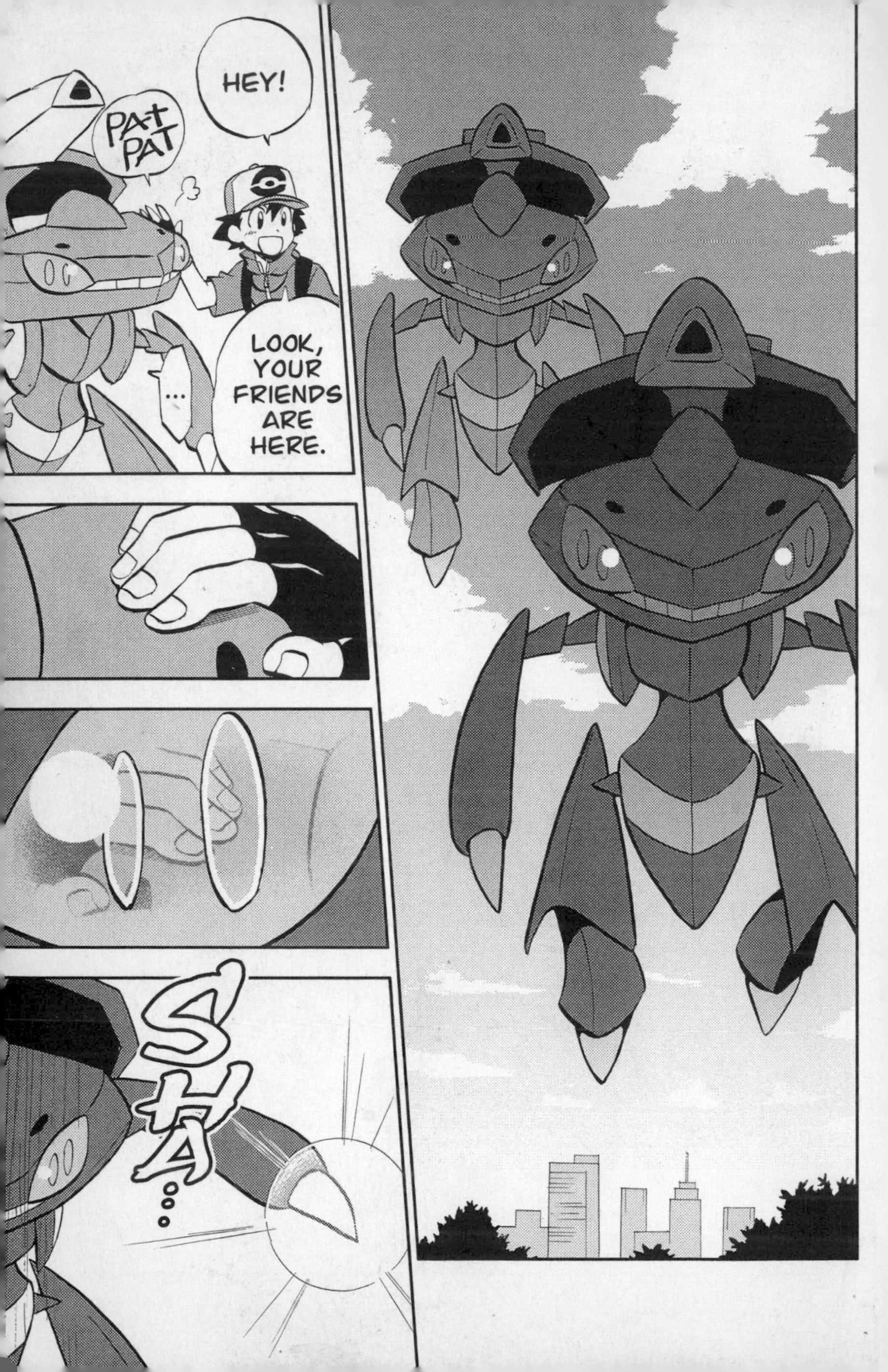
HEY!
PAT PAT
LOOK, YOUR FRIENDS ARE HERE.
...
SHA...

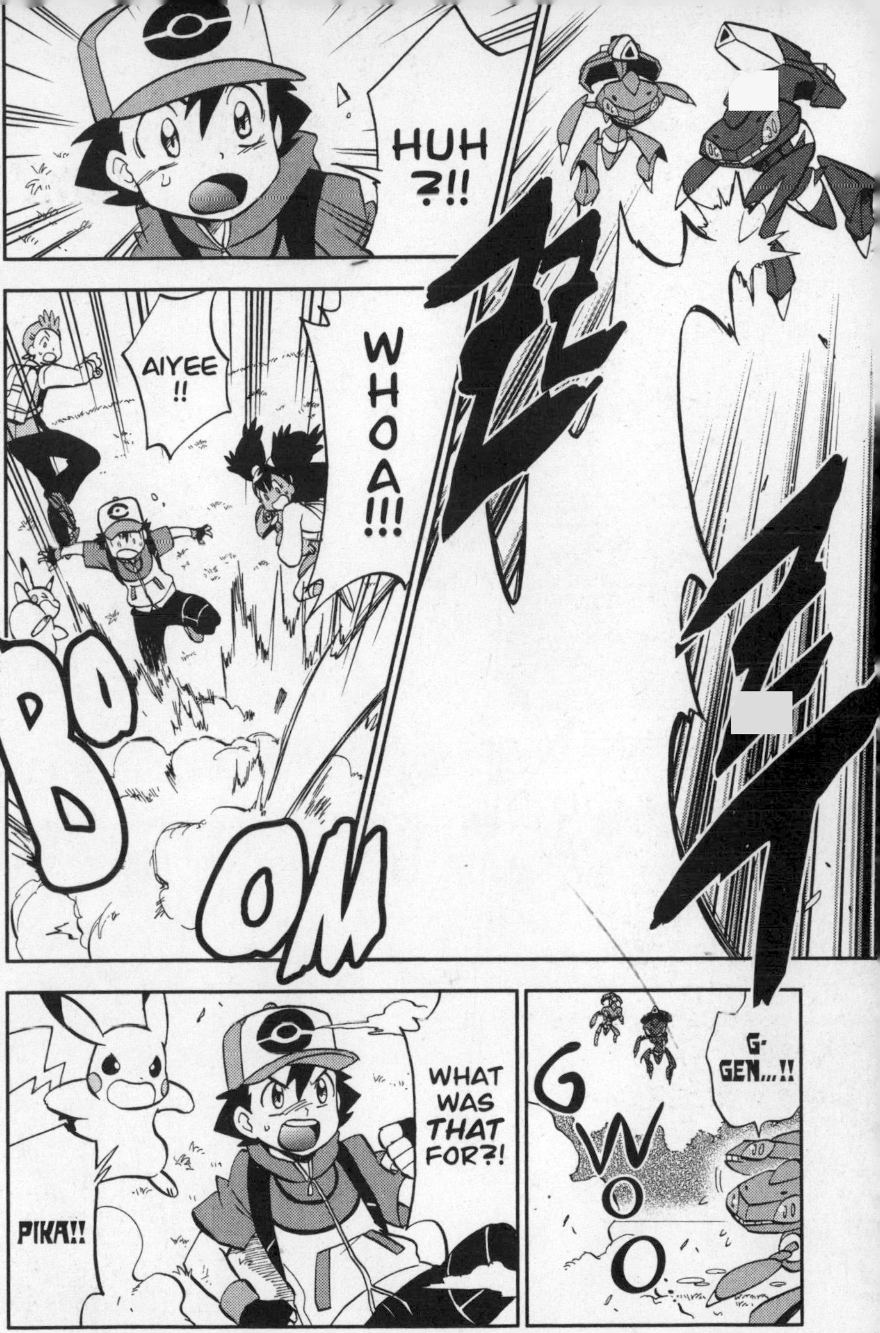
HUH ?!!
AIYEE !!
WHOA!!!
BOOM
G-GEN...!!
GWOO
WHAT WAS THAT FOR?!
PIKA!!

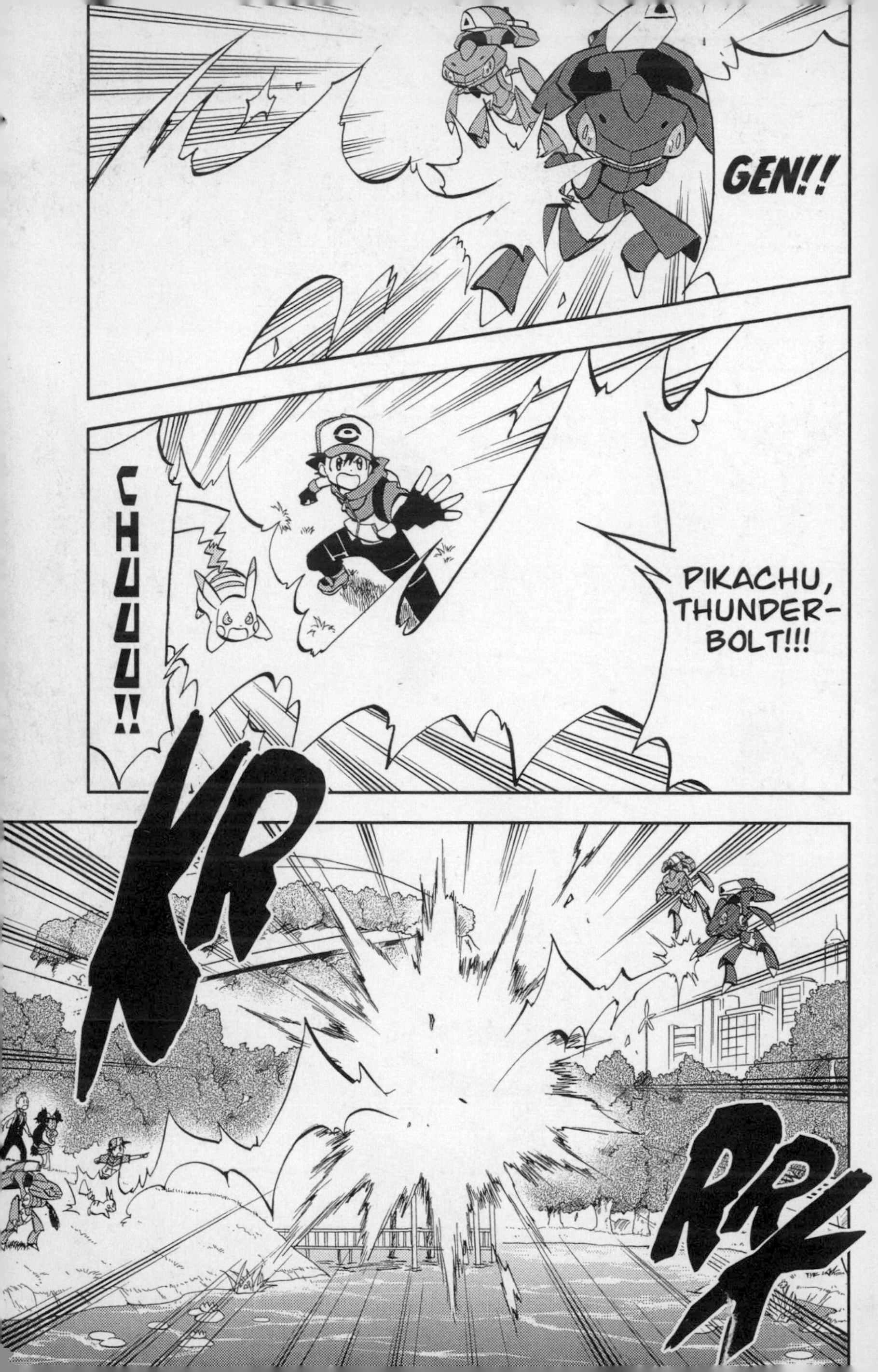
GEN!!
PIKACHU, THUNDER-BOLT!!!
CHUUUU!!
KR
RRK

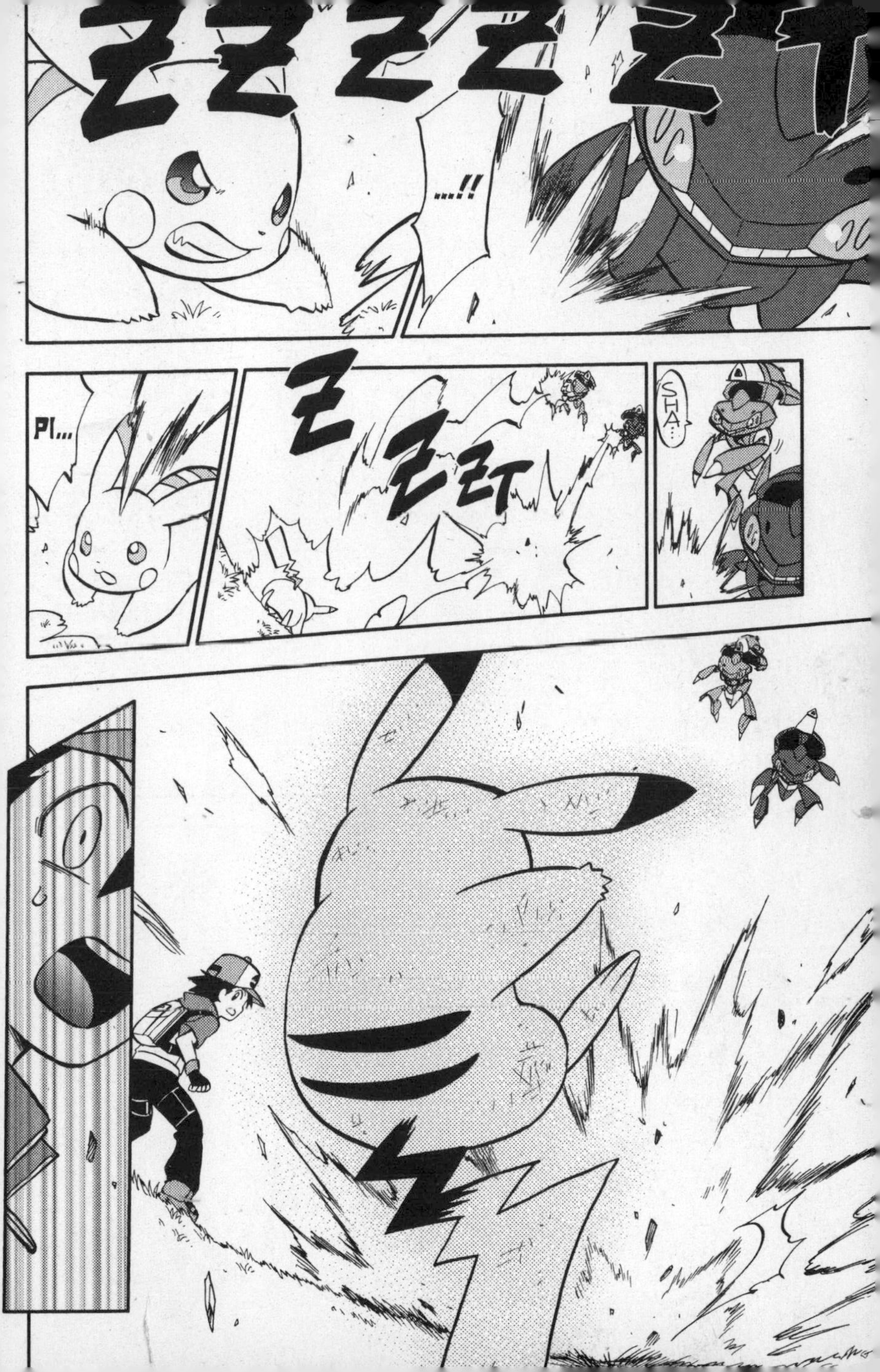

ZZZZZT
...!!
SHA...
ZZZT
PI...

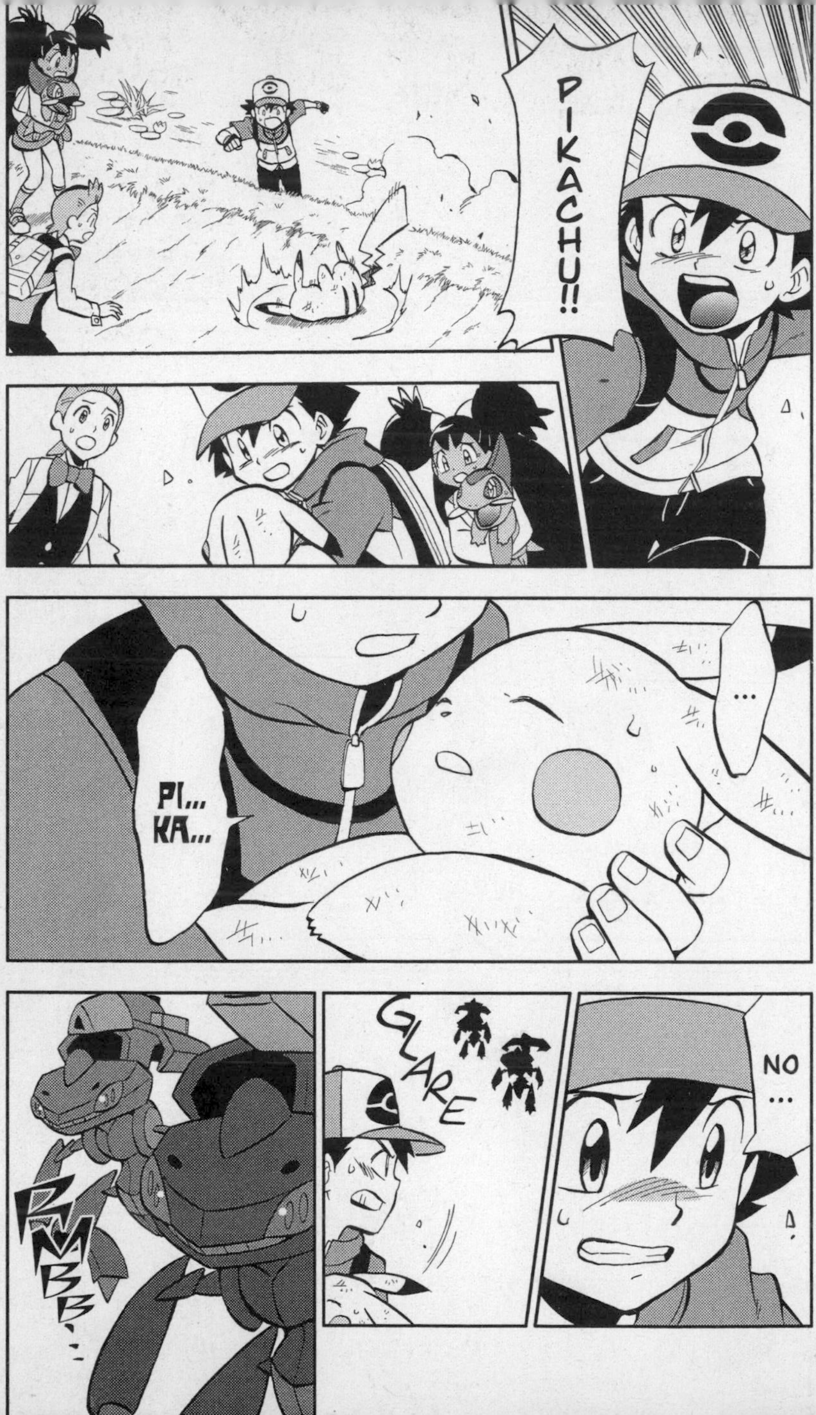
PIKACHU!!
...
PI... KA...
NO ...
GLARE
RMBB...

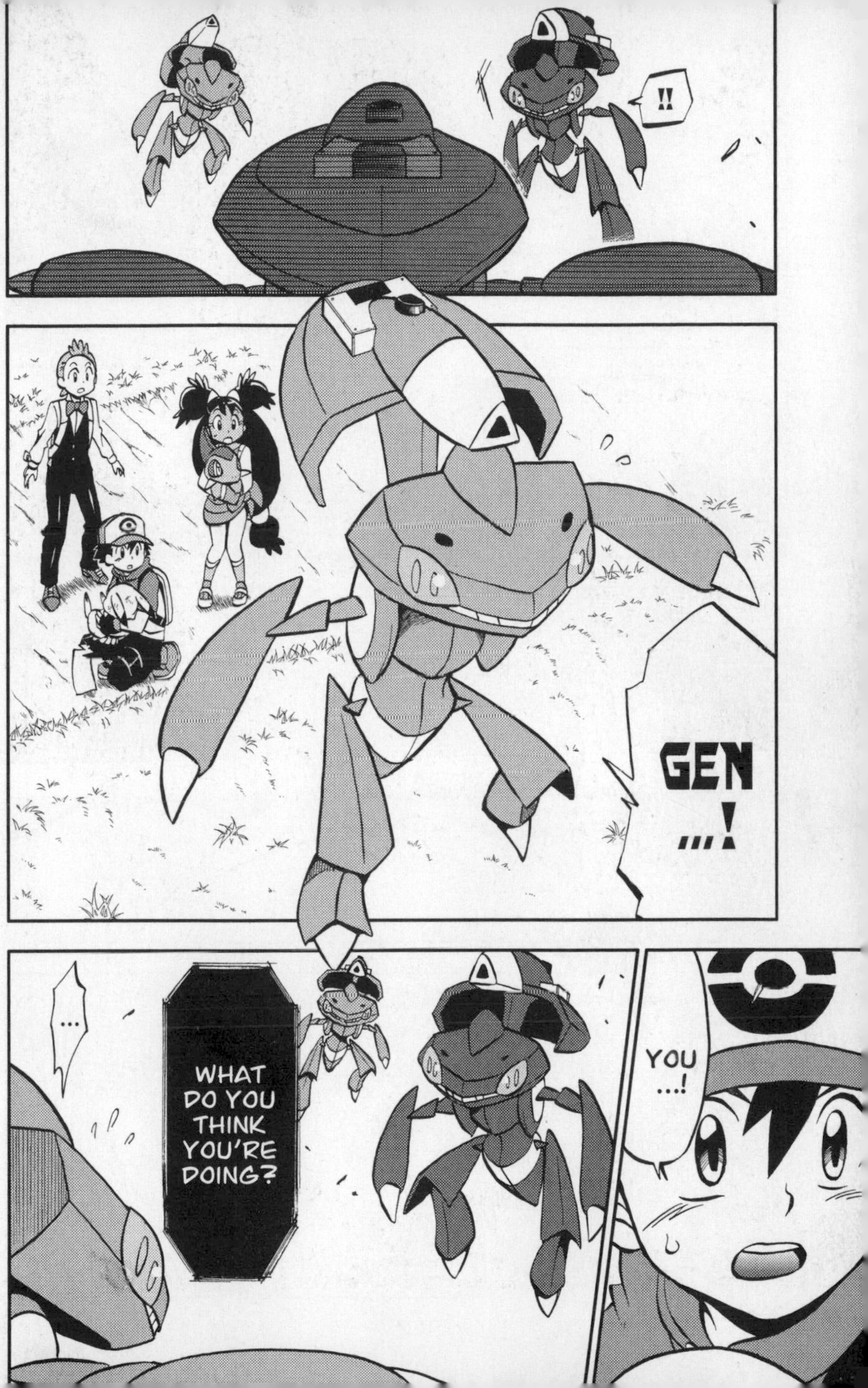
!!
GEN ...!
YOU ...!
WHAT DO YOU THINK YOU'RE DOING?
...

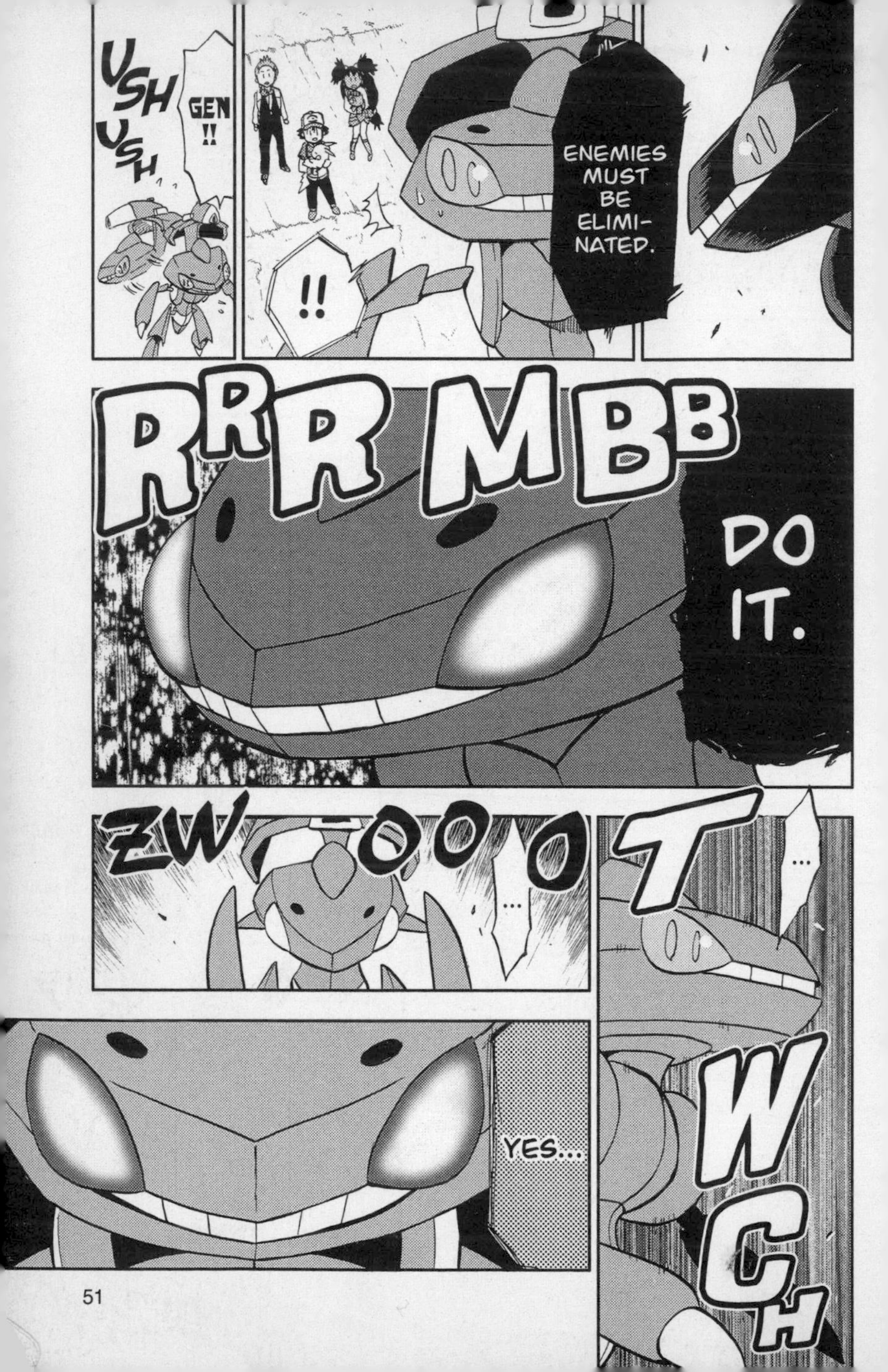
ENEMIES MUST BE ELIMINATED.
!!
GEN !!
USH USH
DO IT.
RRRMBB
...
WCH
ZWOOOT
...
YES...

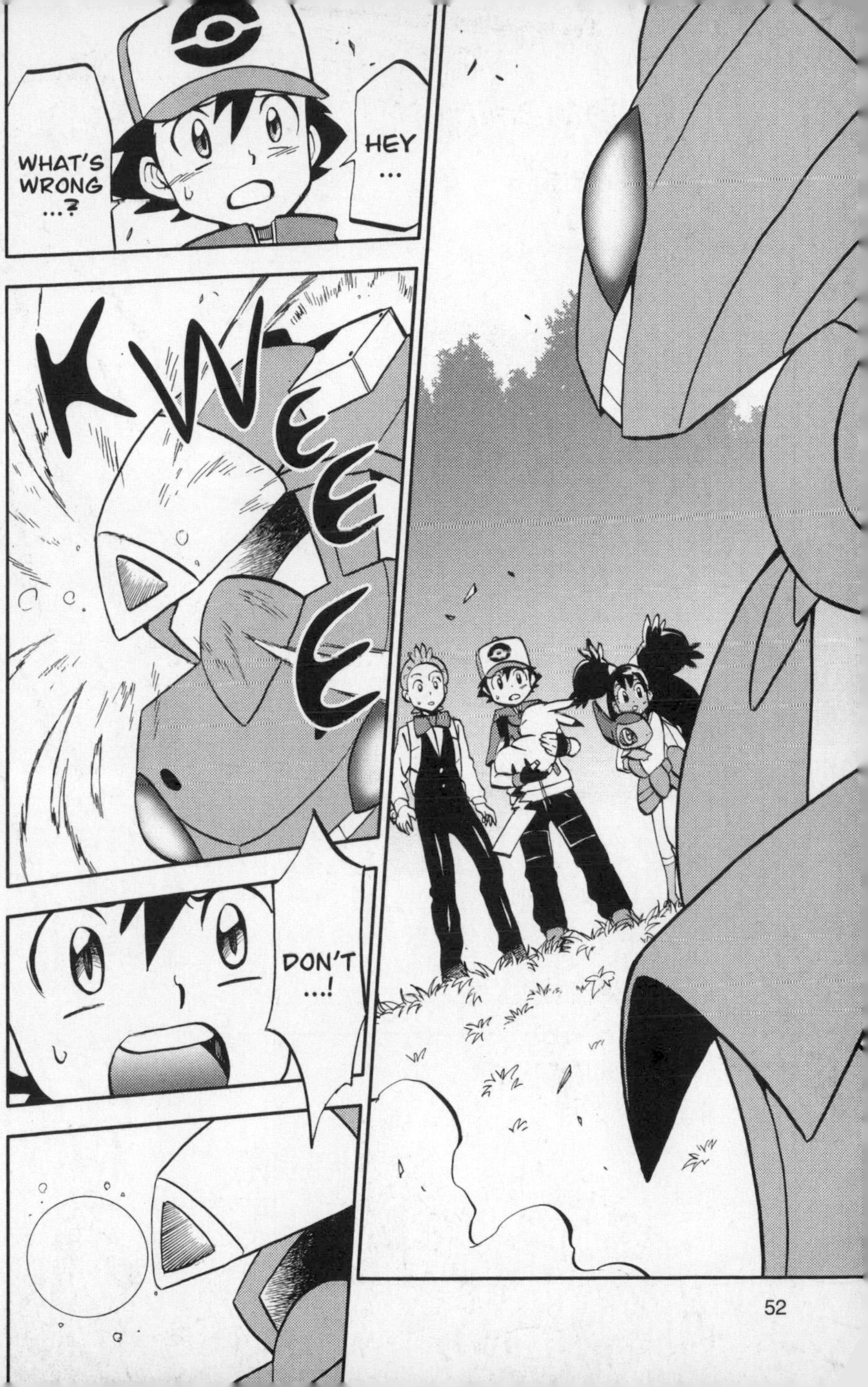
HEY ...
WHAT'S WRONG ...?
KWEEEE
DON'T ...!

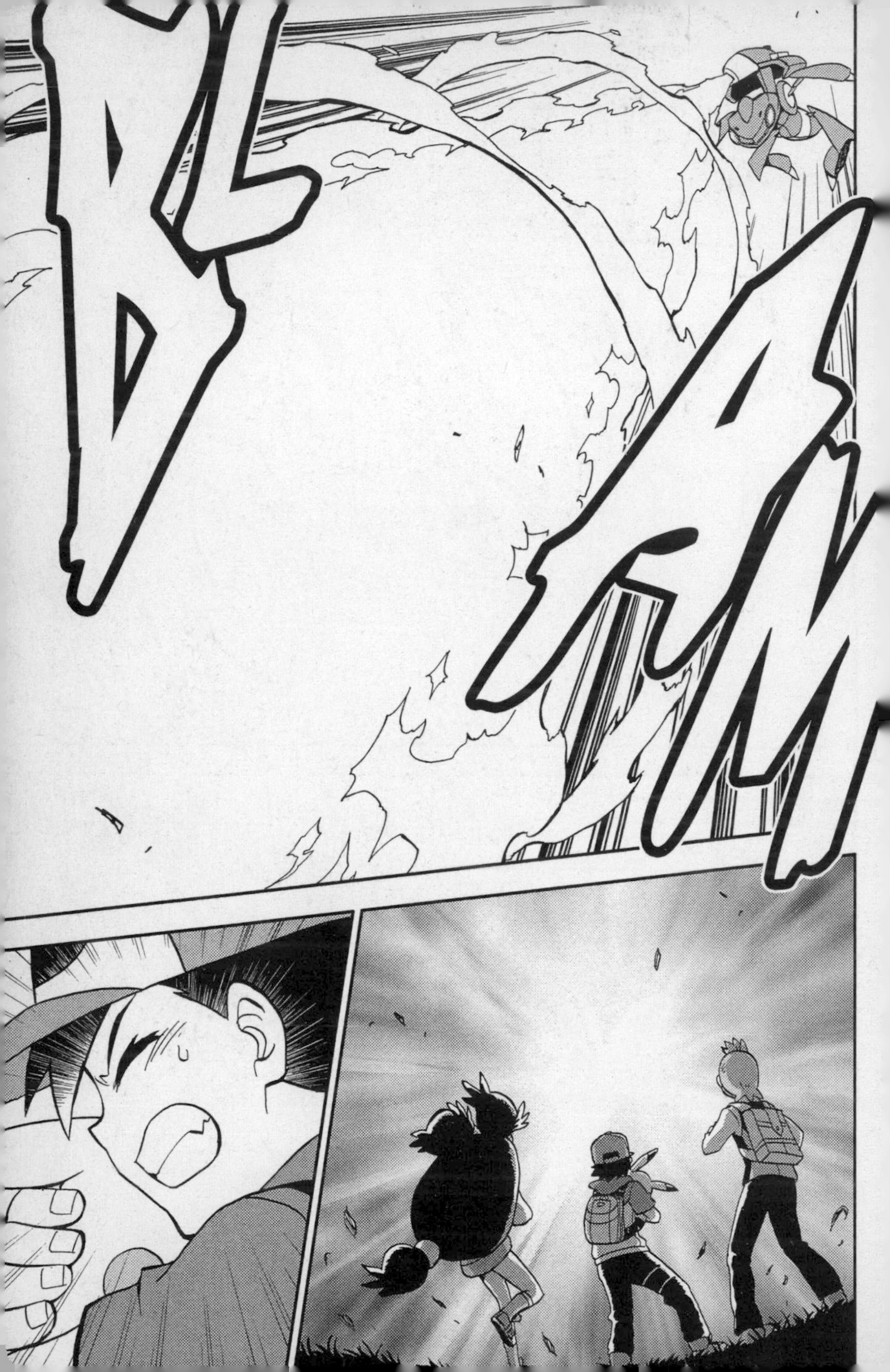

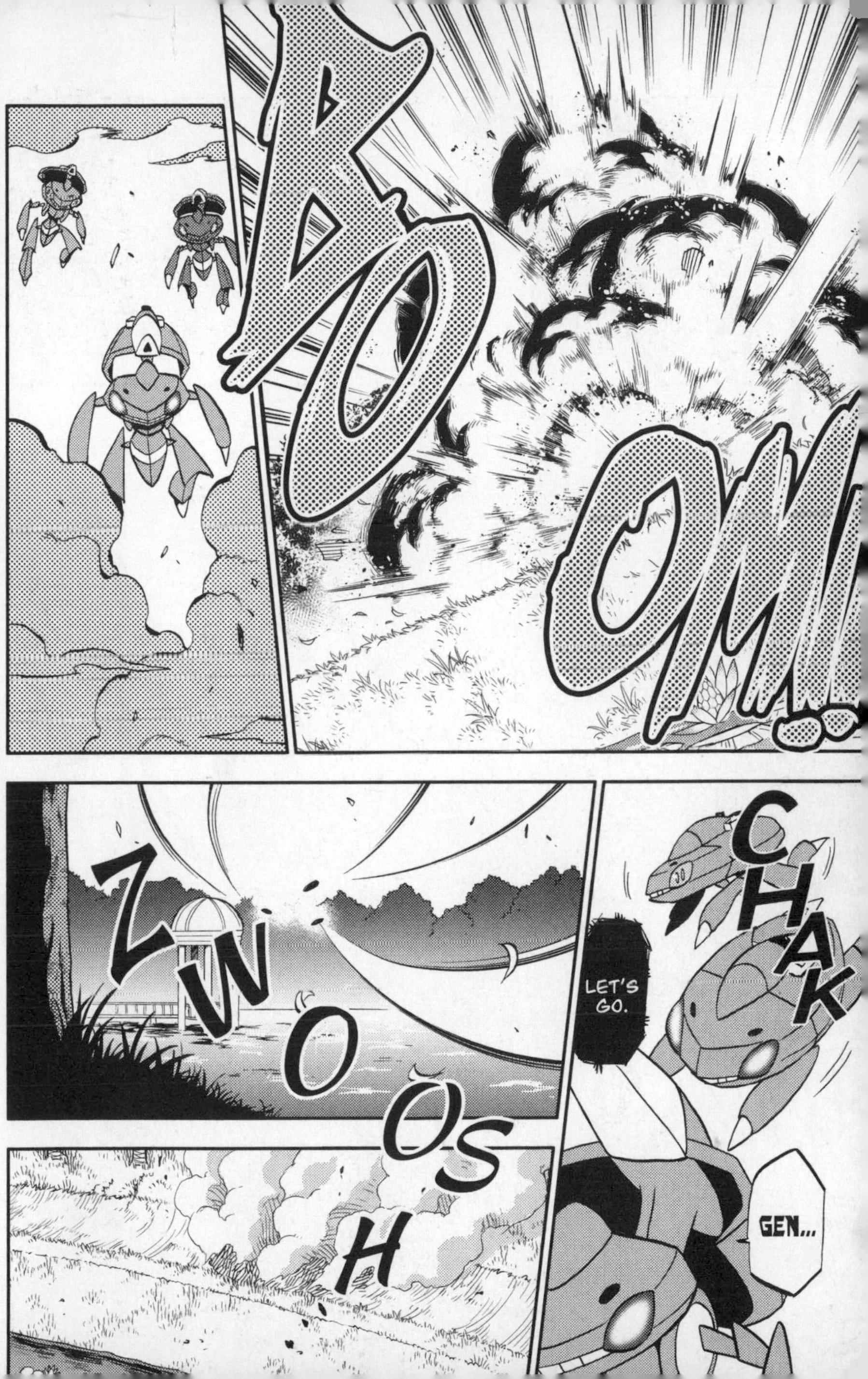
BOOM!!
CHAK
LET'S GO.
GEN...
ZWOOSH

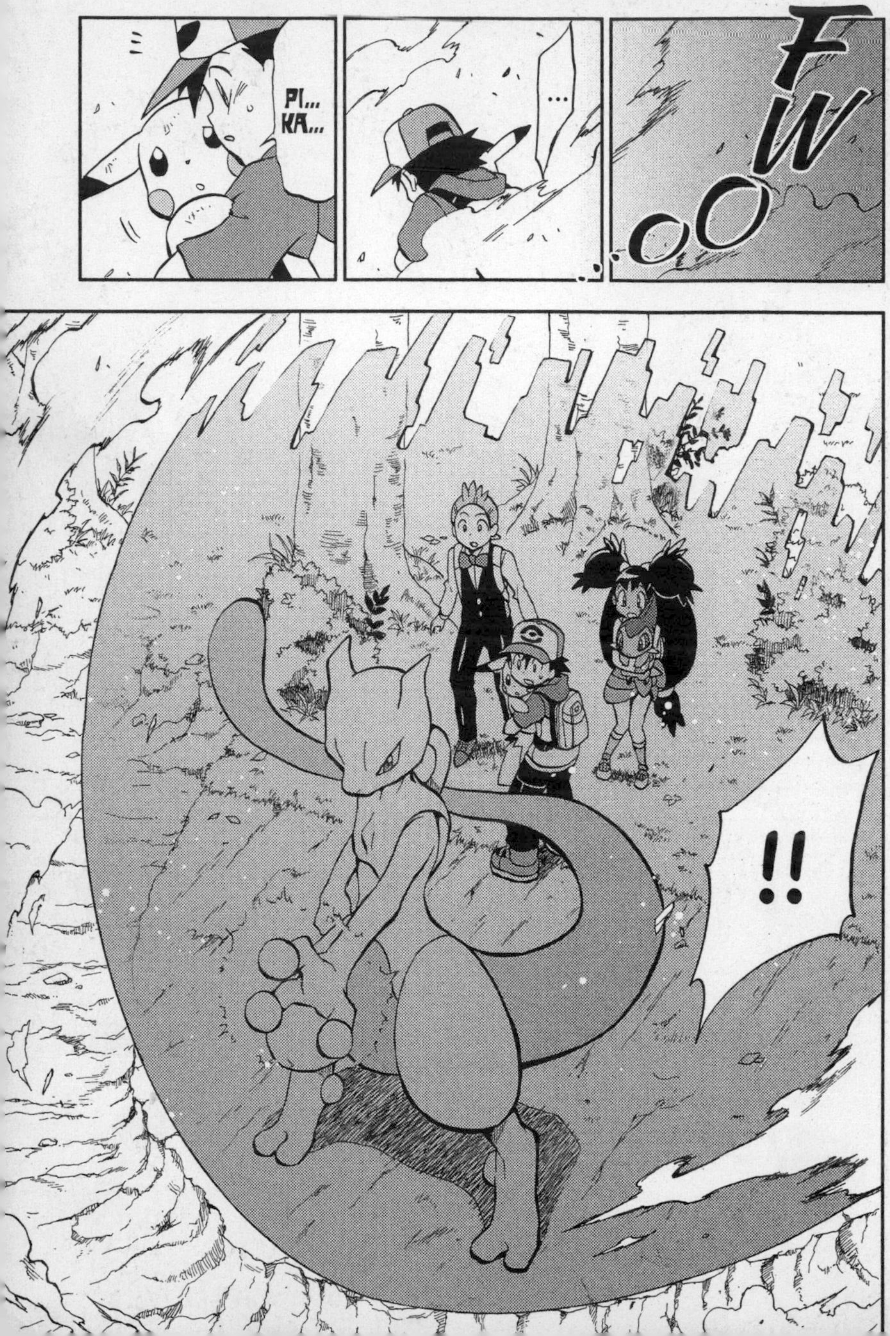
FWOOO
...
PI... KA...
!!

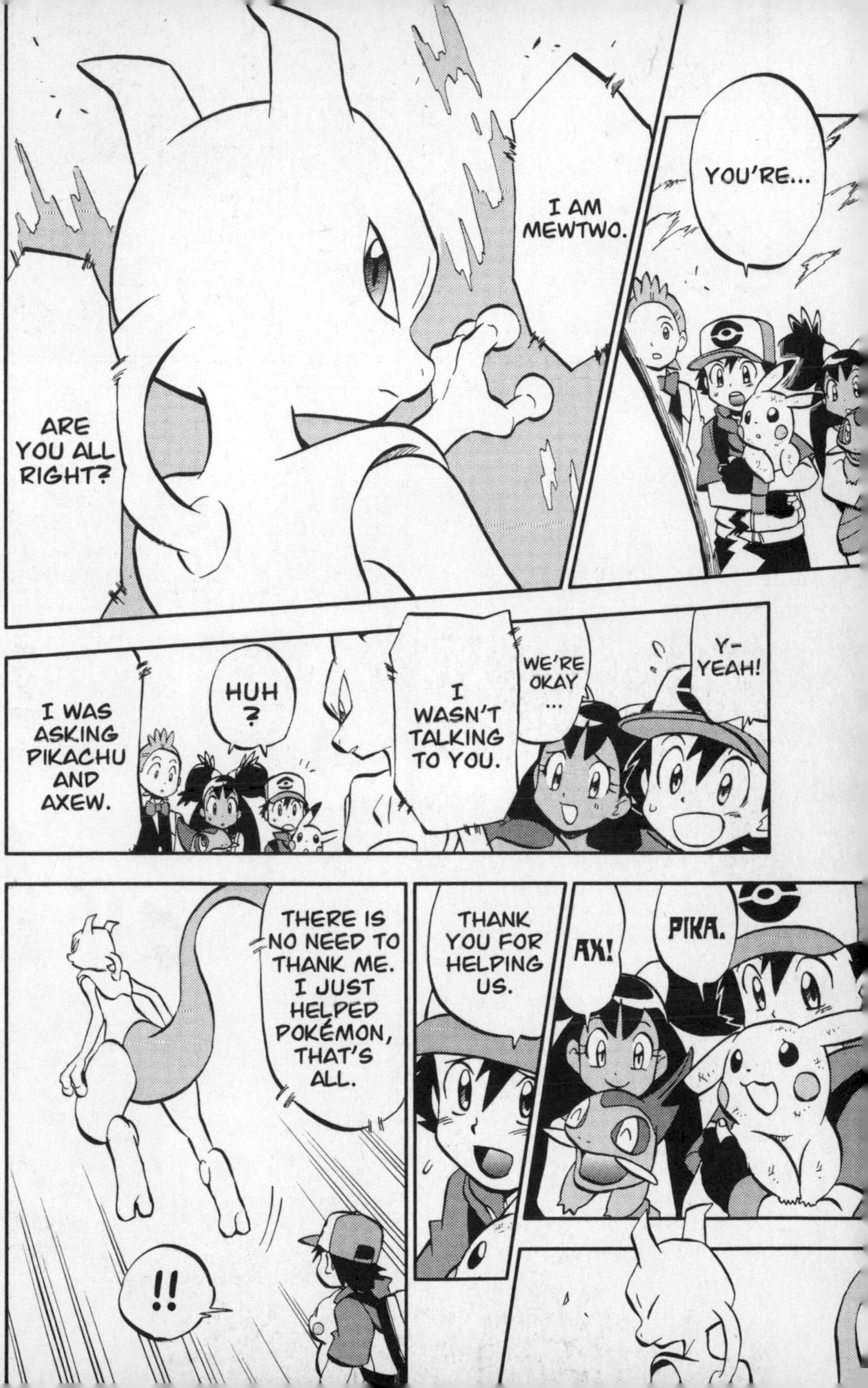
YOU'RE...
I AM MEWTWO.
ARE YOU ALL RIGHT?
Y-YEAH!
WE'RE OKAY...
I WASN'T TALKING TO YOU.
HUH?
I WAS ASKING PIKACHU AND AXEW.
PIKA.
AX!
THANK YOU FOR HELPING US.
THERE IS NO NEED TO THANK ME. I JUST HELPED POKÉMON, THAT'S ALL.
!!

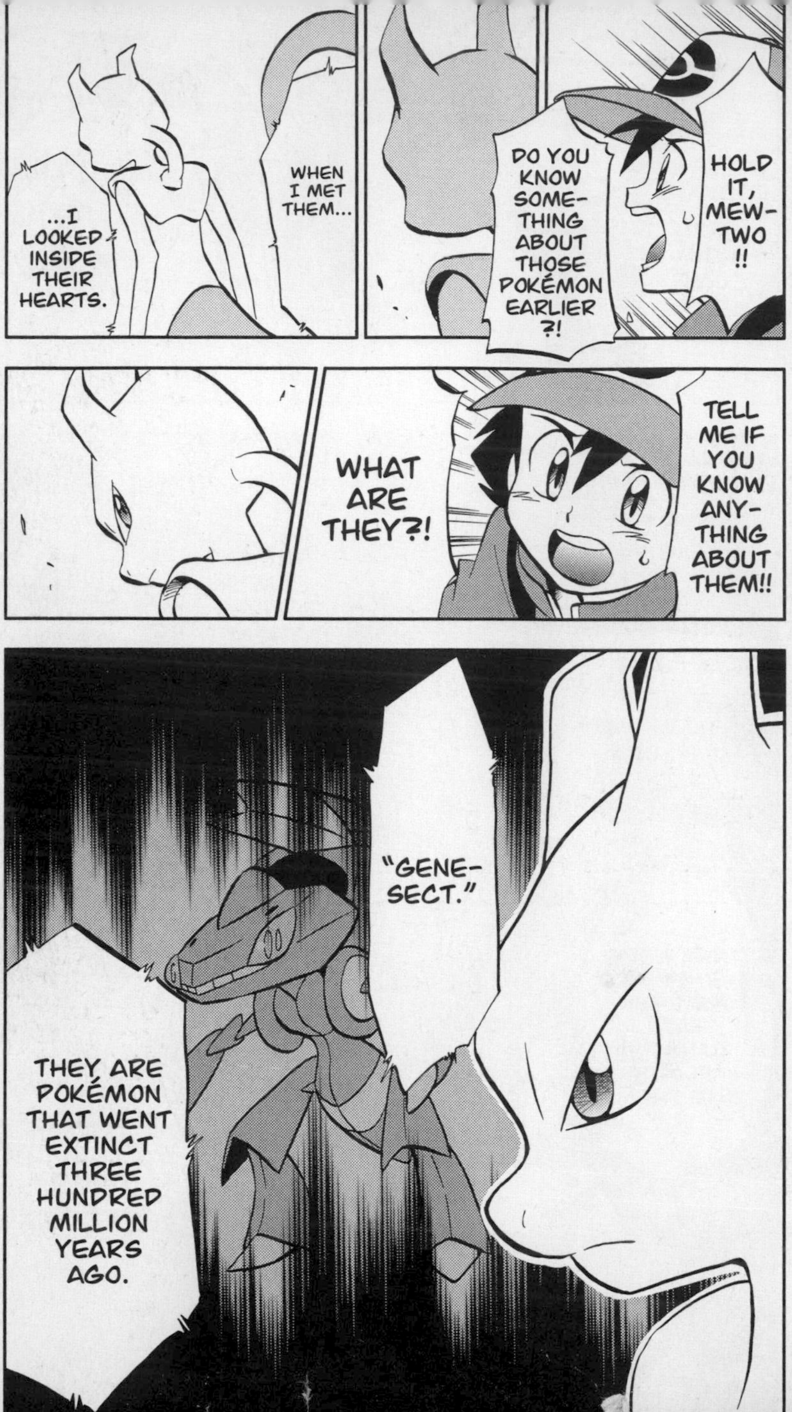
HOLD IT, MEW-TWO!!
DO YOU KNOW SOME-THING ABOUT THOSE POKÉMON EARLIER?!
WHEN I MET THEM...
...I LOOKED INSIDE THEIR HEARTS.
TELL ME IF YOU KNOW ANY-THING ABOUT THEM!!
WHAT ARE THEY?!
"GENE-SECT."
THEY ARE POKÉMON THAT WENT EXTINCT THREE HUNDRED MILLION YEARS AGO.

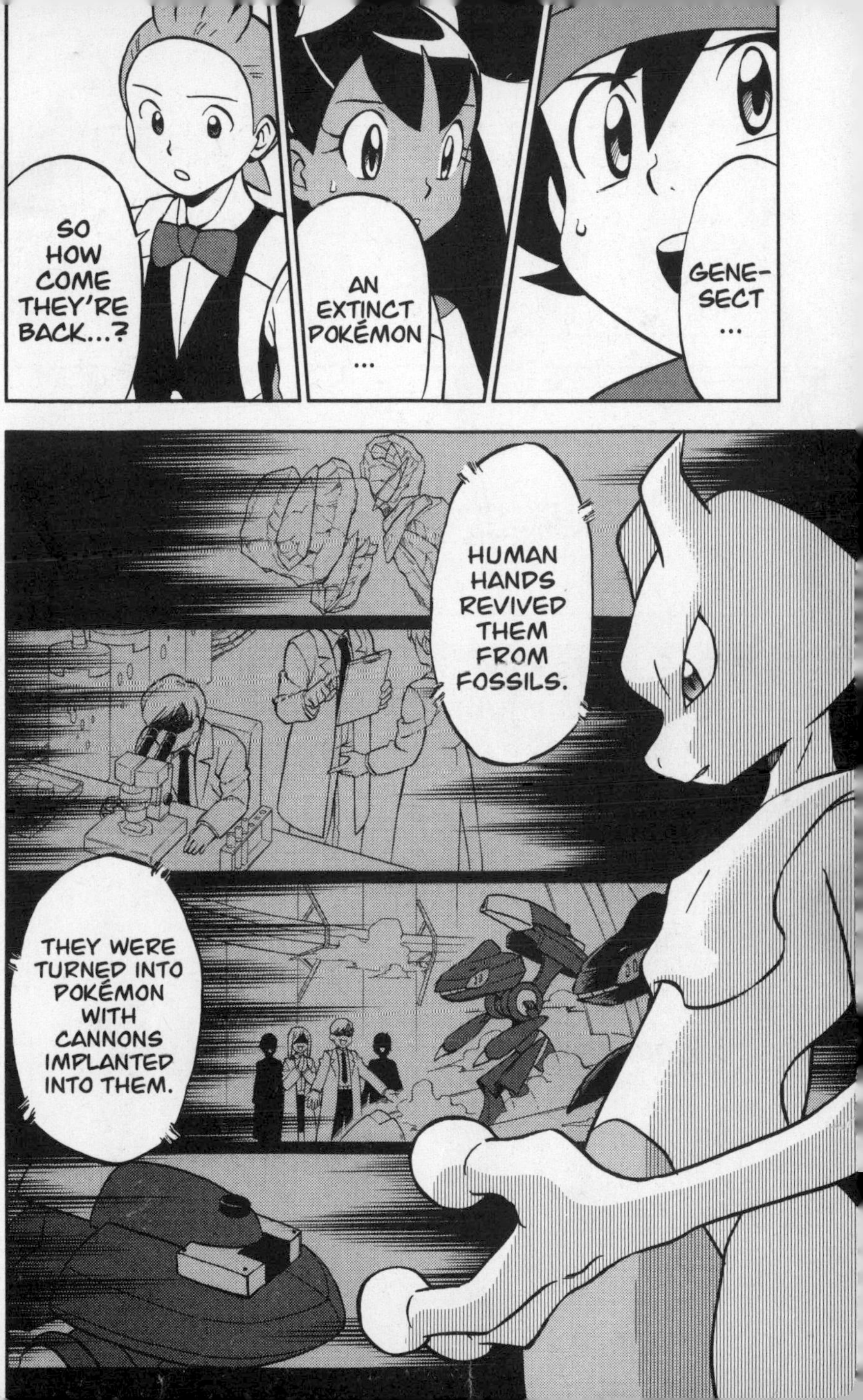
GENE-SECT...
AN EXTINCT POKÉMON...
SO HOW COME THEY'RE BACK...?
HUMAN HANDS REVIVED THEM FROM FOSSILS.
THEY WERE TURNED INTO POKÉMON WITH CANNONS IMPLANTED INTO THEM.

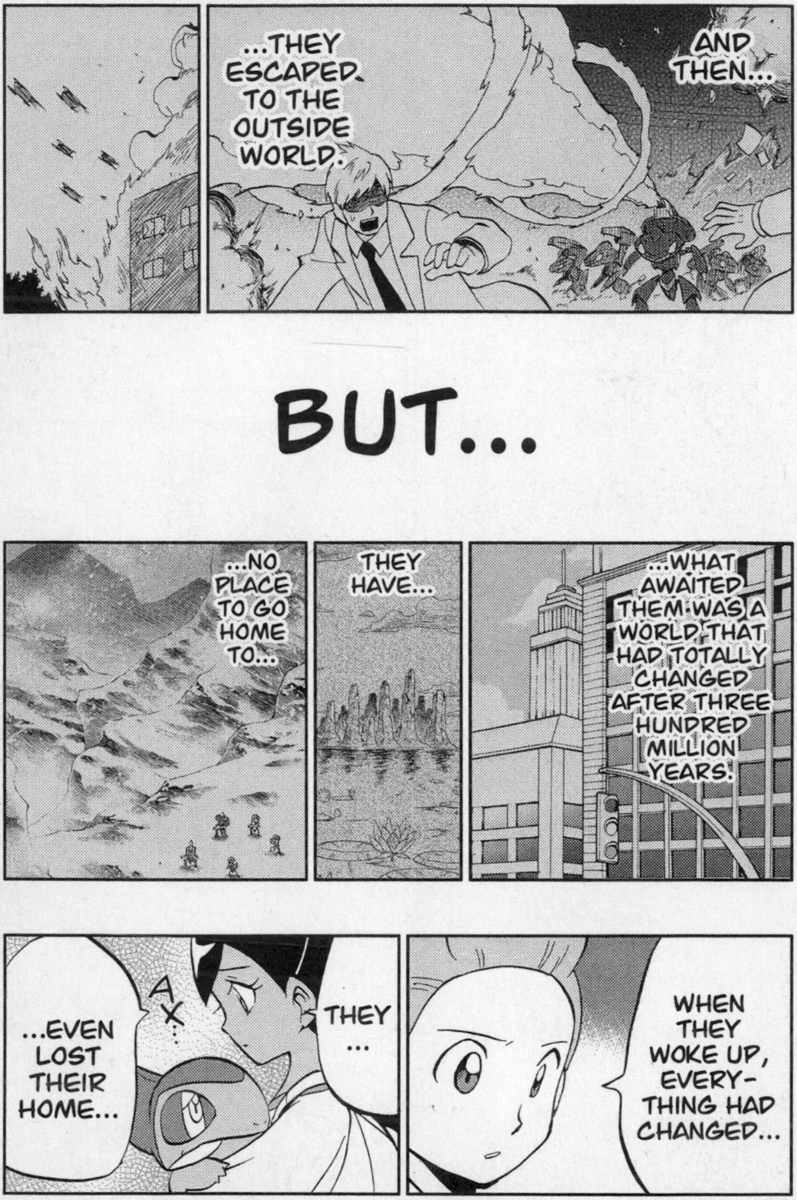
AND THEN...
...THEY ESCAPED TO THE OUTSIDE WORLD.
BUT...
...WHAT AWAITED THEM WAS A WORLD THAT HAD TOTALLY CHANGED AFTER THREE HUNDRED MILLION YEARS.
THEY HAVE...
...NO PLACE TO GO HOME TO...
WHEN THEY WOKE UP, EVERYTHING HAD CHANGED...
THEY ...
...EVEN LOST THEIR HOME...

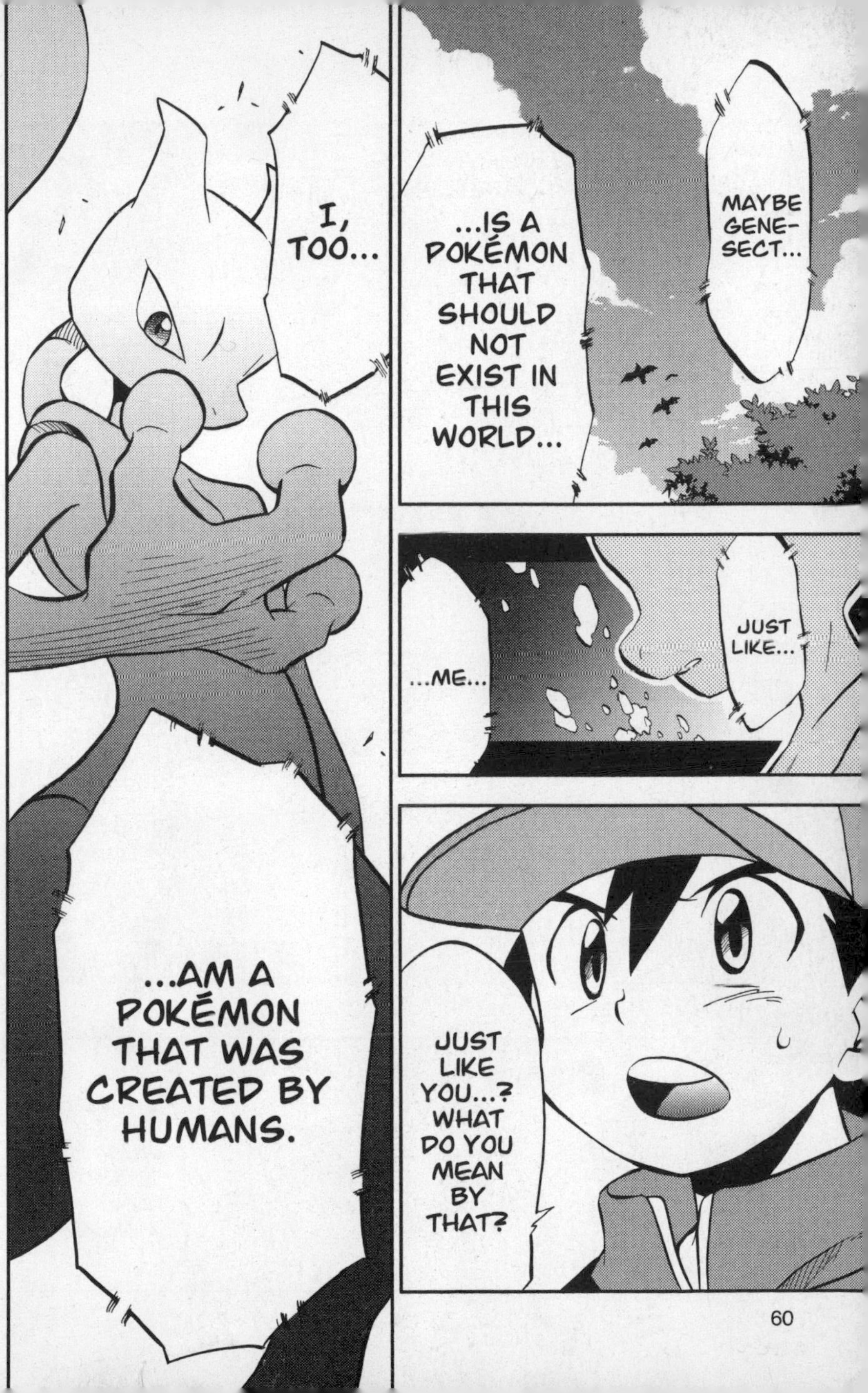
MAYBE GENE-SECT...
...IS A POKÉMON THAT SHOULD NOT EXIST IN THIS WORLD...
JUST LIKE...
...ME...
JUST LIKE YOU...? WHAT DO YOU MEAN BY THAT?
I, TOO...
...AM A POKÉMON THAT WAS CREATED BY HUMANS.

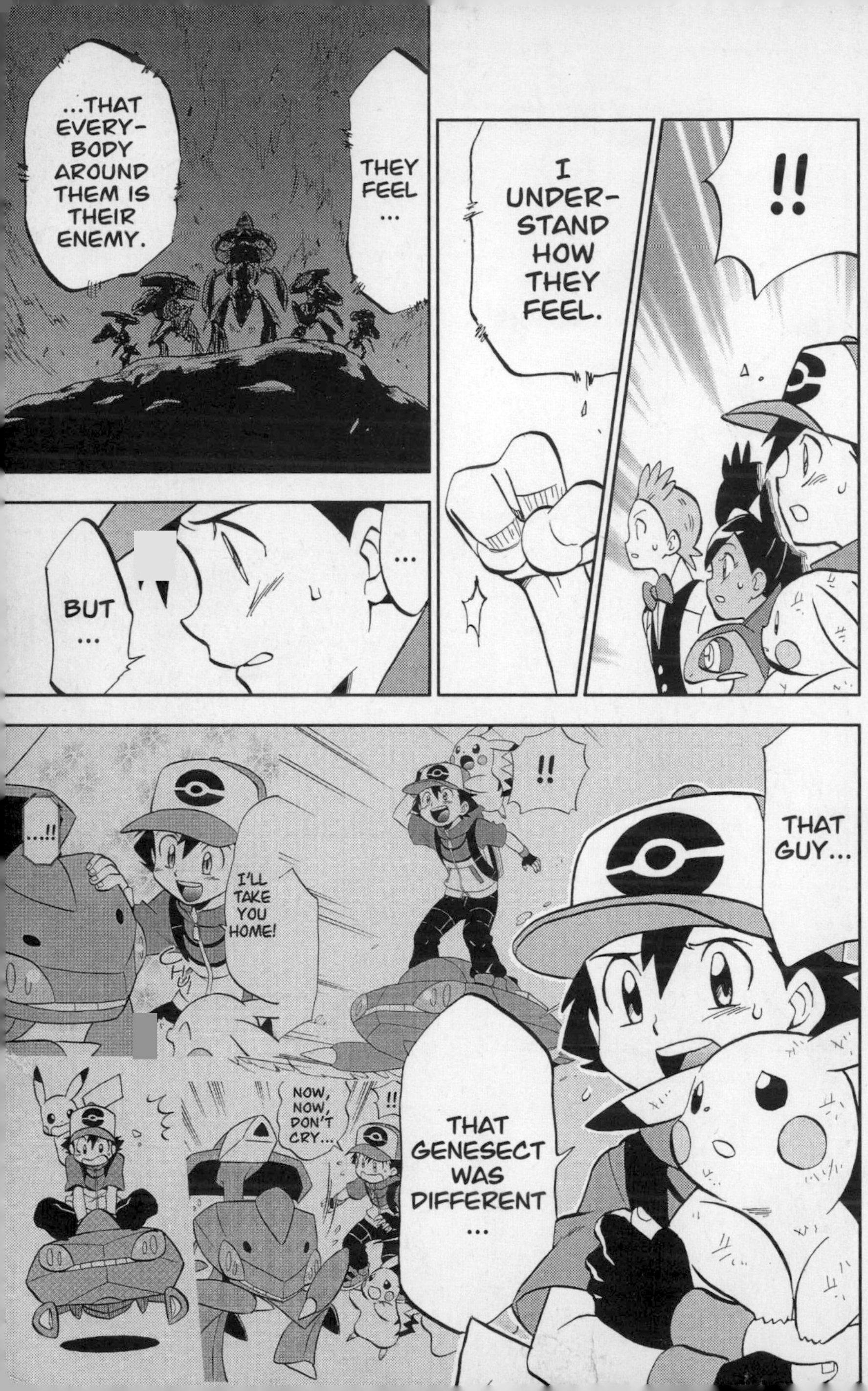
THEY FEEL ...
...THAT EVERY-BODY AROUND THEM IS THEIR ENEMY.
BUT ...
...
I UNDER-STAND HOW THEY FEEL.
!!
THAT GUY...
THAT GENESECT WAS DIFFERENT ...
!!
I'LL TAKE YOU HOME!
...!!
!!
NOW, NOW, DON'T CRY...

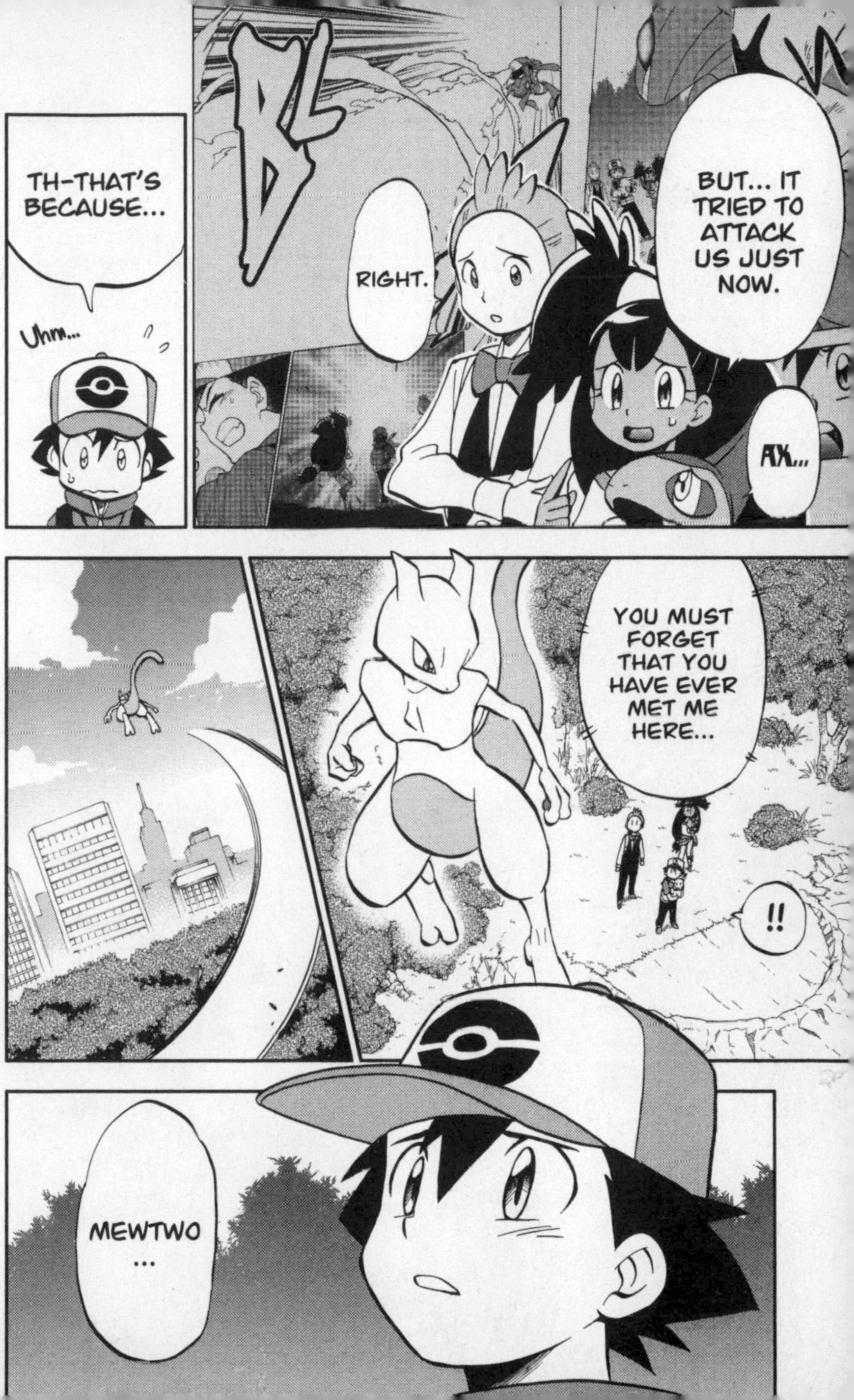
BUT... IT TRIED TO ATTACK US JUST NOW.
RIGHT.
AX...
TH-THAT'S BECAUSE...
Uhm...
YOU MUST FORGET THAT YOU HAVE EVER MET ME HERE...
!!
MEWTWO ...

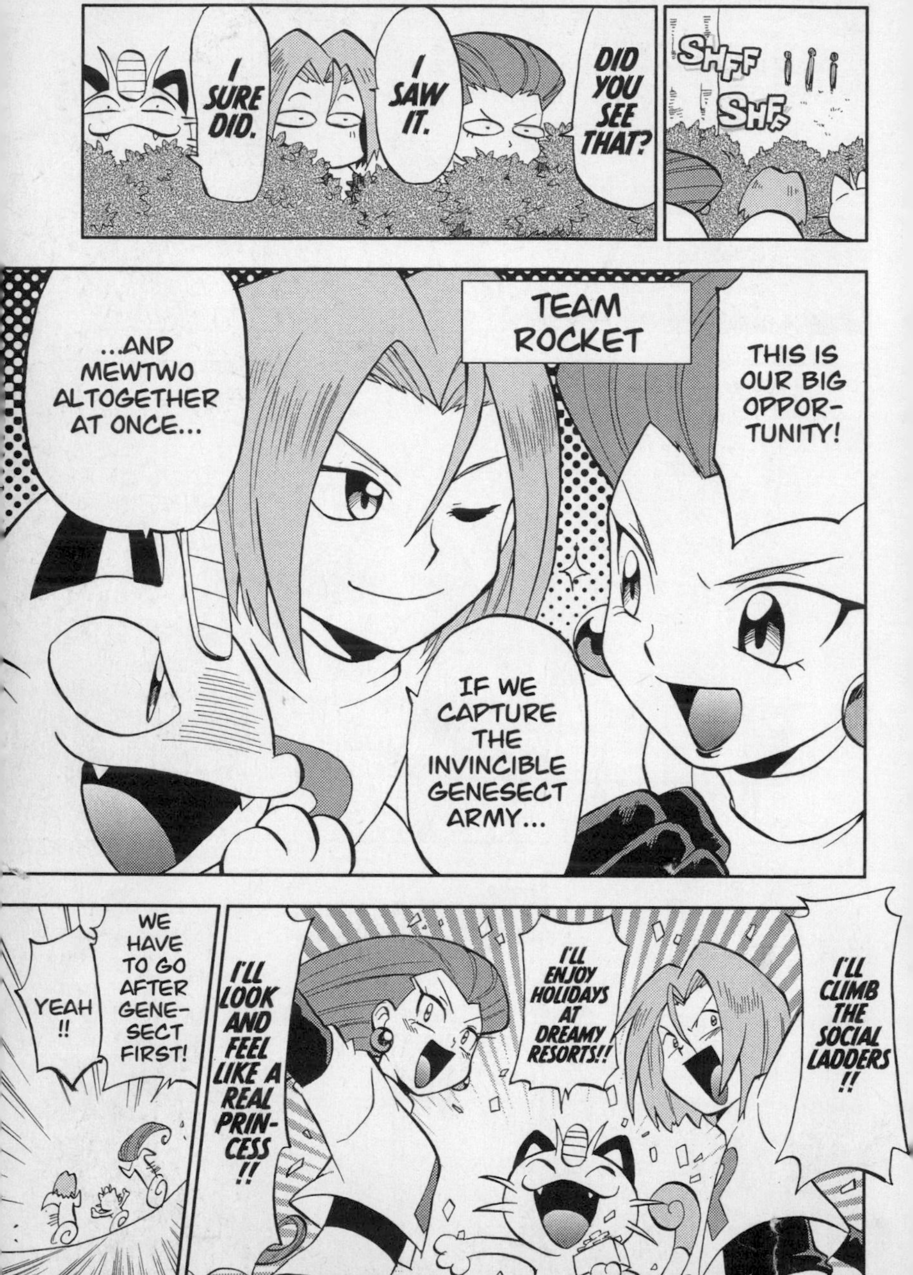
SHFF
SHFF
DID YOU SEE THAT?
I SAW IT.
I SURE DID.
TEAM ROCKET
THIS IS OUR BIG OPPORTUNITY!
...AND MEWTWO ALTOGETHER AT ONCE...
IF WE CAPTURE THE INVINCIBLE GENESECT ARMY...
I'LL CLIMB THE SOCIAL LADDERS!!
I'LL ENJOY HOLIDAYS AT DREAMY RESORTS!!
I'LL LOOK AND FEEL LIKE A REAL PRINCESS!!
WE HAVE TO GO AFTER GENESECT FIRST!
YEAH!!

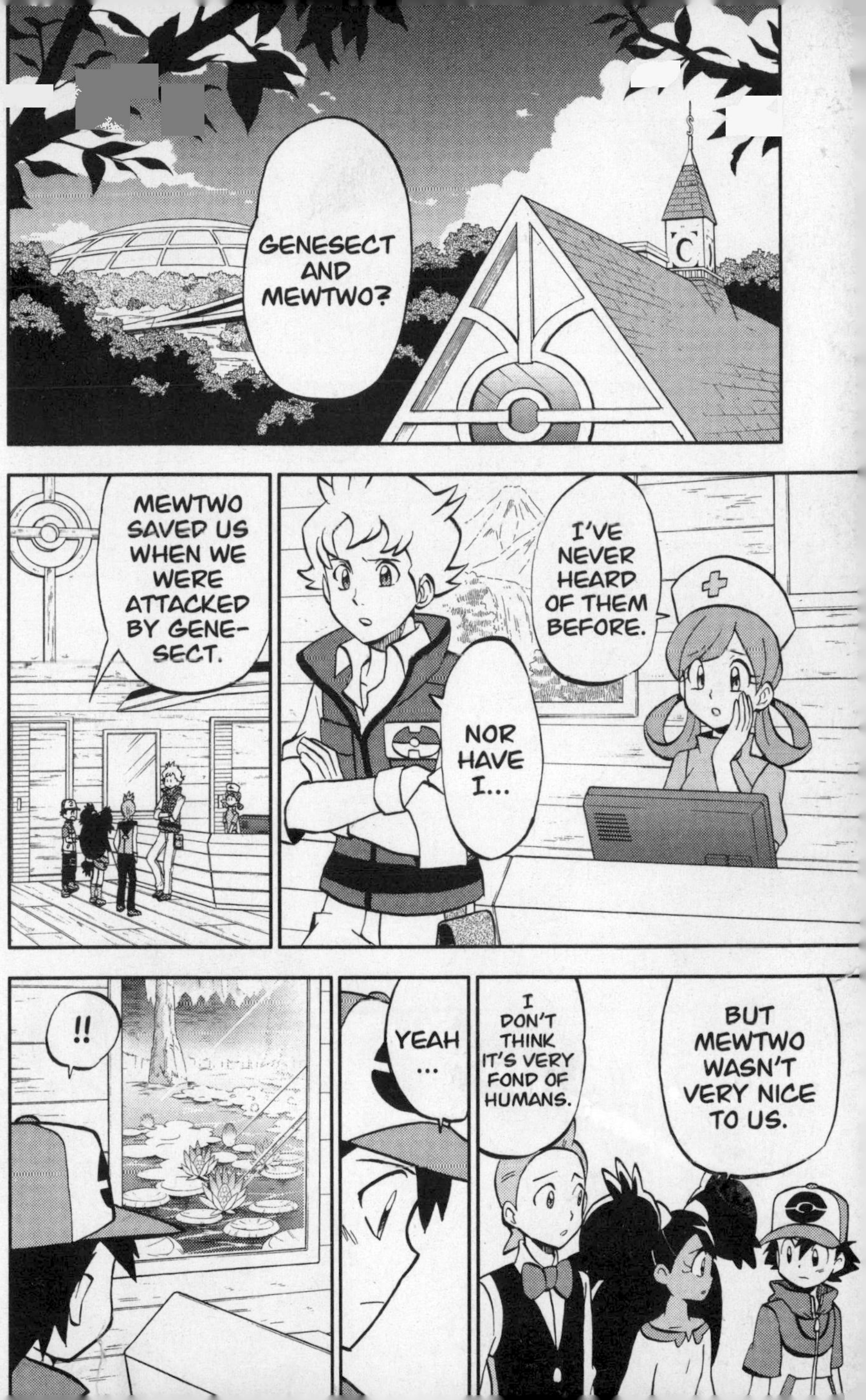
GENESECT AND MEWTWO?
I'VE NEVER HEARD OF THEM BEFORE.
NOR HAVE I...
MEWTWO SAVED US WHEN WE WERE ATTACKED BY GENE-SECT.
BUT MEWTWO WASN'T VERY NICE TO US.
I DON'T THINK IT'S VERY FOND OF HUMANS.
YEAH...
!!

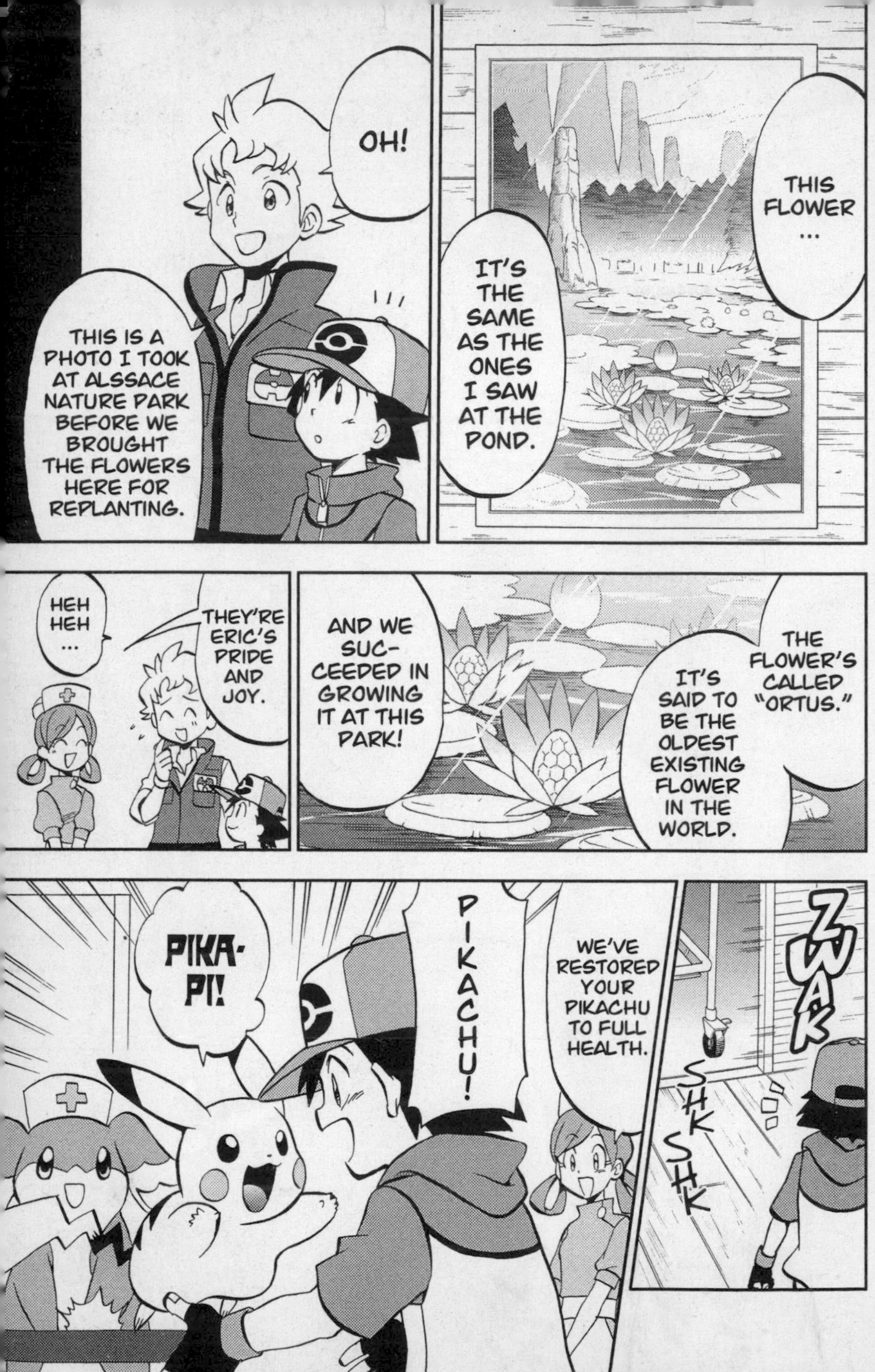
THIS FLOWER ...
IT'S THE SAME AS THE ONES I SAW AT THE POND.
OH!
THIS IS A PHOTO I TOOK AT ALSSACE NATURE PARK BEFORE WE BROUGHT THE FLOWERS HERE FOR REPLANTING.
THE FLOWER'S CALLED "ORTUS."
IT'S SAID TO BE THE OLDEST EXISTING FLOWER IN THE WORLD.
AND WE SUC-CEEDED IN GROWING IT AT THIS PARK!
THEY'RE ERIC'S PRIDE AND JOY.
HEH HEH ...
ZWAK
SHK SHK
WE'VE RESTORED YOUR PIKACHU TO FULL HEALTH.
PIKACHU!
PIKA-PI!

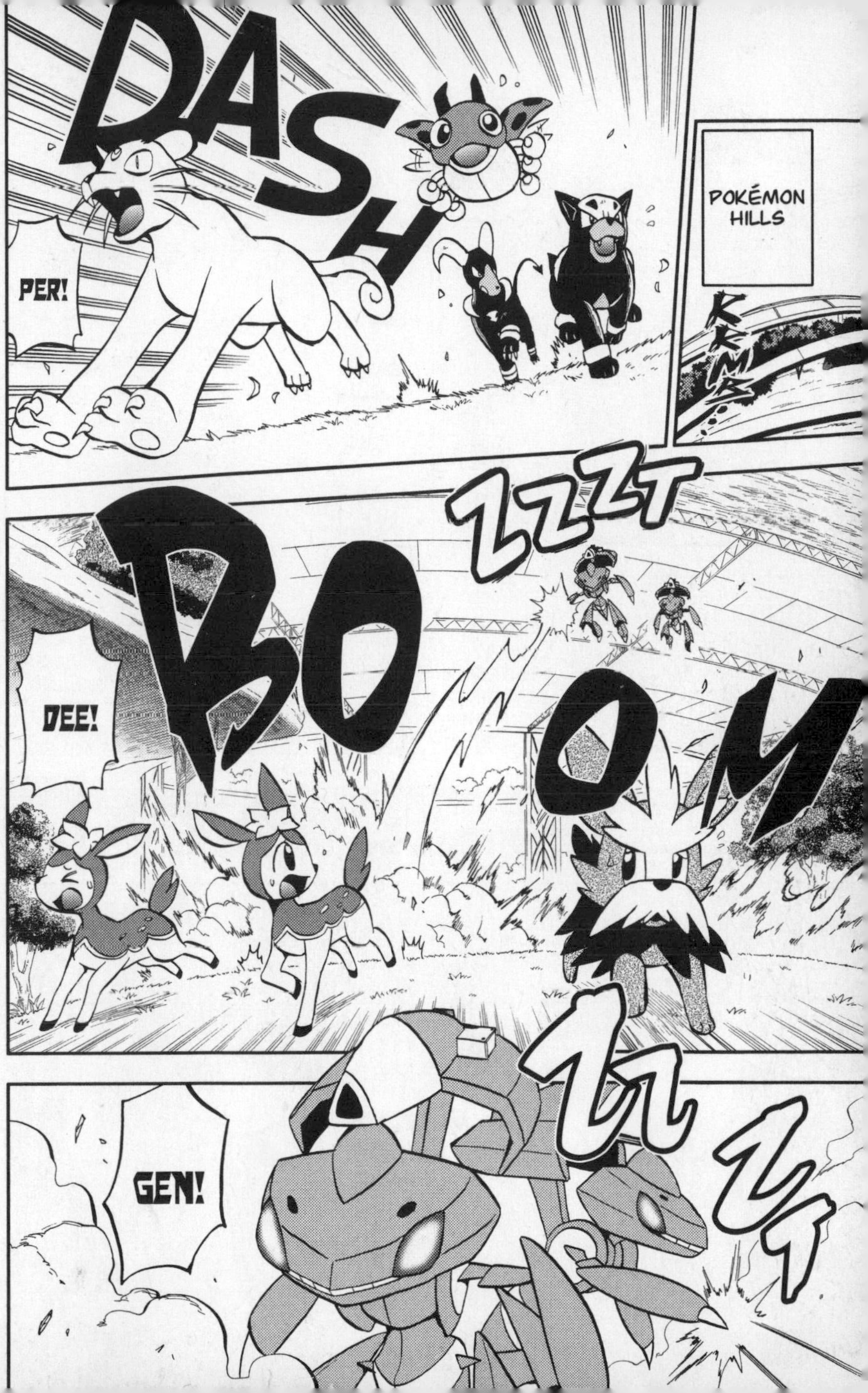
POKÉMON HILLS
RRMB...
DASH
PER!
ZZZT
BOOM
DEE!
ZZ
ZZ
GEN!

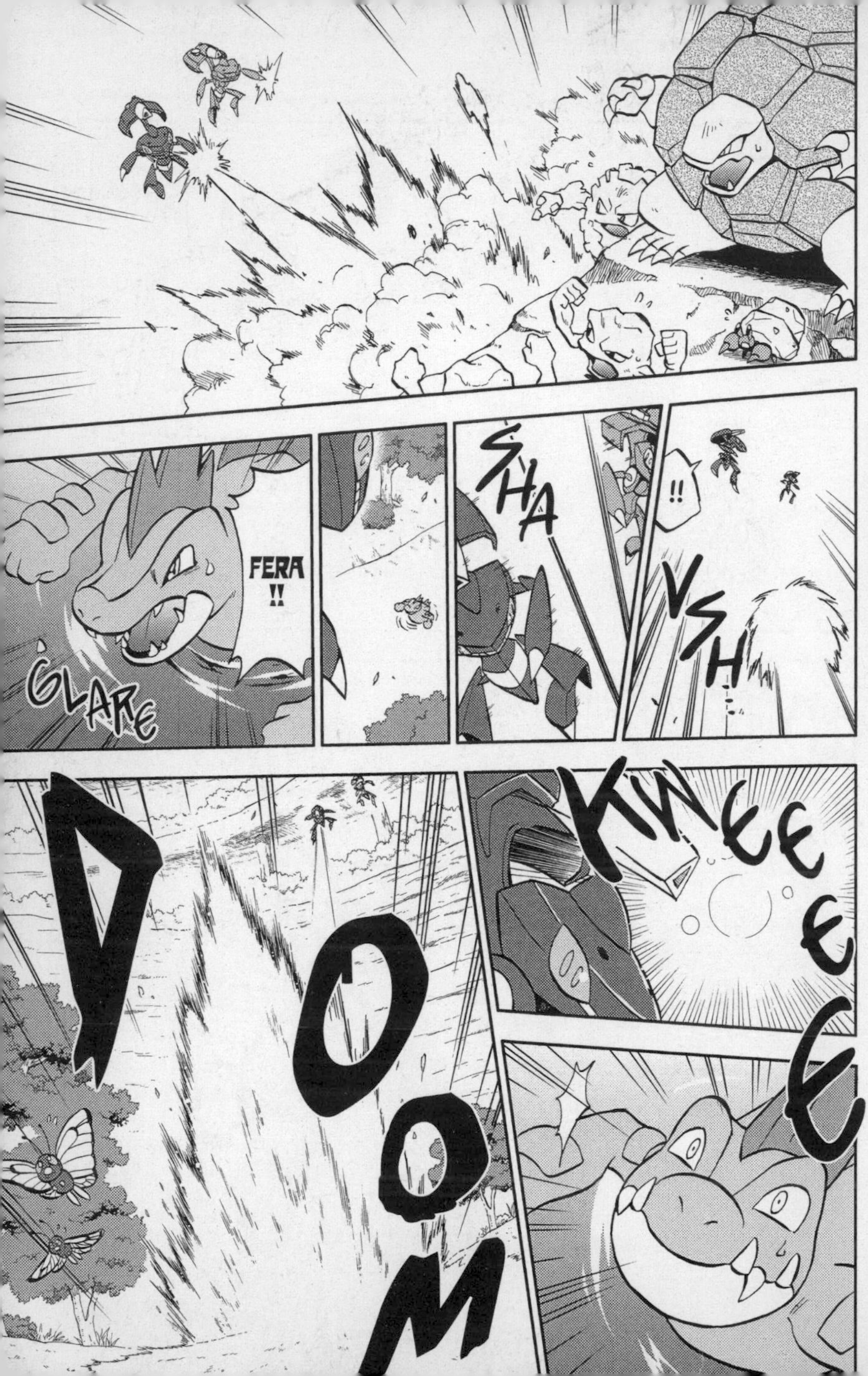
!!
VSH
SHA
FERA !!
GLARE
KWEEEEE
DOOOM

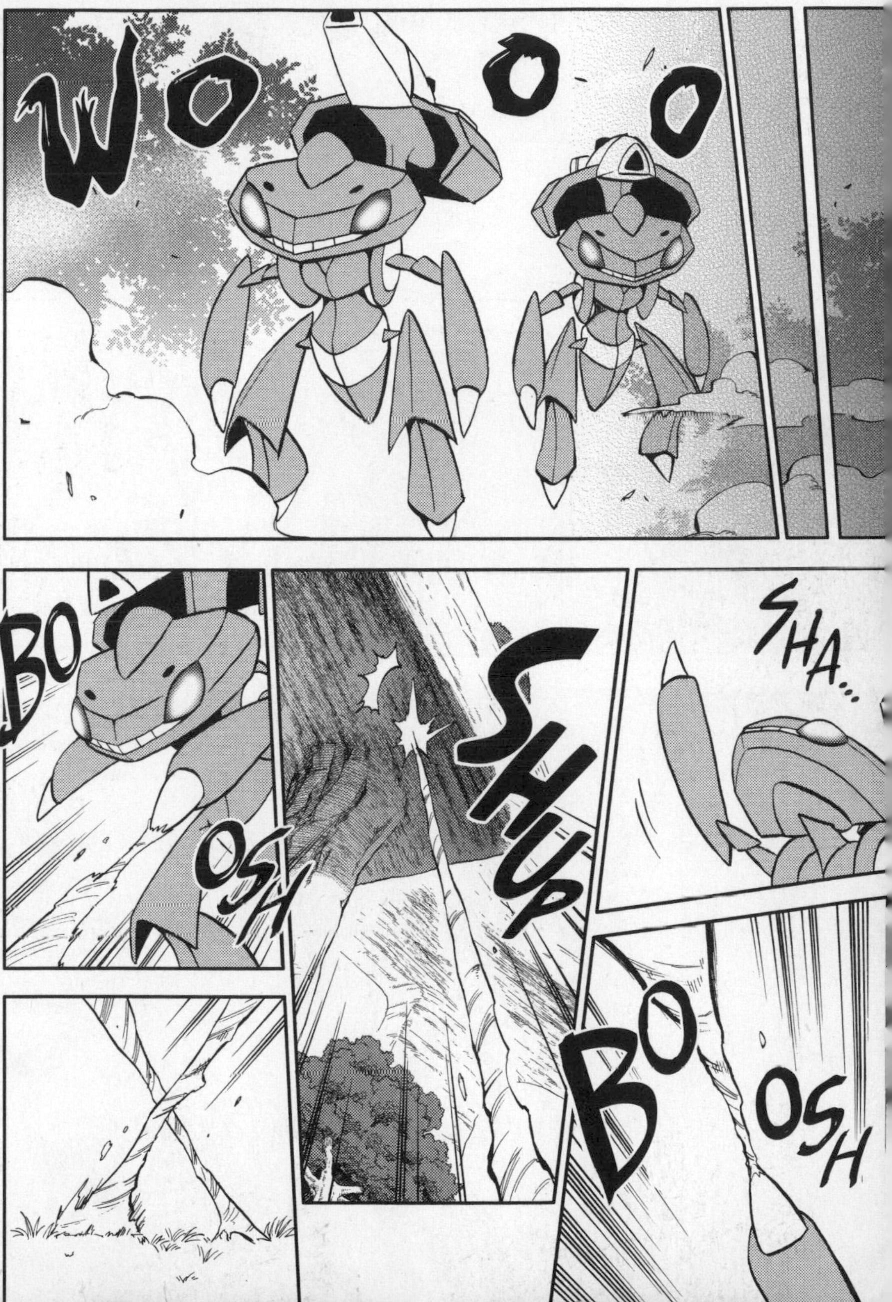
WOOOO
SHA...
BOOSH
SHUP
BOOSH

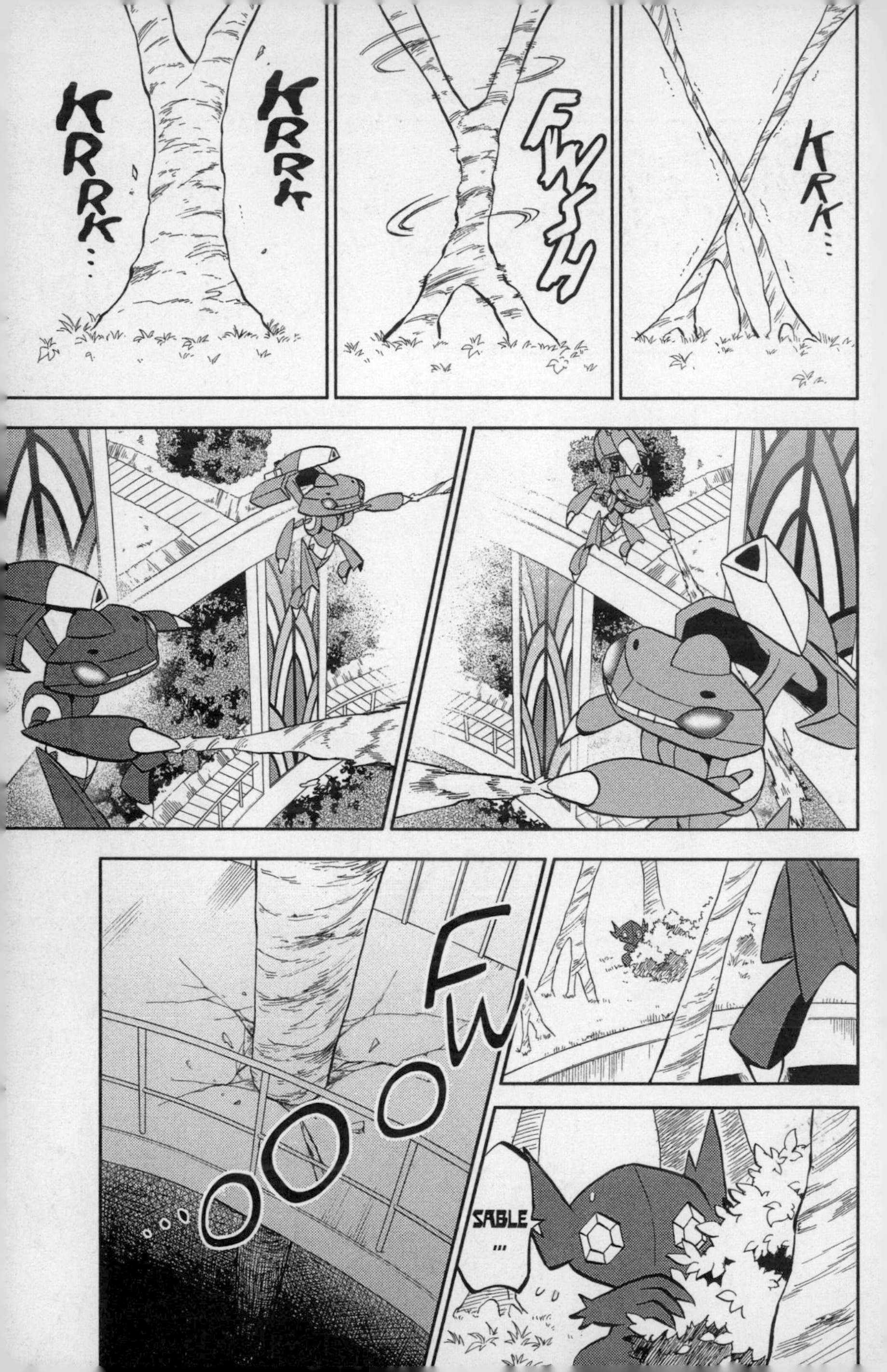
KRK...
FWSH
KRRK
KRRK...
FWOOO
SABLE...

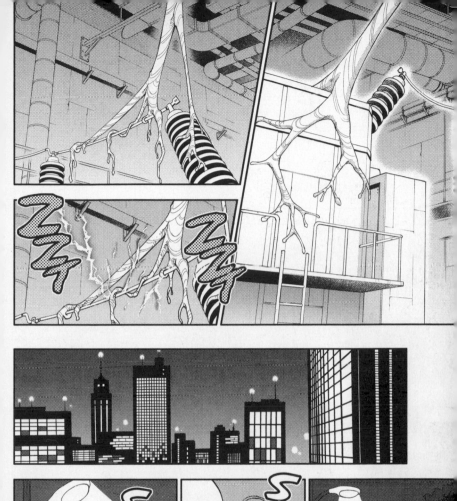

SHHHNG

It turned on again...

HUH?

SHUP

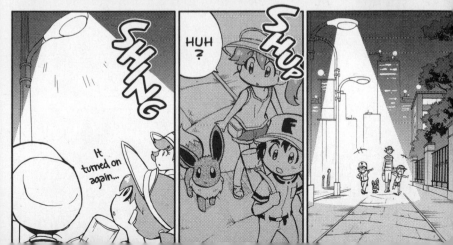

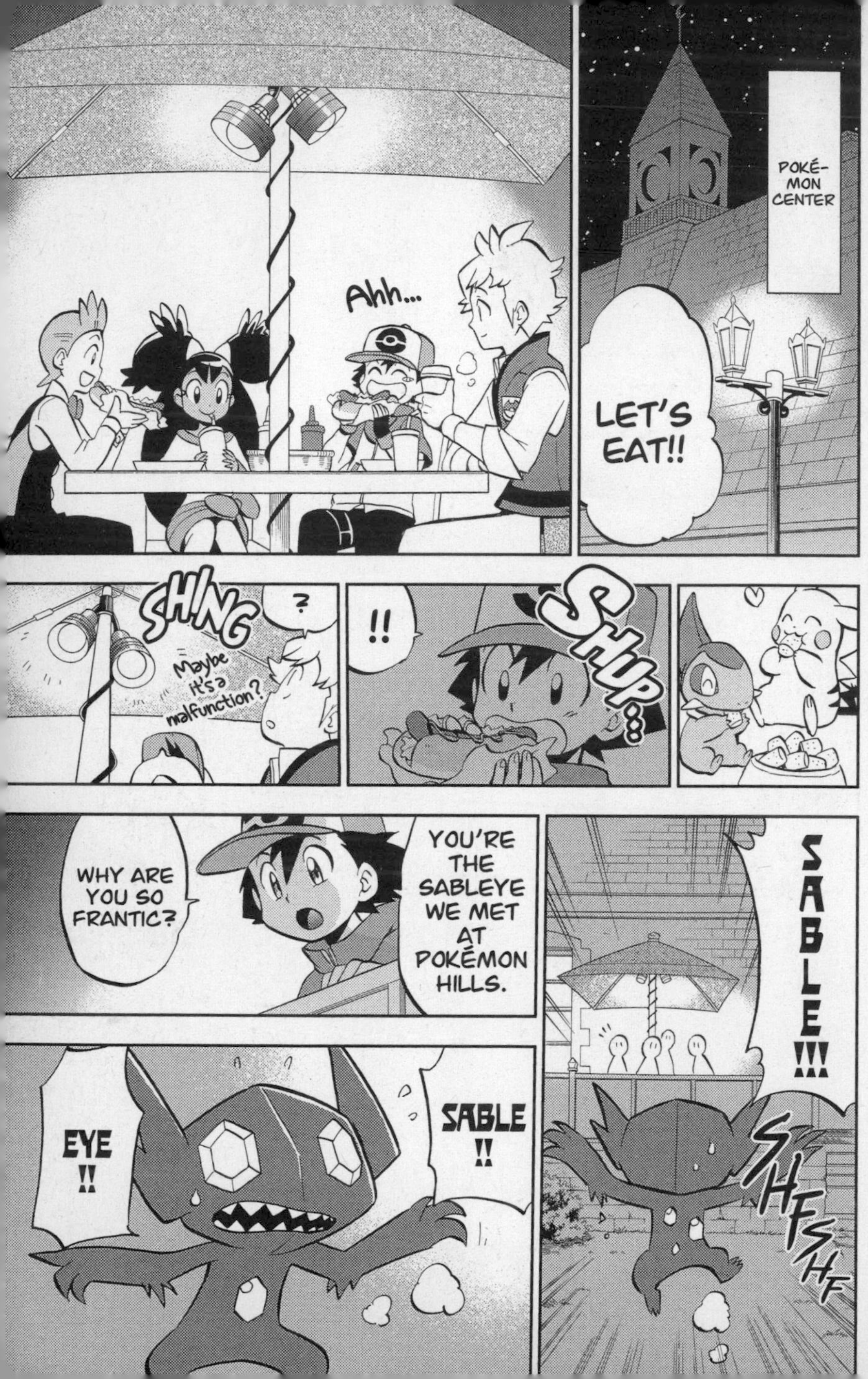
POKÉ-
MON
CENTER
LET'S EAT!!
Ahh...
SHUP..
!!
SHING
?
Maybe it's a malfunction?
SABLE!!!
SHFSHF
YOU'RE THE SABLEYE WE MET AT POKÉMON HILLS.
WHY ARE YOU SO FRANTIC?
SABLE!!
EYE!!

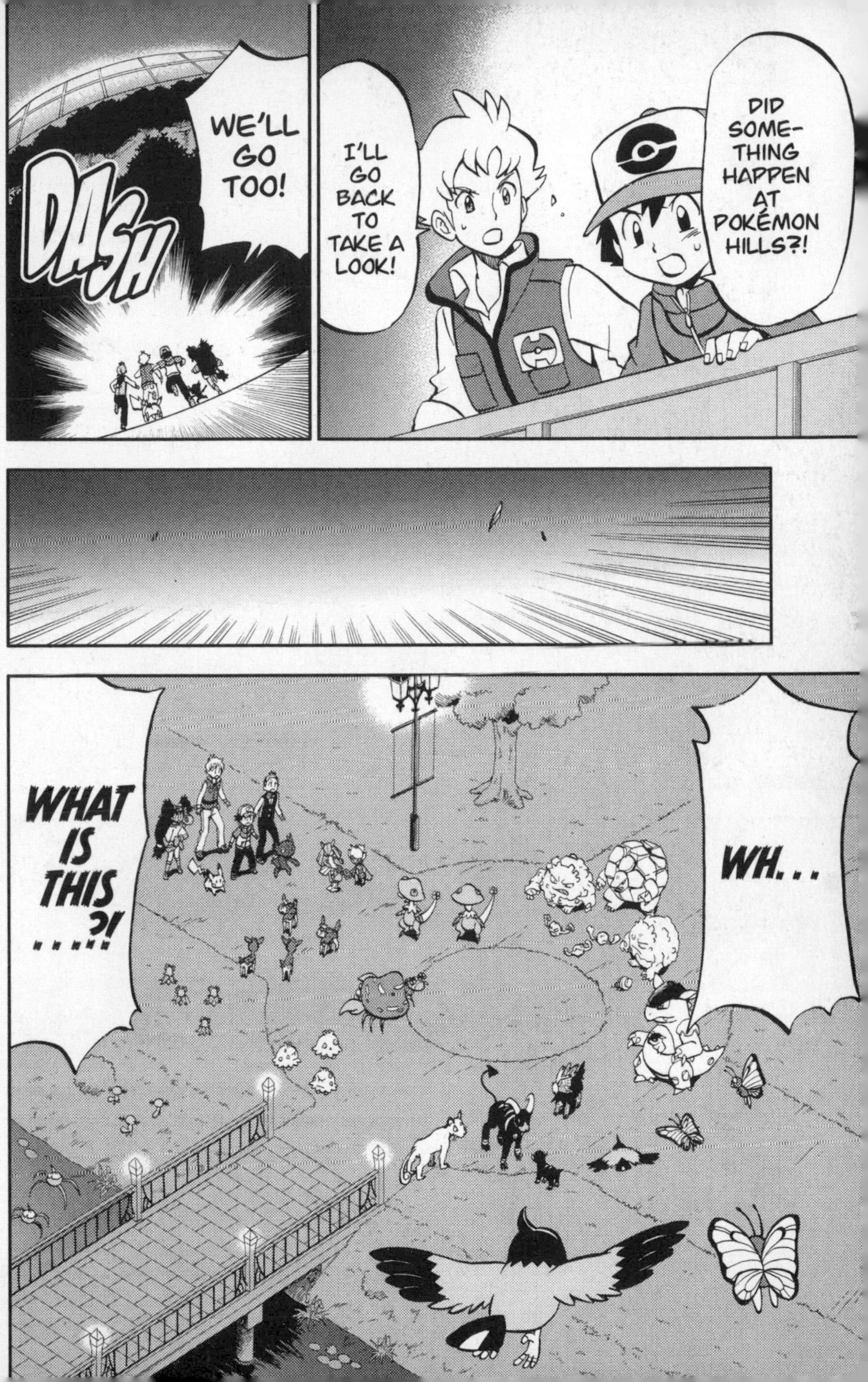
DID SOMETHING HAPPEN AT POKÉMON HILLS?!
I'LL GO BACK TO TAKE A LOOK!
WE'LL GO TOO!
DASH
WH...
WHAT IS THIS .....?!

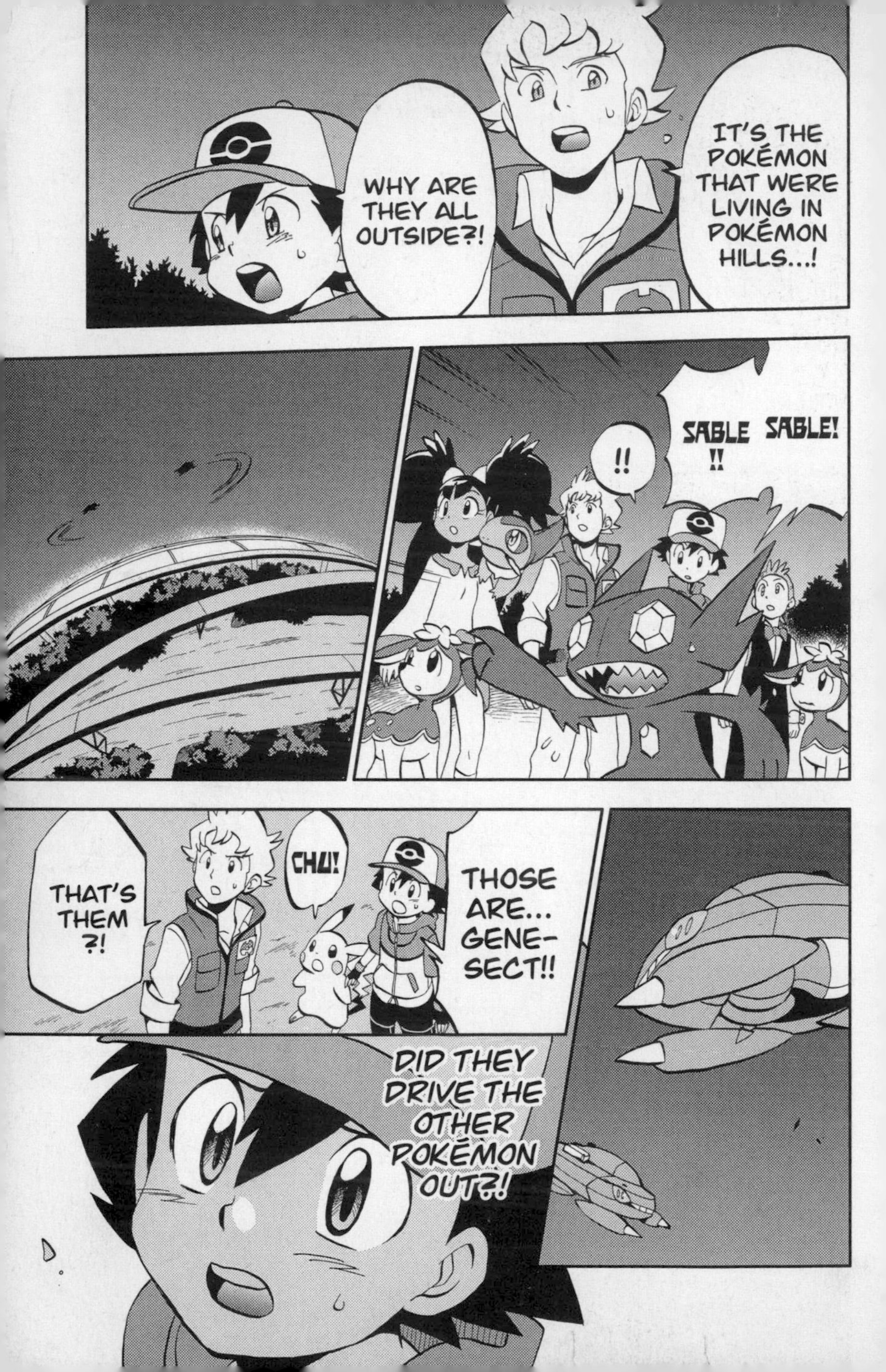
IT'S THE POKÉMON THAT WERE LIVING IN POKÉMON HILLS...!
WHY ARE THEY ALL OUTSIDE?!
SABLE!
SABLE!!
!!
THOSE ARE... GENE-SECT!!
CHU!
THAT'S THEM?!
DID THEY DRIVE THE OTHER POKÉMON OUT?!

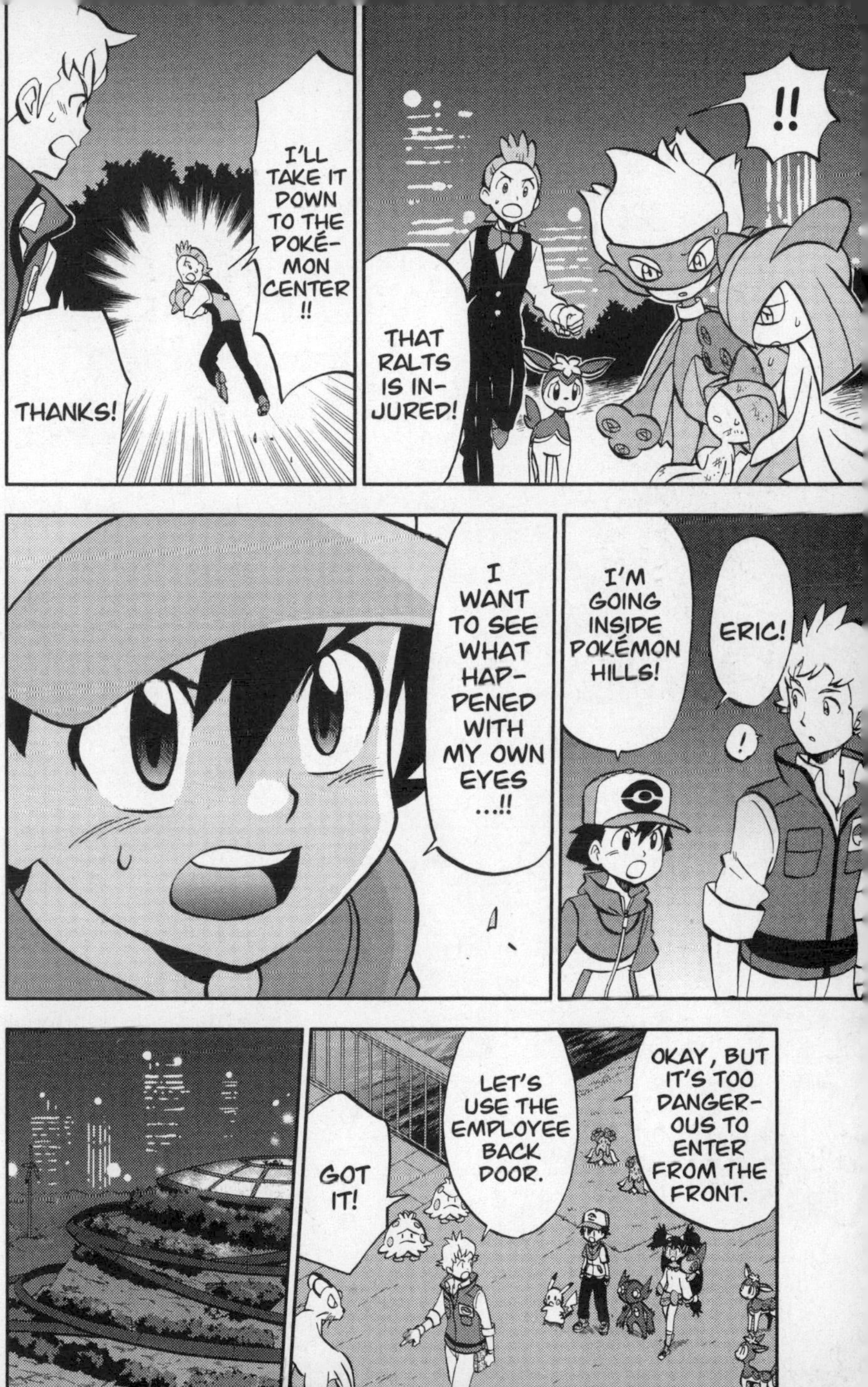
!!
THAT RALTS IS INJURED!
I'LL TAKE IT DOWN TO THE POKÉMON CENTER!!
THANKS!
ERIC!
!
I'M GOING INSIDE POKÉMON HILLS!
I WANT TO SEE WHAT HAPPENED WITH MY OWN EYES ...!!
OKAY, BUT IT'S TOO DANGEROUS TO ENTER FROM THE FRONT.
LET'S USE THE EMPLOYEE BACK DOOR.
GOT IT!

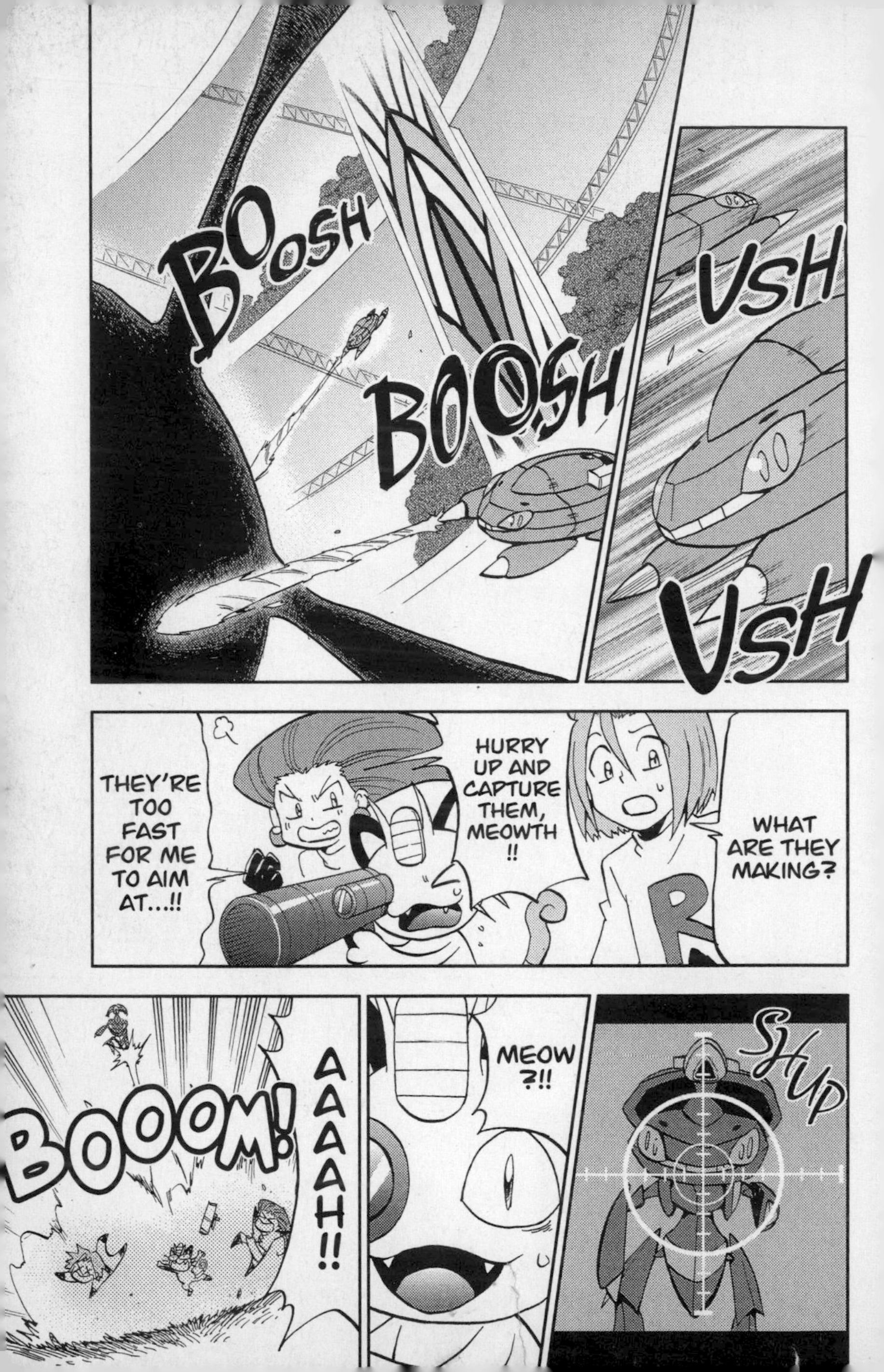
VSH
VSH
BOOSH
BOOSH
WHAT ARE THEY MAKING?
HURRY UP AND CAPTURE THEM, MEOWTH!!
THEY'RE TOO FAST FOR ME TO AIM AT...!!
SHUP
MEOW?!!
AAAAAH!!
BOOOM!

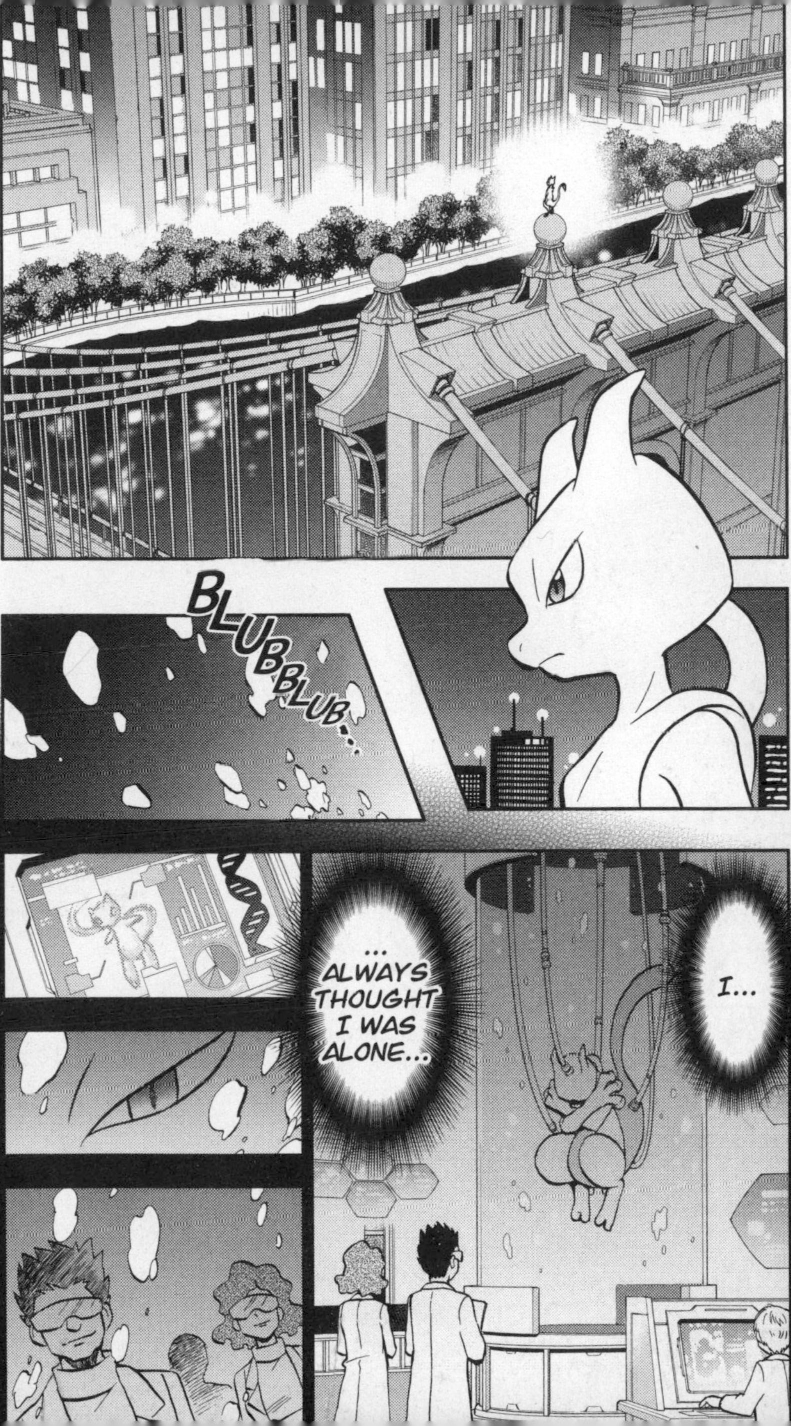
BLUBBLUB...
I...
... ALWAYS THOUGHT I WAS ALONE...

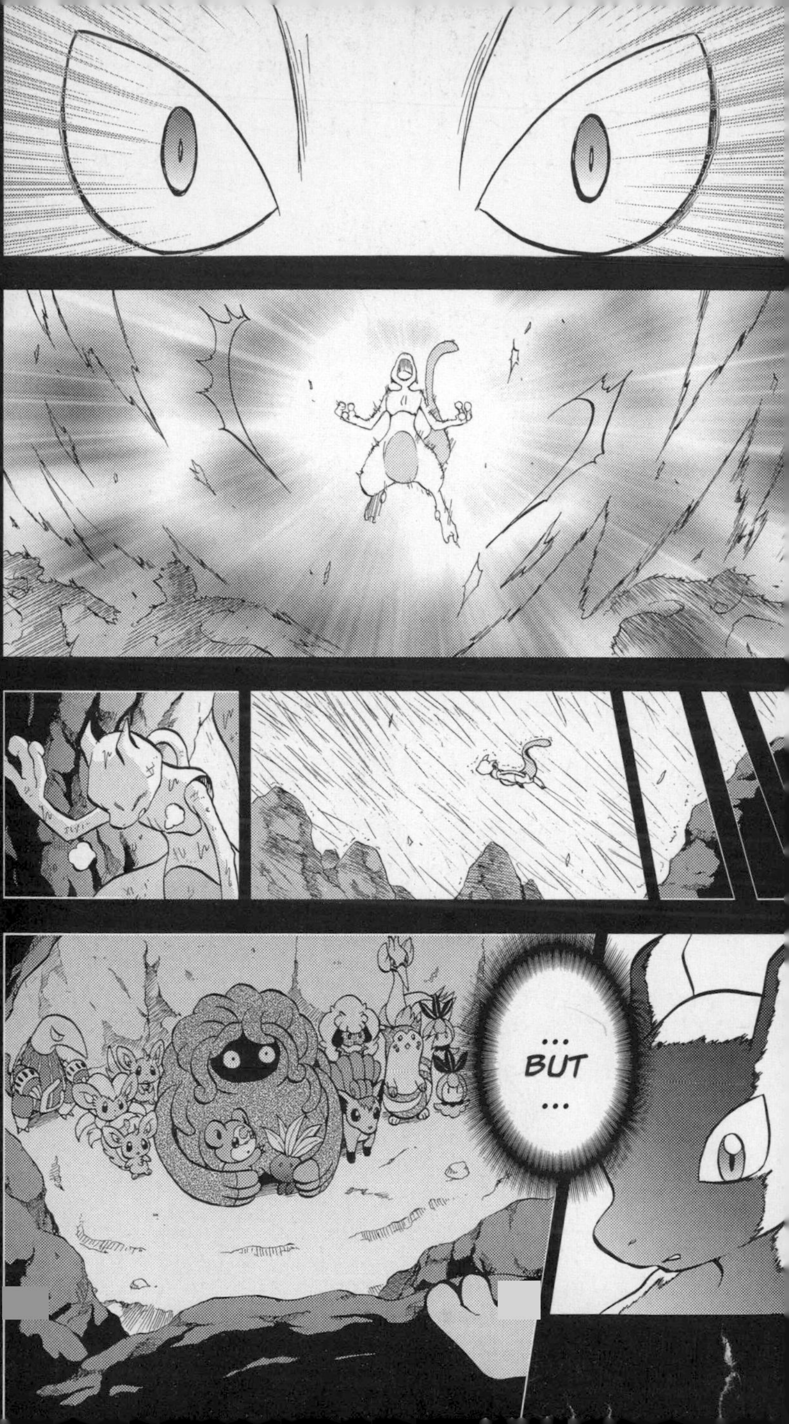
...BUT...

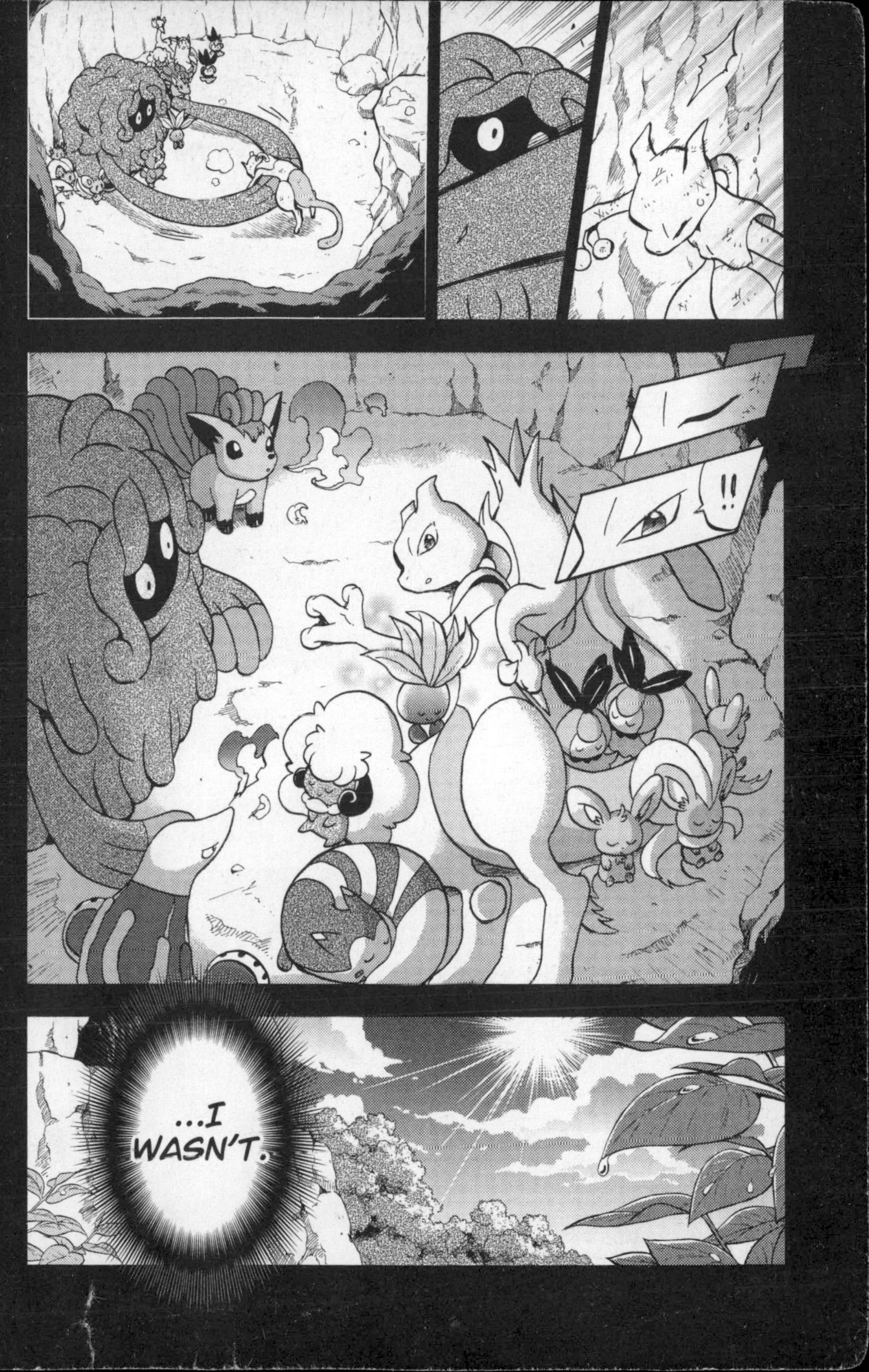
!!
...I WASN'T.

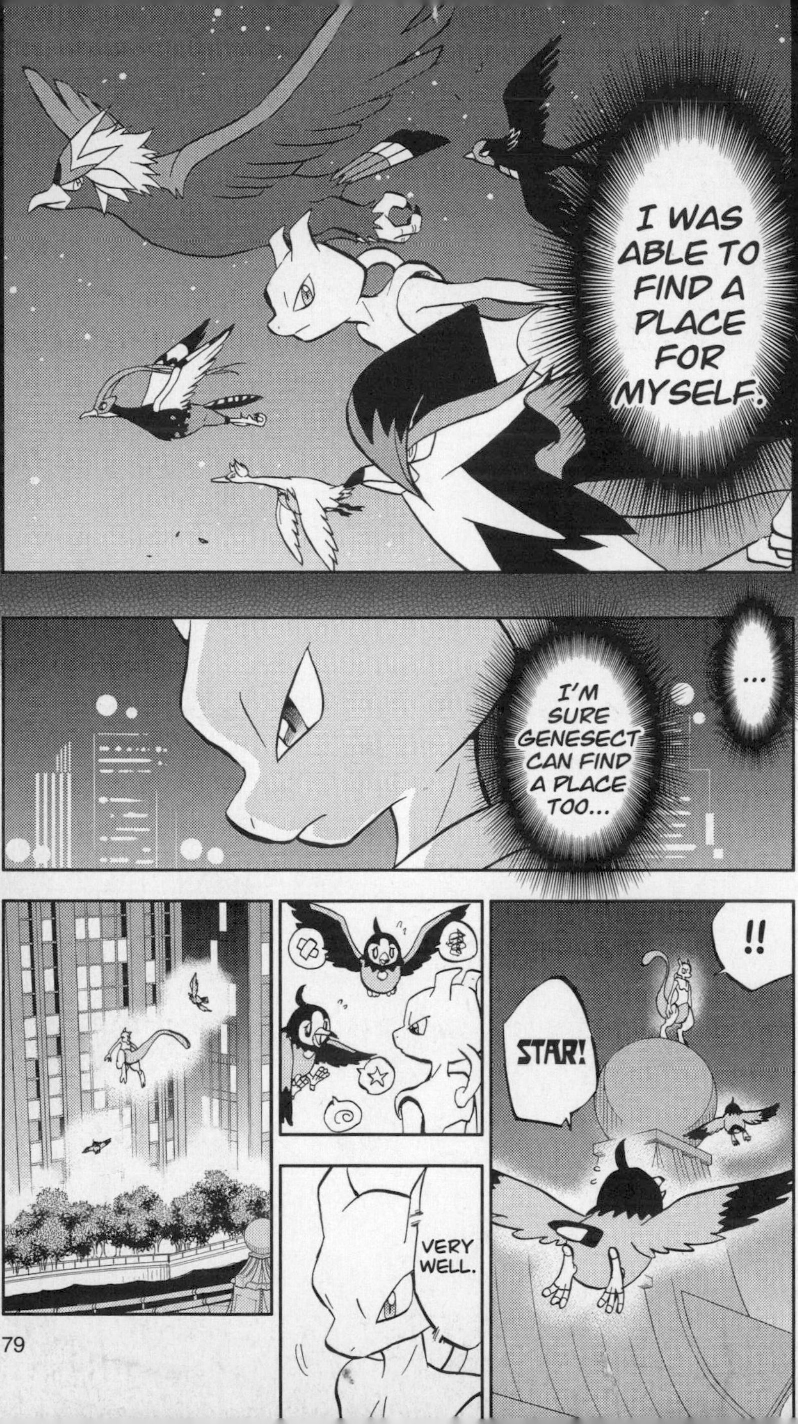

I WAS ABLE TO FIND A PLACE FOR MYSELF.
...
I'M SURE GENESECT CAN FIND A PLACE TOO...
!!
STAR!
VERY WELL.

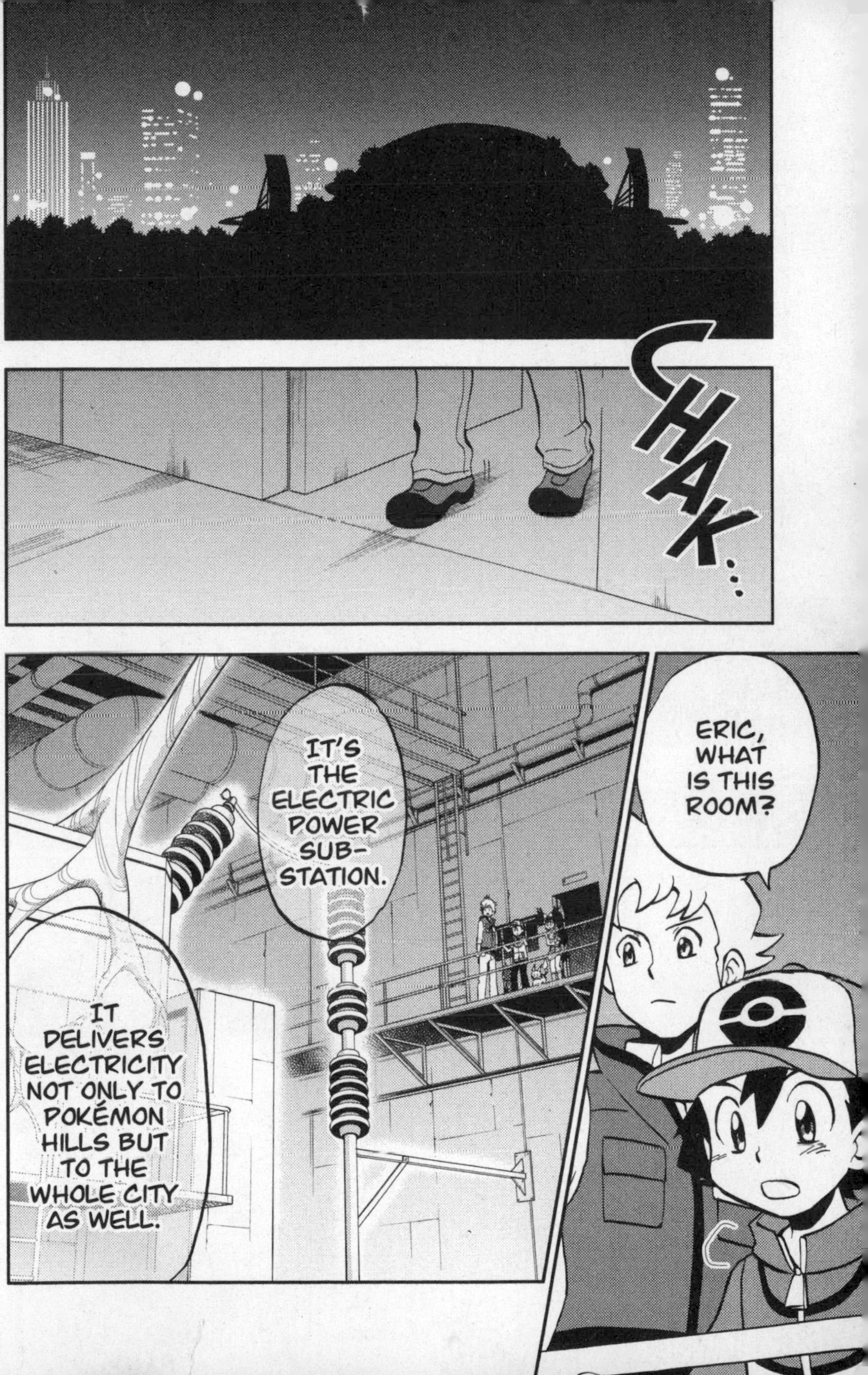
CHAK...
ERIC, WHAT IS THIS ROOM?
IT'S THE ELECTRIC POWER SUB-STATION.
IT DELIVERS ELECTRICITY NOT ONLY TO POKÉMON HILLS BUT TO THE WHOLE CITY AS WELL.

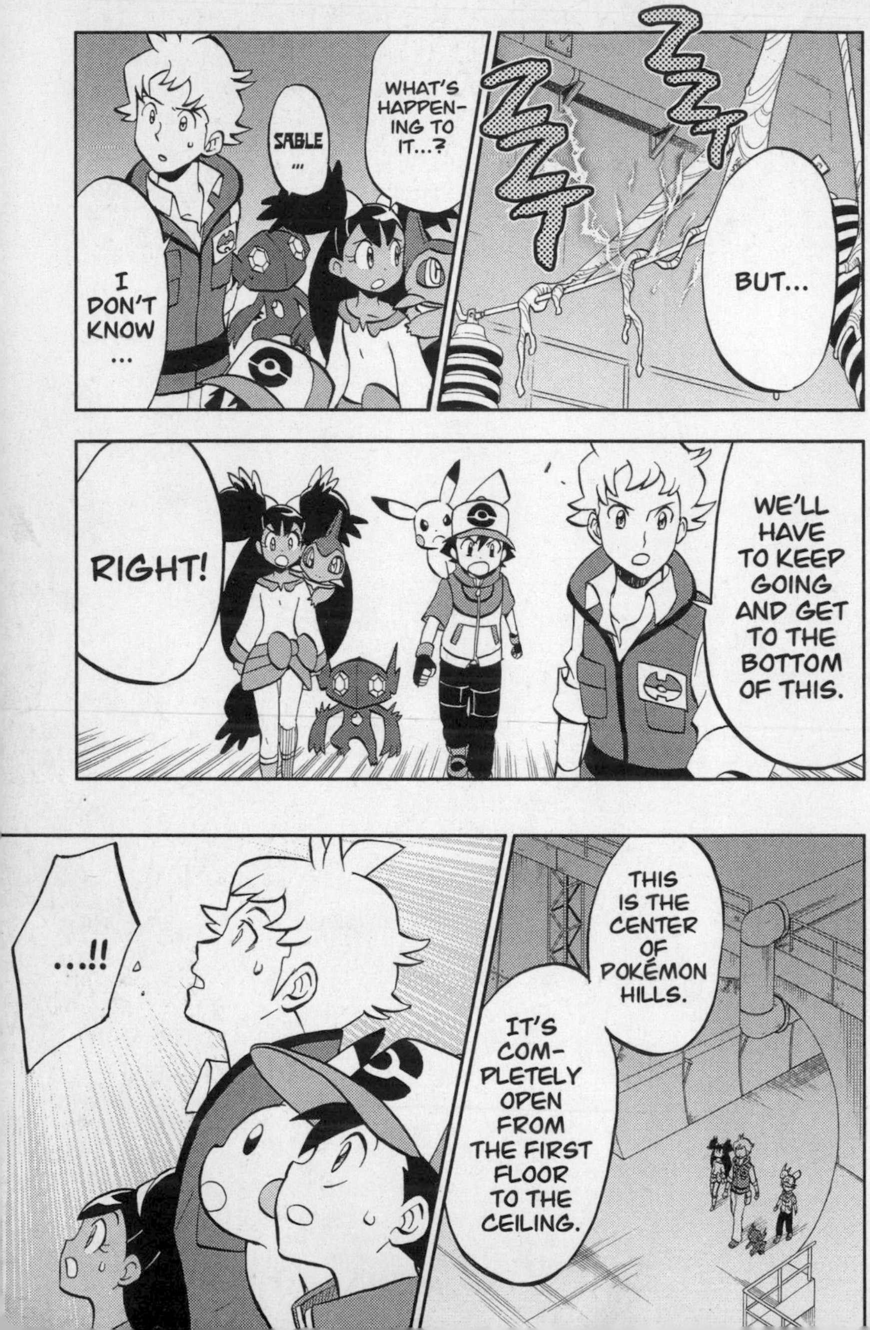
BUT...
WHAT'S HAPPEN-ING TO IT...?
SABLE ...
I DON'T KNOW ...
WE'LL HAVE TO KEEP GOING AND GET TO THE BOTTOM OF THIS.
RIGHT!
THIS IS THE CENTER OF POKÉMON HILLS.
IT'S COM-PLETELY OPEN FROM THE FIRST FLOOR TO THE CEILING.
...!!

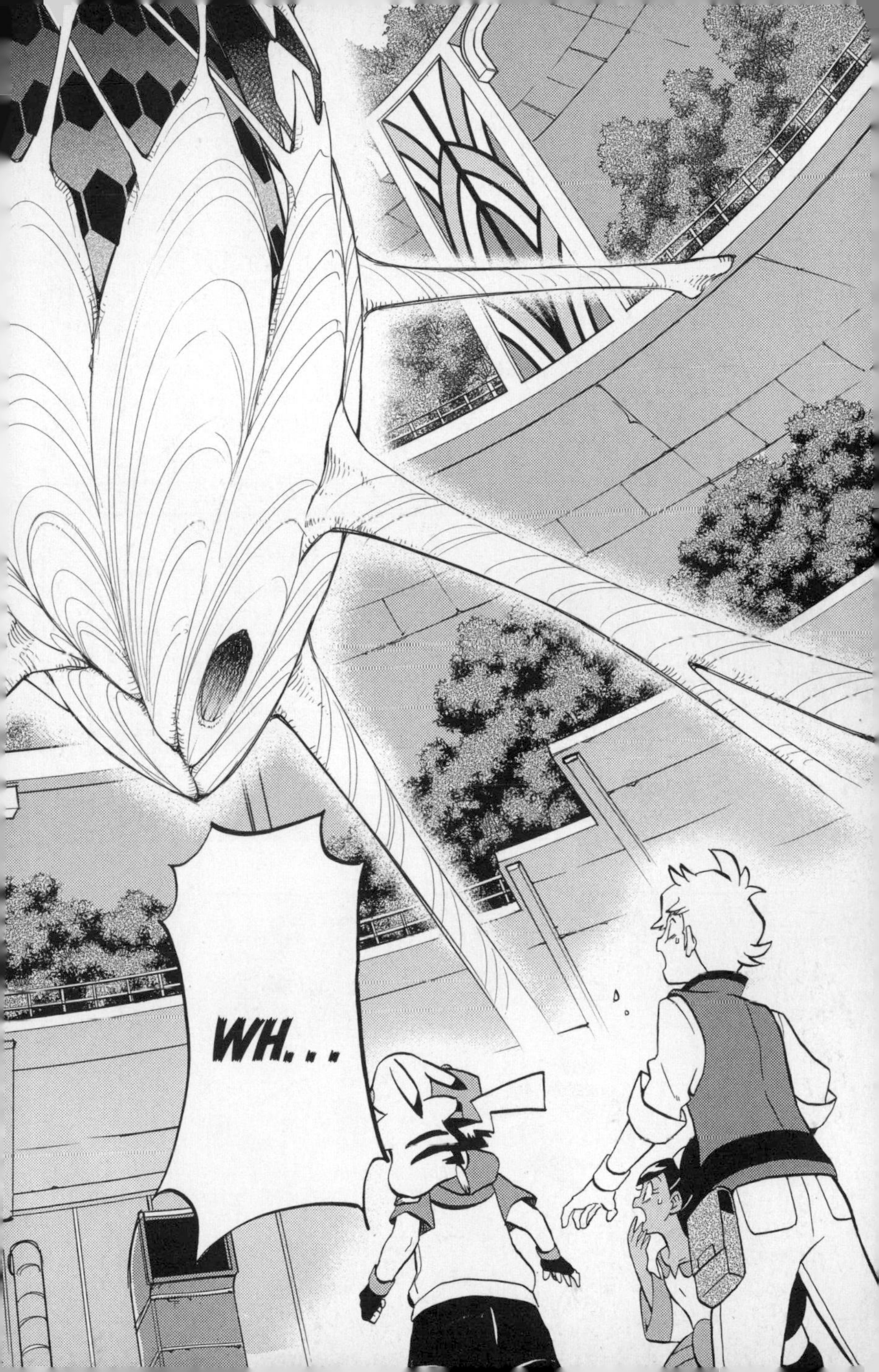
WH...

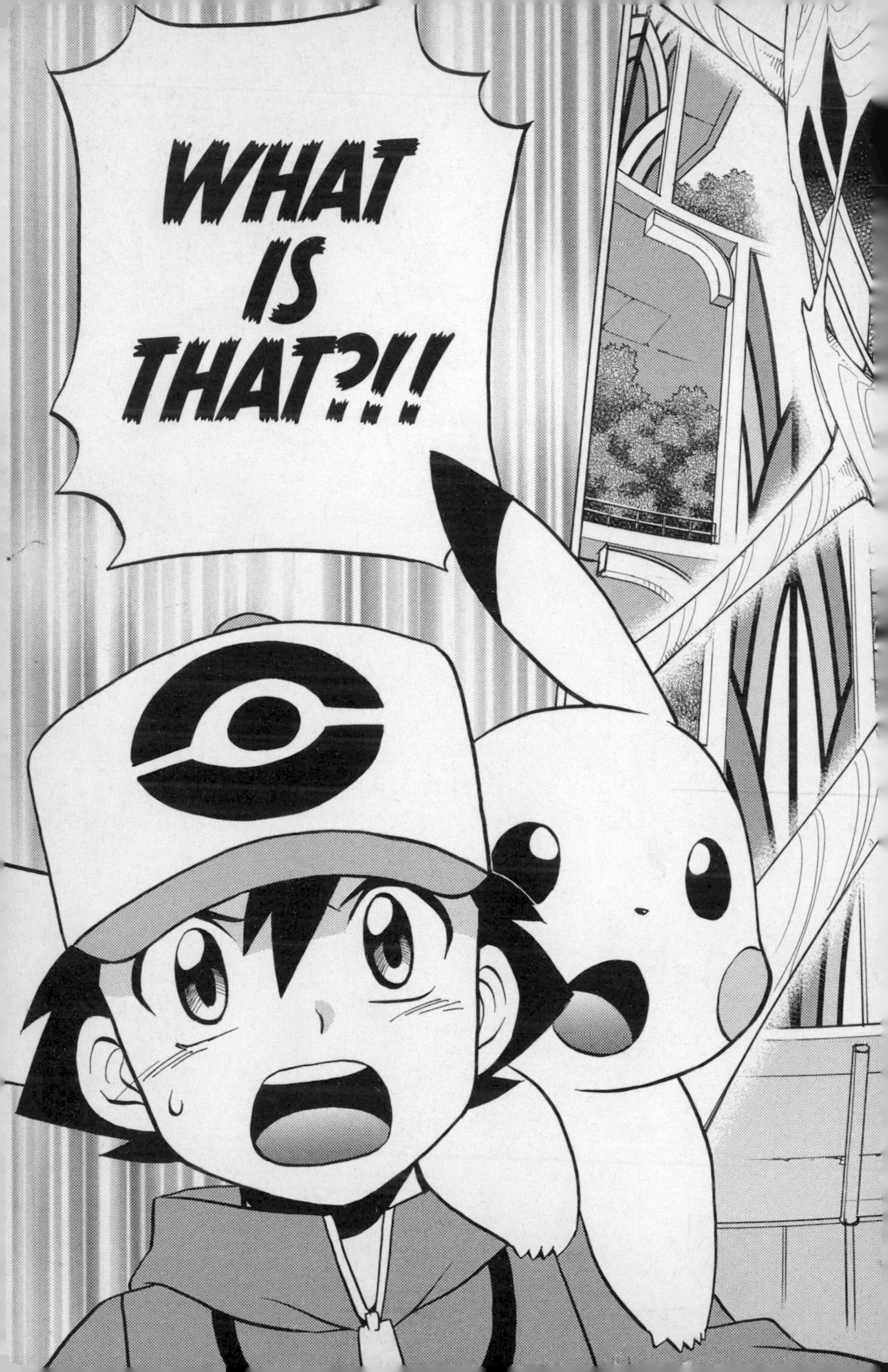
WHAT IS THAT?!!

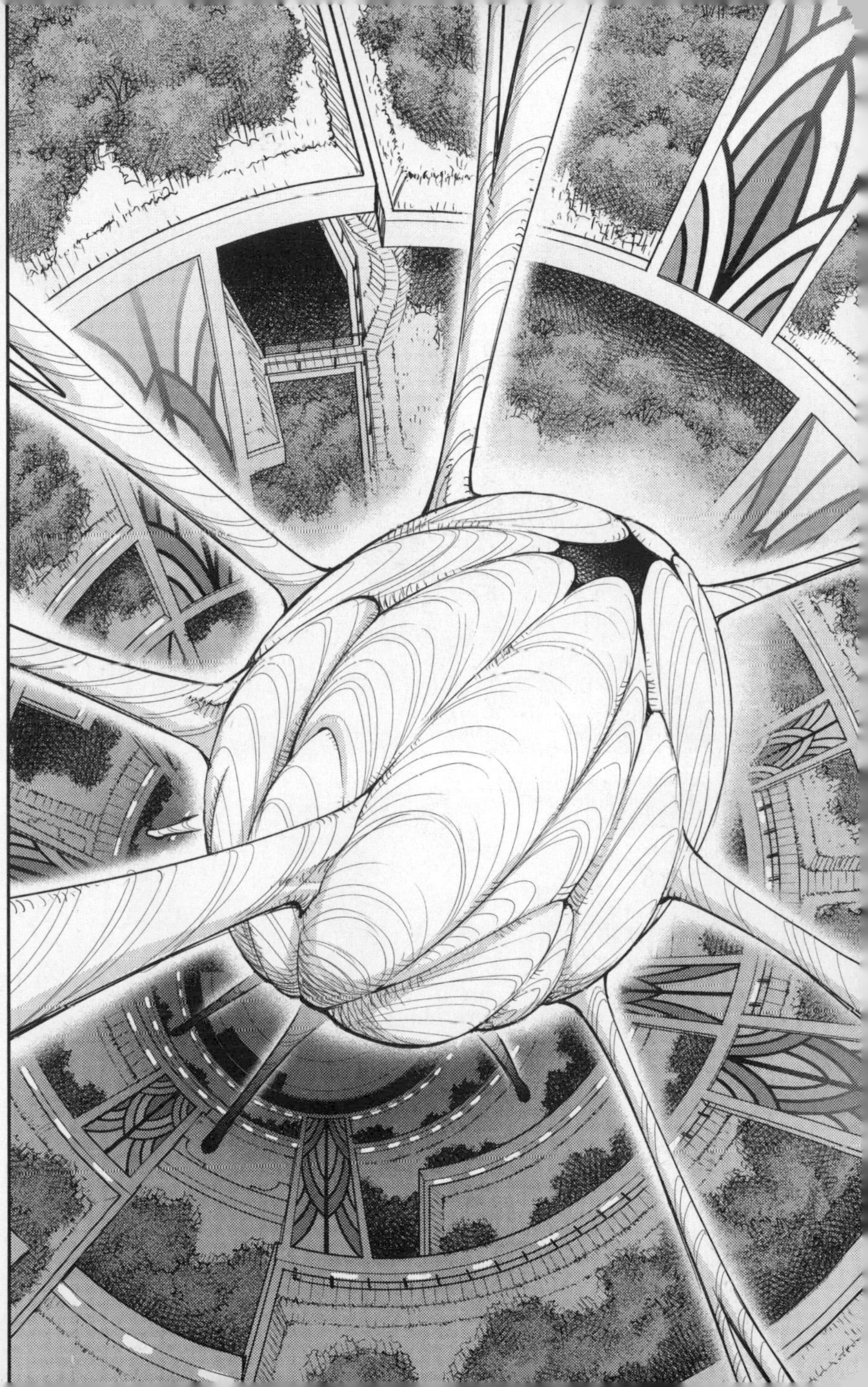

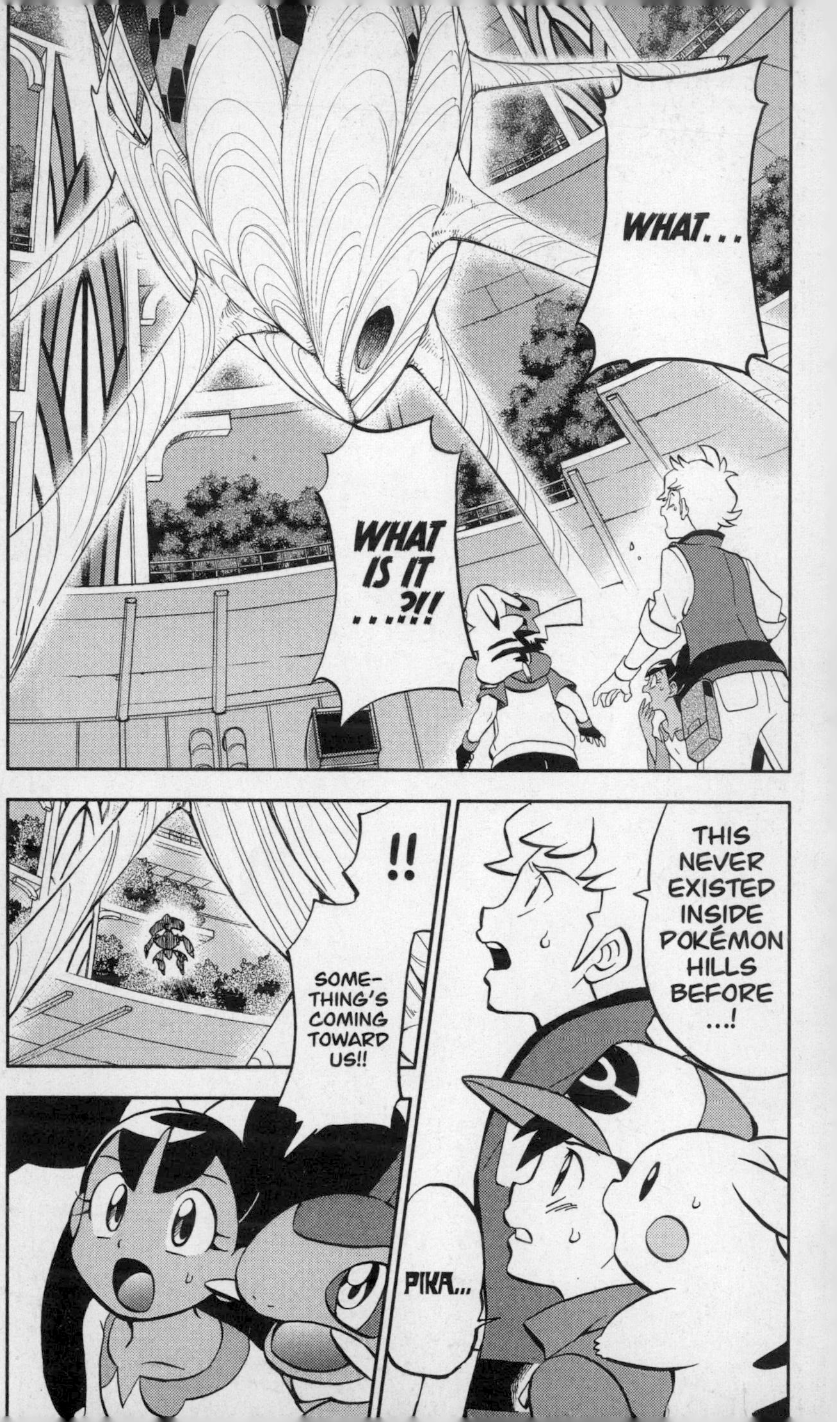
WHAT...
WHAT IS IT ...?!!
THIS NEVER EXISTED INSIDE POKÉMON HILLS BEFORE ...!
!!
SOME-THING'S COMING TOWARD US!!
PIKA...

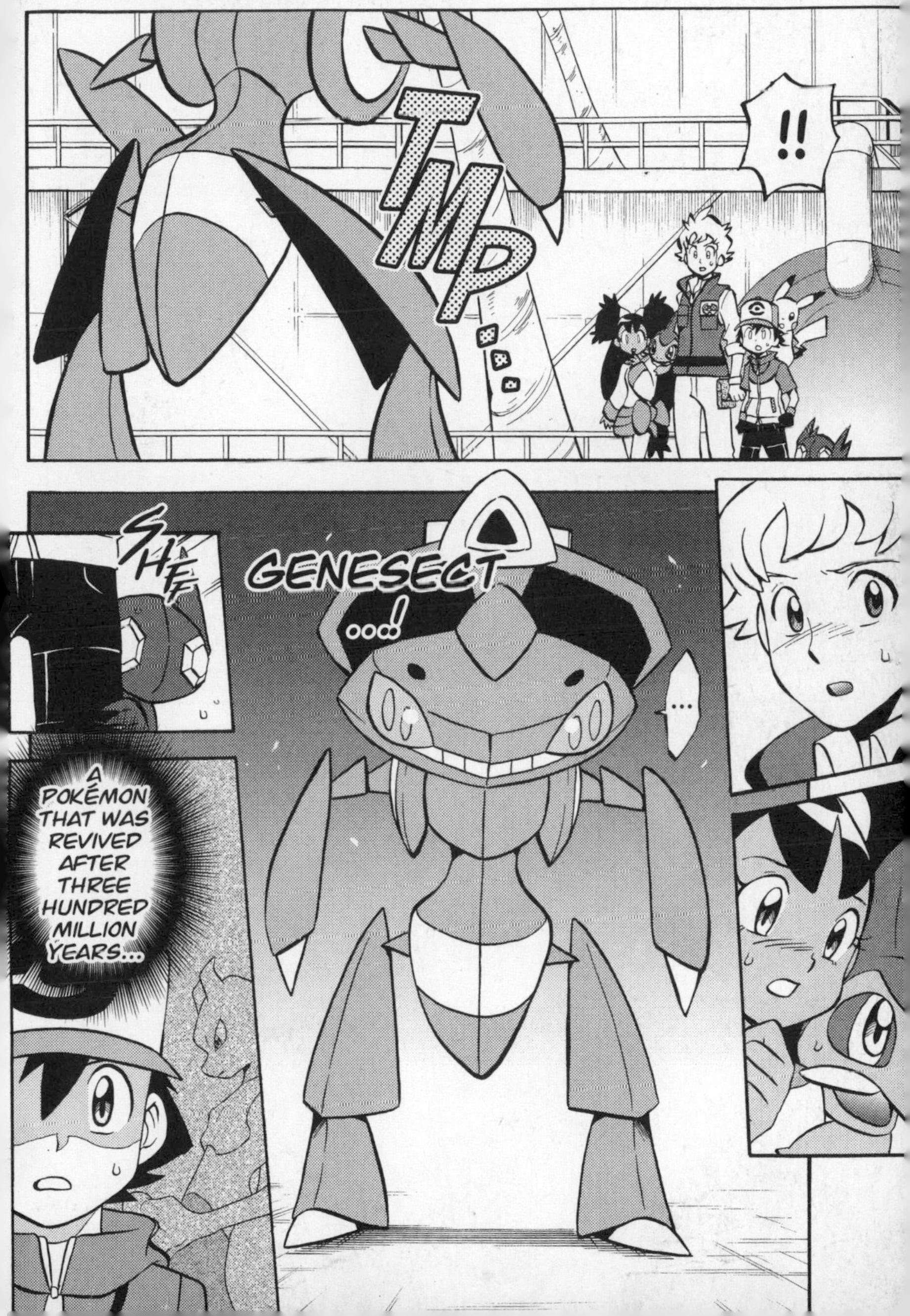
!!
TMP
...
GENESECT ...!
SHFF
A POKÉMON THAT WAS REVIVED AFTER THREE HUNDRED MILLION YEARS...

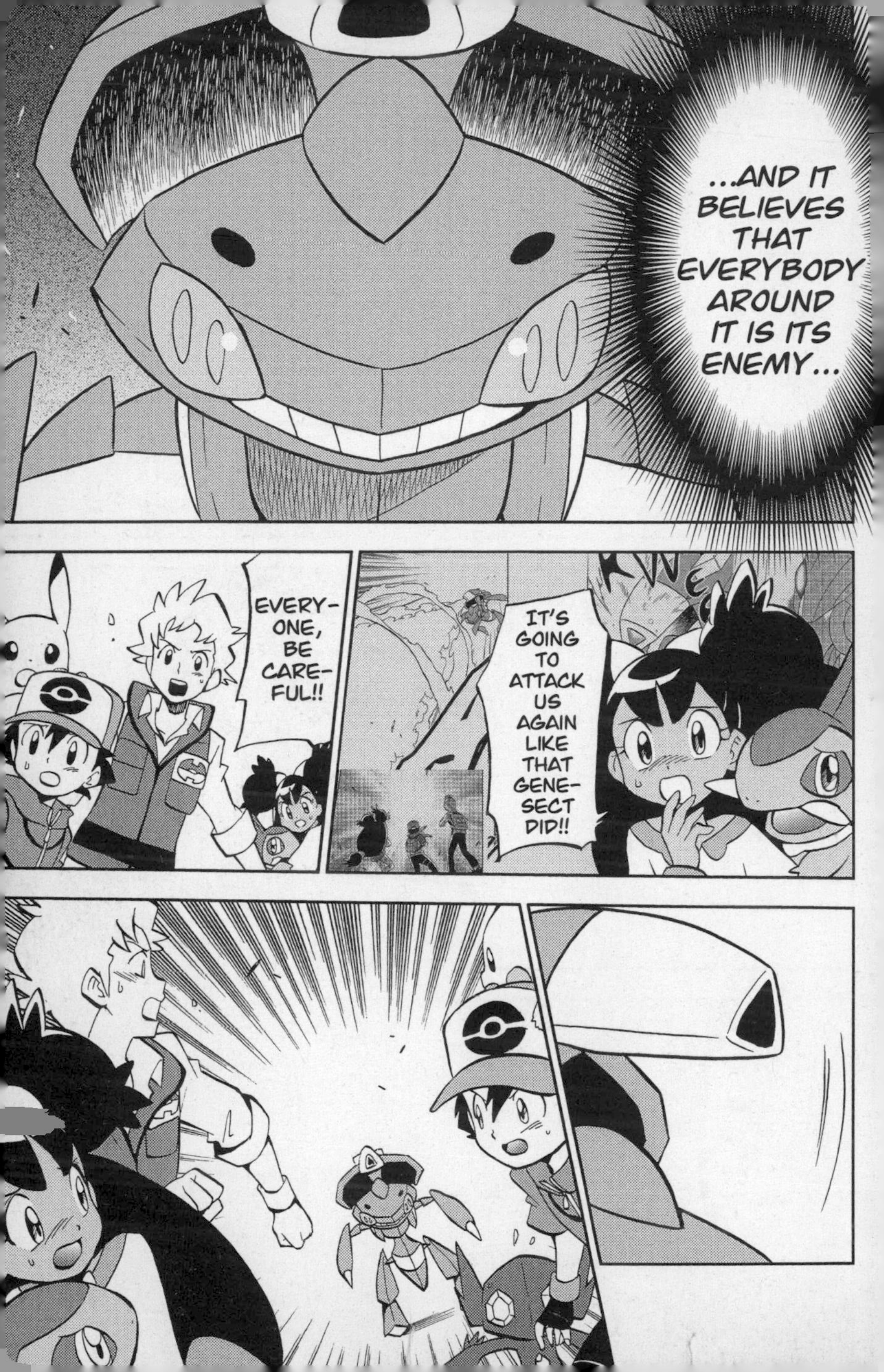
...AND IT BELIEVES THAT EVERYBODY AROUND IT IS ITS ENEMY...
IT'S GOING TO ATTACK US AGAIN LIKE THAT GENE-SECT DID!!
EVERY-ONE, BE CARE-FUL!!

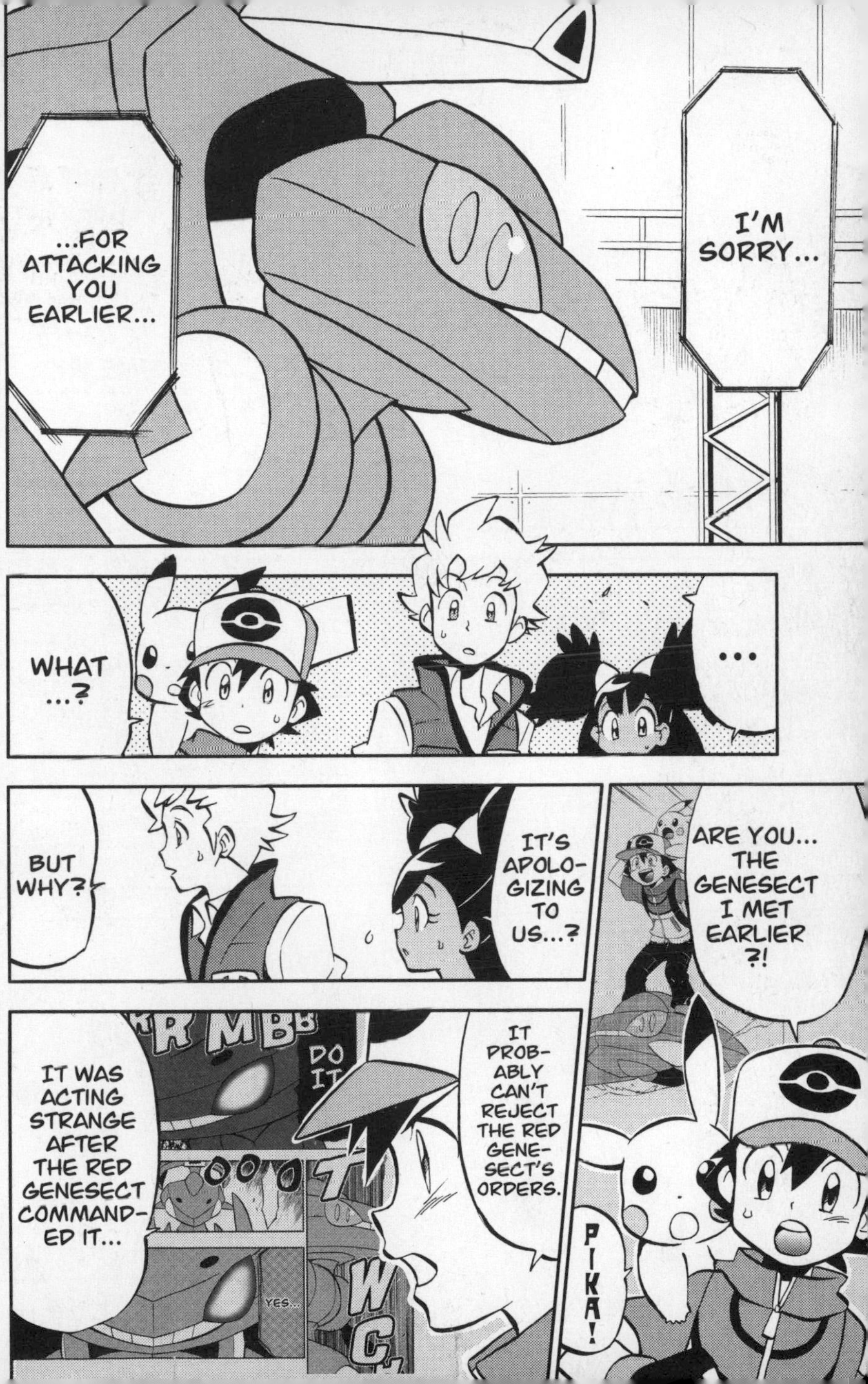
I'M SORRY...
...FOR ATTACKING YOU EARLIER...
...
WHAT ...?
ARE YOU... THE GENESECT I MET EARLIER ?!
IT'S APOLOGIZING TO US...?
BUT WHY?
PIKA!
IT PROBABLY CAN'T REJECT THE RED GENESECT'S ORDERS.
DO IT
IT WAS ACTING STRANGE AFTER THE RED GENESECT COMMANDED IT...
YES...

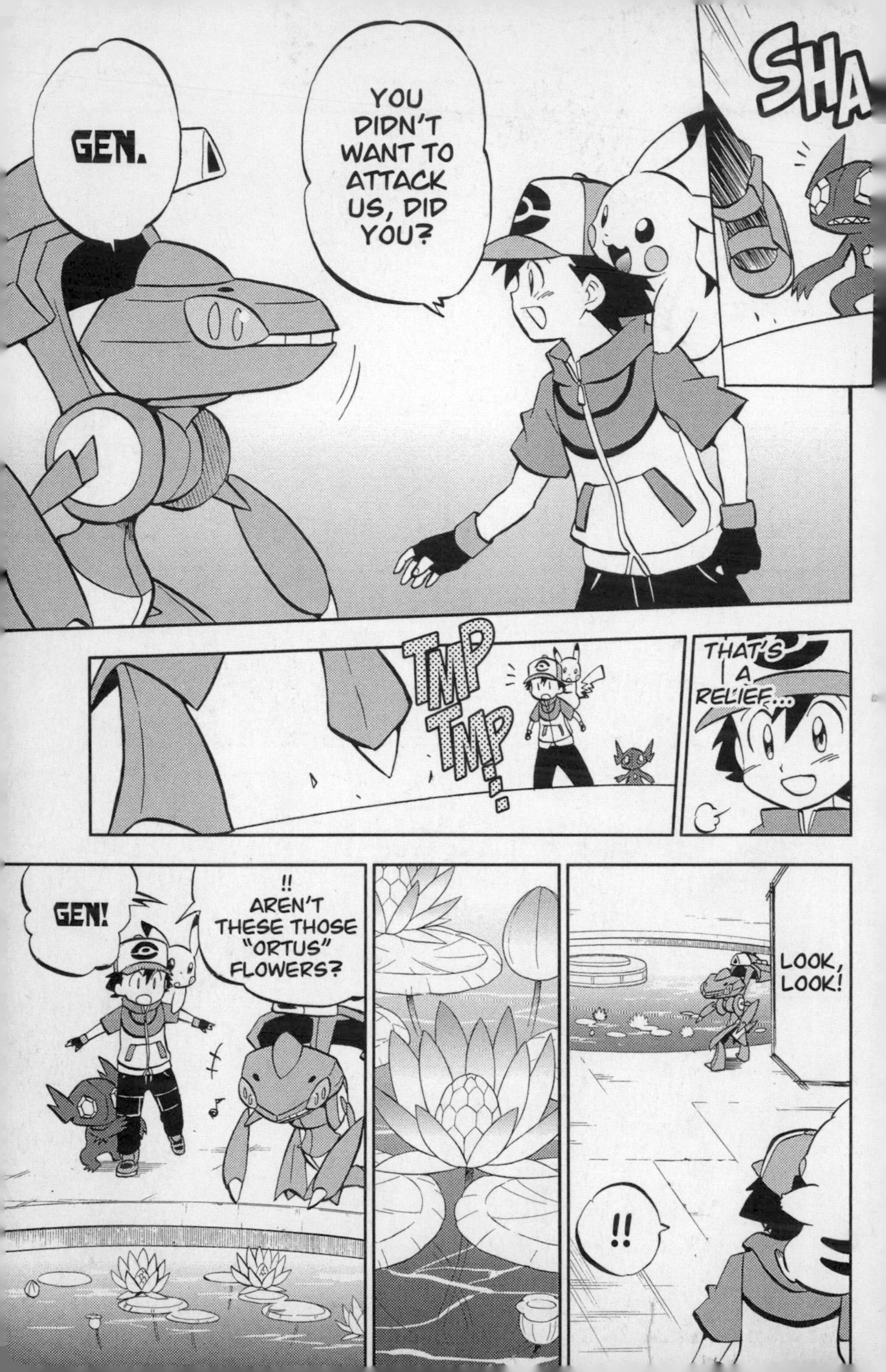
SHA
YOU DIDN'T WANT TO ATTACK US, DID YOU?
GEN.
THAT'S A RELIEF...
TMP TMP...
LOOK, LOOK!
!!
!! AREN'T THESE THOSE "ORTUS" FLOWERS?
GEN!

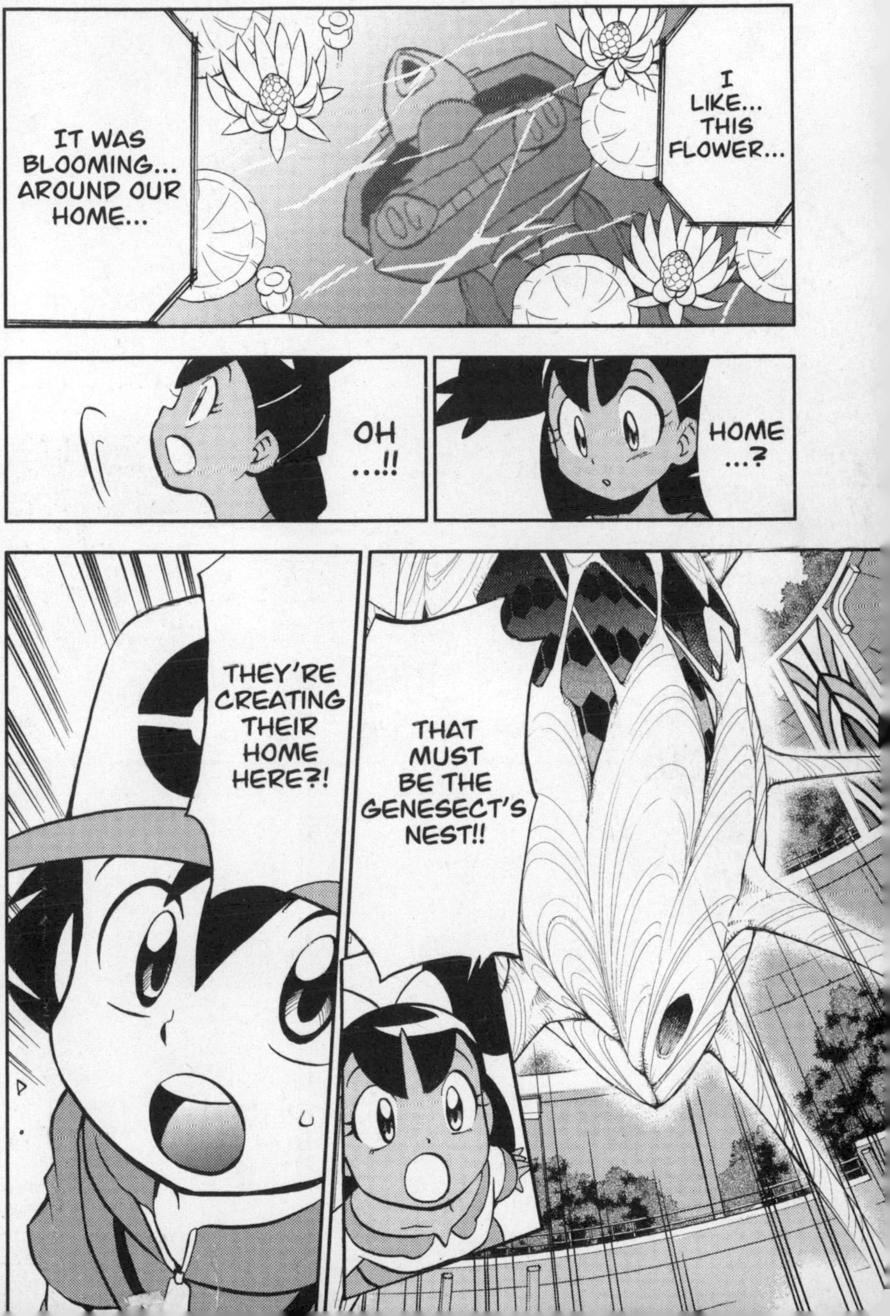
I LIKE... THIS FLOWER...
IT WAS BLOOMING... AROUND OUR HOME...
HOME ...?
OH ...!!
THAT MUST BE THE GENESECT'S NEST!!
THEY'RE CREATING THEIR HOME HERE?!

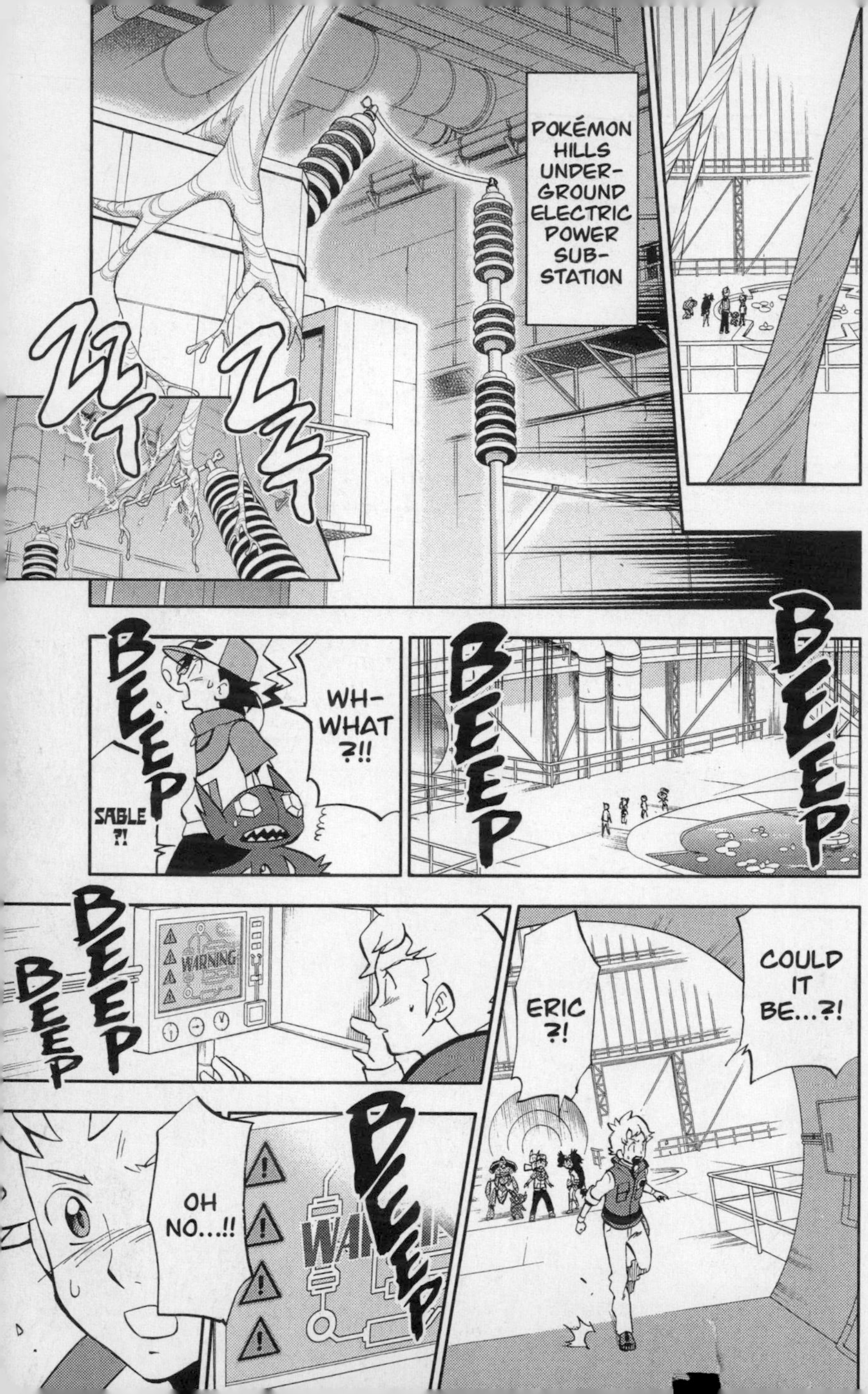
POKÉMON HILLS UNDER-GROUND ELECTRIC POWER SUB-STATION
ZZZT
ZZZT
BEEEP
BEEEP
BEEEP
WH-WHAT?!!
SABLE?!
COULD IT BE...?!
ERIC?!
BEEEP
BEEP
OH NO...!!
BEEEP

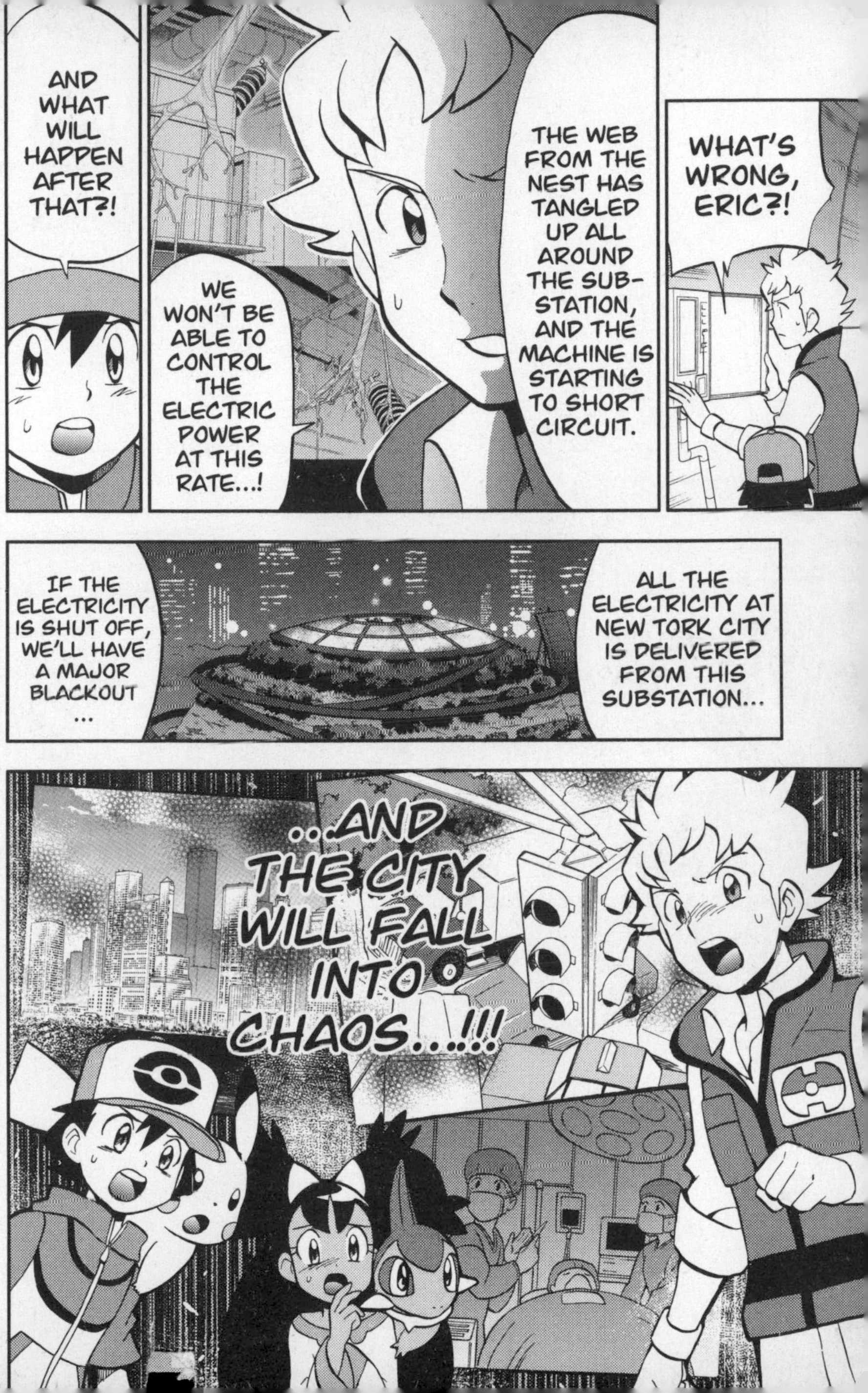
WHAT'S WRONG, ERIC?!
THE WEB FROM THE NEST HAS TANGLED UP ALL AROUND THE SUB-STATION, AND THE MACHINE IS STARTING TO SHORT CIRCUIT.
WE WON'T BE ABLE TO CONTROL THE ELECTRIC POWER AT THIS RATE...!
AND WHAT WILL HAPPEN AFTER THAT?!
ALL THE ELECTRICITY AT NEW TORK CITY IS DELIVERED FROM THIS SUBSTATION...
IF THE ELECTRICITY IS SHUT OFF, WE'LL HAVE A MAJOR BLACKOUT ...
...AND THE CITY WILL FALL INTO CHAOS...!!!

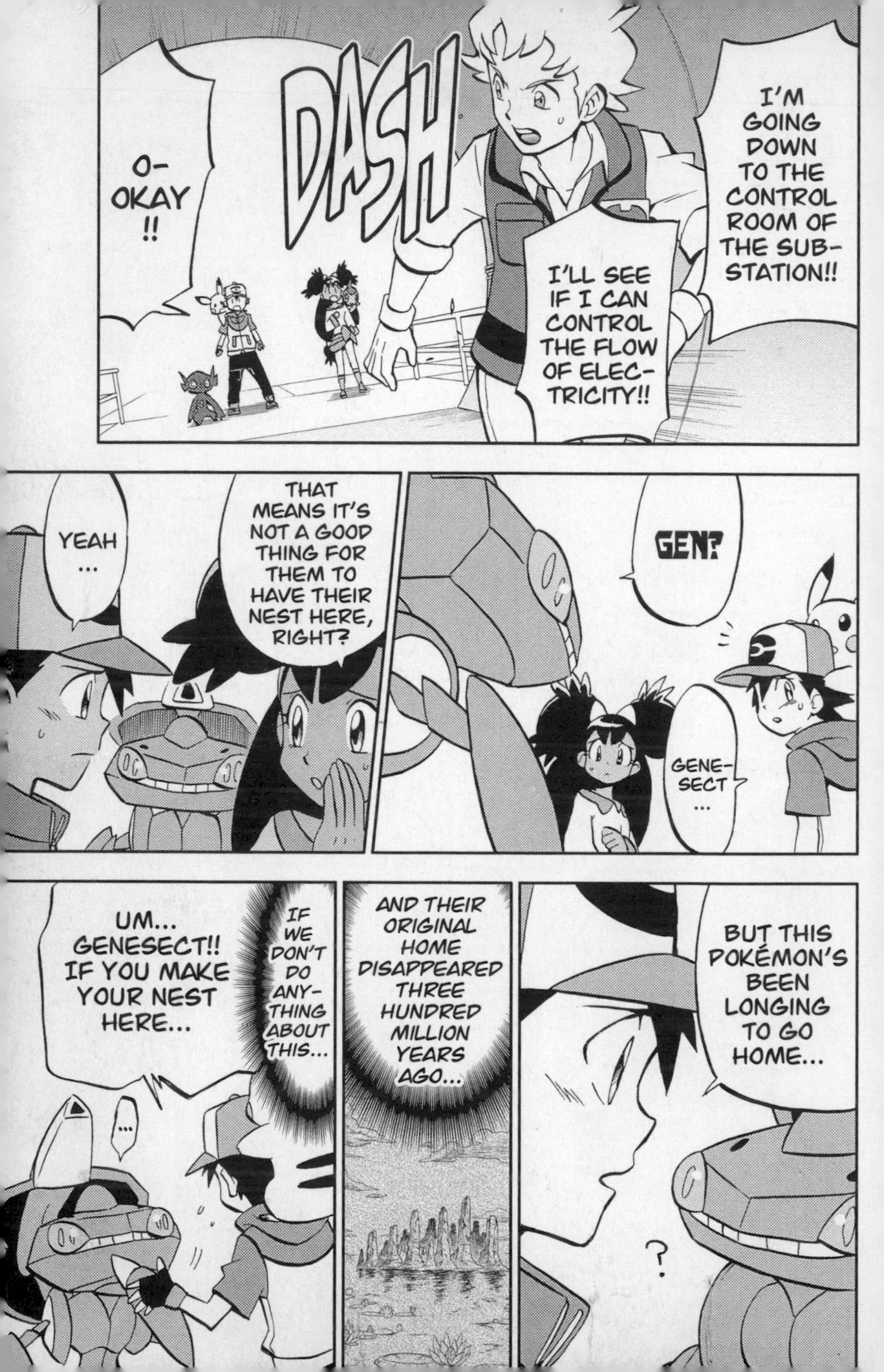
I'M GOING DOWN TO THE CONTROL ROOM OF THE SUB-STATION!!
I'LL SEE IF I CAN CONTROL THE FLOW OF ELEC-TRICITY!!
DASH
O-OKAY!!
GEN?
GENE-SECT ...
THAT MEANS IT'S NOT A GOOD THING FOR THEM TO HAVE THEIR NEST HERE, RIGHT?
YEAH ...
BUT THIS POKÉMON'S BEEN LONGING TO GO HOME...
?
AND THEIR ORIGINAL HOME DISAPPEARED THREE HUNDRED MILLION YEARS AGO...
IF WE DON'T DO ANYTHING ABOUT THIS...
UM... GENESECT!! IF YOU MAKE YOUR NEST HERE...
...

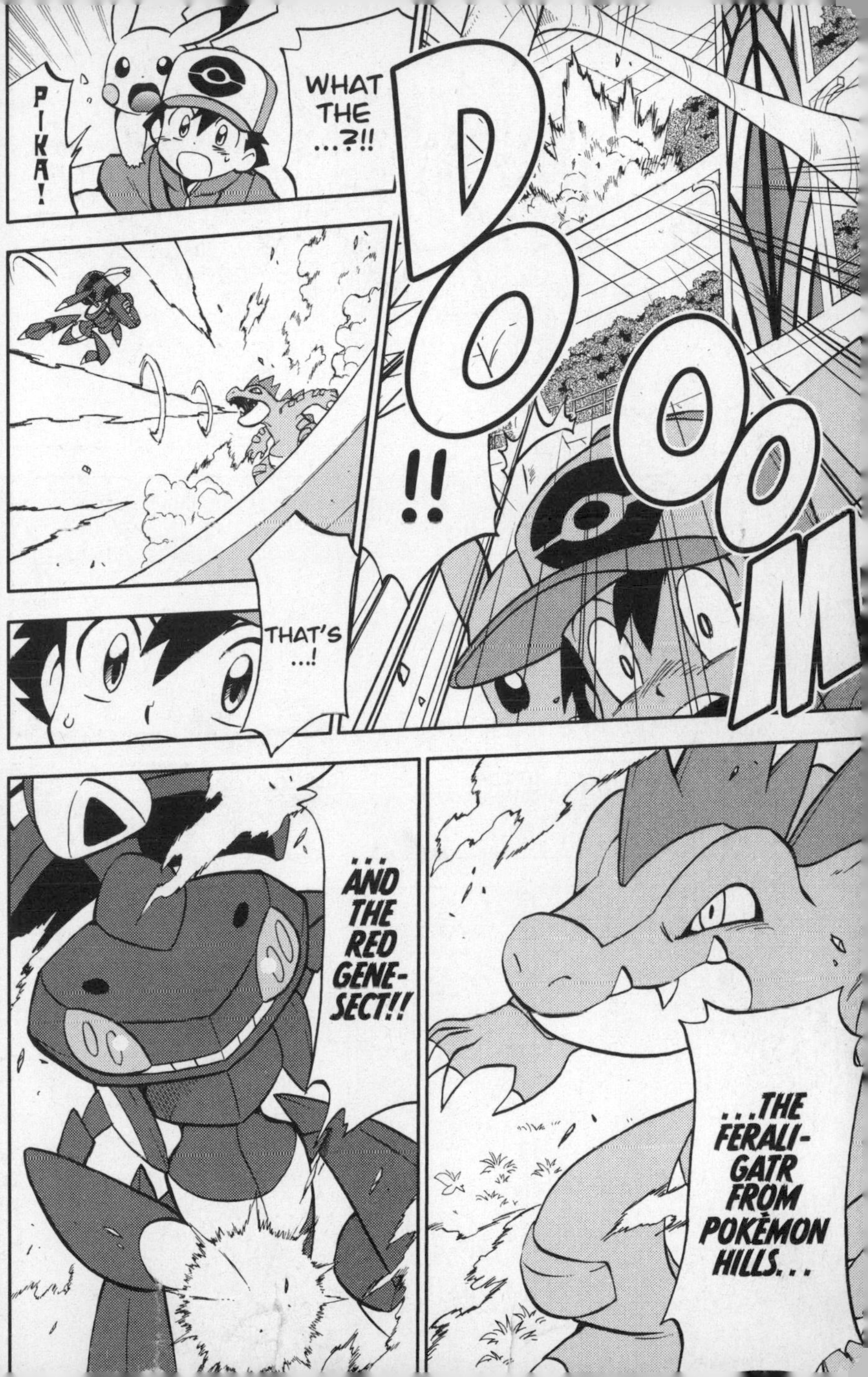
DOOOOOM!!
WHAT THE ...?!!
PIKA!
THAT'S ...!
...THE FERALI-GATR FROM POKÉMON HILLS...
...AND THE RED GENE-SECT!!

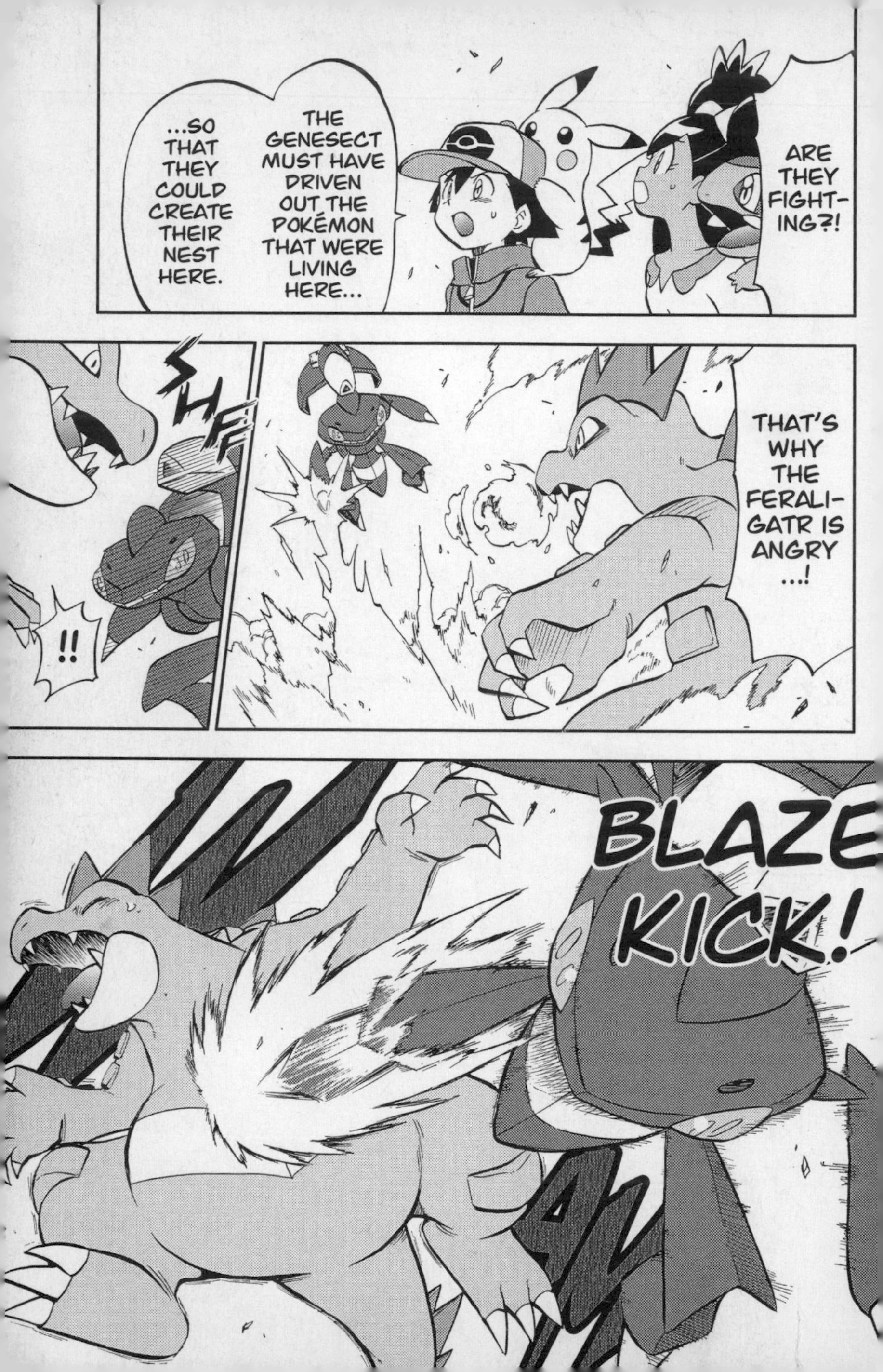
ARE THEY FIGHTING?!
THE GENESECT MUST HAVE DRIVEN OUT THE POKÉMON THAT WERE LIVING HERE...
...SO THAT THEY COULD CREATE THEIR NEST HERE.
THAT'S WHY THE FERALIGATR IS ANGRY...!
SHFF
!!
BLAZE KICK!

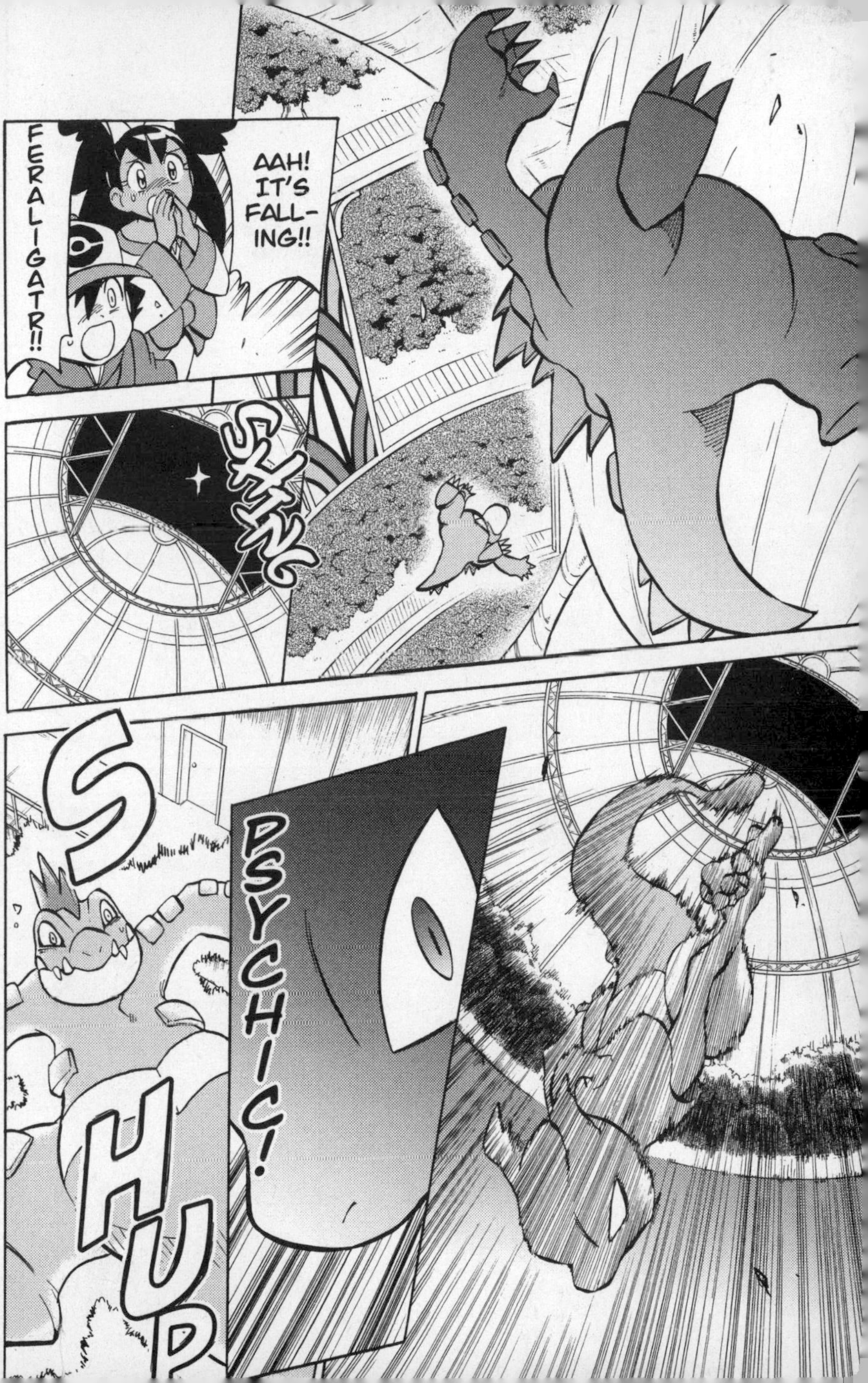
AAH! IT'S FALL-ING!!
FERALIGATR!!
SHING
PSYCHIC!
SHUP

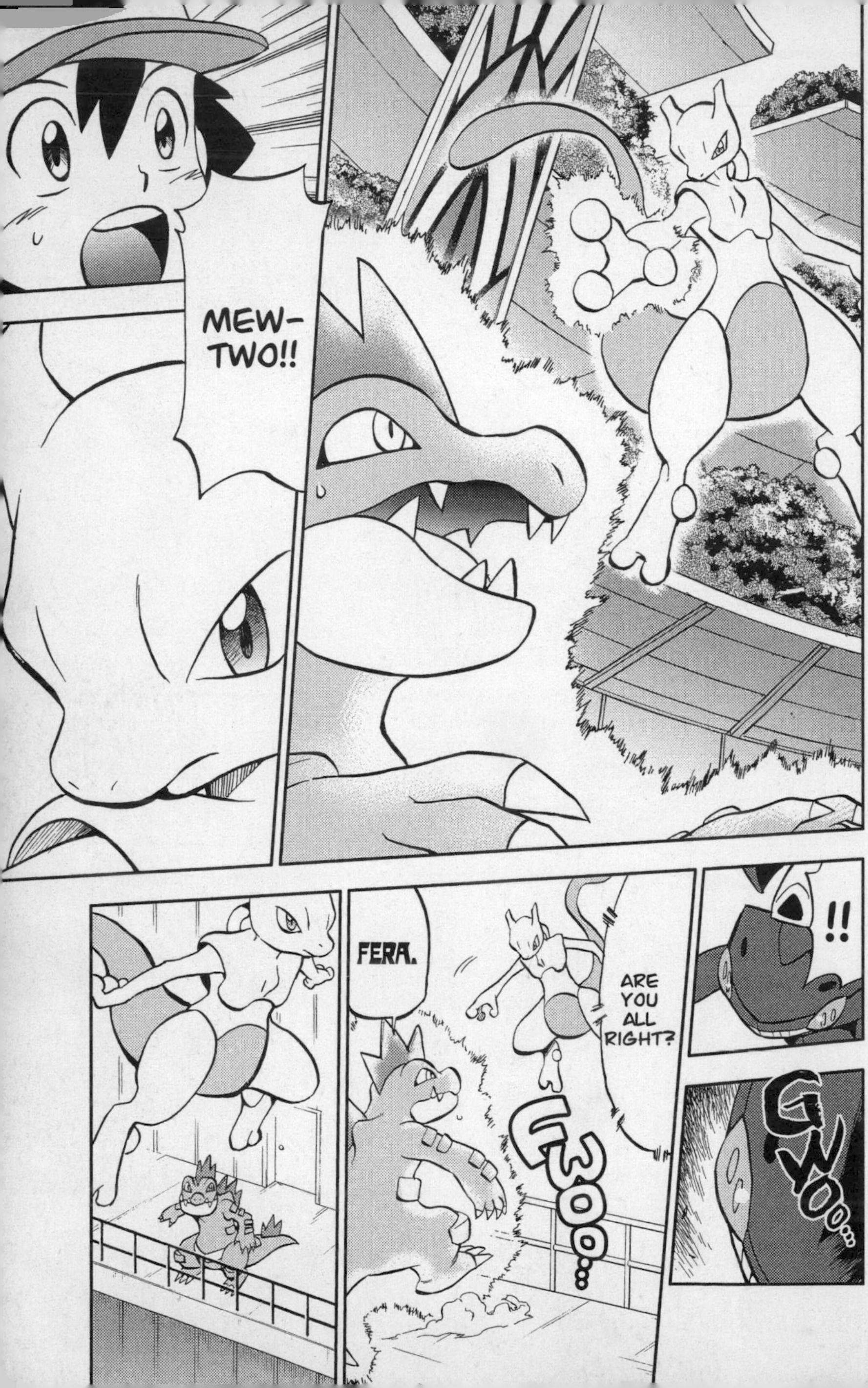
MEW-TWO!!
!!
GWOO...
ARE YOU ALL RIGHT?
FERA.
GWOO...

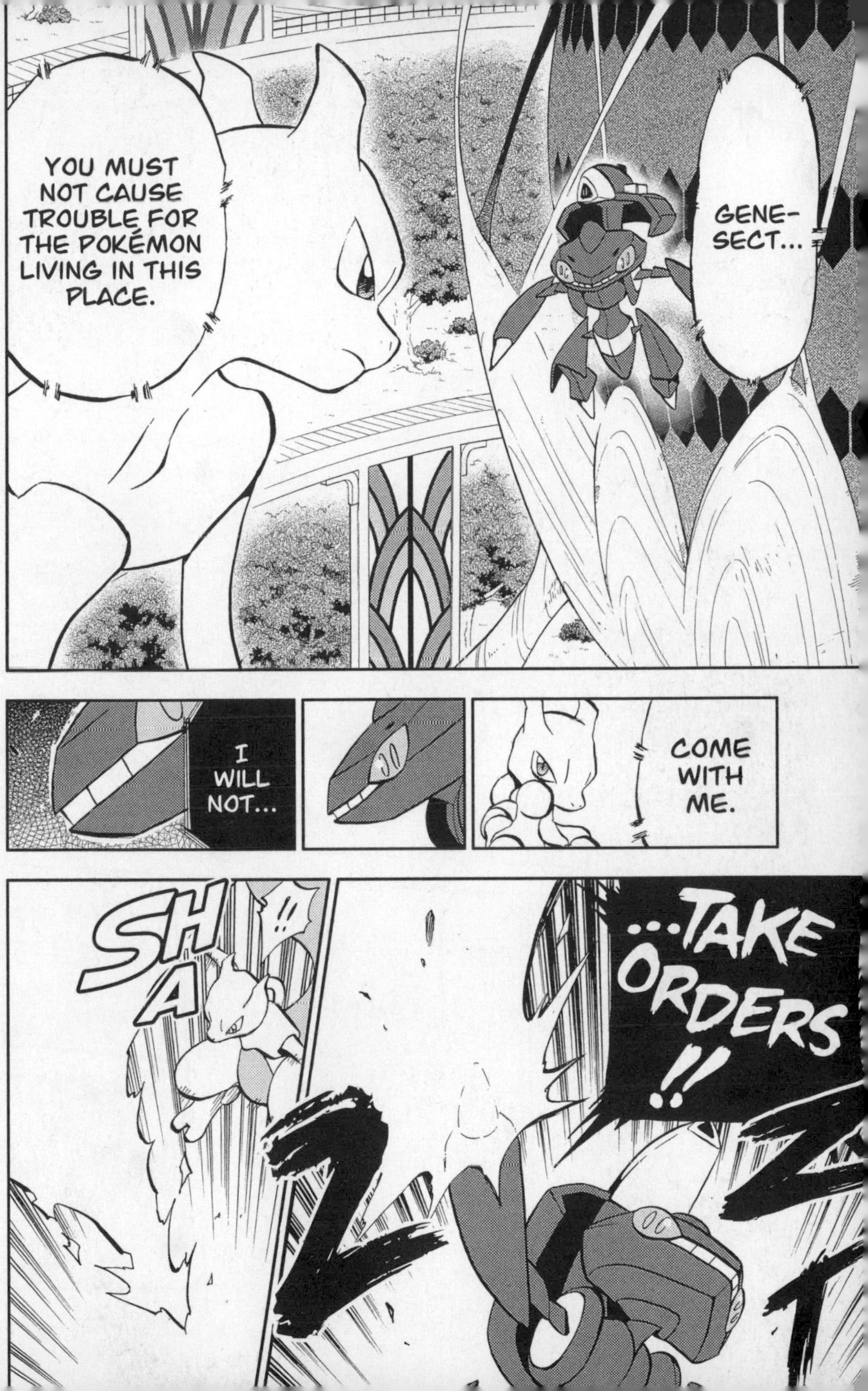
GENE-SECT...
YOU MUST NOT CAUSE TROUBLE FOR THE POKÉMON LIVING IN THIS PLACE.
COME WITH ME.
I WILL NOT...
...TAKE ORDERS!!
!!
SHA

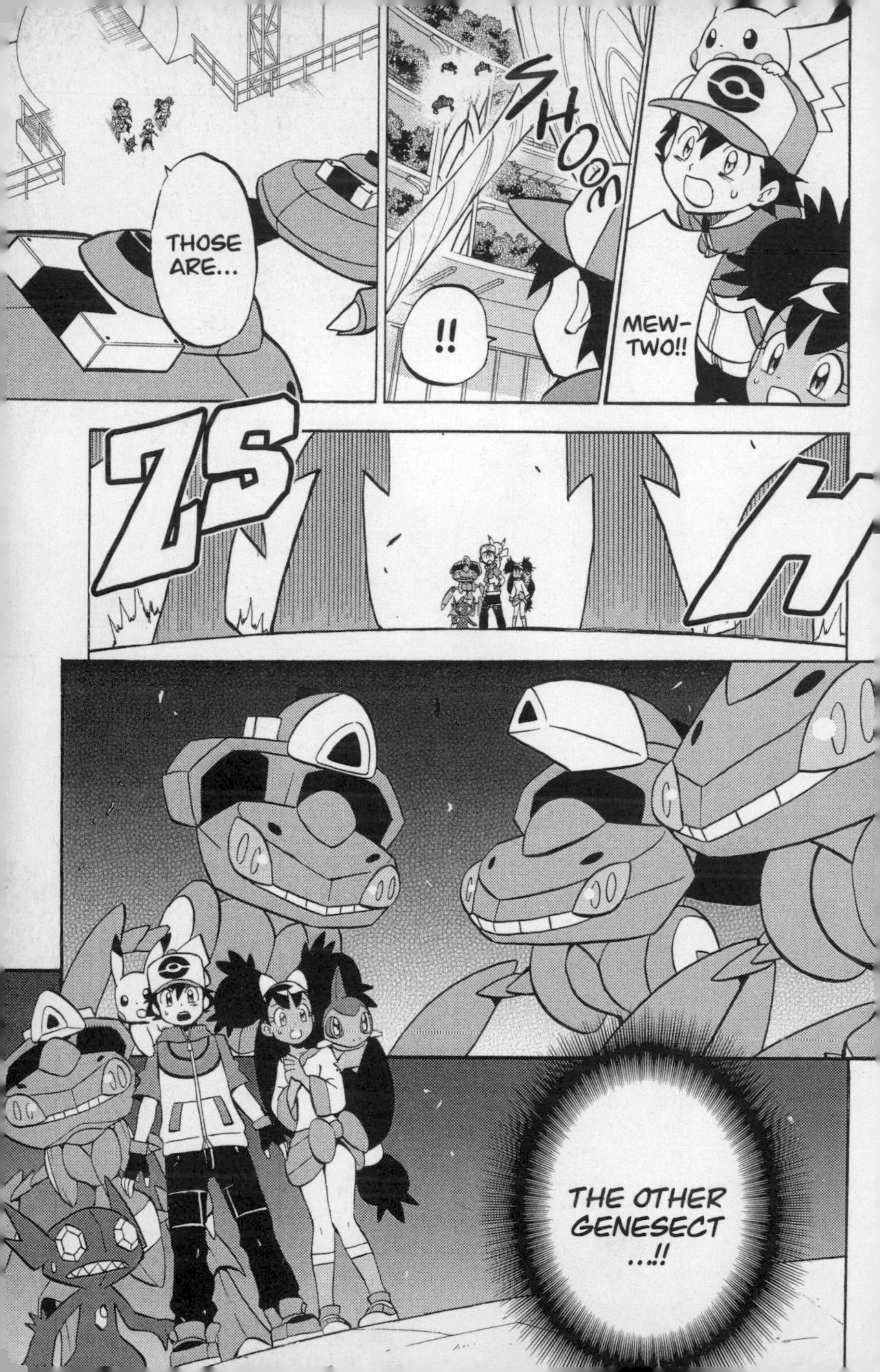
MEW-TWO!!
SHOOM
!!
THOSE ARE...
ZS
H
THE OTHER GENESECT ...!!

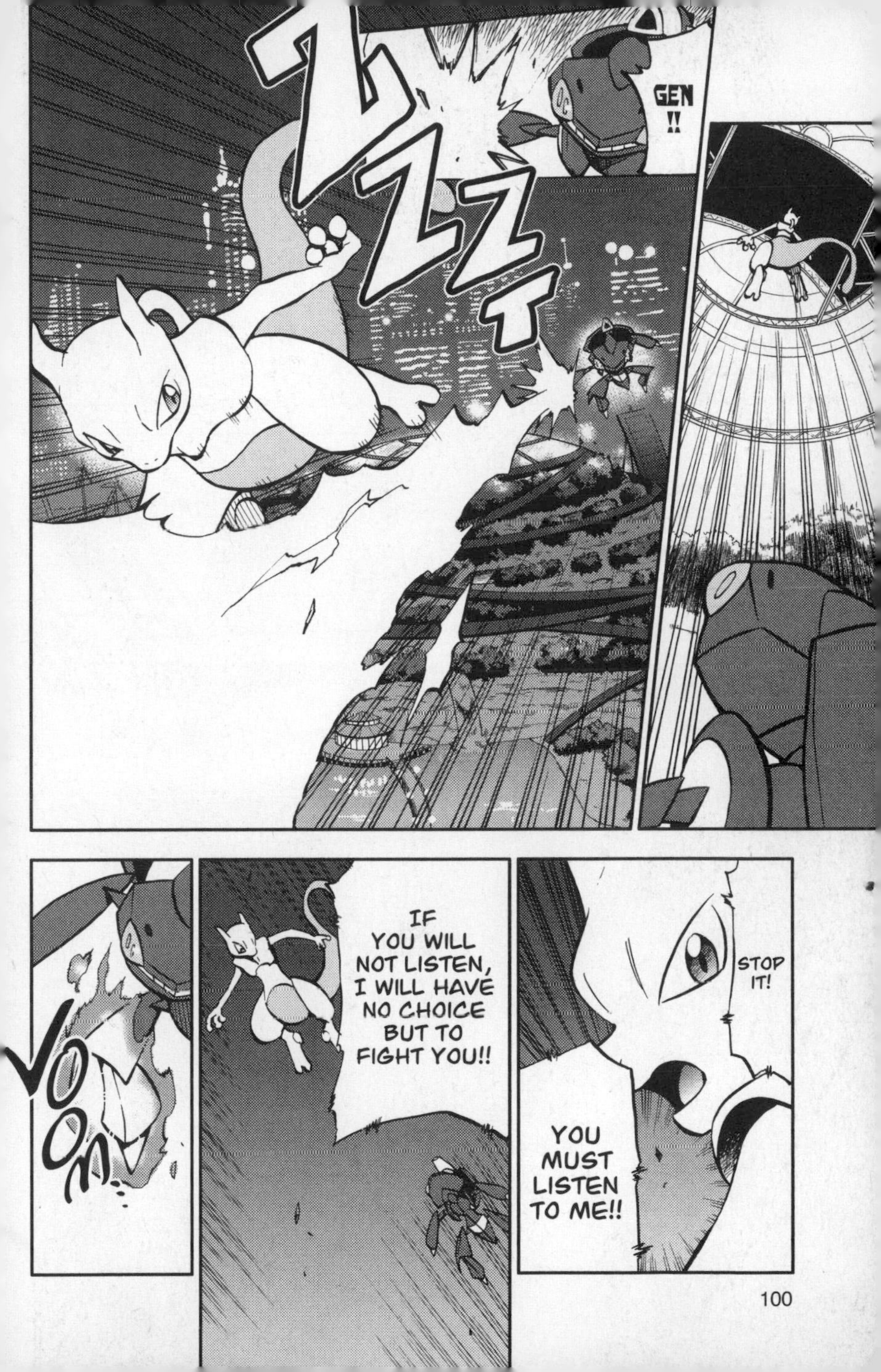
GEN !!
ZZZZT
STOP IT!
YOU MUST LISTEN TO ME!!
IF YOU WILL NOT LISTEN, I WILL HAVE NO CHOICE BUT TO FIGHT YOU!!
VOOOM

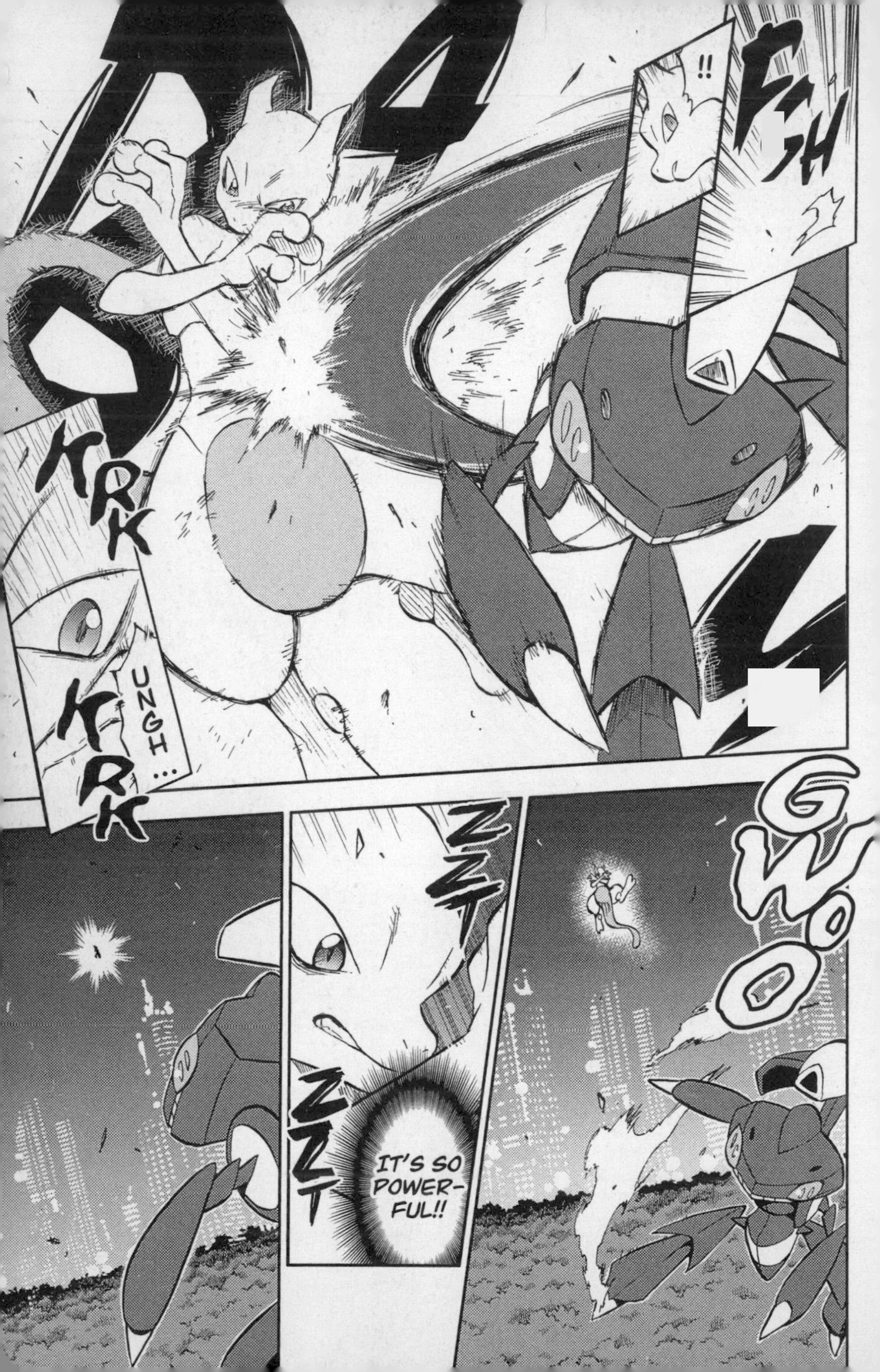
!!
FSH
KRK
UNGH...
KRK
GWOO
ZZT
ZZT
IT'S SO POWER-FUL!!

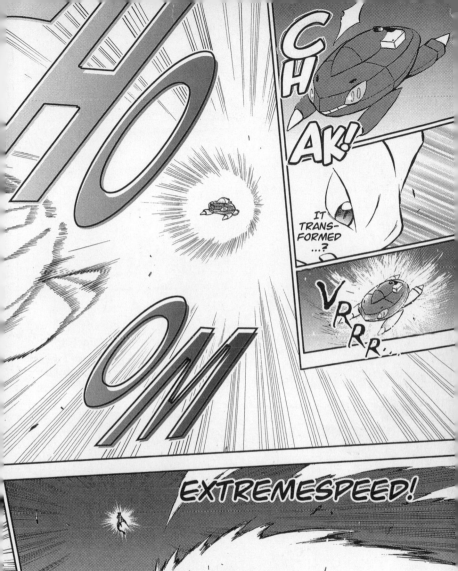

CH

AK!

IT TRANS-FORMED ...?

VRrrr

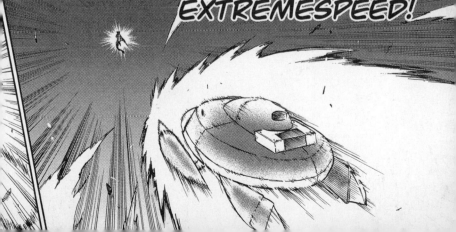

EXTREMESPEED!

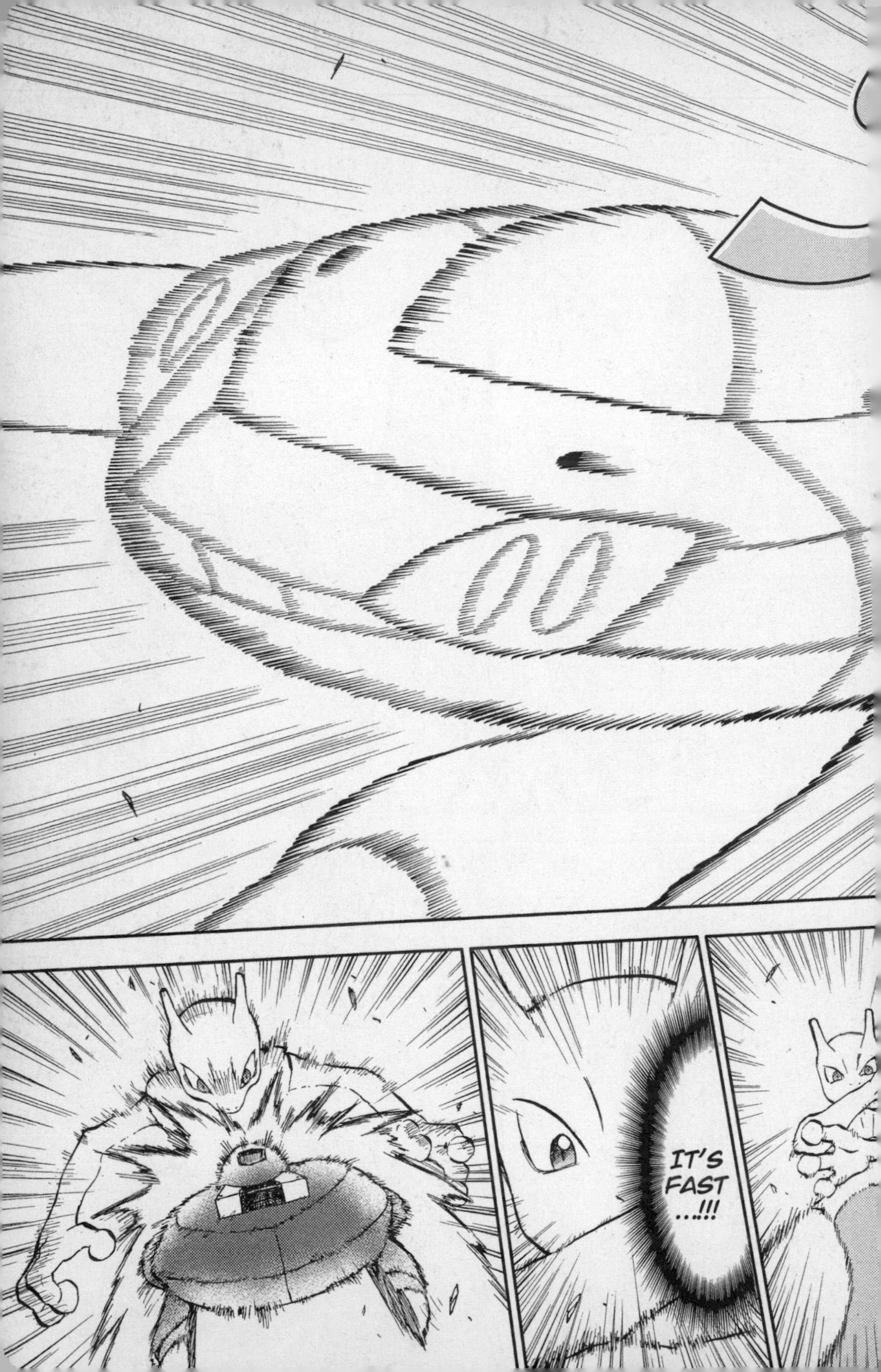
IT'S FAST ...!!!

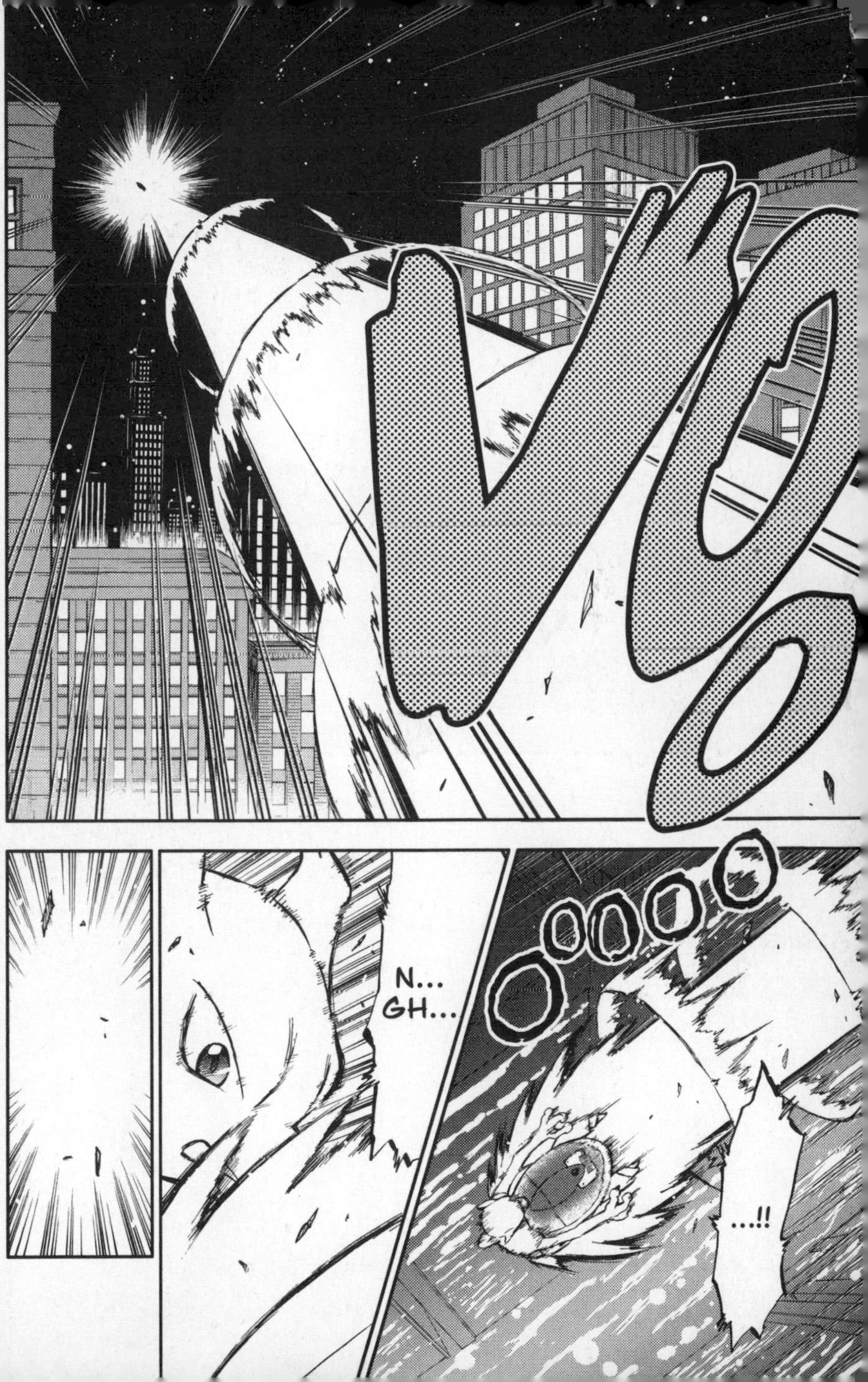
...!!
N...
GH...

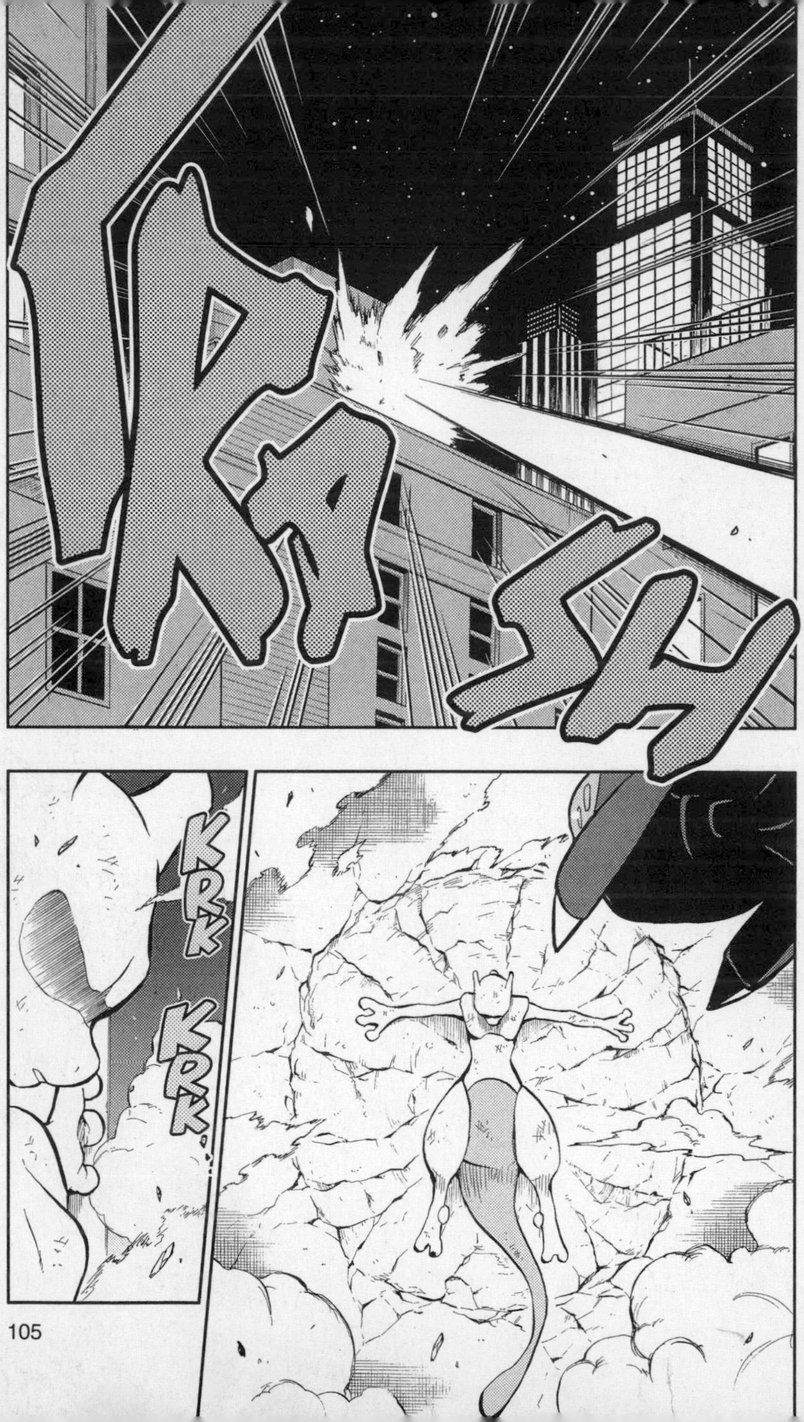
KRK
KRK

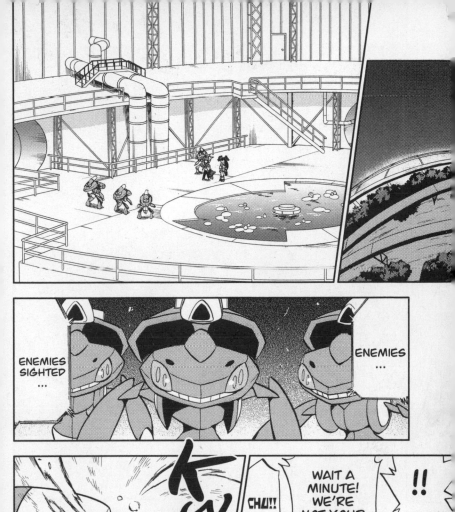

ENEMIES
SIGHTED
...

ENEMIES
...

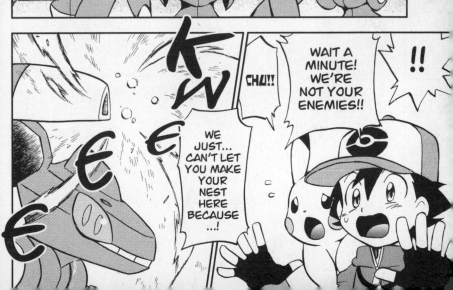

WAIT A
MINUTE!
WE'RE
NOT YOUR
ENEMIES!!

!!

CHU!!

WE
JUST...
CAN'T LET
YOU MAKE
YOUR
NEST
HERE
BECAUSE
...!

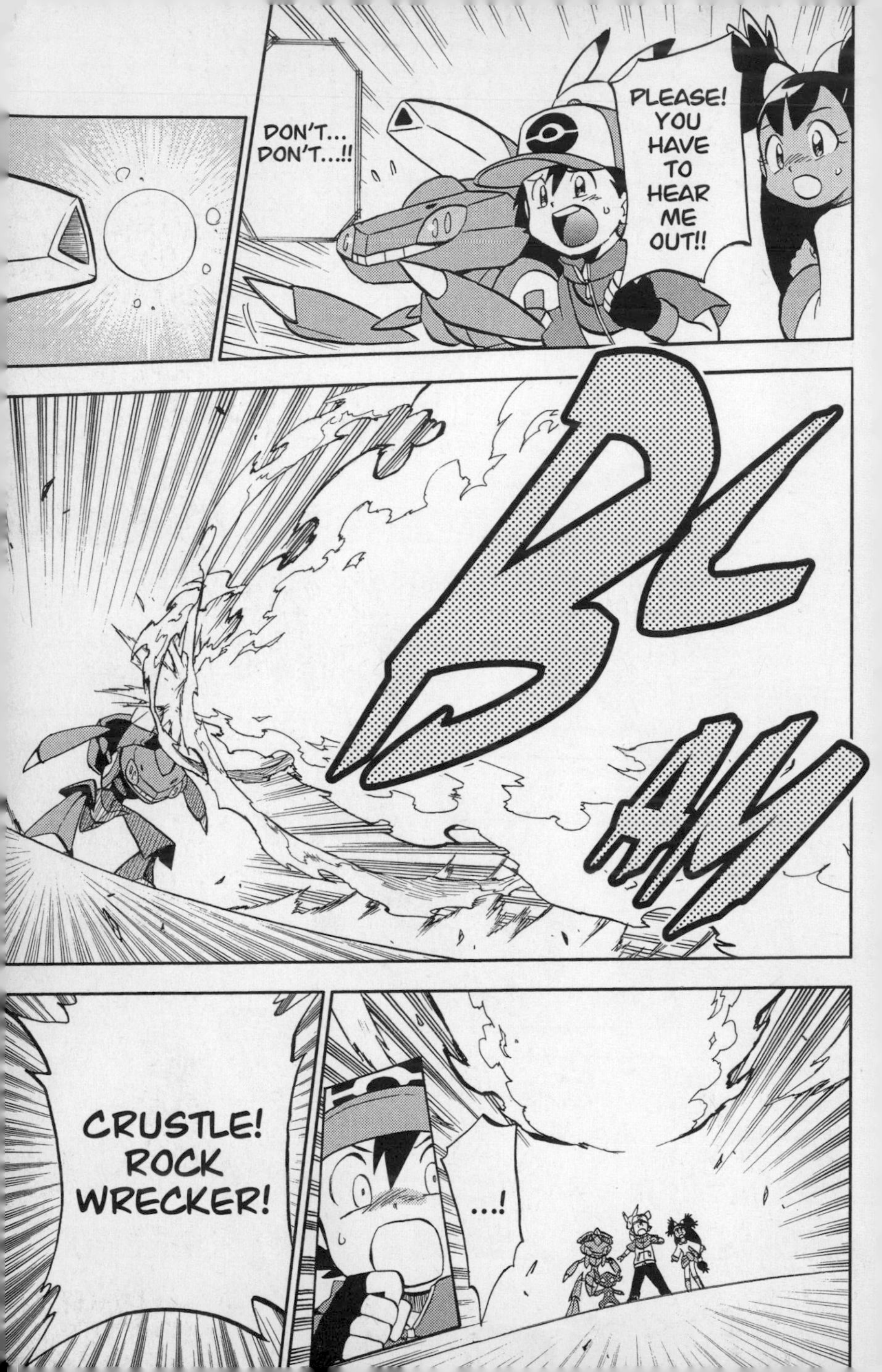
PLEASE! YOU HAVE TO HEAR ME OUT!!
DON'T... DON'T...!!
...!
CRUSTLE! ROCK WRECKER!

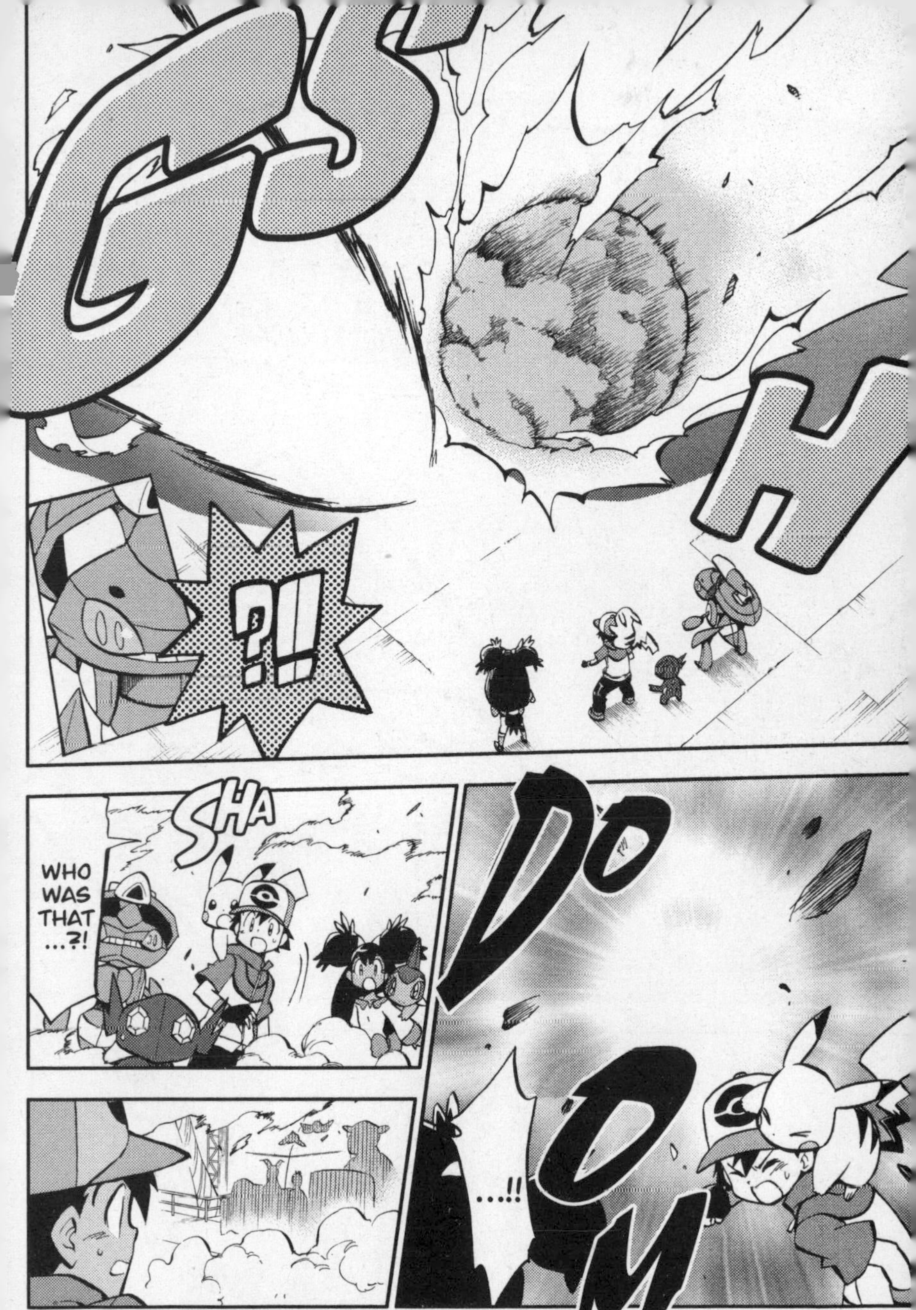
?!!
DOOM
...!!
SHA
WHO WAS THAT ...?!

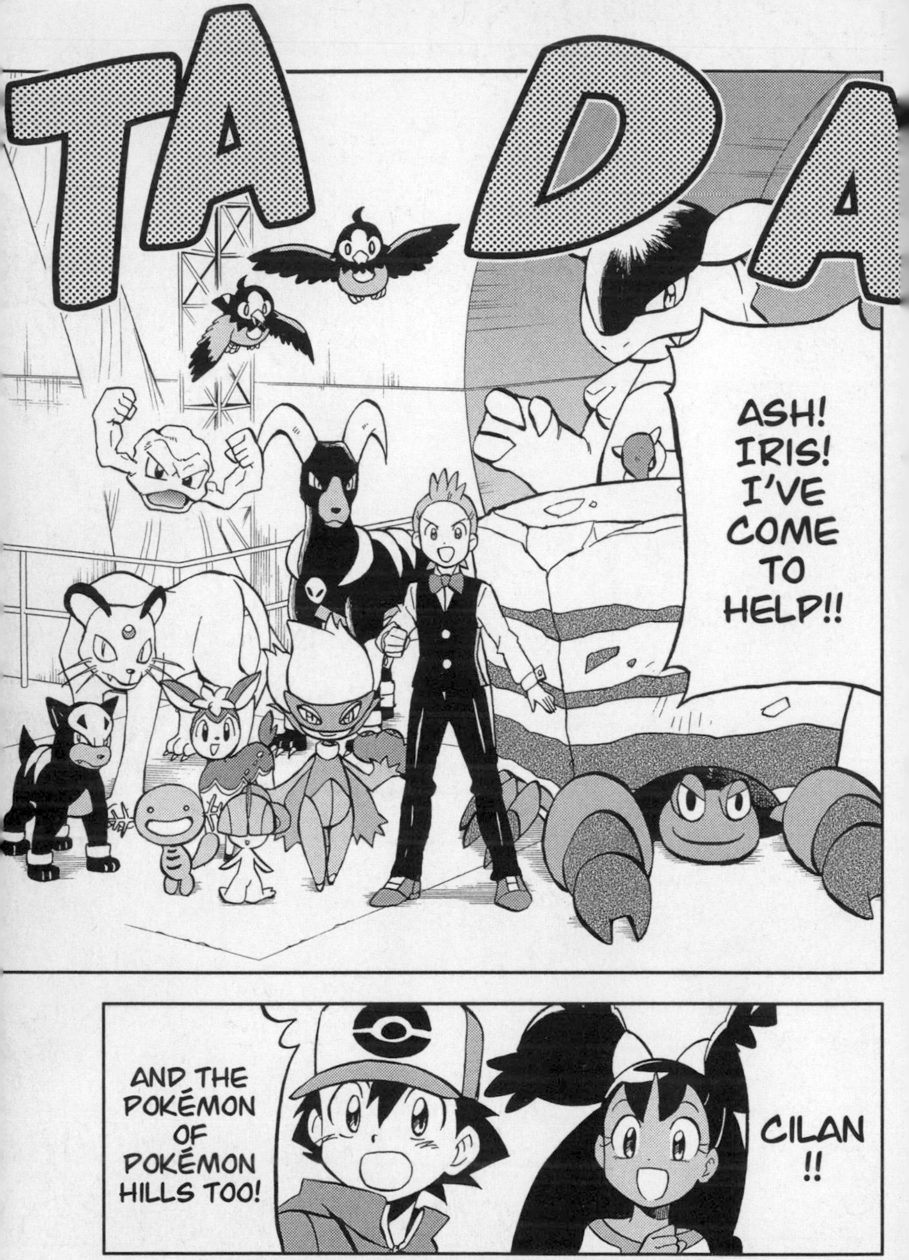
TA DA
ASH! IRIS! I'VE COME TO HELP!!
CILAN!!
AND THE POKÉMON OF POKÉMON HILLS TOO!

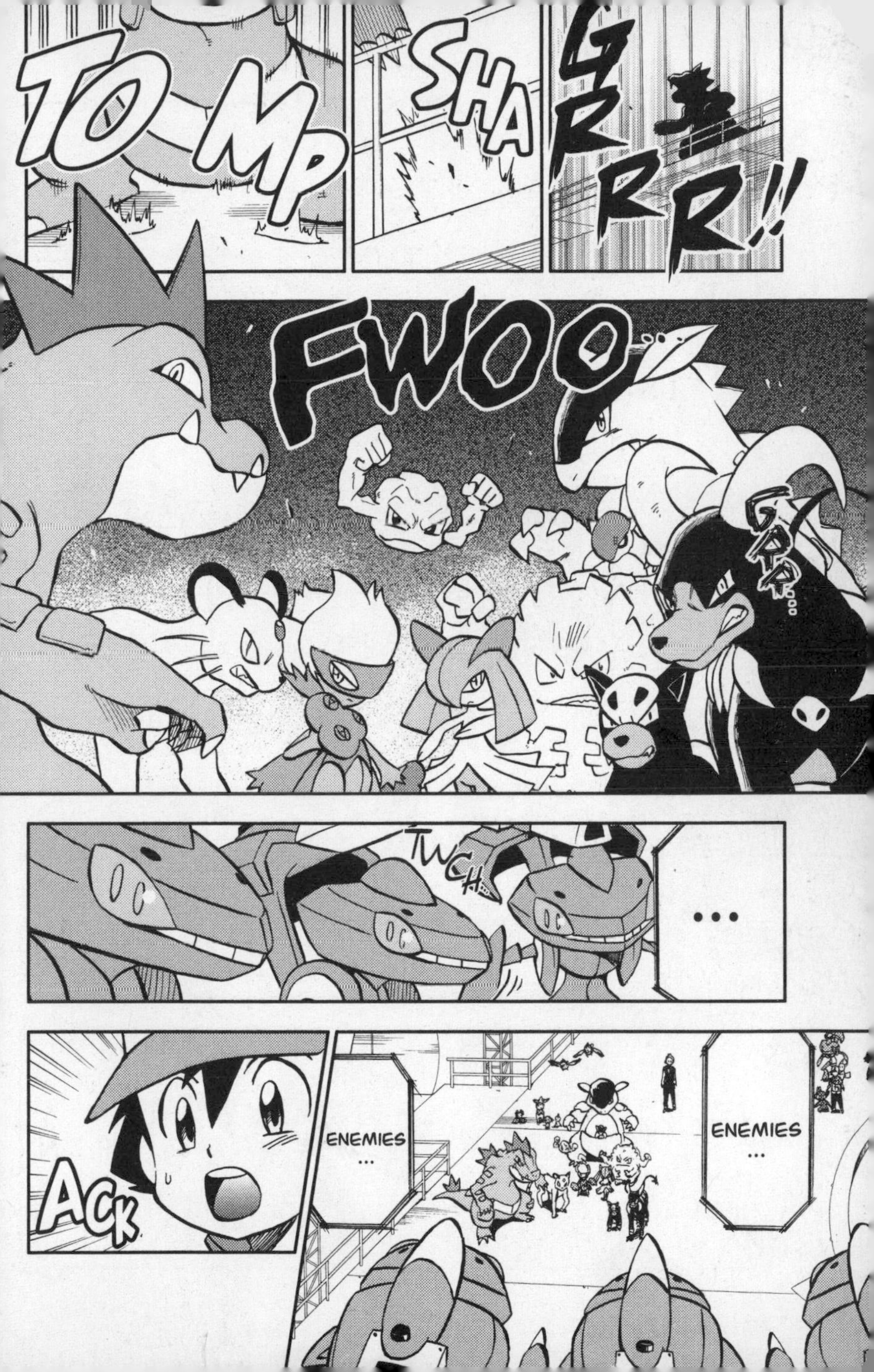
GRRRR!!
SHA
TOMP
FWOO
GRRR...
TWCH
...
ENEMIES ...
ENEMIES ...
ACK

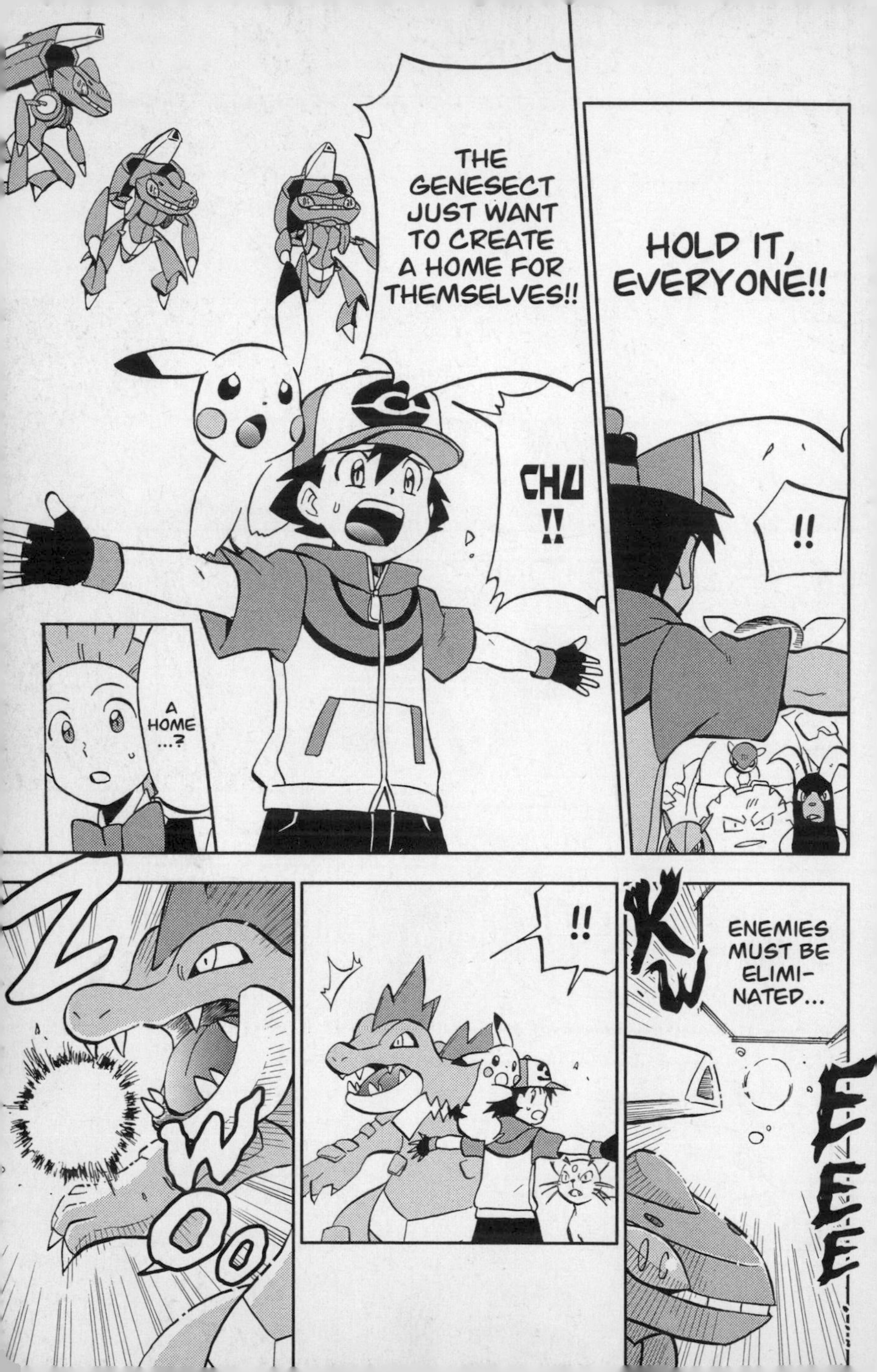
HOLD IT, EVERYONE!!
!!
THE GENESECT JUST WANT TO CREATE A HOME FOR THEMSELVES!!
CHU !!
A HOME ...?
KW
ENEMIES MUST BE ELIMI-NATED...
EEEE
!!
ZWOO

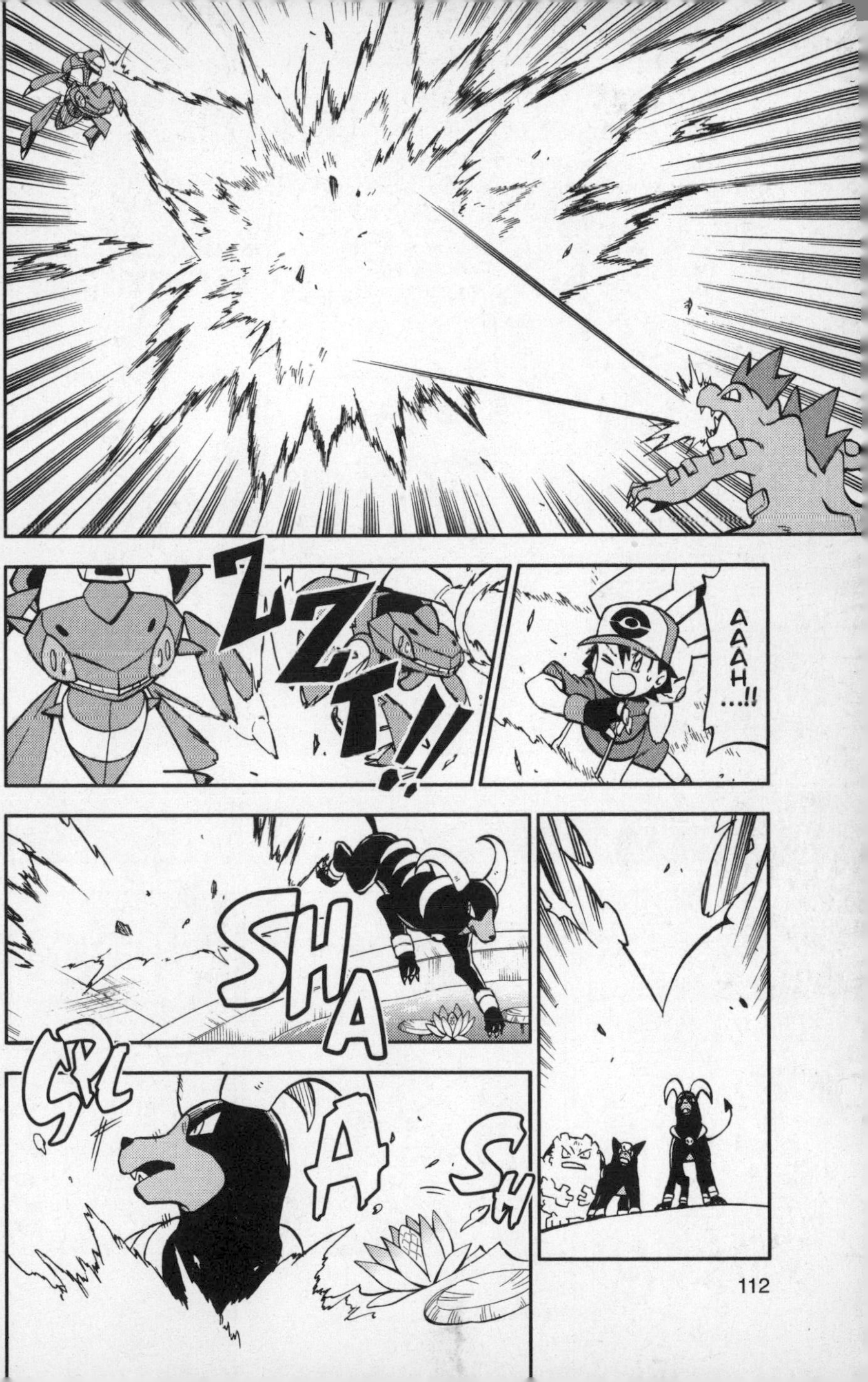
AAAH...!!
ZZZT!!
SHA
SPLASH

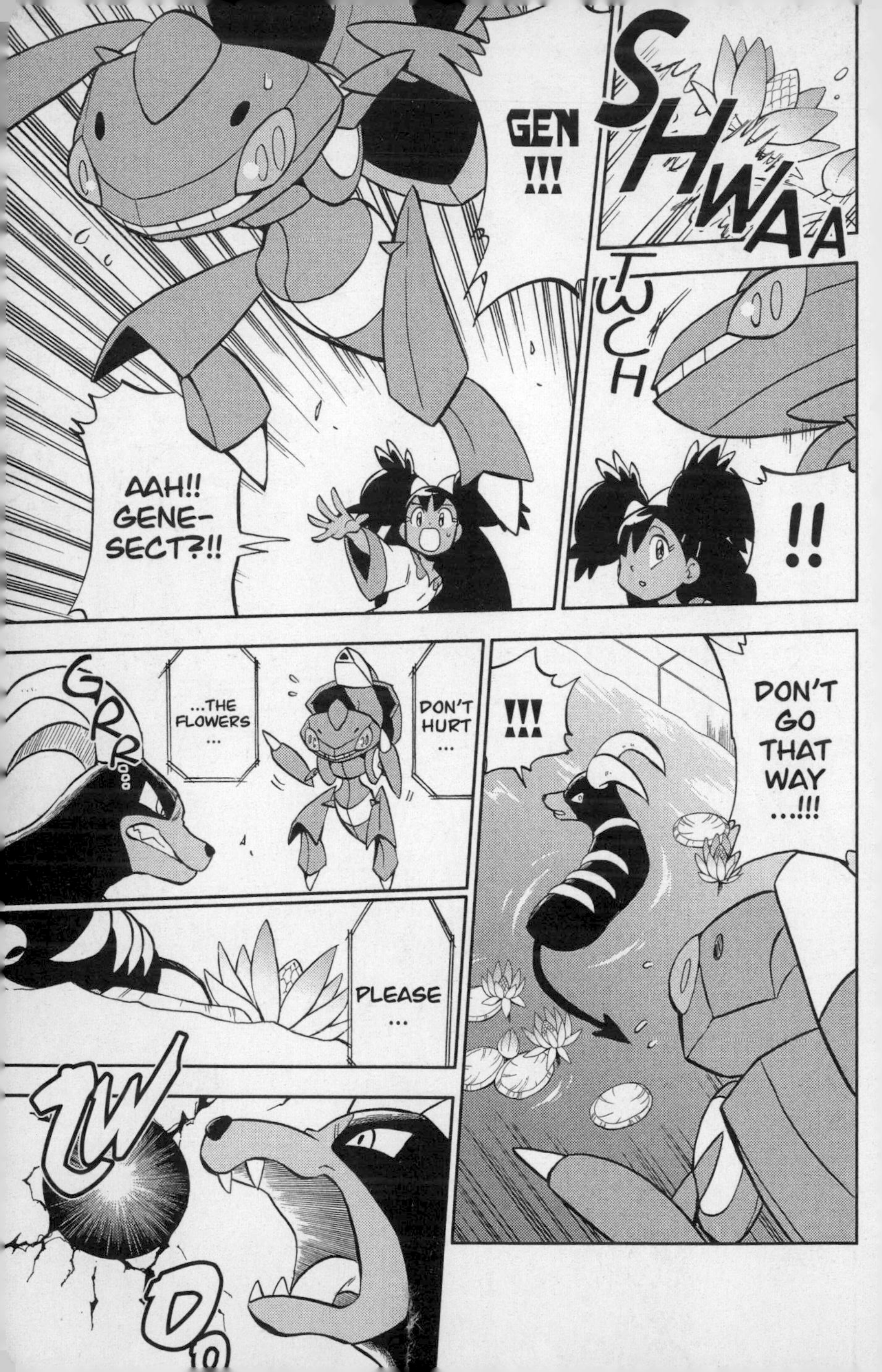
SHWAA
TWCH
!!
GEN!!!
AAH!! GENE-SECT?!!
DON'T GO THAT WAY...!!!
!!!
DON'T HURT...
...THE FLOWERS...
GRR
PLEASE...
TW
D

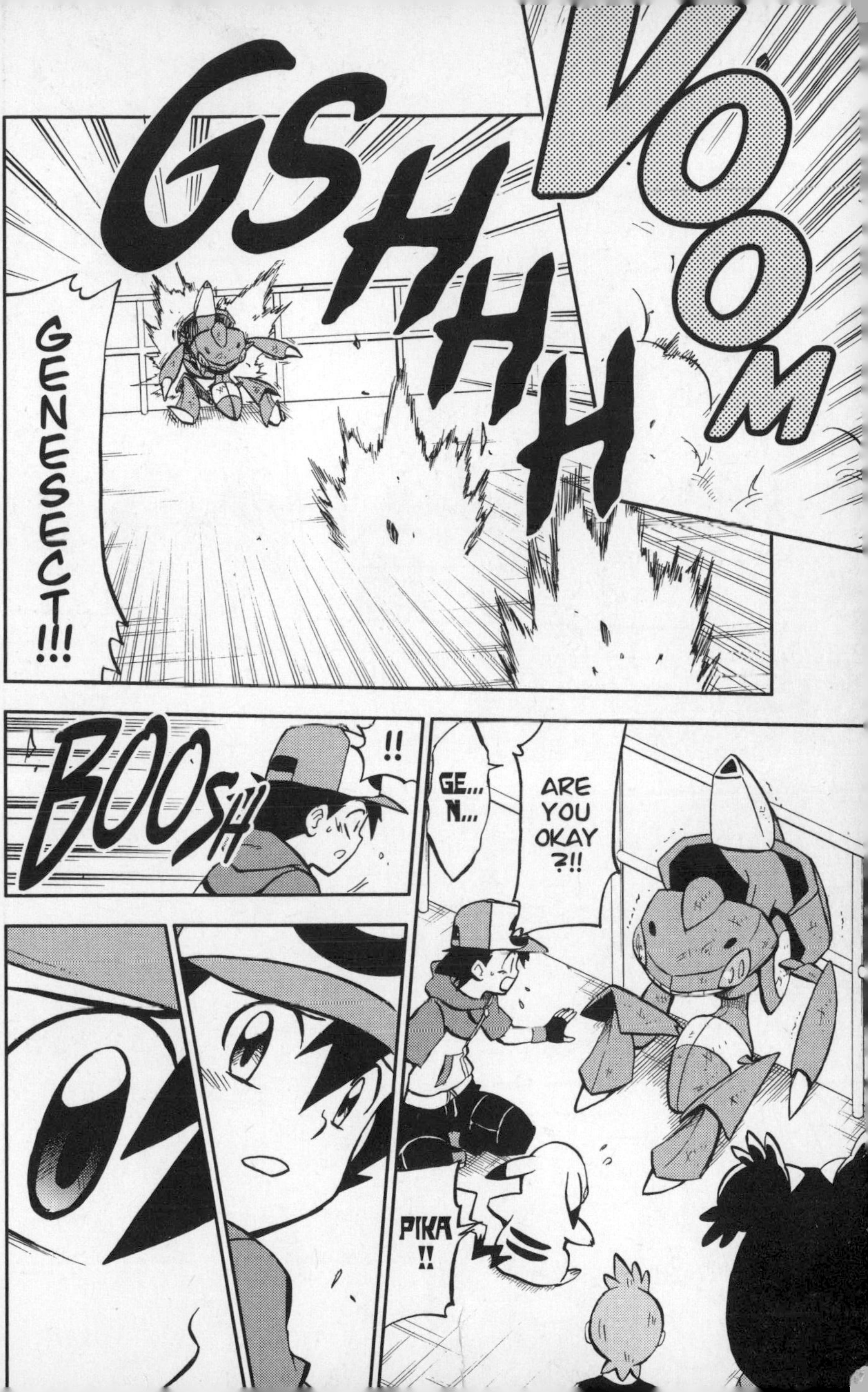
VOOM
GSHHHH
GENESECT!!!
ARE YOU OKAY?!!
GE... N...
PIKA!!
!!
BOOSH

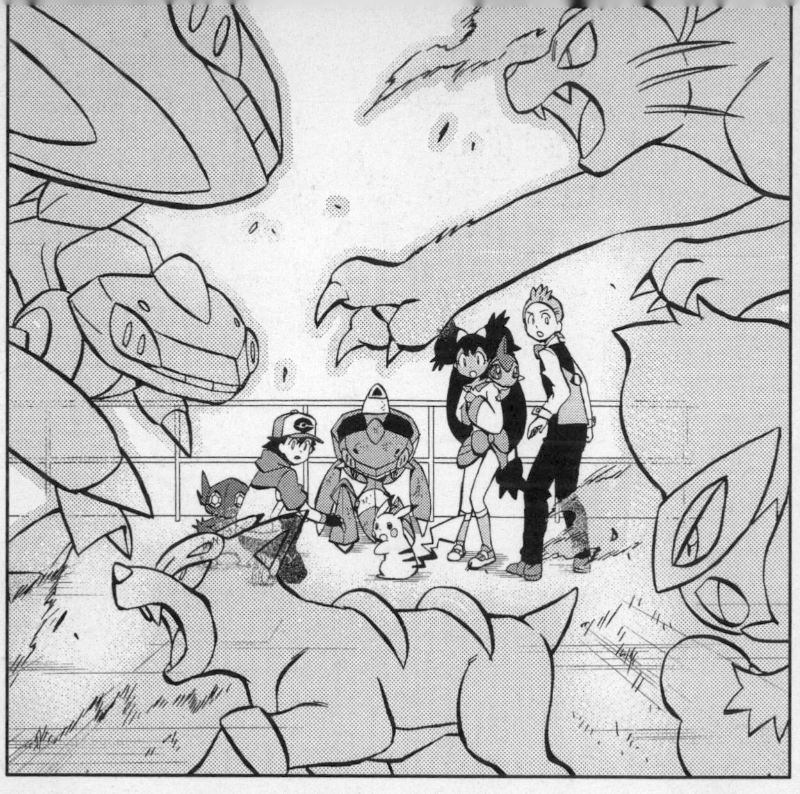

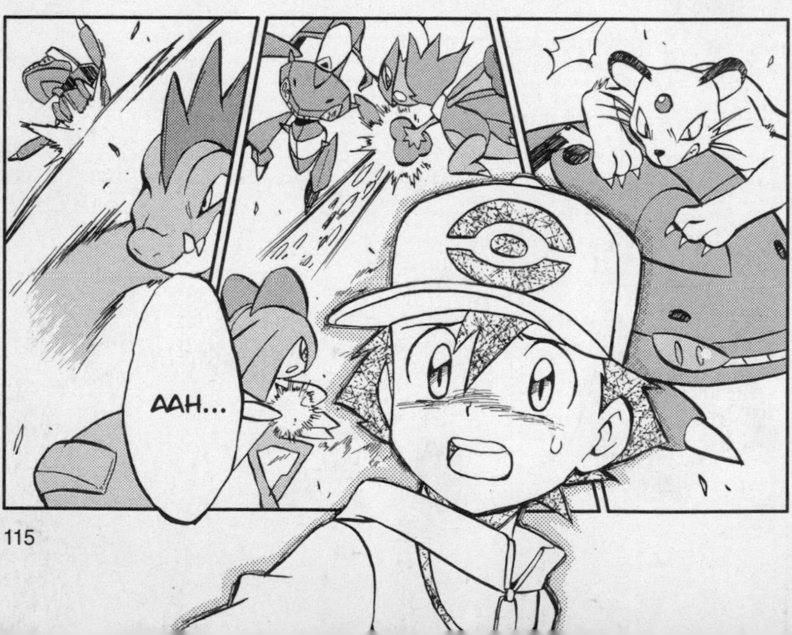
AAH...

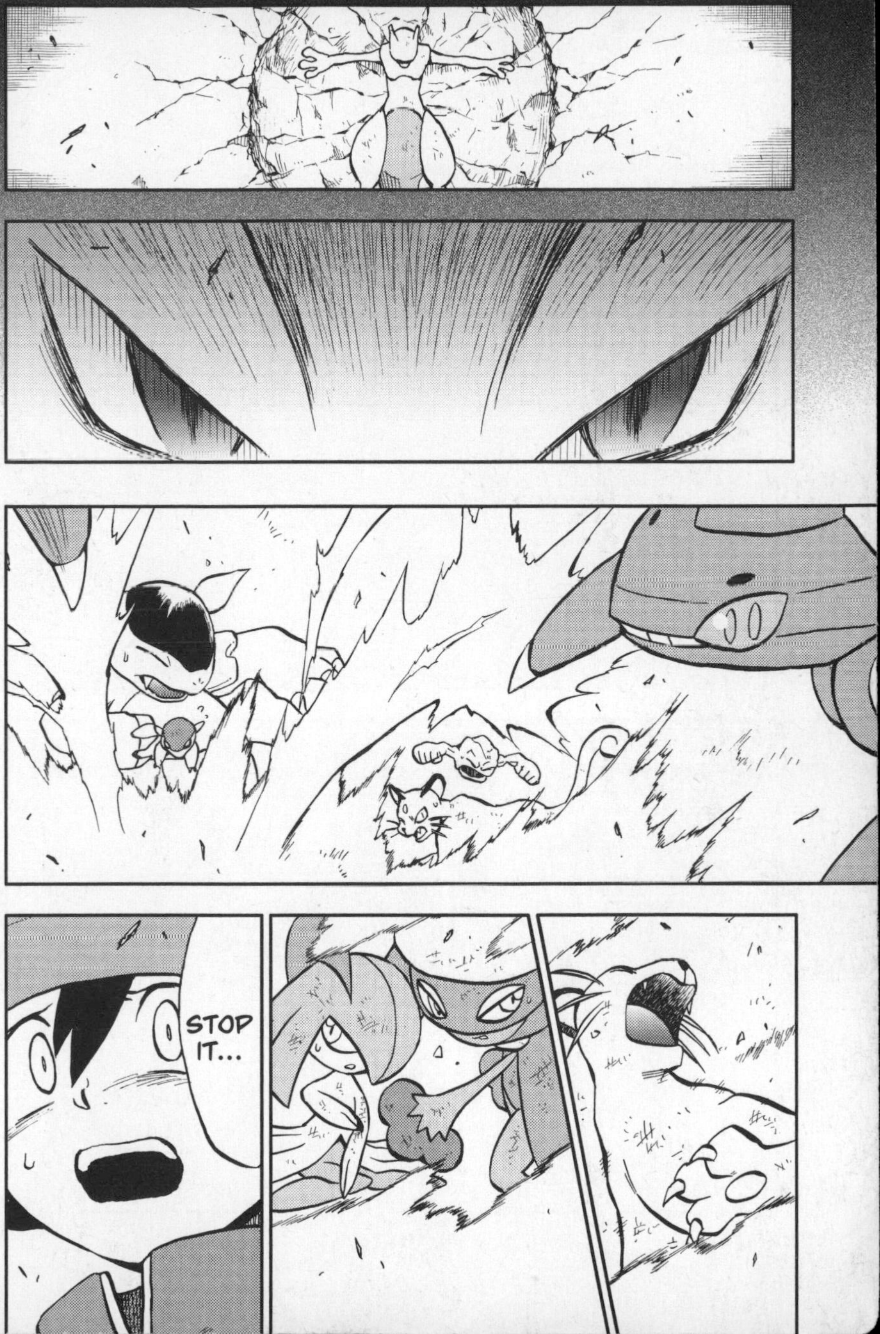
STOP IT...

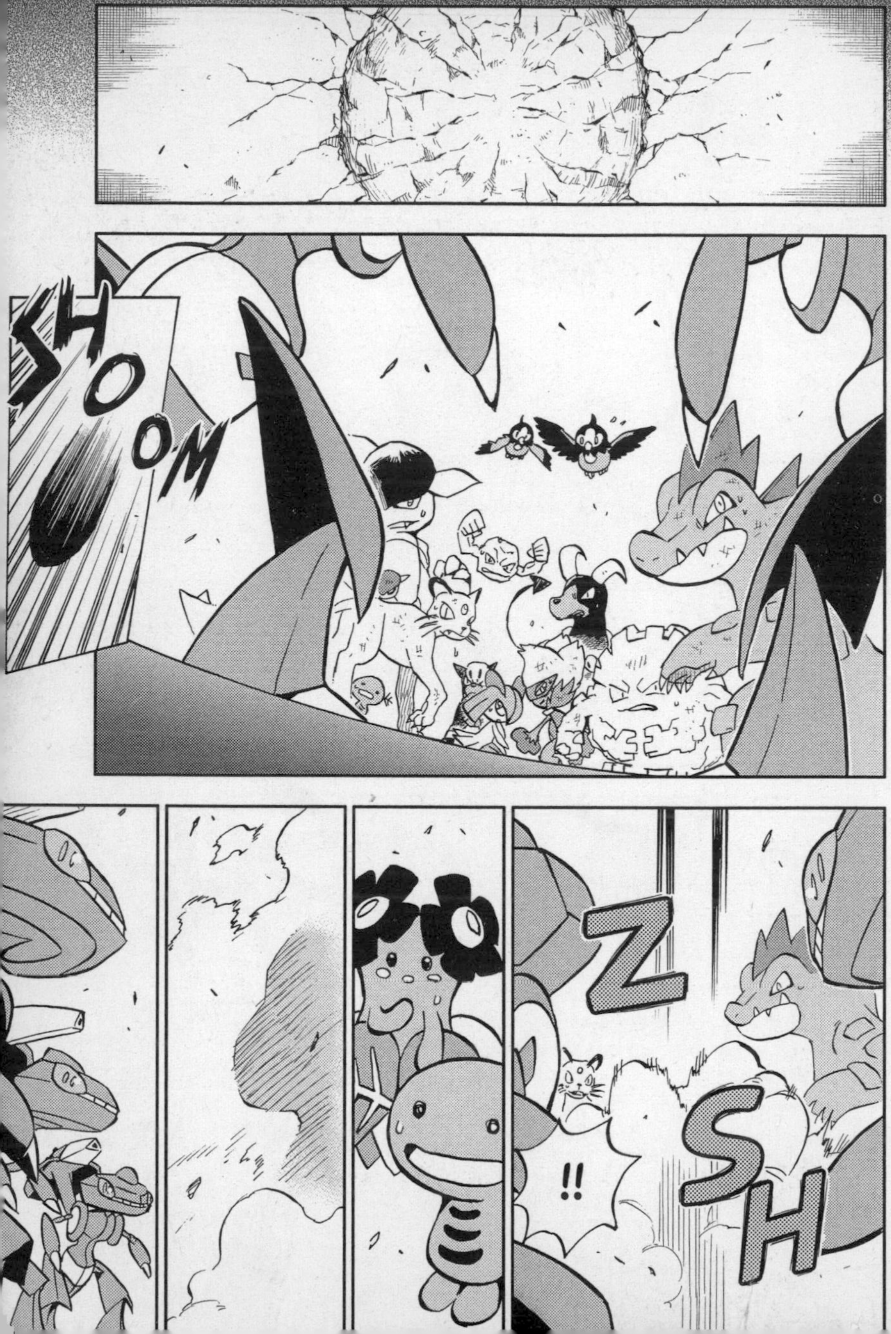
SHOOM
ZSH
!!

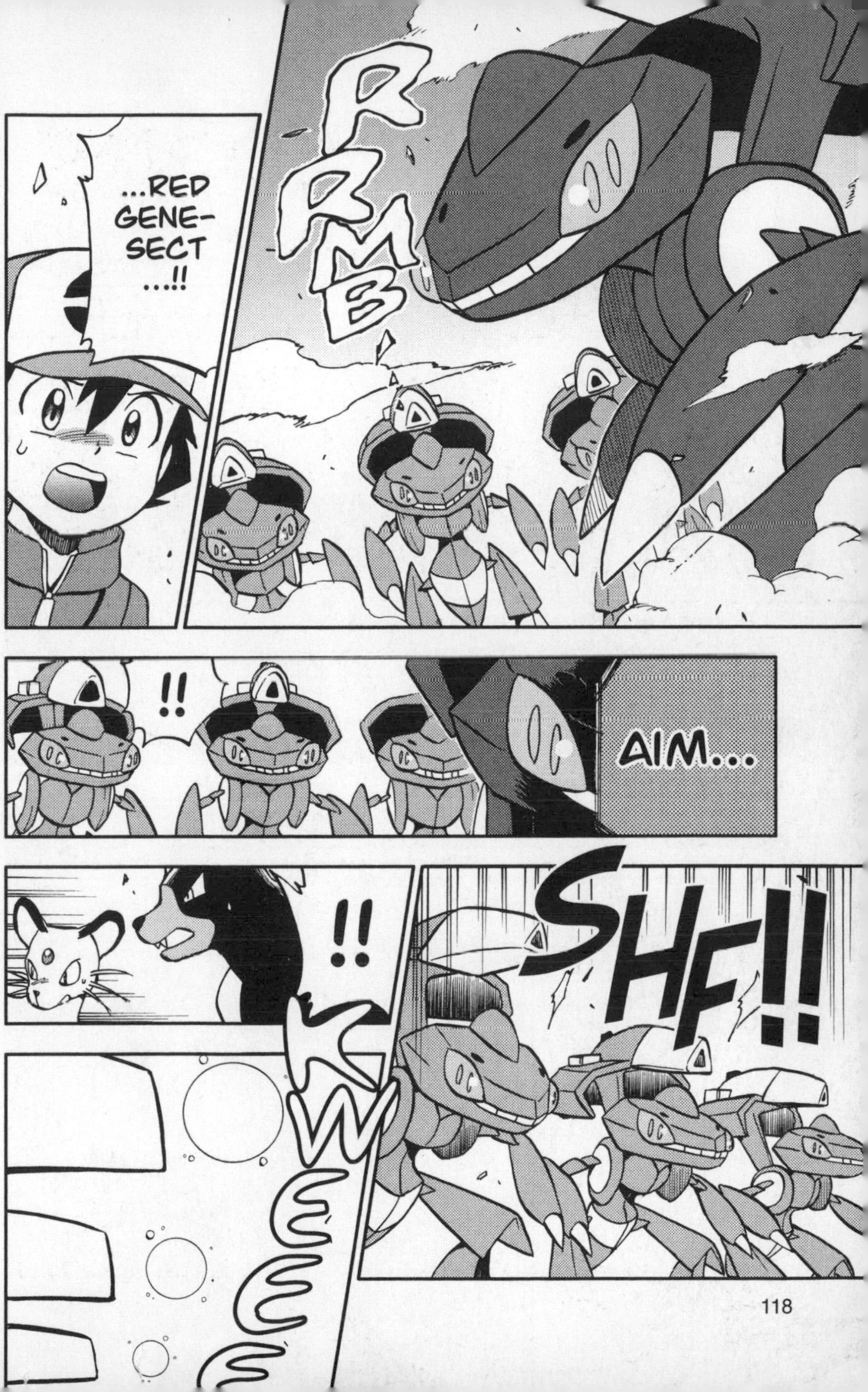
RRMB
...RED GENE-SECT ...!!
AIM...
!!
SHF!!
!!
WEEE

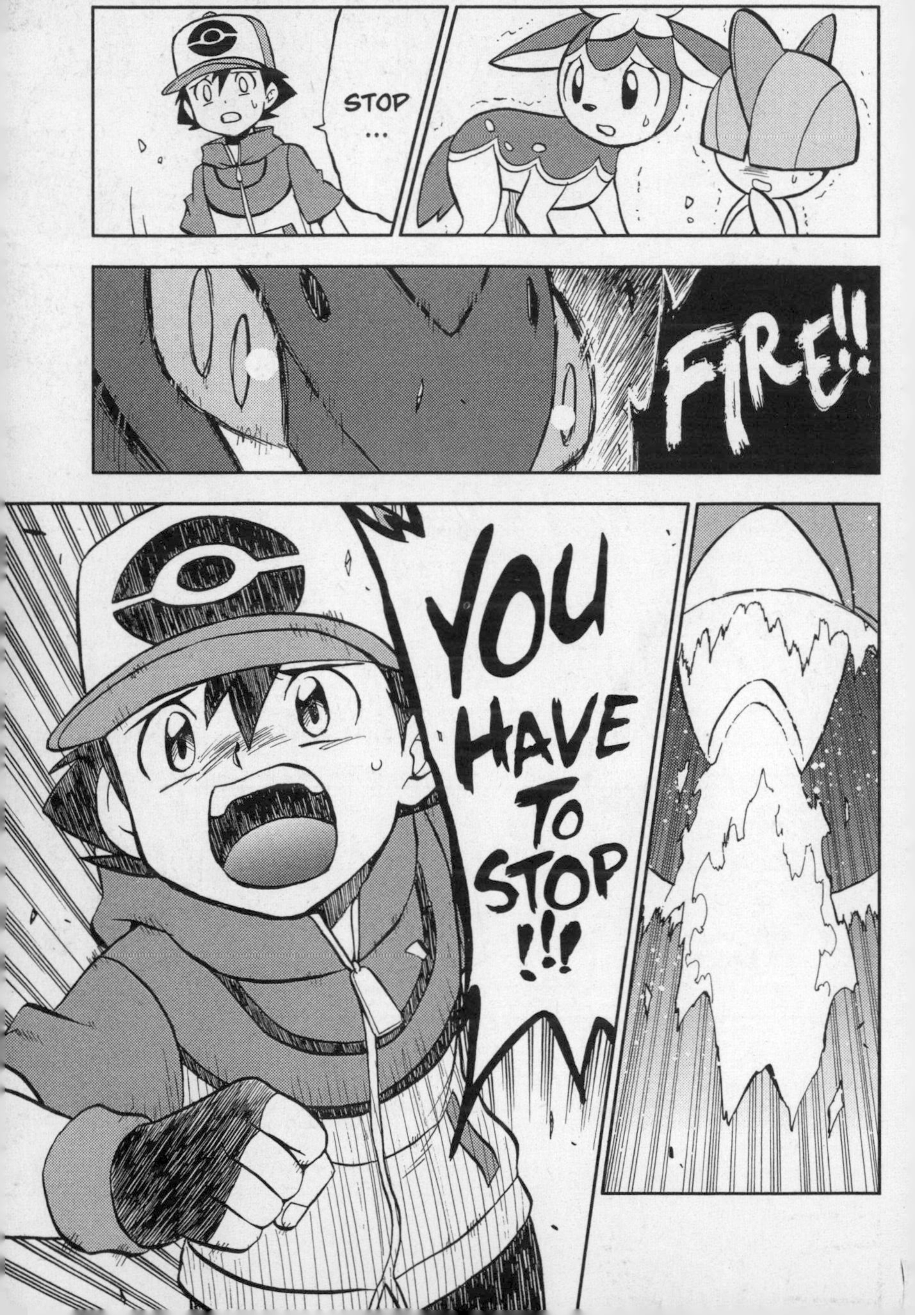
STOP ...
FIRE!!
YOU HAVE TO STOP !!!

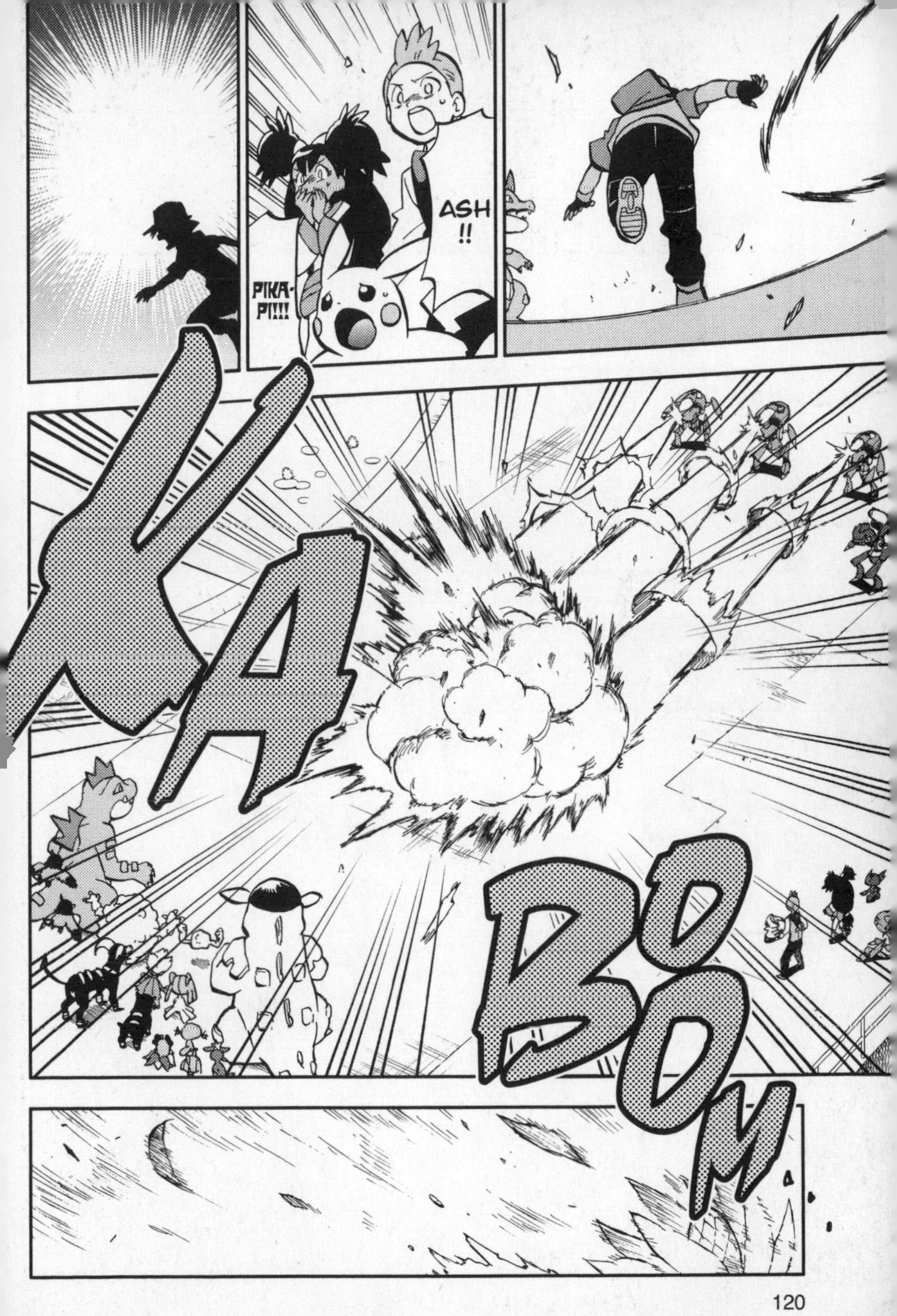
ASH!!
PIKA-PI!!!
KA
BOOM

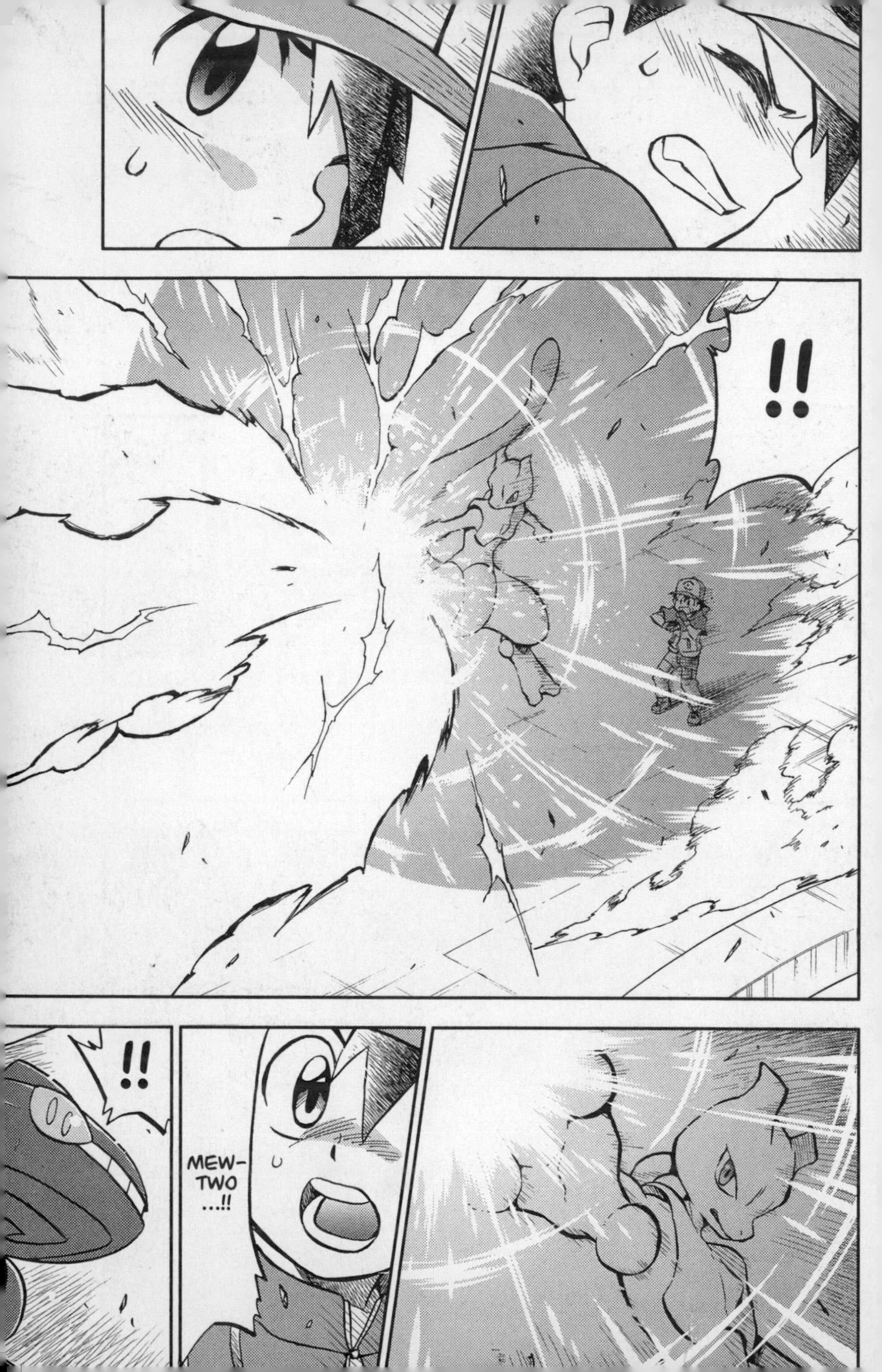
!!
MEW-
TWO
...!!
!!

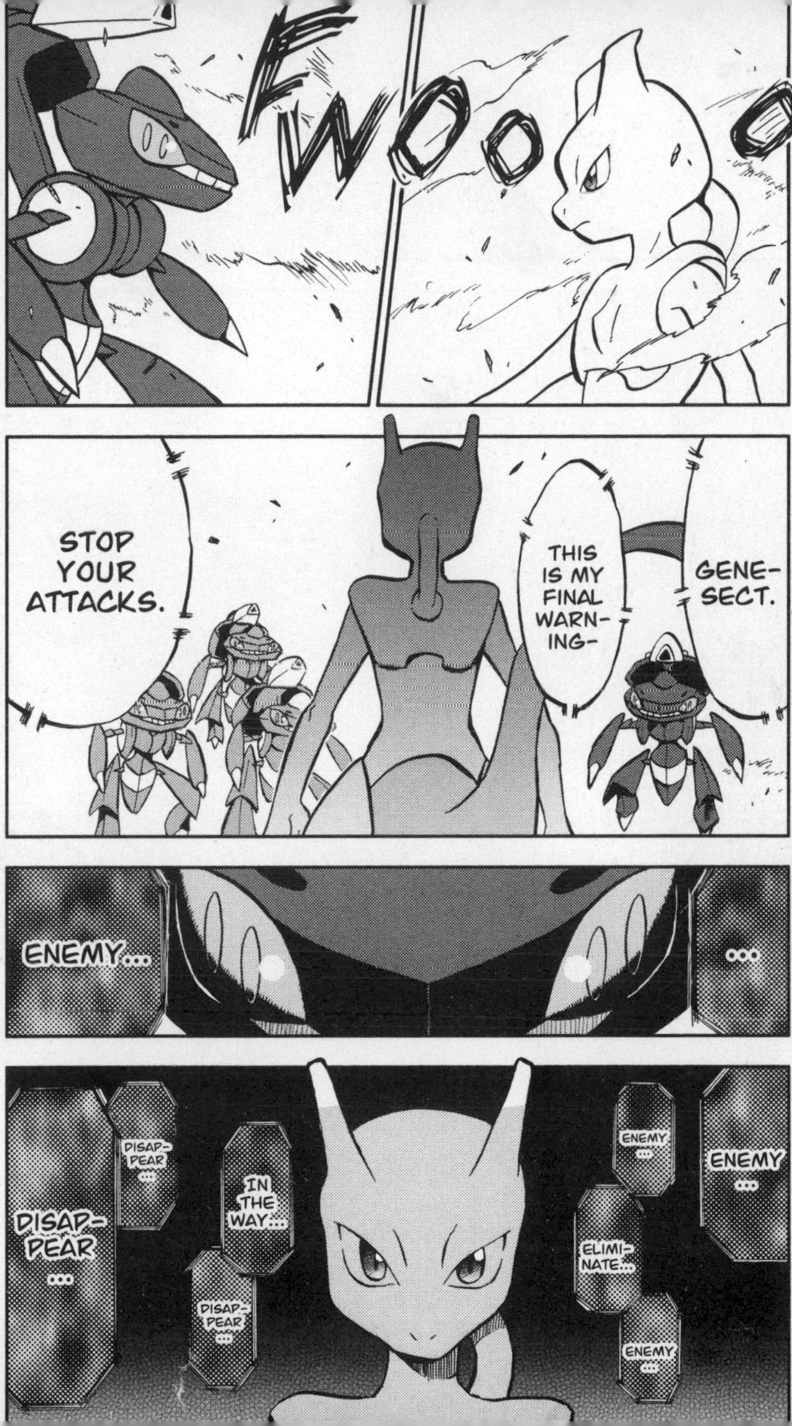
FWOOO...
GENE-SECT.
THIS IS MY FINAL WARN-ING-
STOP YOUR ATTACKS.
...
ENEMY...
ENEMY...
ENEMY...
ELIMI-NATE...
ENEMY...
IN THE WAY...
DISAP-PEAR...
DISAP-PEAR...
DISAP-PEAR...

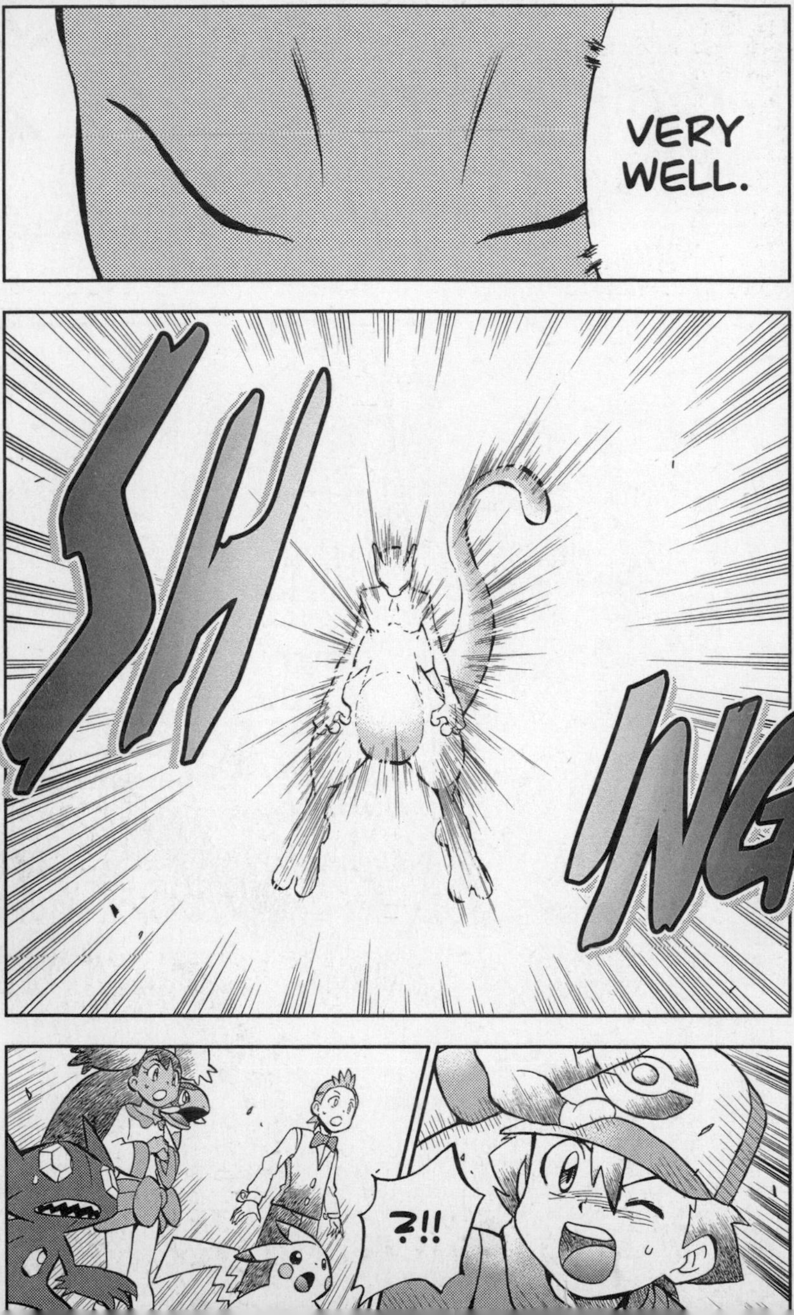
VERY WELL.
SHING
?!!

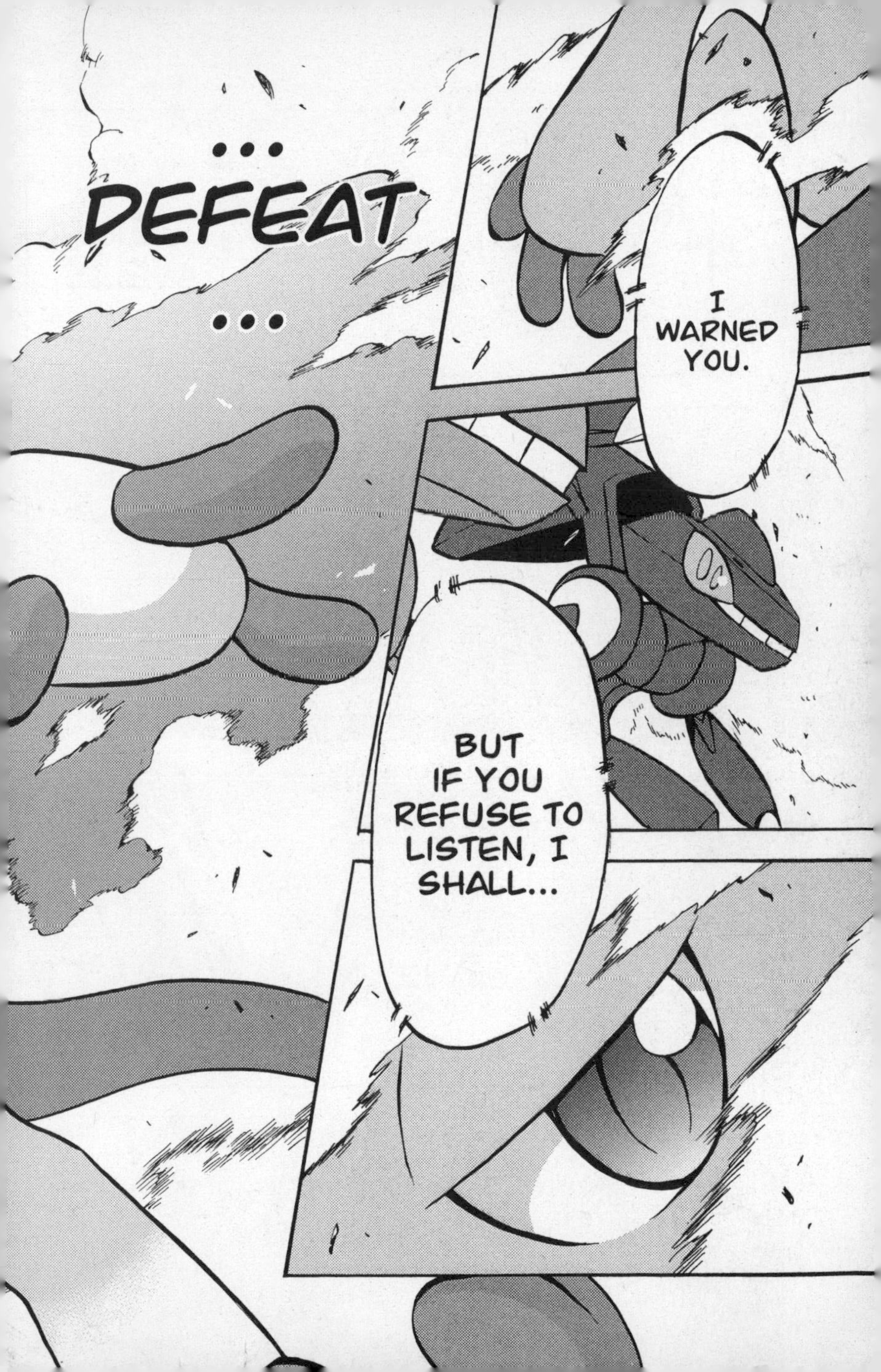
I WARNED YOU.
BUT IF YOU REFUSE TO LISTEN, I SHALL...
... DEFEAT ...

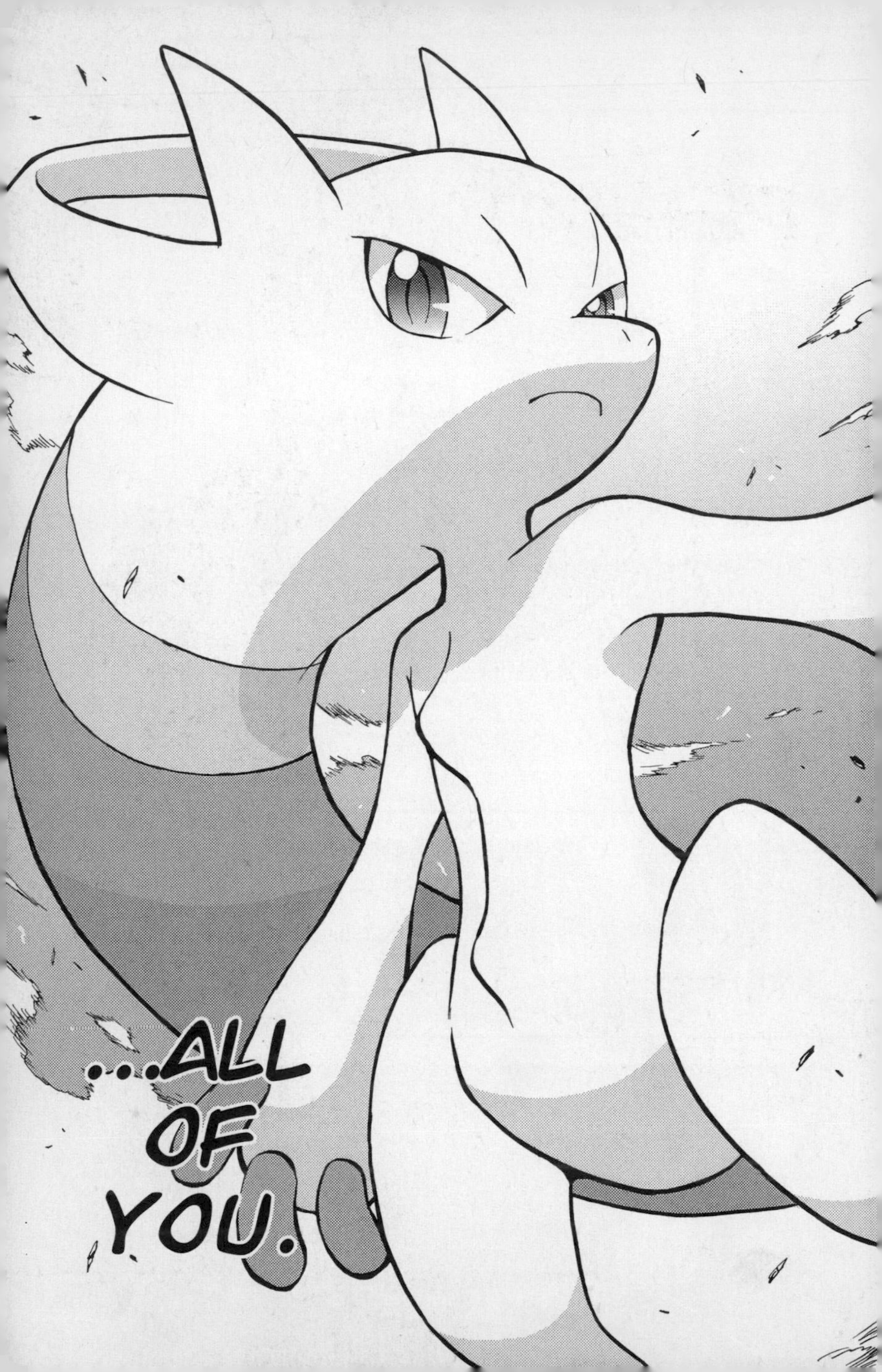
...ALL OF YOU.

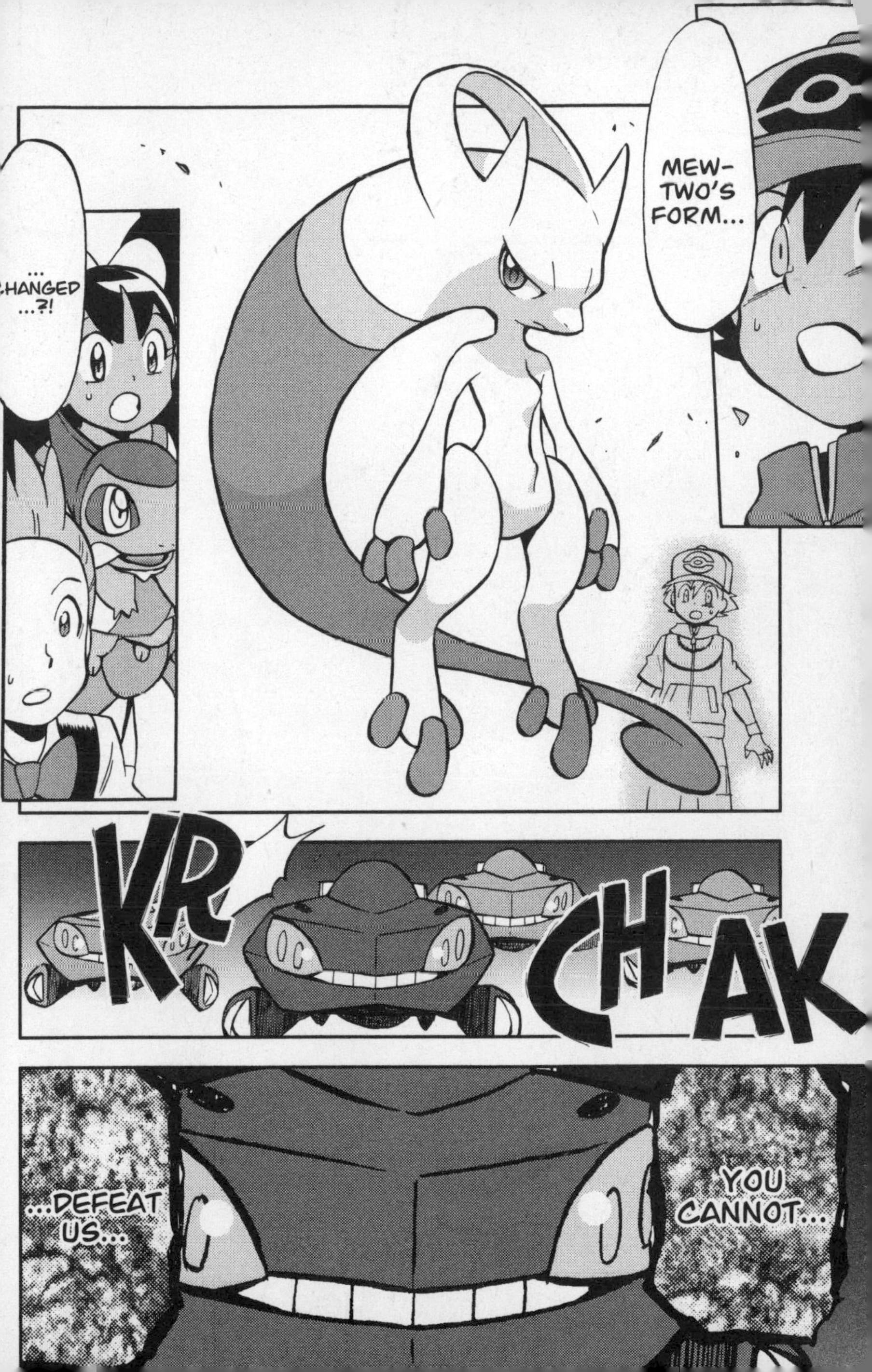
MEW-TWO'S FORM...
...CHANGED ...?!
KRCHAK
YOU CANNOT...
...DEFEAT US...

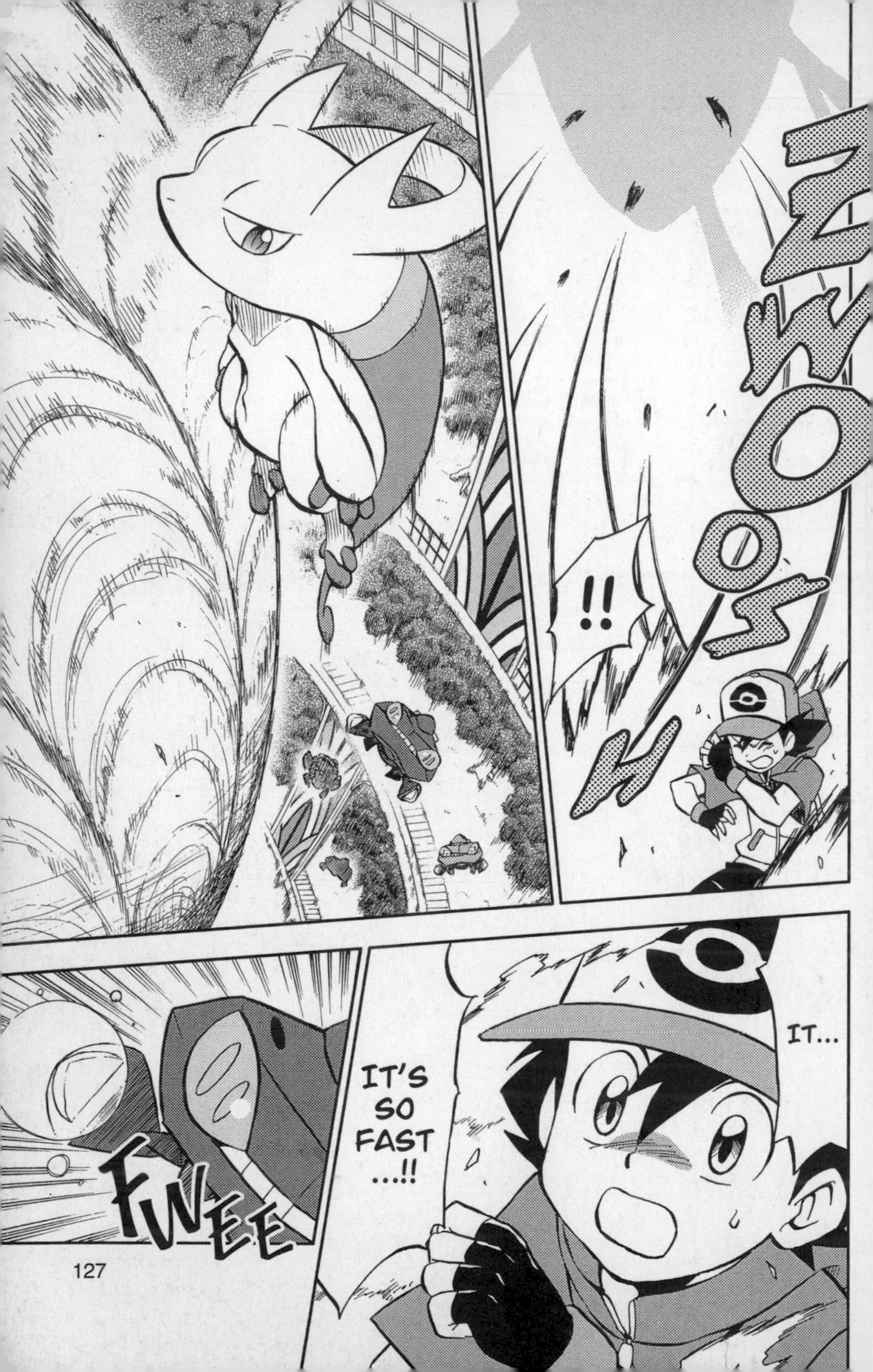
WHOOSH
!!
IT...
IT'S SO FAST ...!!
FWEE

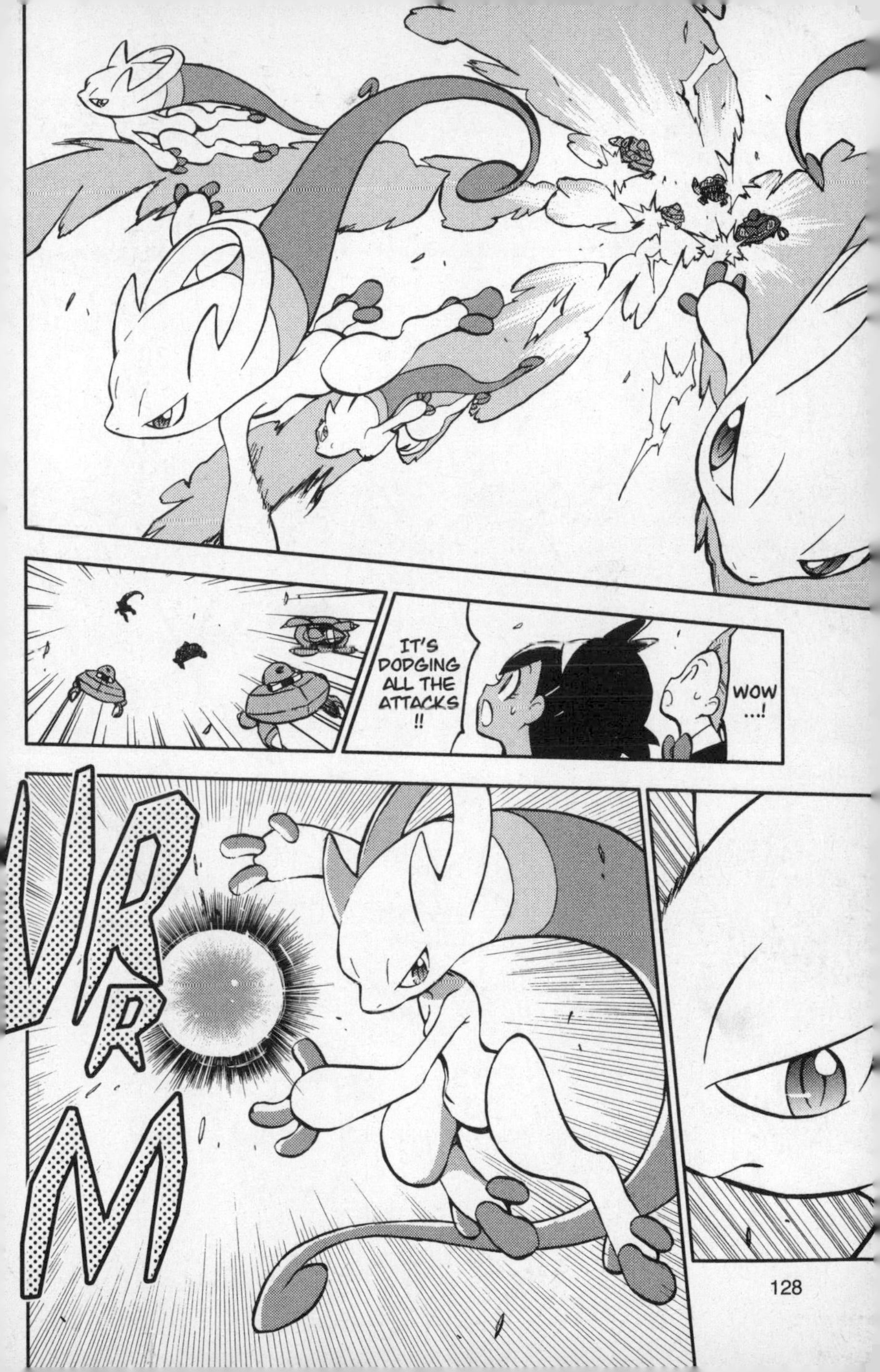
WOW ...!
IT'S DODGING ALL THE ATTACKS !!
VRRM

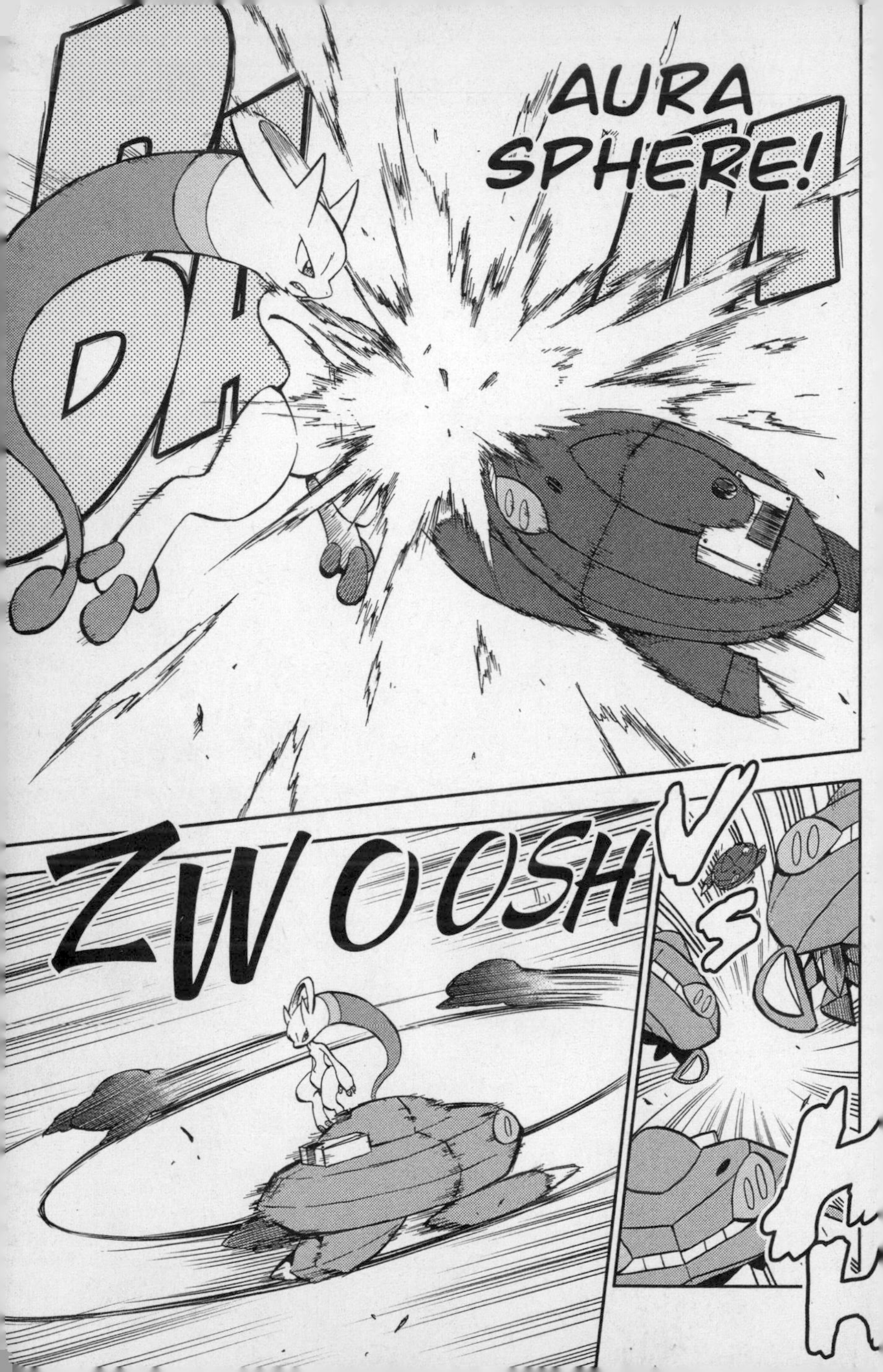
AURA SPHERE!
ZWOOSH

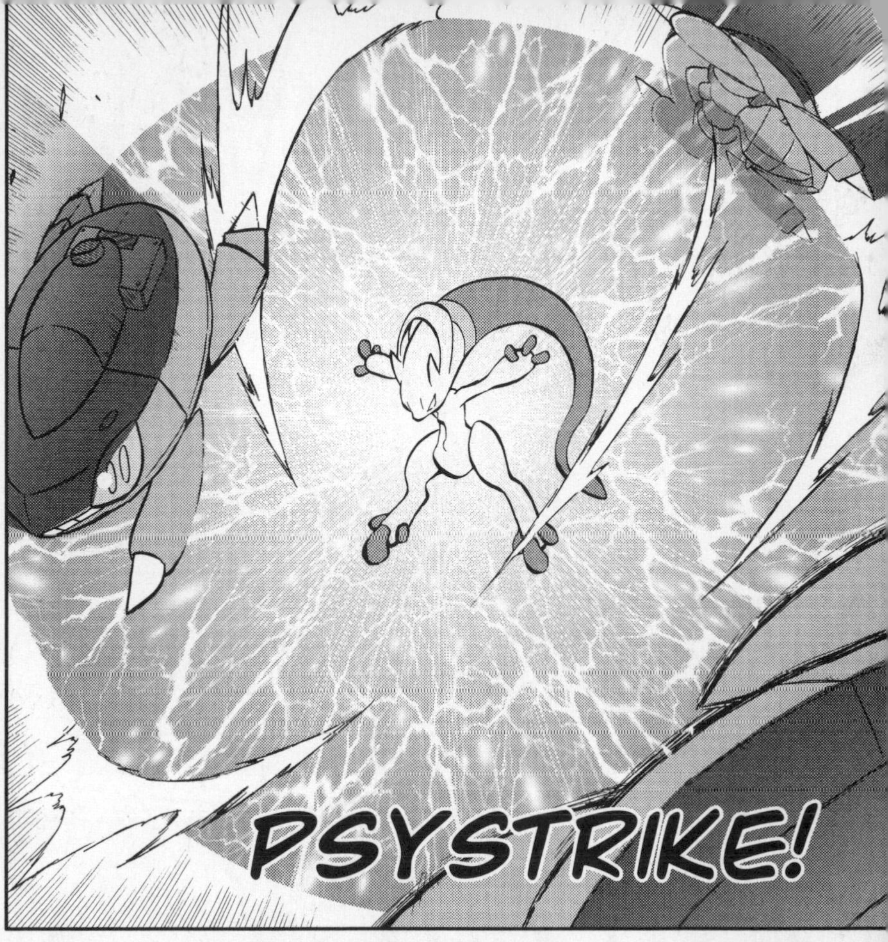
PSYSTRIKE!

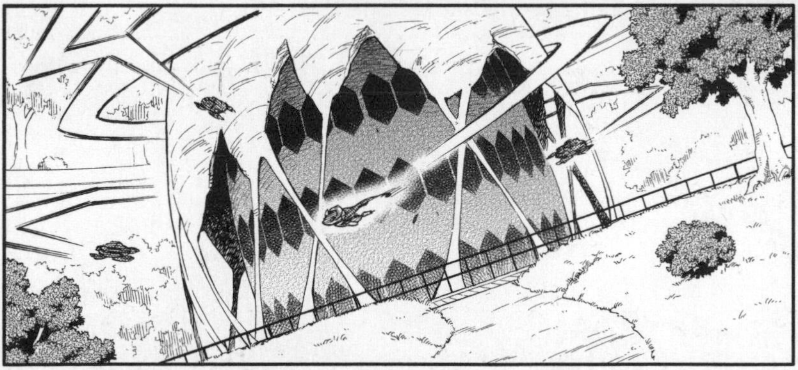

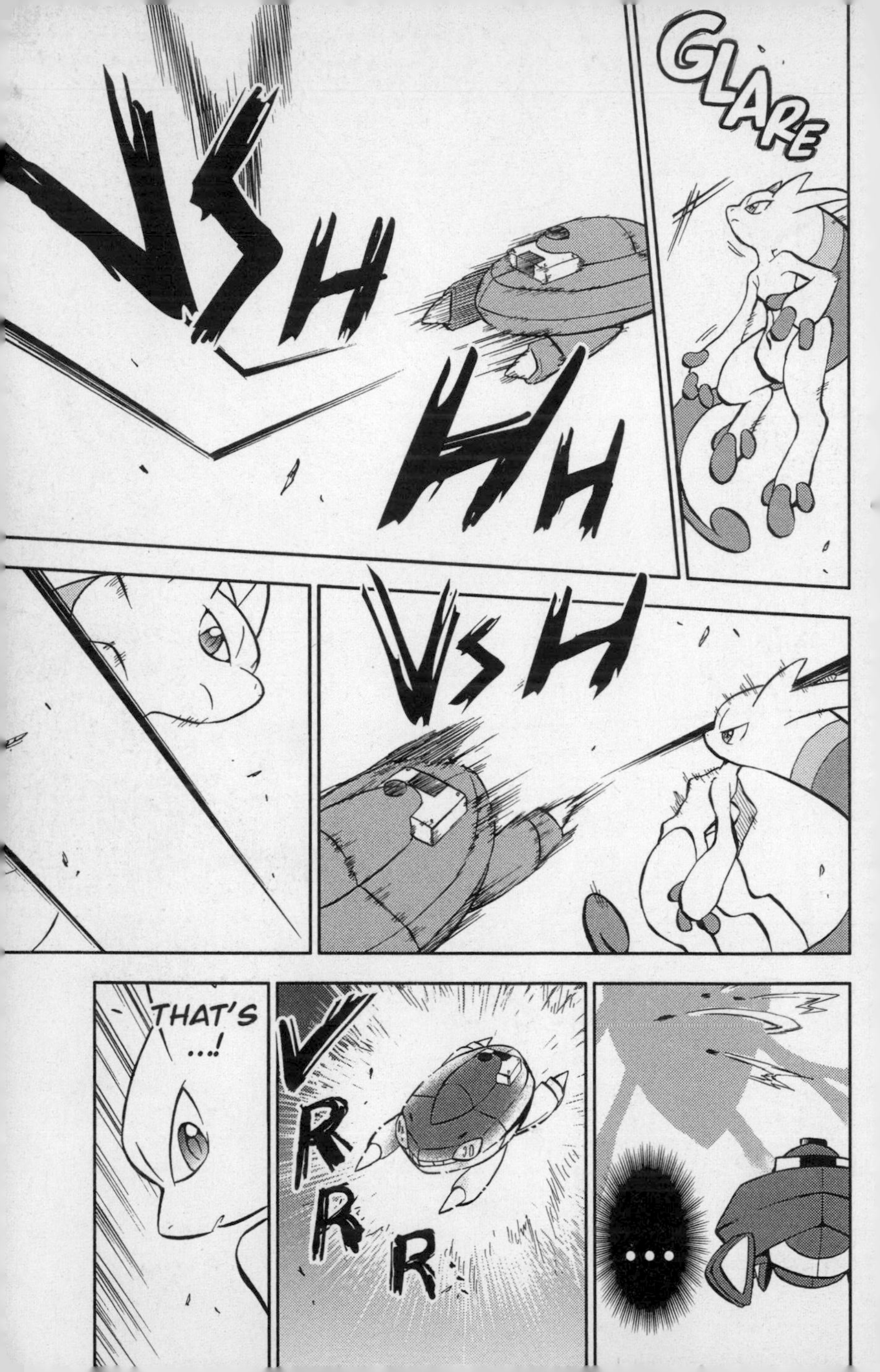
GLARE
VSHHHH
VSH
...
VRRRR
THAT'S ...!

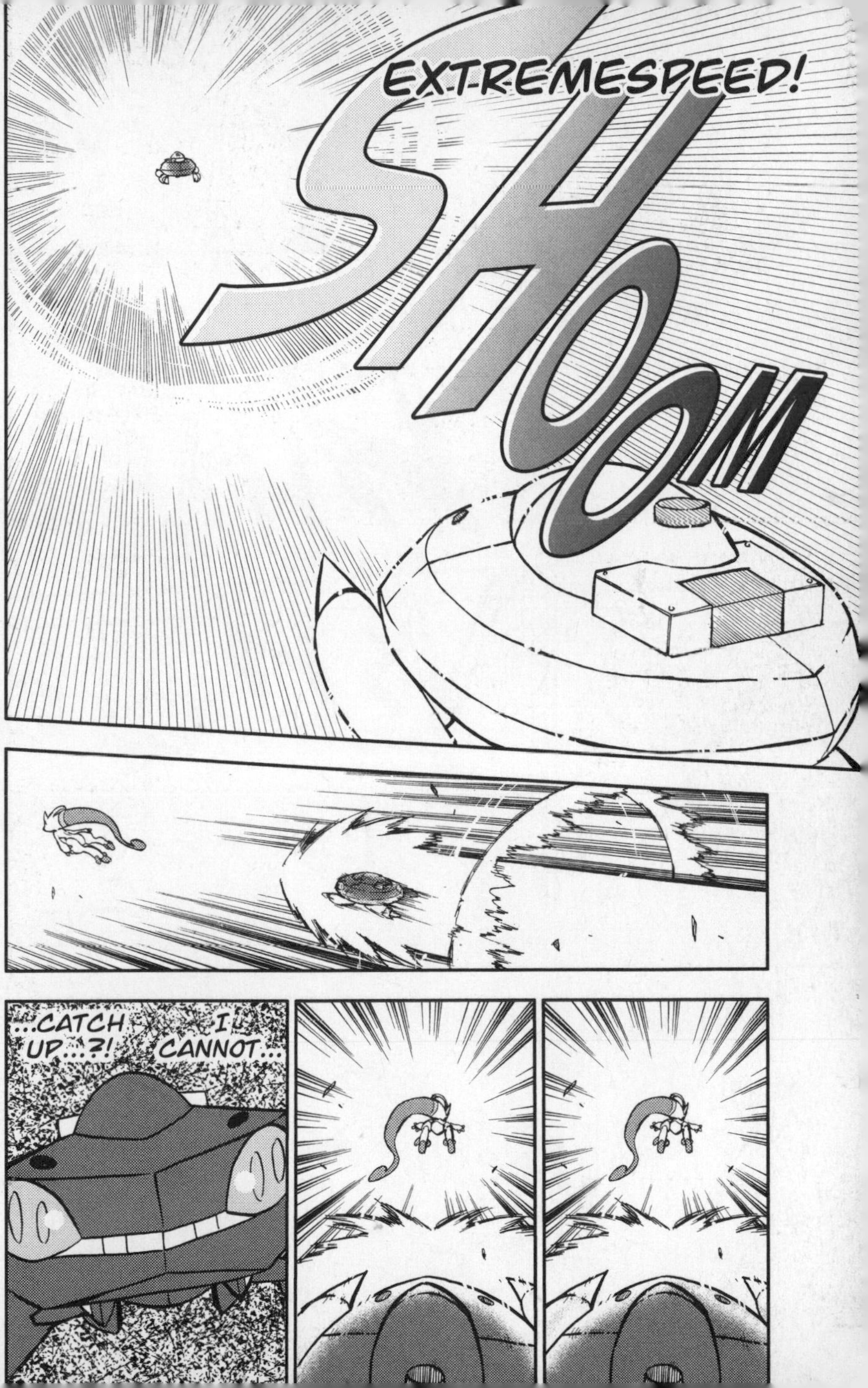
EXTREMESPEED!
SHOOM
I CANNOT...
...CATCH UP...?!

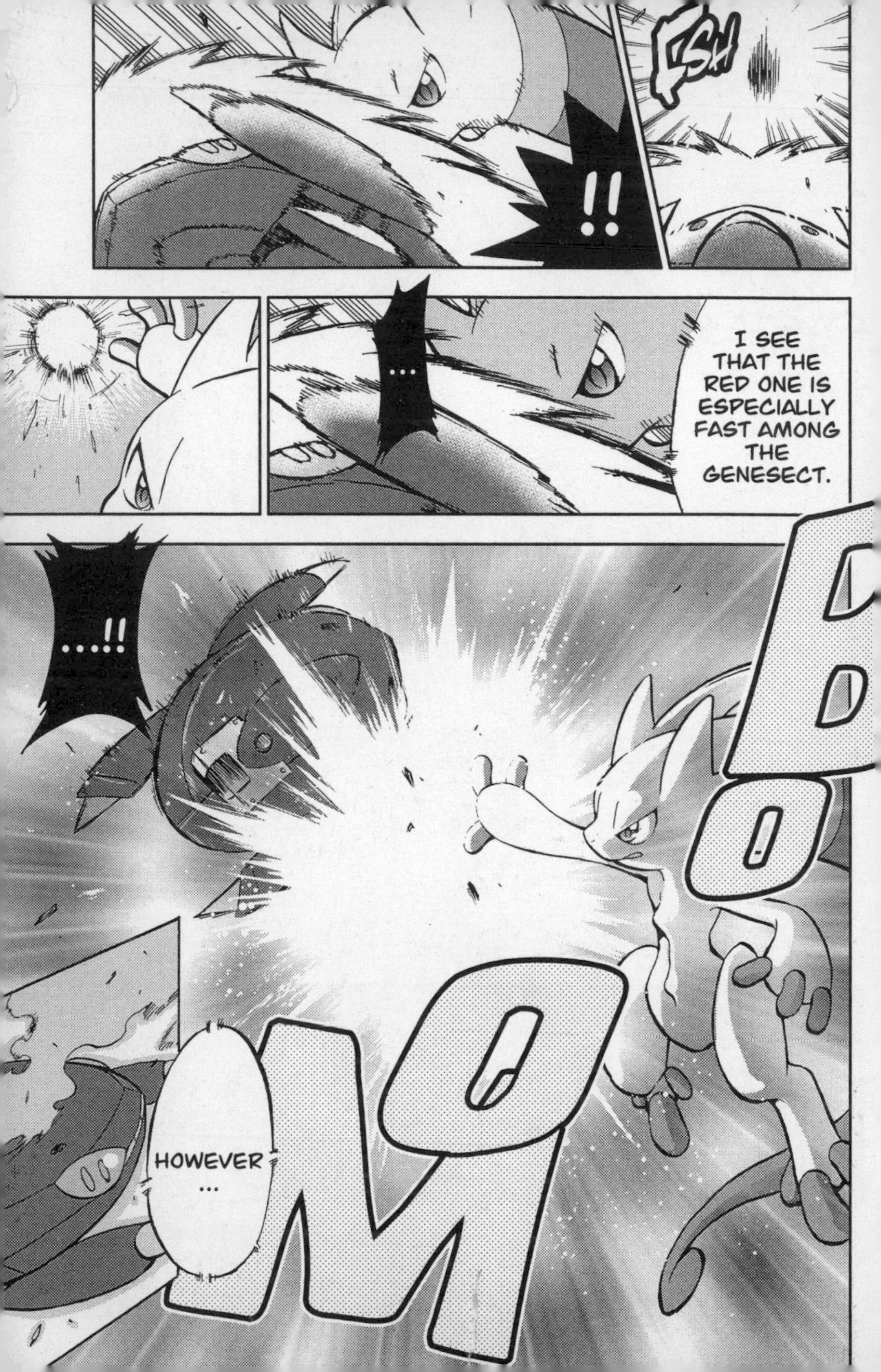
FSH
!!
I SEE THAT THE RED ONE IS ESPECIALLY FAST AMONG THE GENESECT.
...
....!!
HOWEVER ...

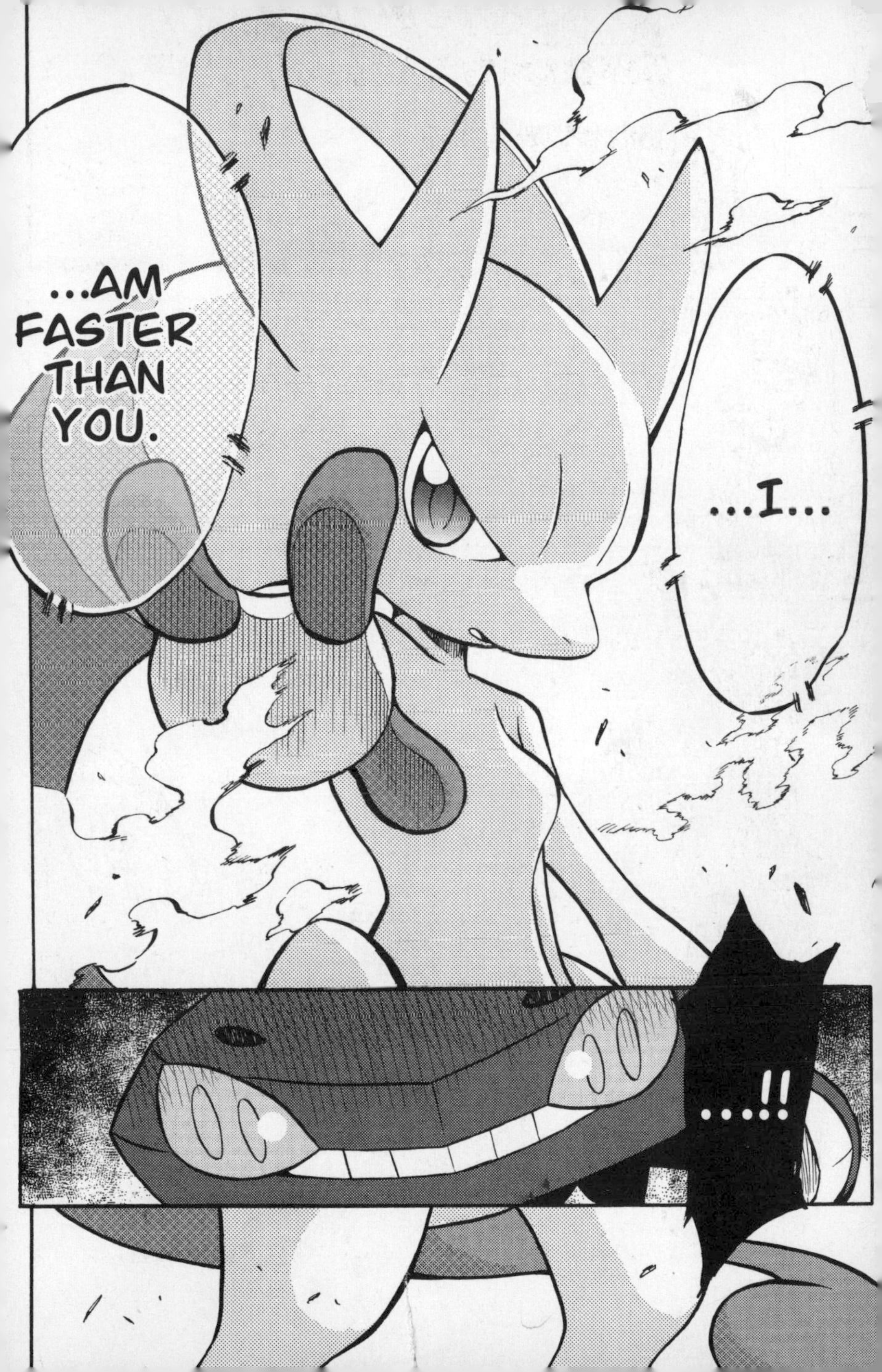
...I...
...AM FASTER THAN YOU.
....!!

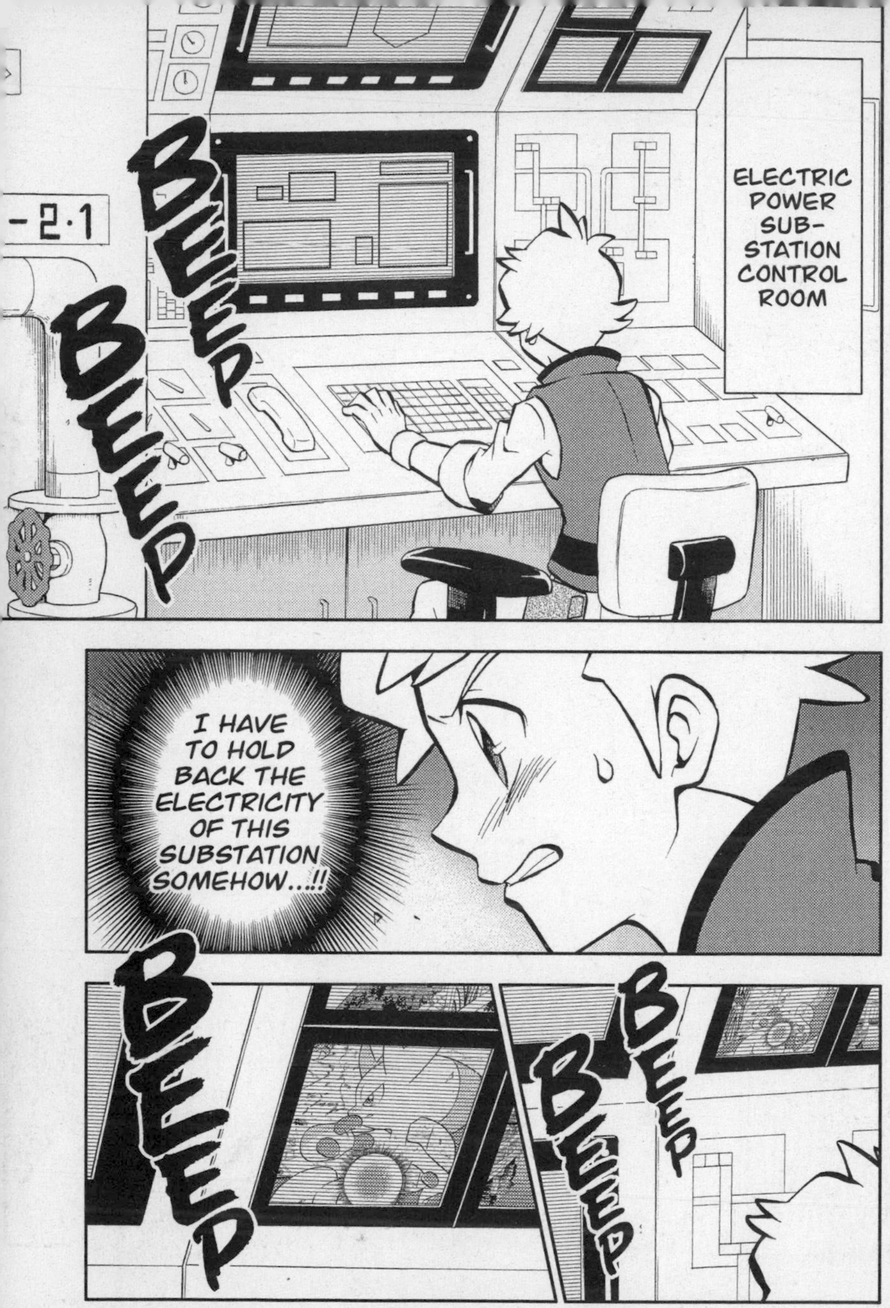
ELECTRIC POWER SUB-STATION CONTROL ROOM
-2·1
BEEP
BEEEP
I HAVE TO HOLD BACK THE ELECTRICITY OF THIS SUBSTATION SOMEHOW...!!
BEEP
BEEEP
BEEEP

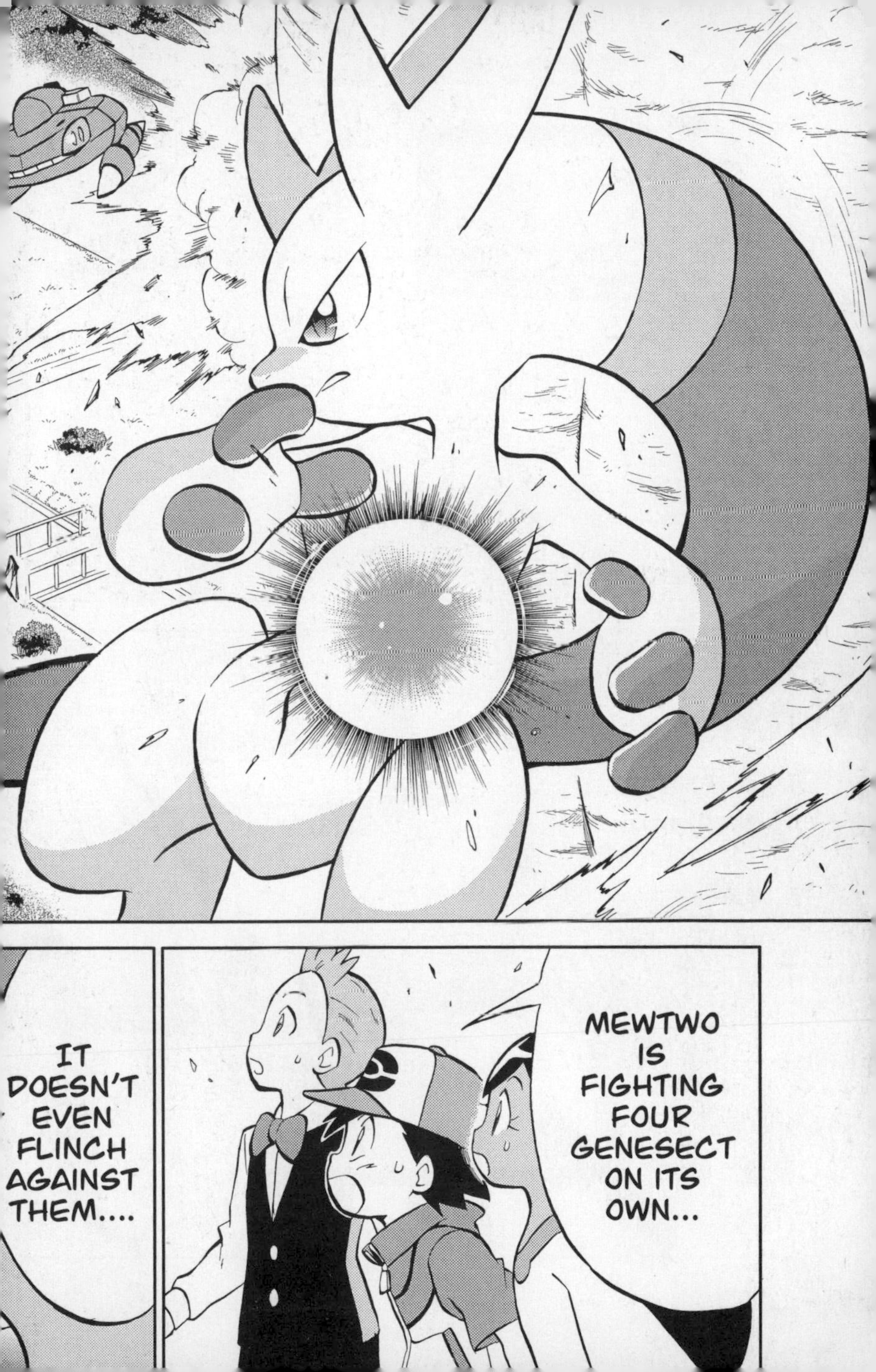
MEWTWO IS FIGHTING FOUR GENESECT ON ITS OWN...
IT DOESN'T EVEN FLINCH AGAINST THEM....

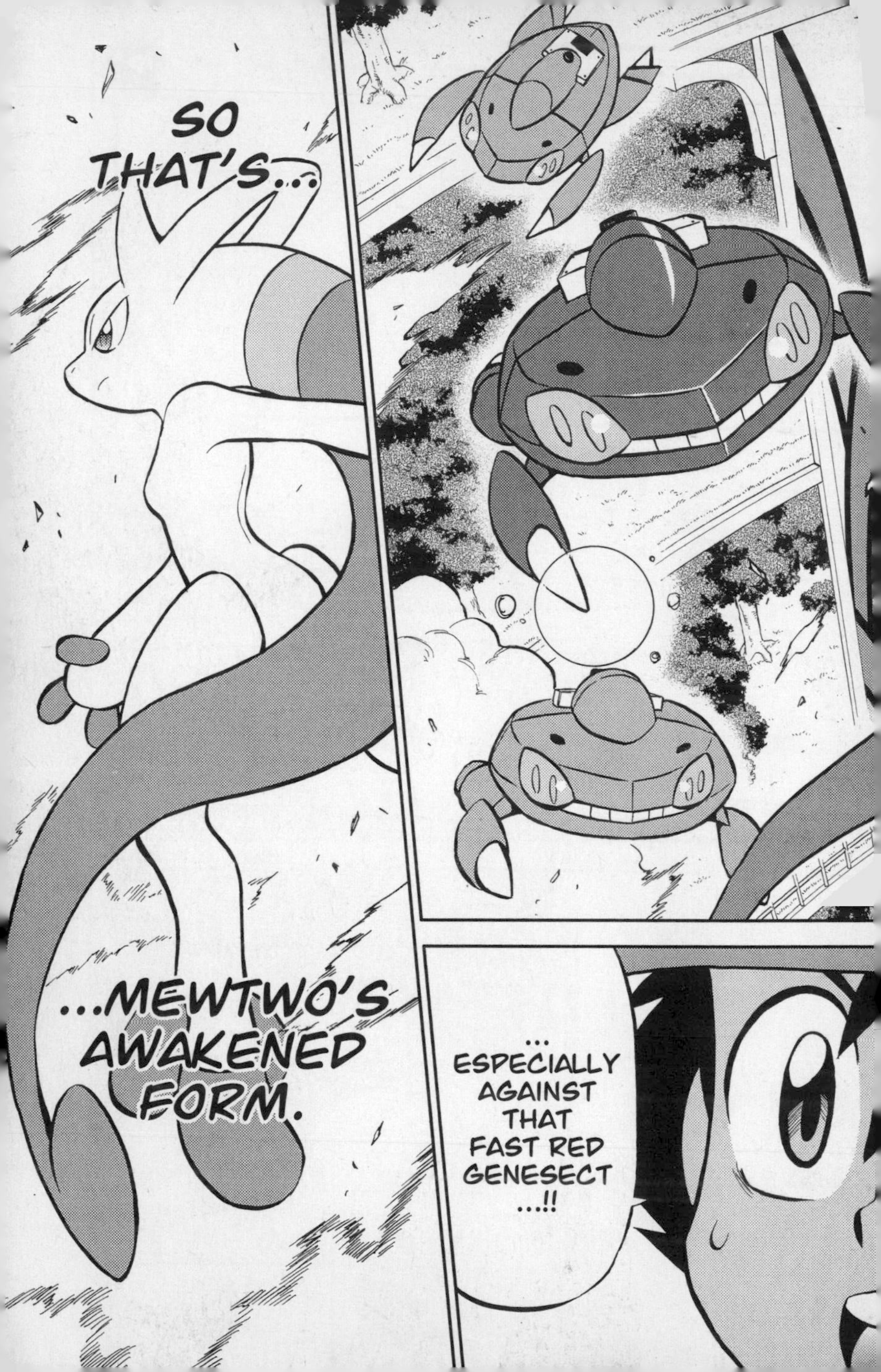
...ESPECIALLY AGAINST THAT FAST RED GENESECT ...!!
SO THAT'S...
...MEWTWO'S AWAKENED FORM.

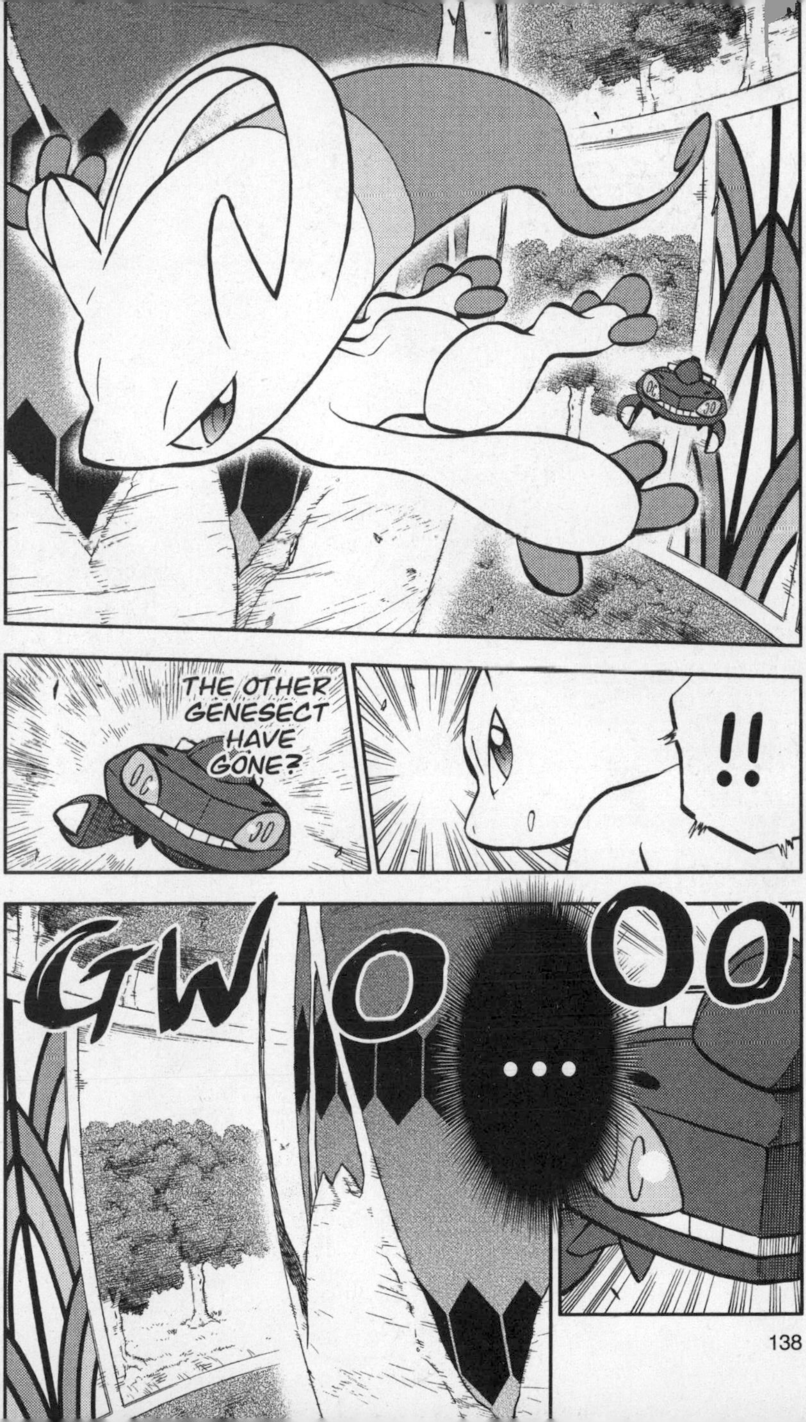
!!
THE OTHER GENESECT HAVE GONE?
GWOOO
...

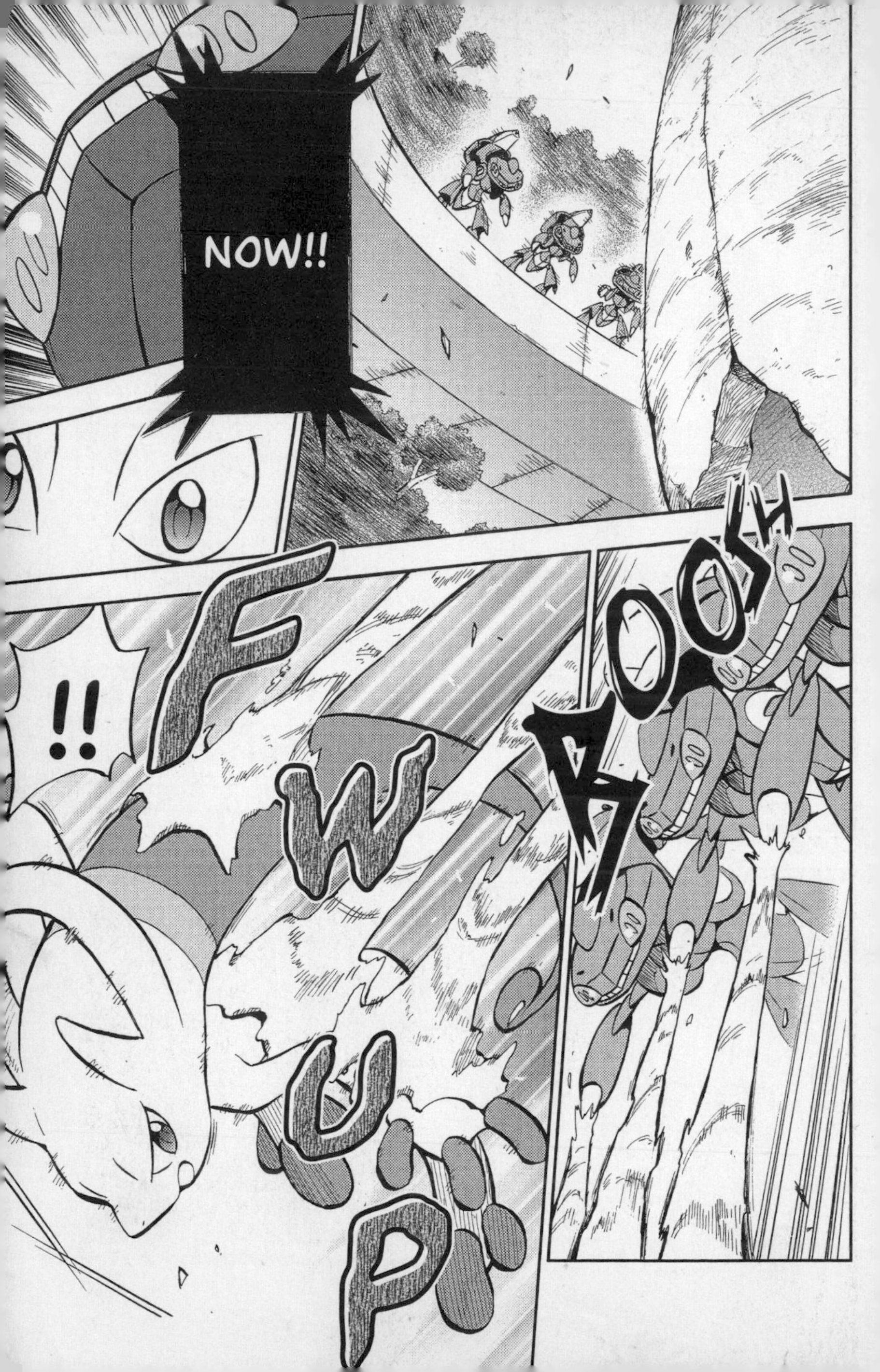
NOW!!
BOOSH
!!
FWUP

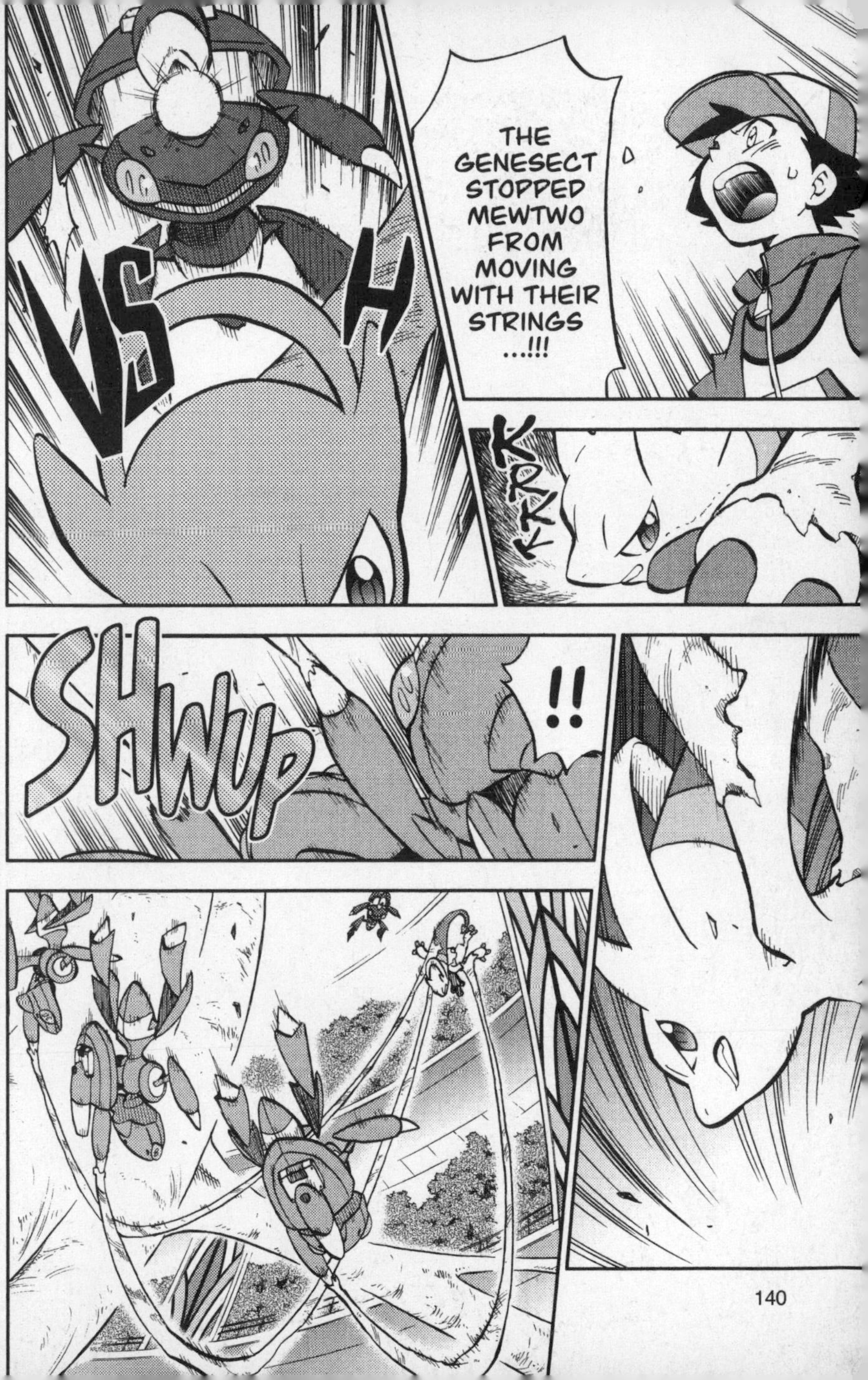
THE GENESECT STOPPED MEWTWO FROM MOVING WITH THEIR STRINGS ...!!!
KRKKK
VSSH
SHWUP
!!

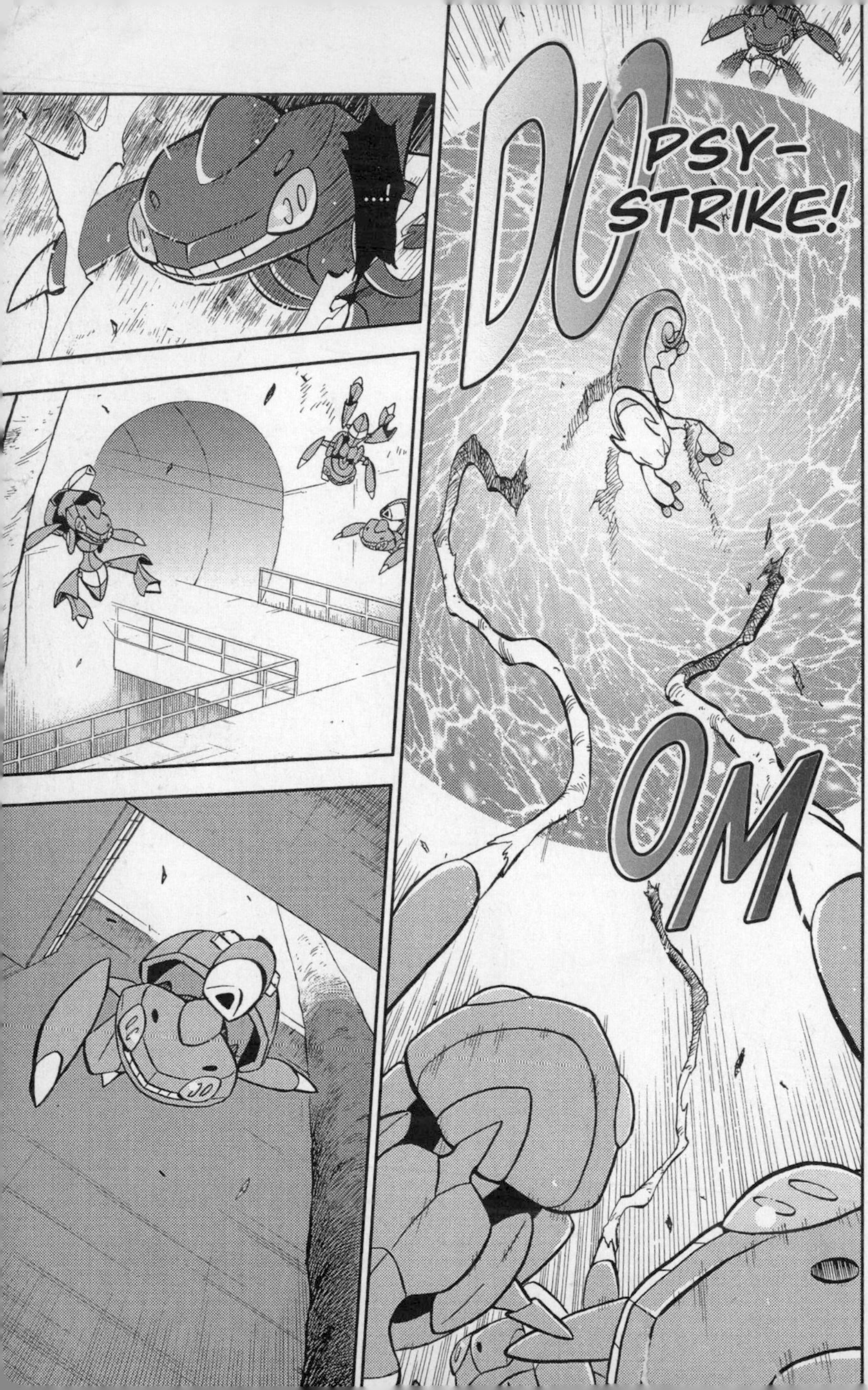
PSY-
STRIKE!
DO
OM
....!

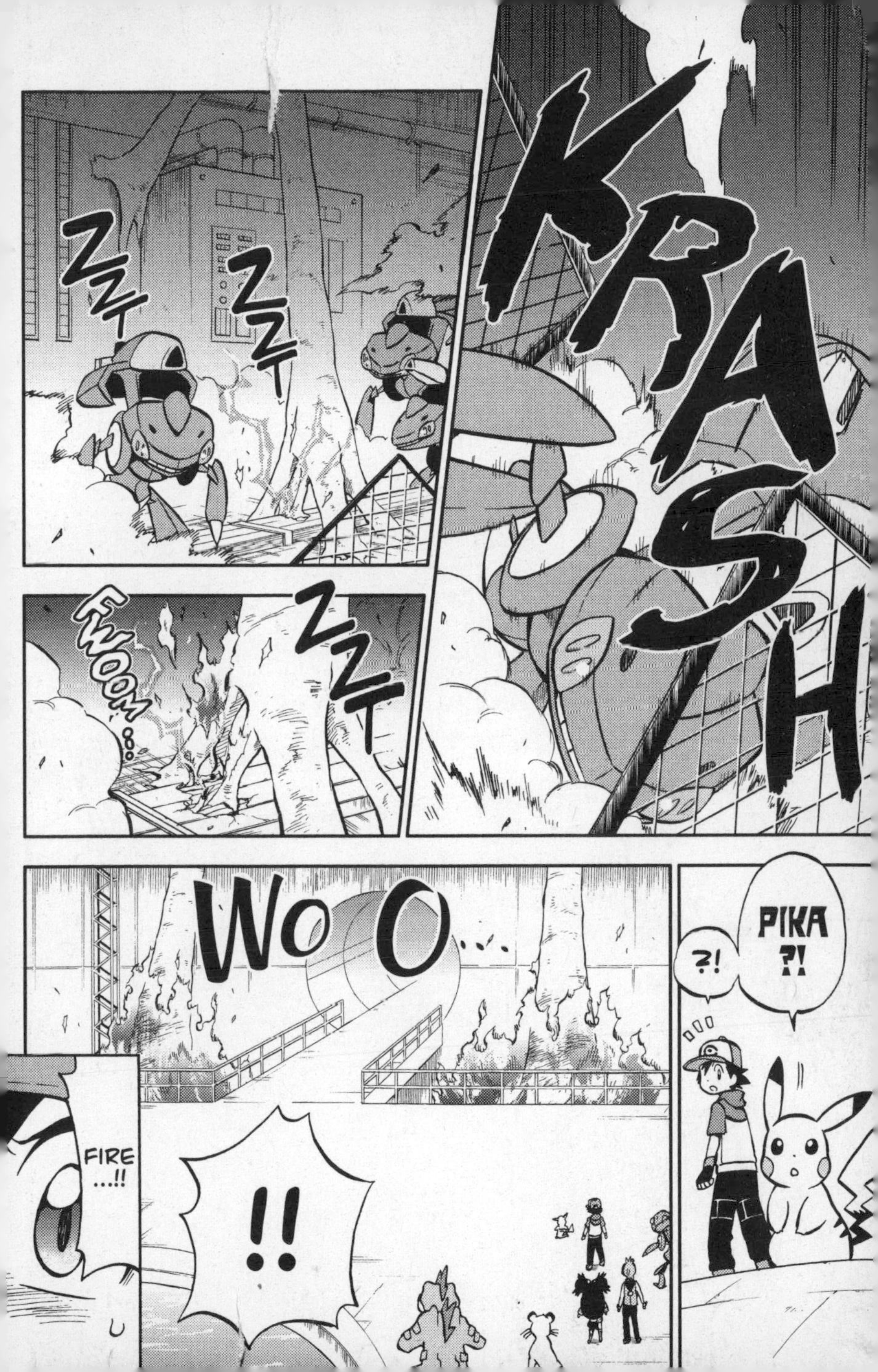
KRASH
ZZZT
ZZZT
ZZZT
FWOOM
PIKA ?!
?!
WOO...
FIRE ...!!
!!

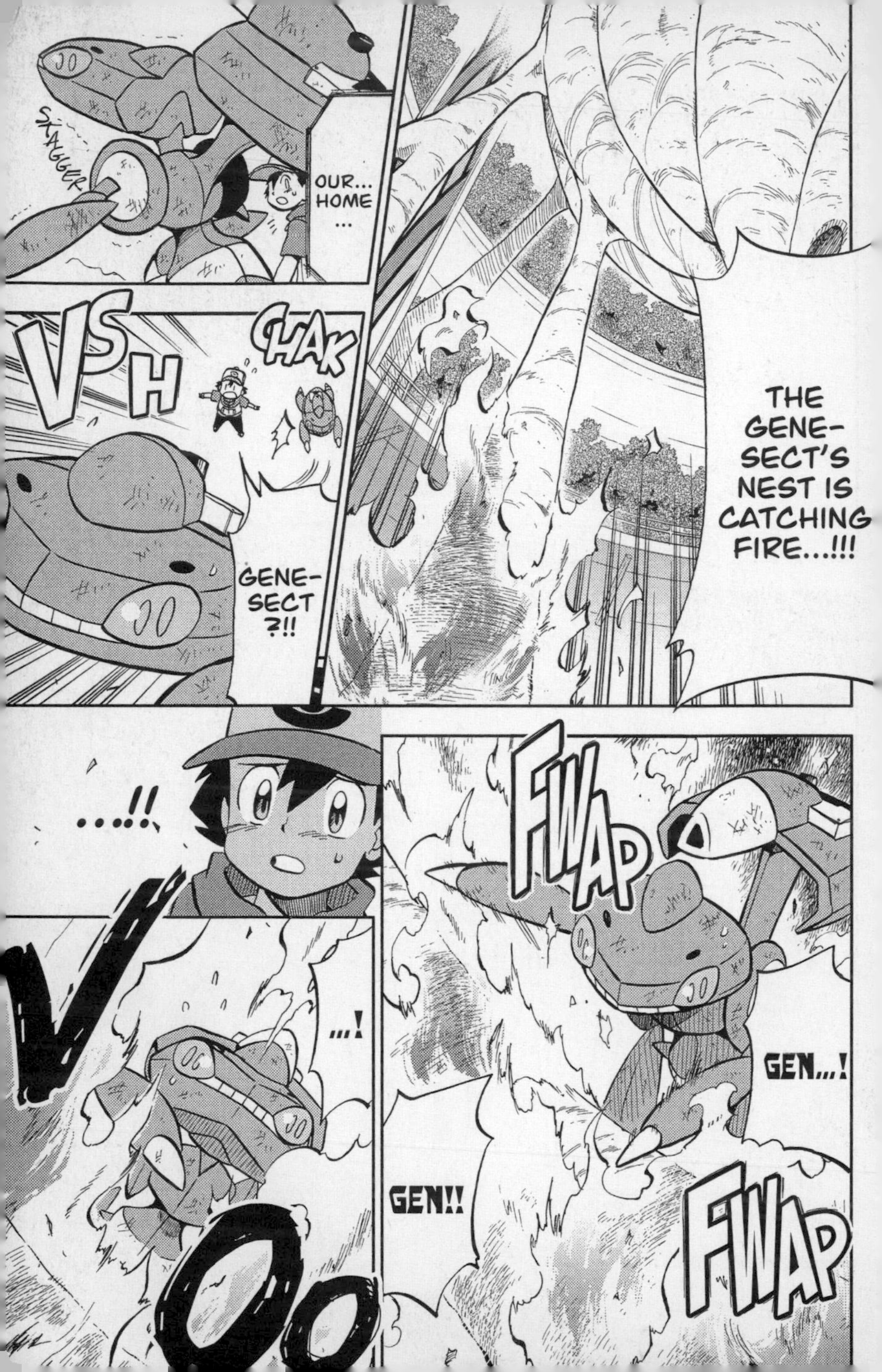
THE GENE-SECT'S NEST IS CATCHING FIRE...!!!
SKAGGER
OUR... HOME ...
VSH
CHAK
GENE-SECT ?!!
FWAP
GEN...!
GEN!!
FWAP
...!!
...!

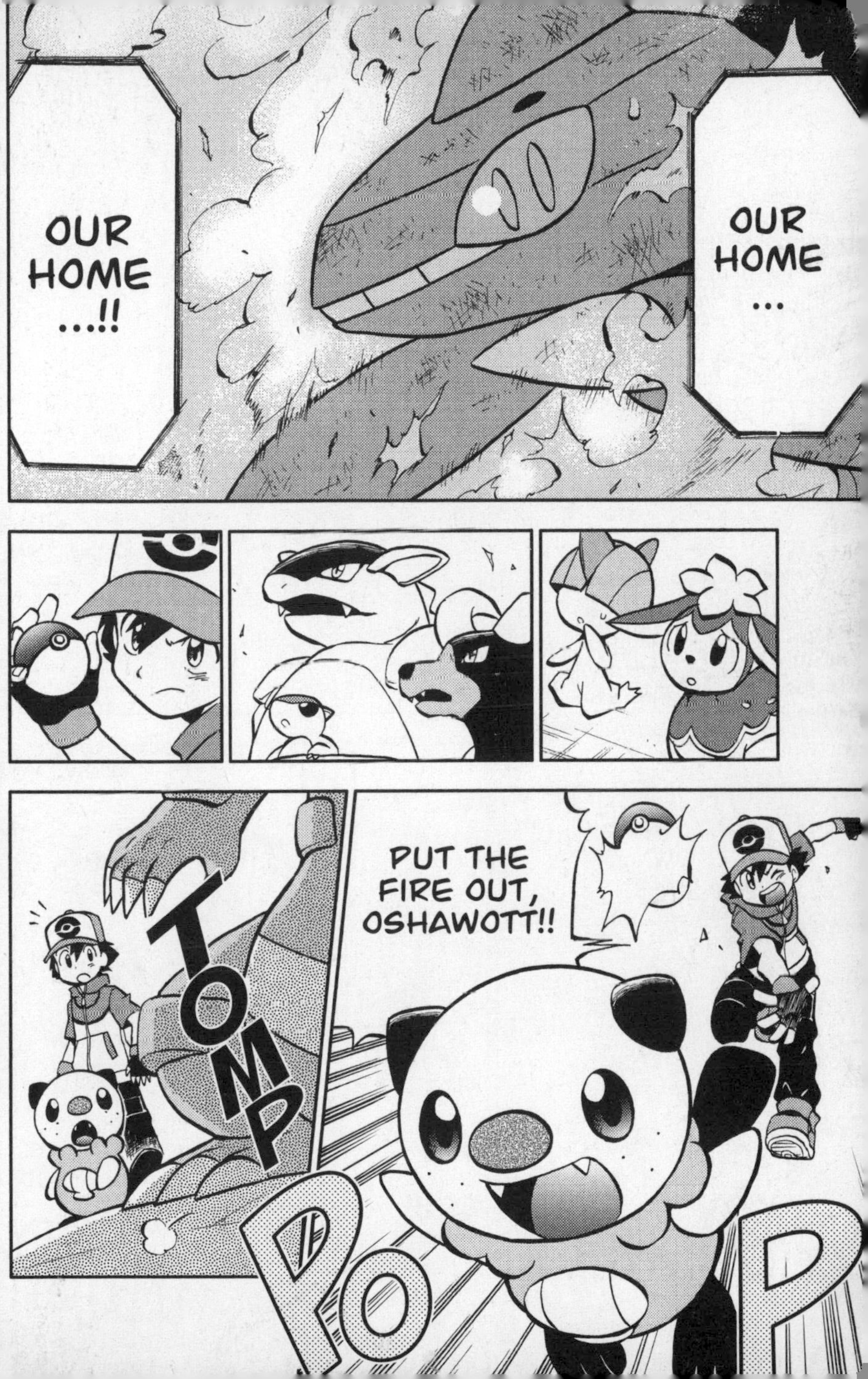
OUR HOME ...
OUR HOME ...!!
PUT THE FIRE OUT, OSHAWOTT!!
POP
TOMP

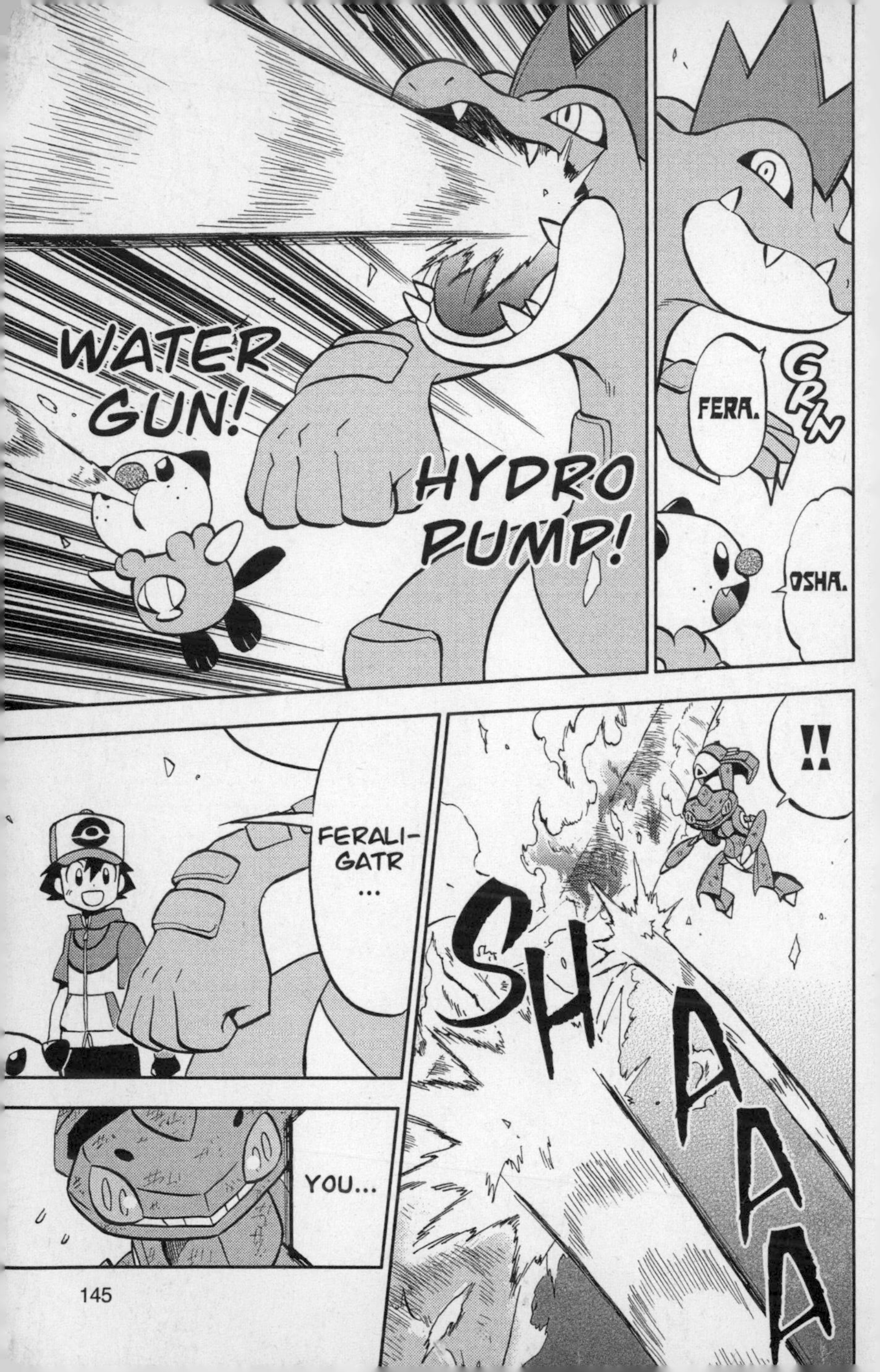
FERA.
GRW
OSHA.
WATER GUN!
HYDRO PUMP!
!!
SHAAAA
FERALI-GATR ...
YOU...

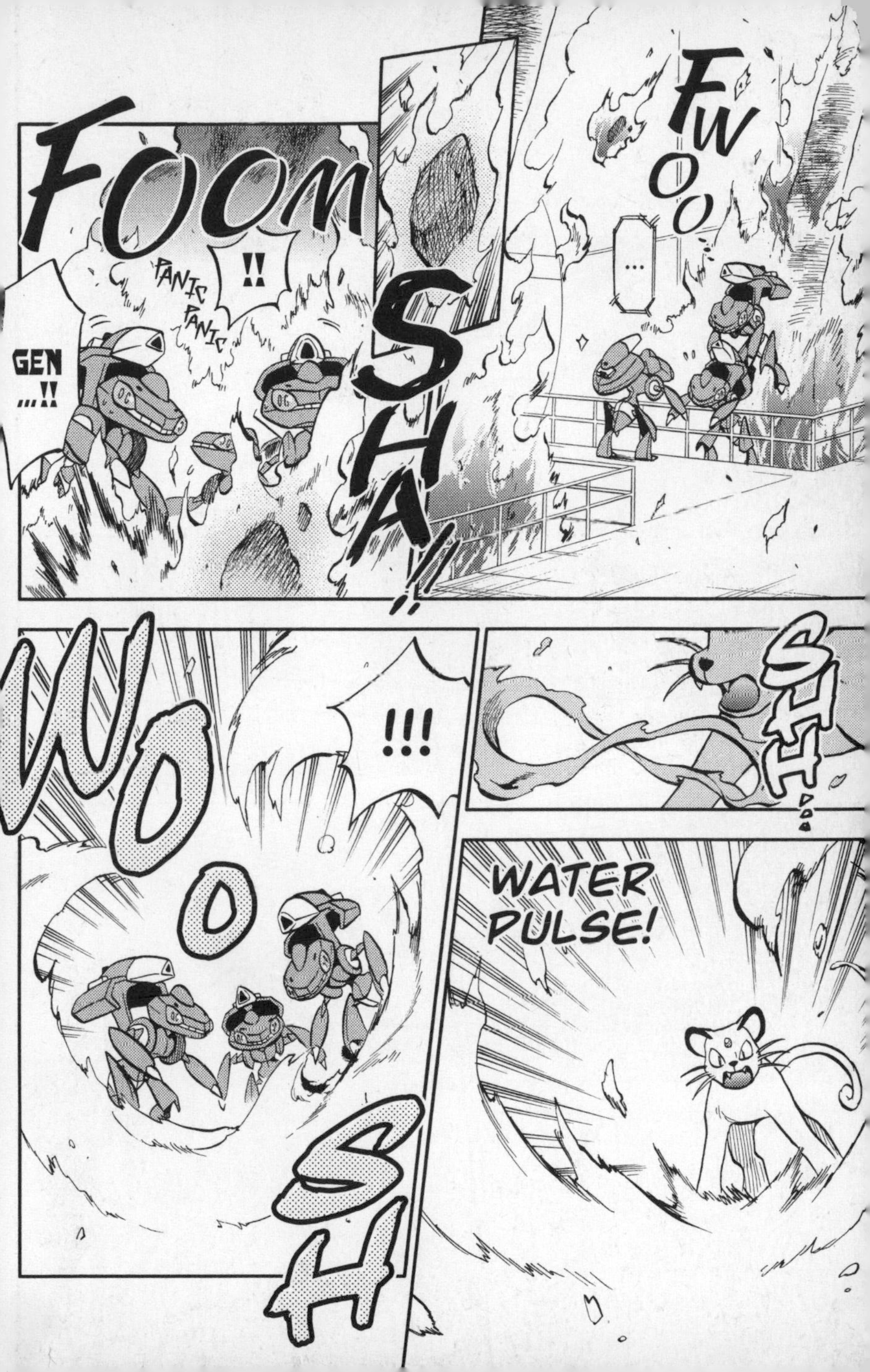
FWOOO
...
SHA!!
FOOM
!!
PANIC PANIC
GEN ...!!
SHH
WATER PULSE!
WOOOSH
!!!

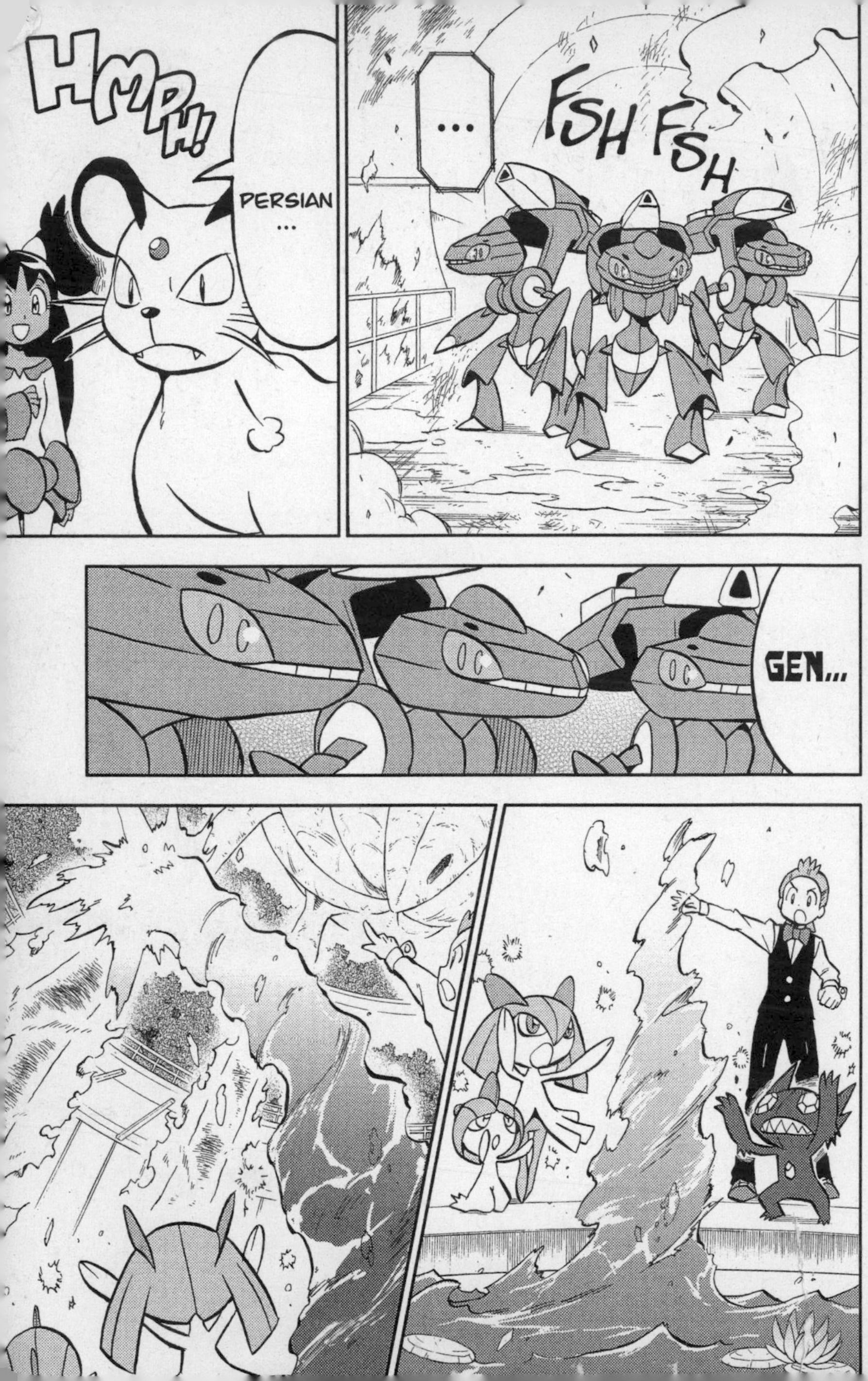
...
FSH FSH
HMPH!
PERSIAN ...
GEN...

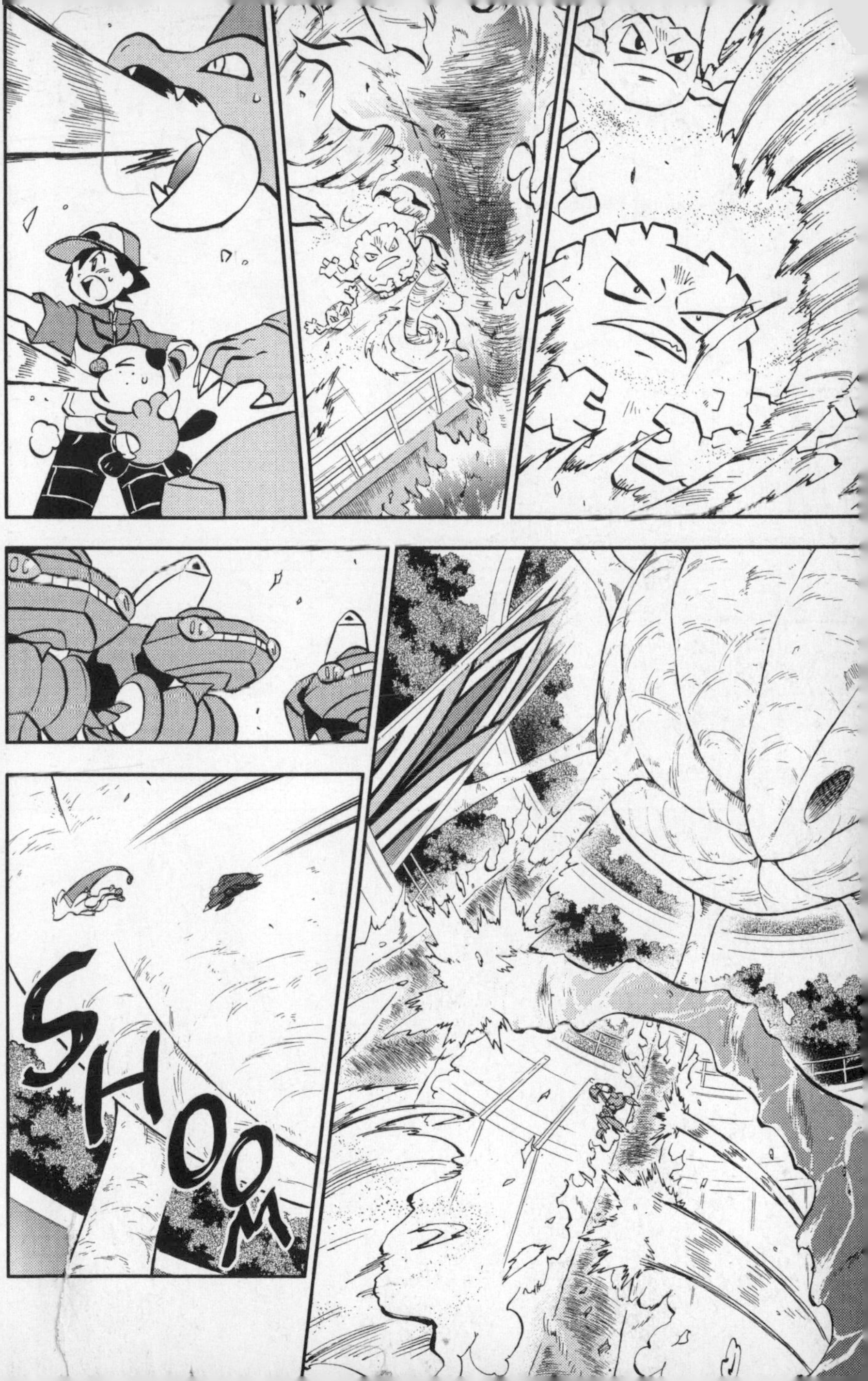
SHOOM

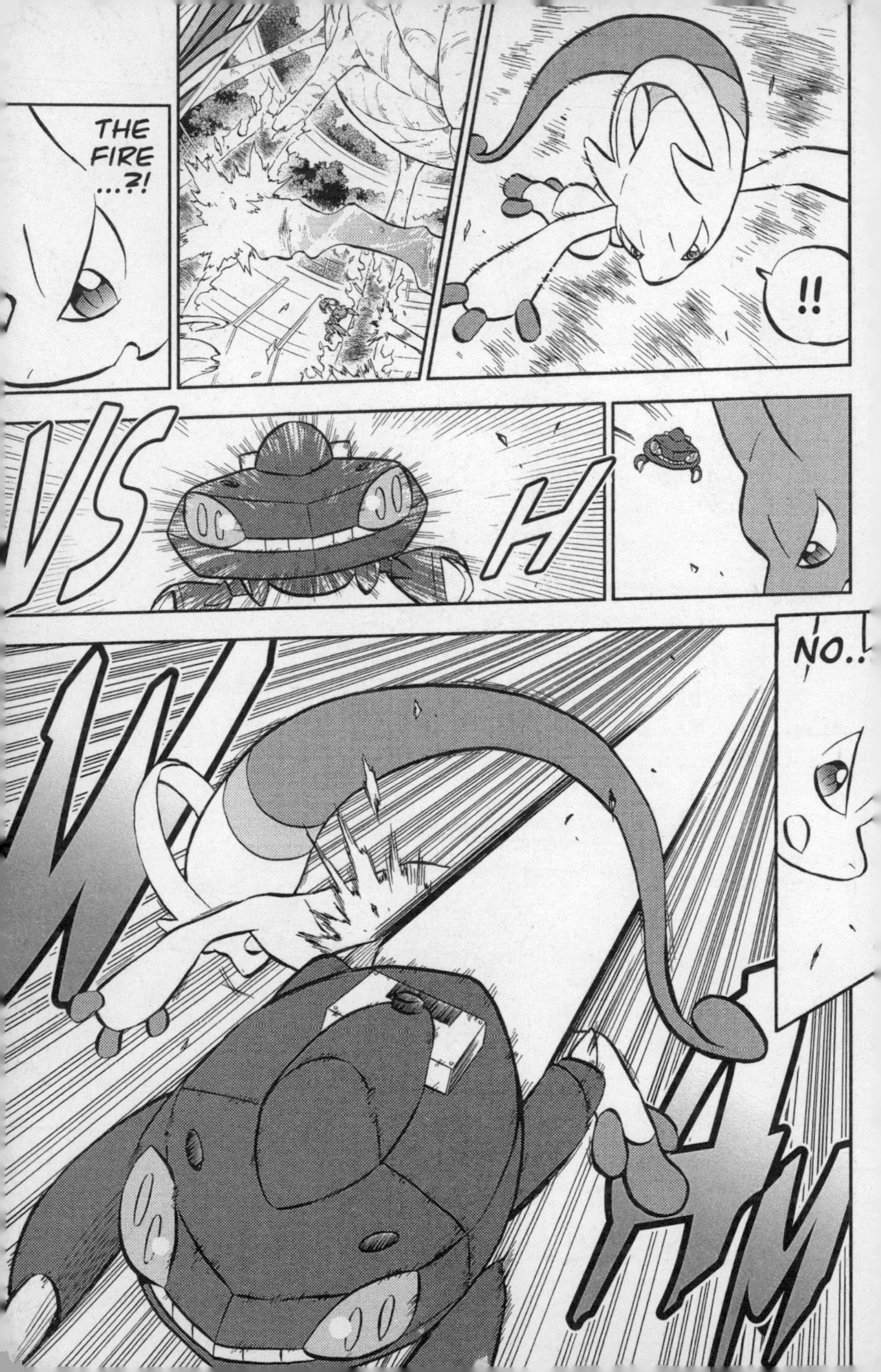
!!
THE FIRE ...?!
NO..!

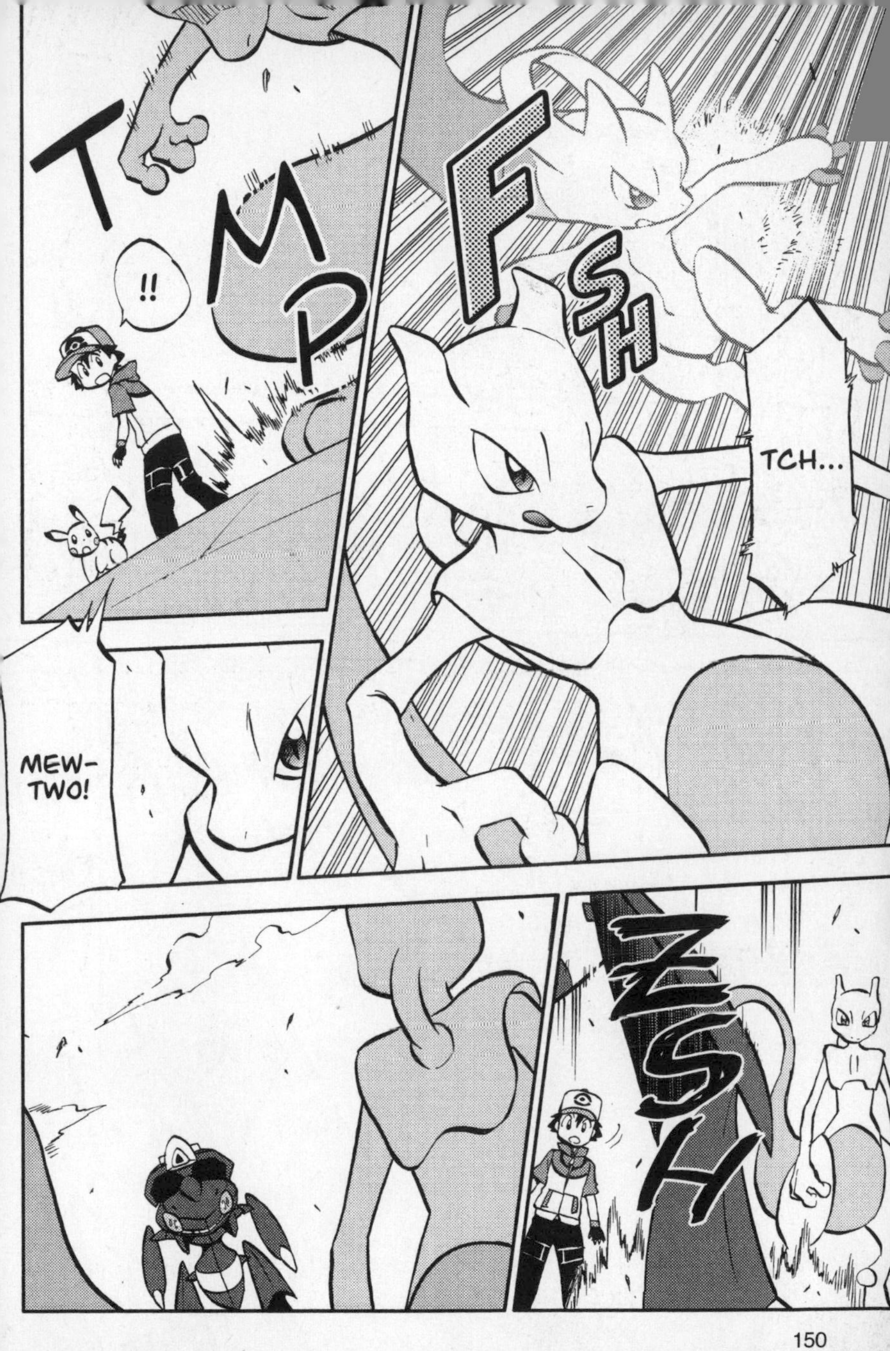
FSH
TCH...
TMP
!!
MEW-TWO!
ZZSH

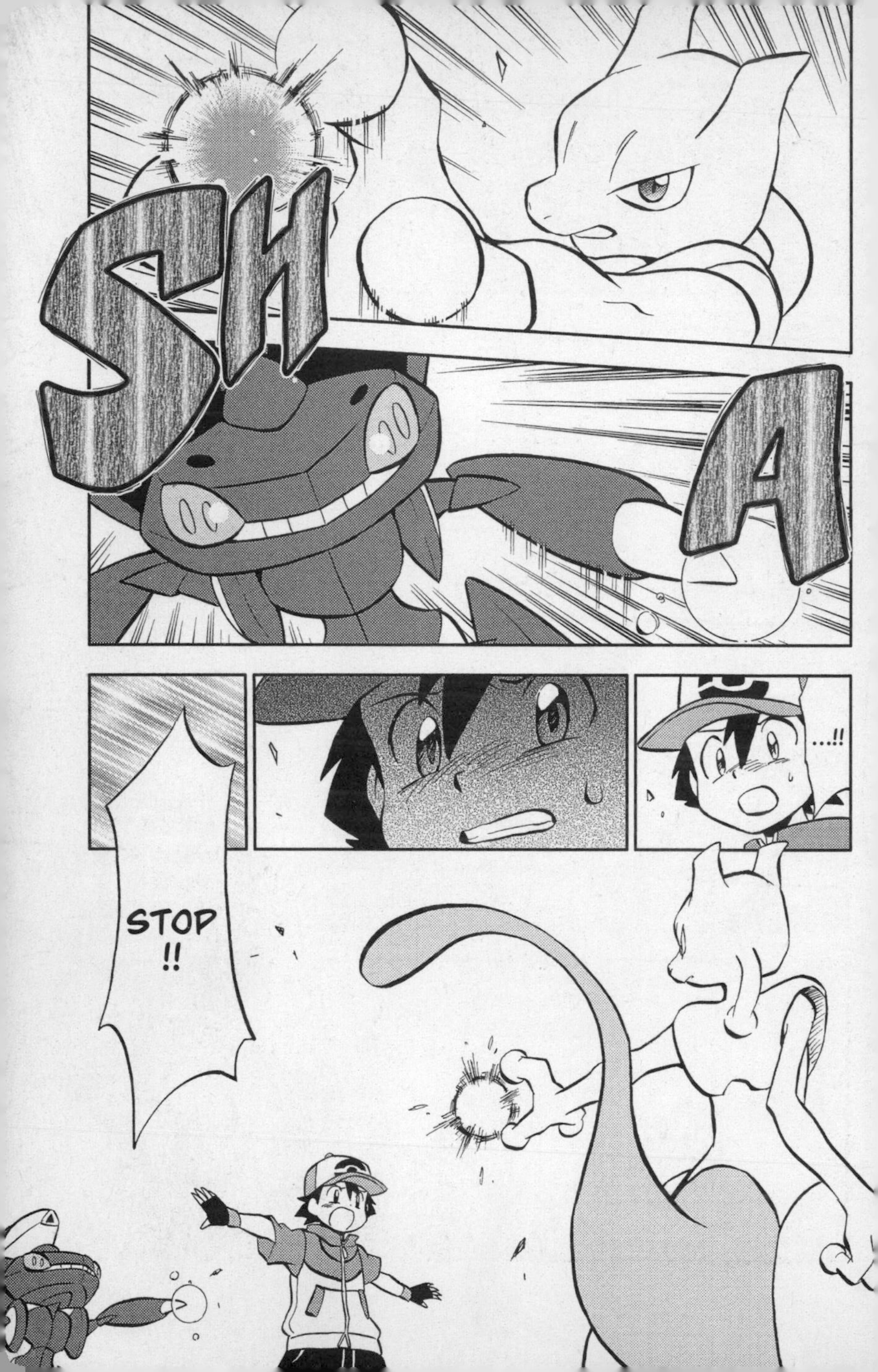
SHA
...!!
STOP !!

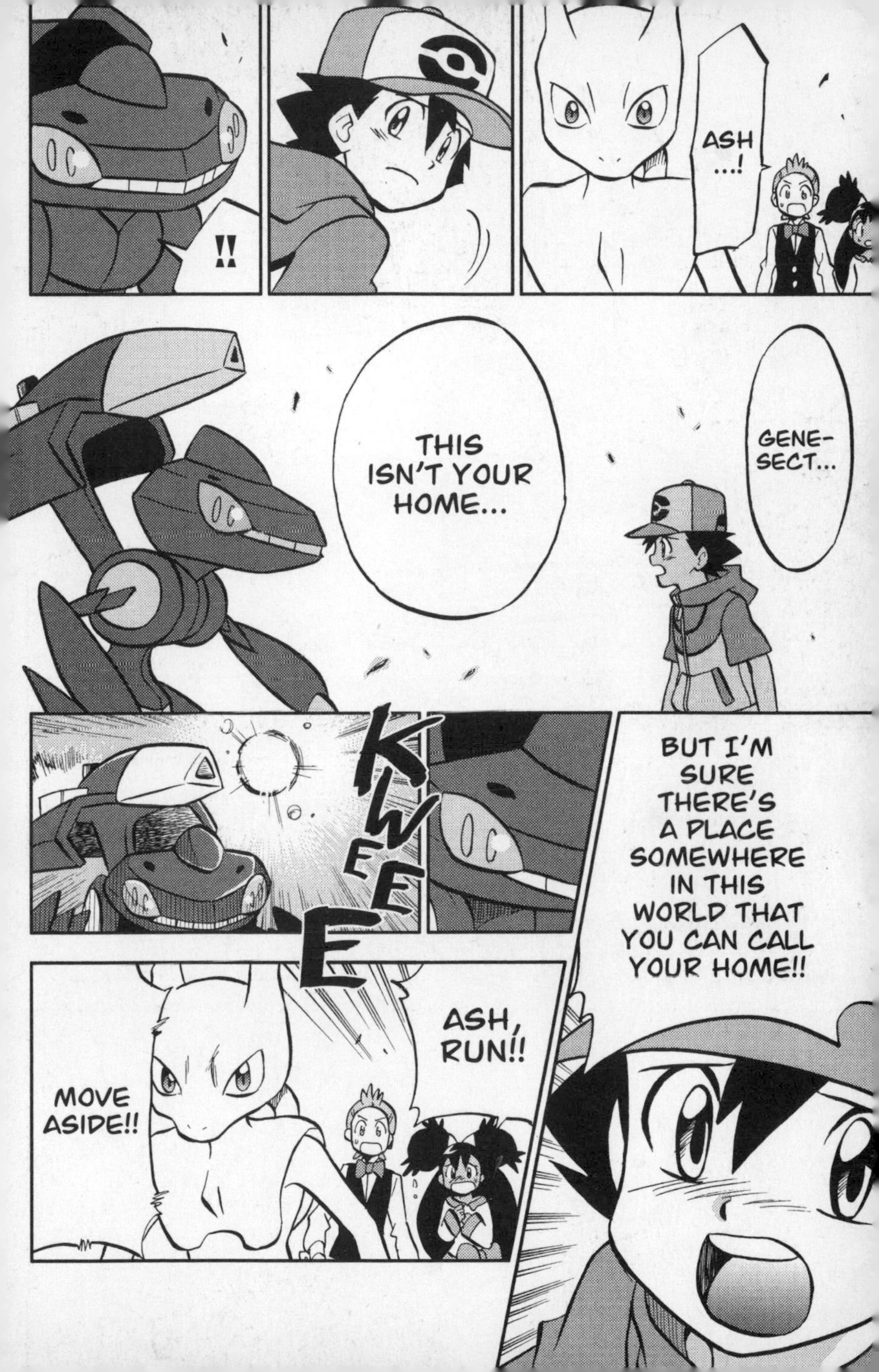
ASH ....!
!!
GENE-SECT...
THIS ISN'T YOUR HOME...
BUT I'M SURE THERE'S A PLACE SOMEWHERE IN THIS WORLD THAT YOU CAN CALL YOUR HOME!!
KWEEE
ASH, RUN!!
MOVE ASIDE!!

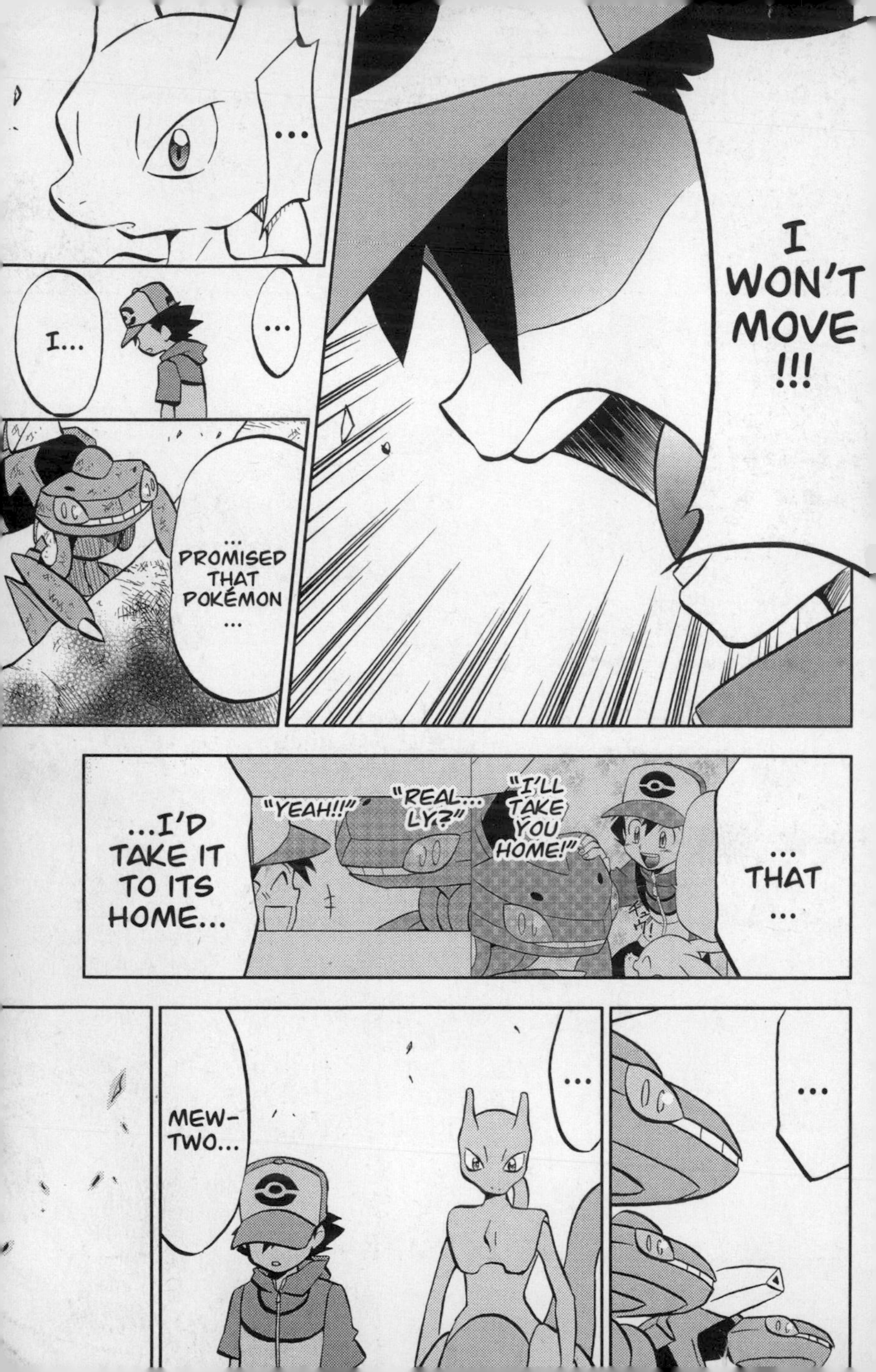

I WON'T MOVE !!!
...
...
I...
... PROMISED THAT POKÉMON ...
... THAT ...
"I'LL TAKE YOU HOME!"
"REAL... LY?"
"YEAH!!"
...I'D TAKE IT TO ITS HOME...
...
...
MEW-TWO...

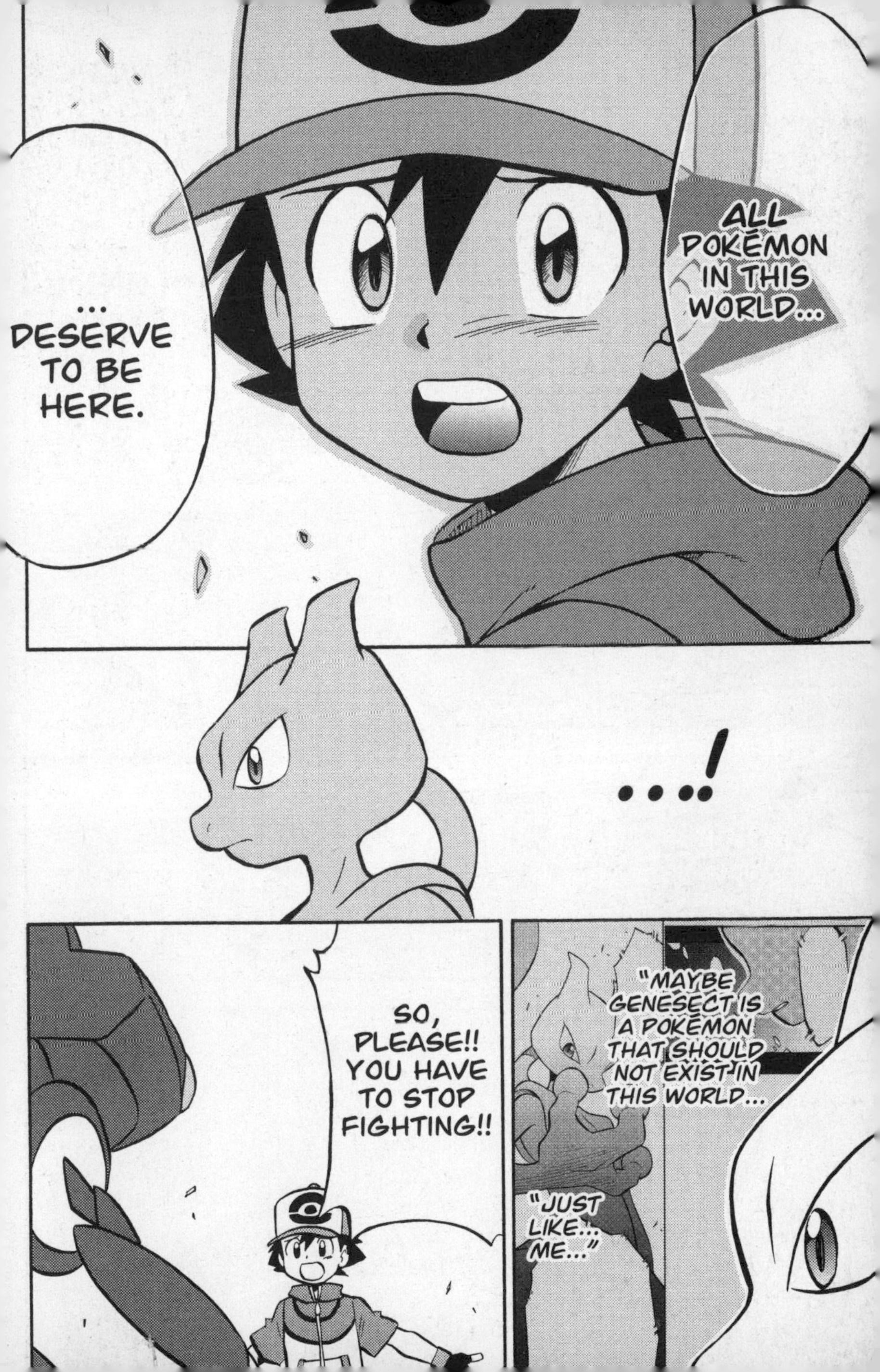
ALL POKÉMON IN THIS WORLD...
... DESERVE TO BE HERE.
...!
"MAYBE GENESECT IS A POKÉMON THAT SHOULD NOT EXIST IN THIS WORLD...
"JUST LIKE... ME..."
SO, PLEASE!! YOU HAVE TO STOP FIGHTING!!

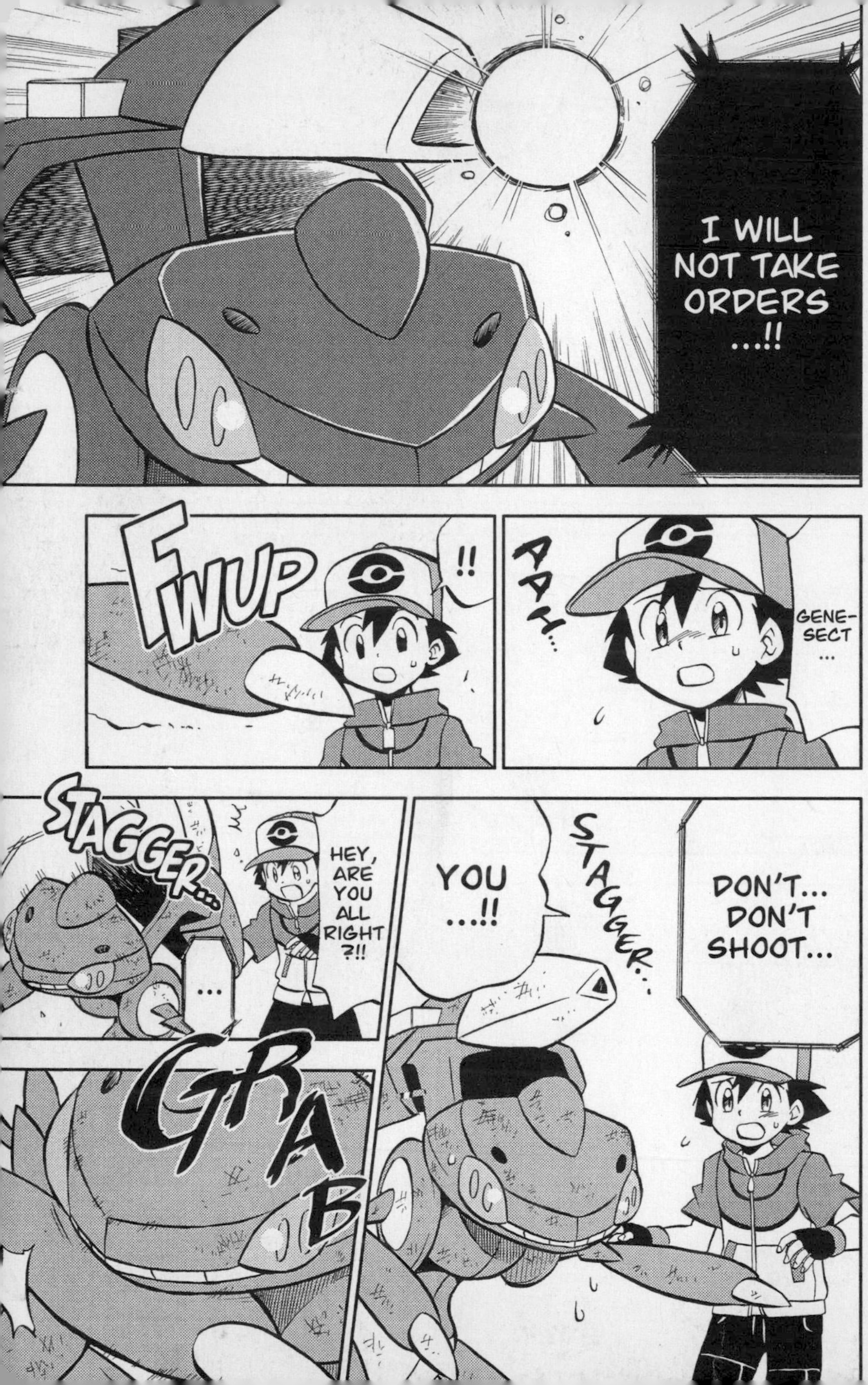
I WILL NOT TAKE ORDERS ....!!
AAH...
GENE-SECT ...
FWUP
!!
DON'T... DON'T SHOOT...
STAGGER...
YOU ....!!
STAGGER...
HEY, ARE YOU ALL RIGHT ?!!
...
GRAB

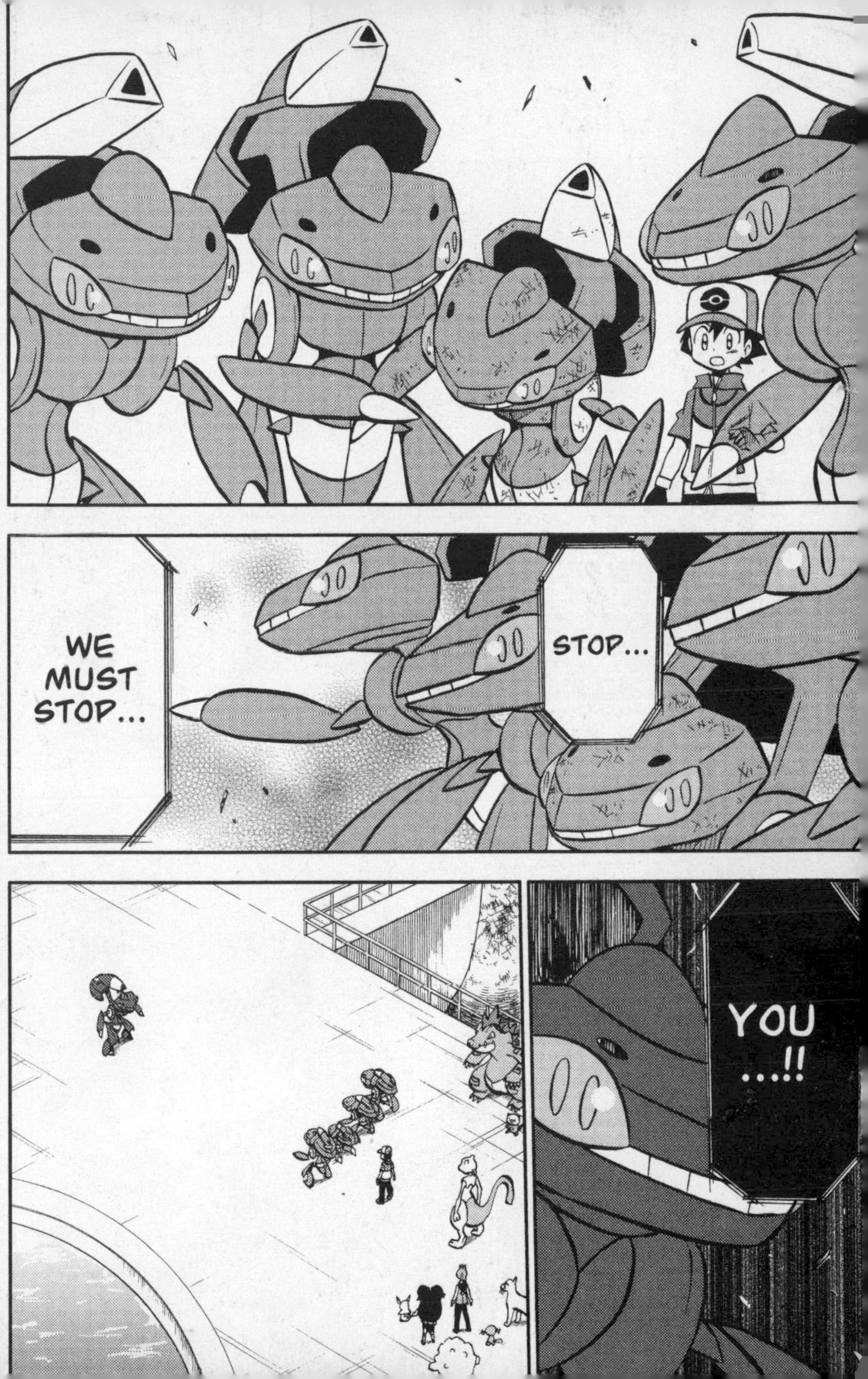
STOP...
WE MUST STOP...
YOU ...!!

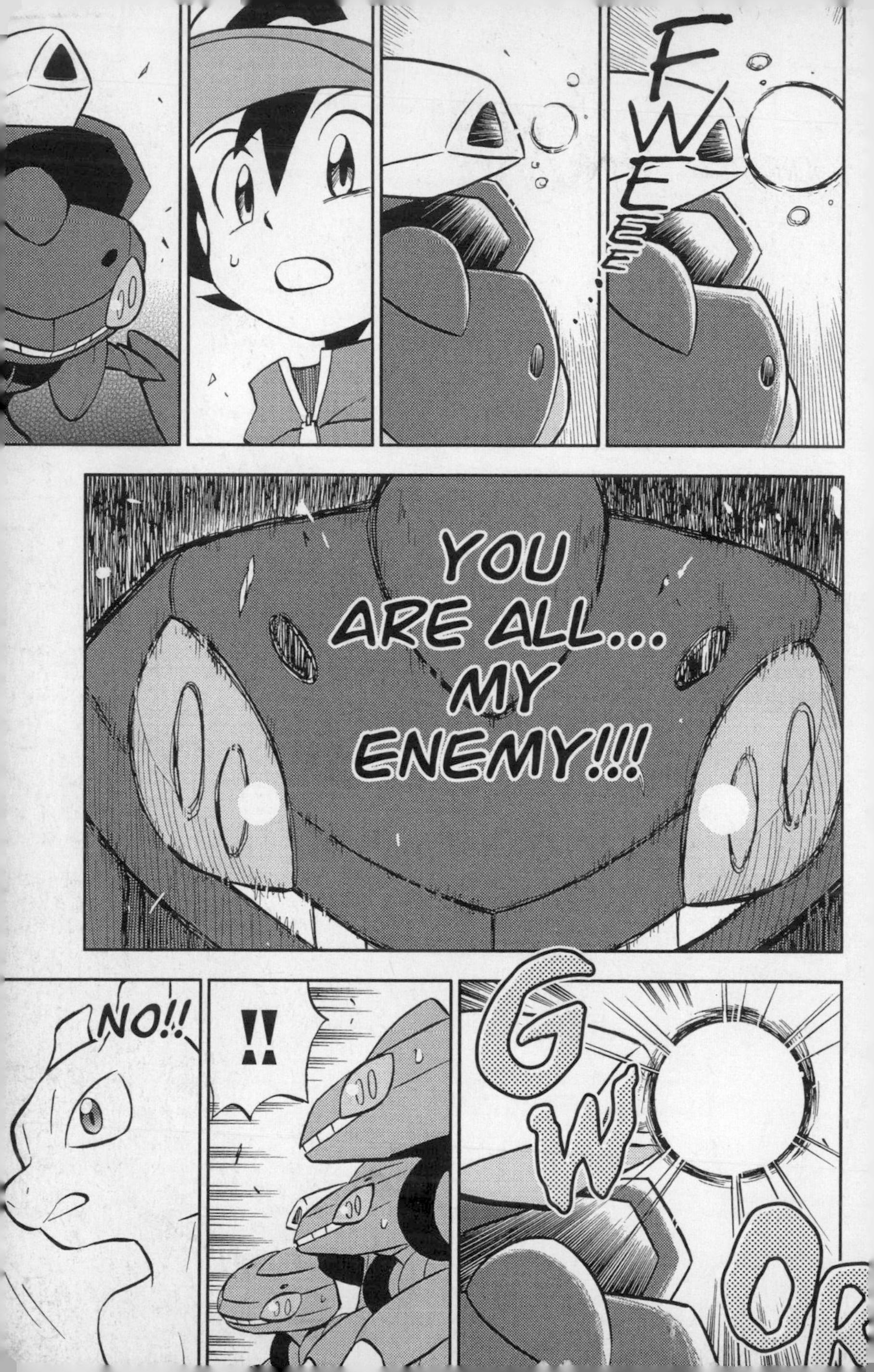
FWEEE
YOU ARE ALL... MY ENEMY!!!
GWOOR
!!
NO!!

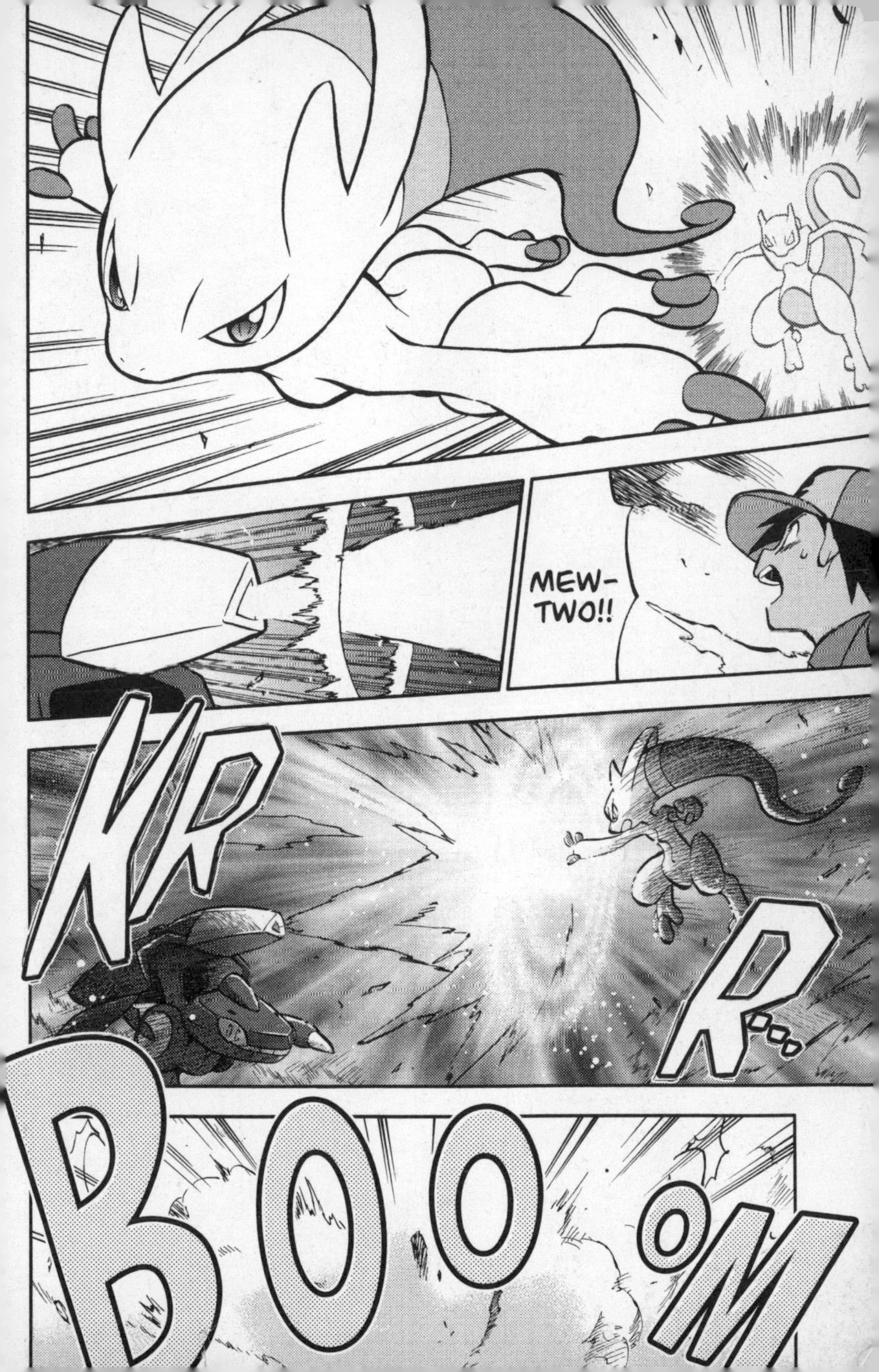
MEW-TWO!!
KR
R...
BOOOM

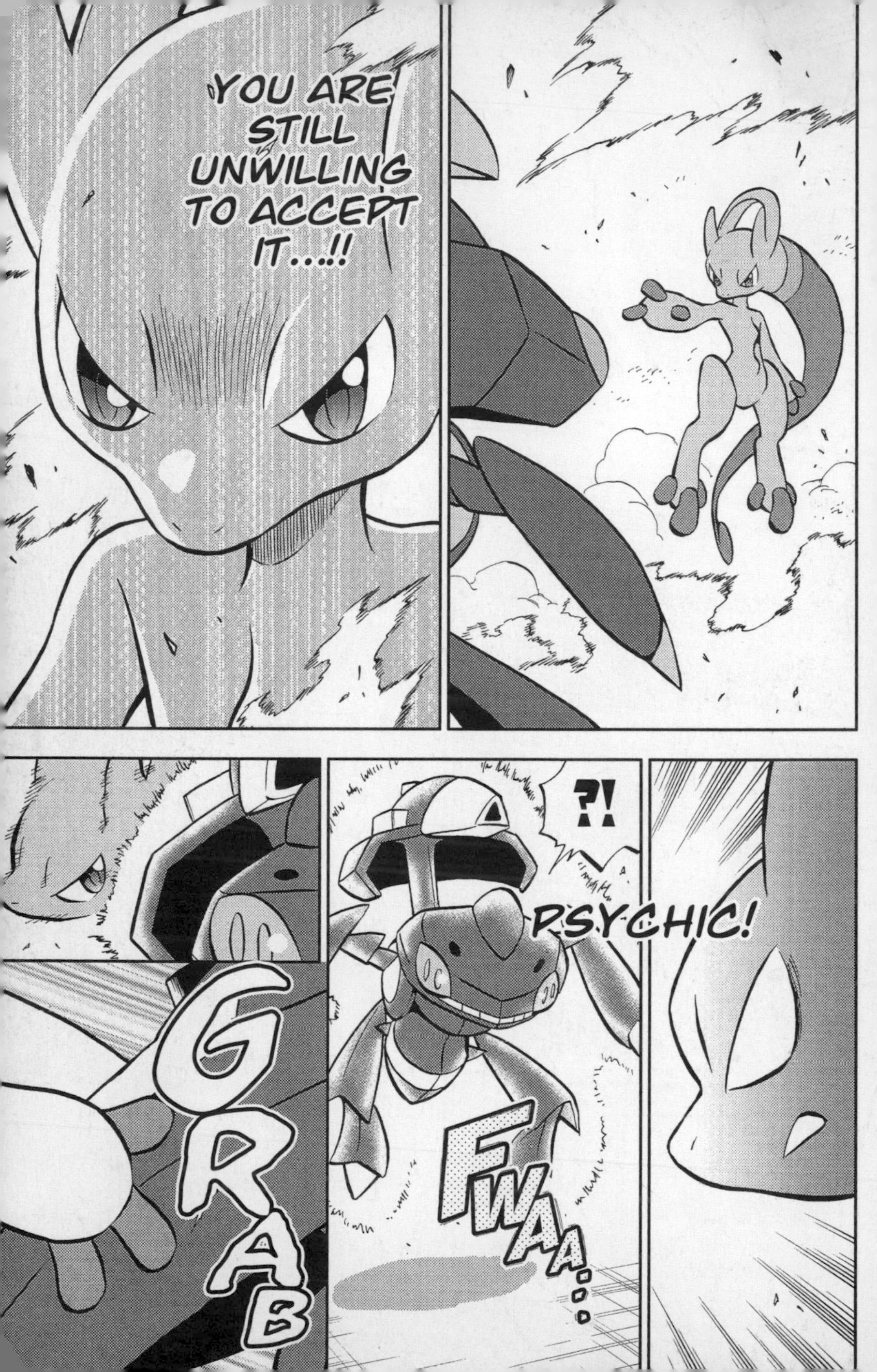
YOU ARE STILL UNWILLING TO ACCEPT IT...!!
?!
PSYCHIC!
FWAA...
GRAB

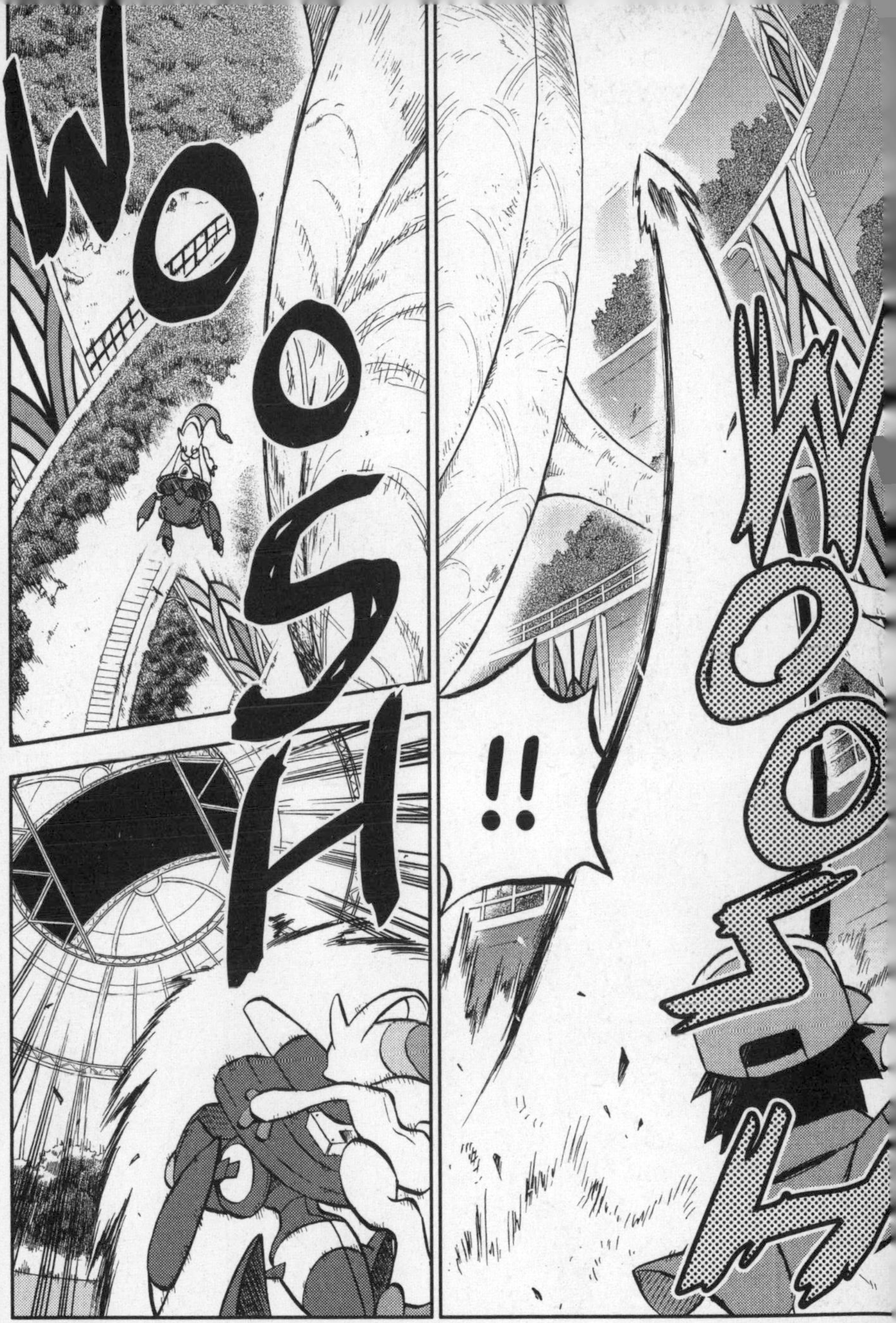
!!
WOOSH
WOOSH

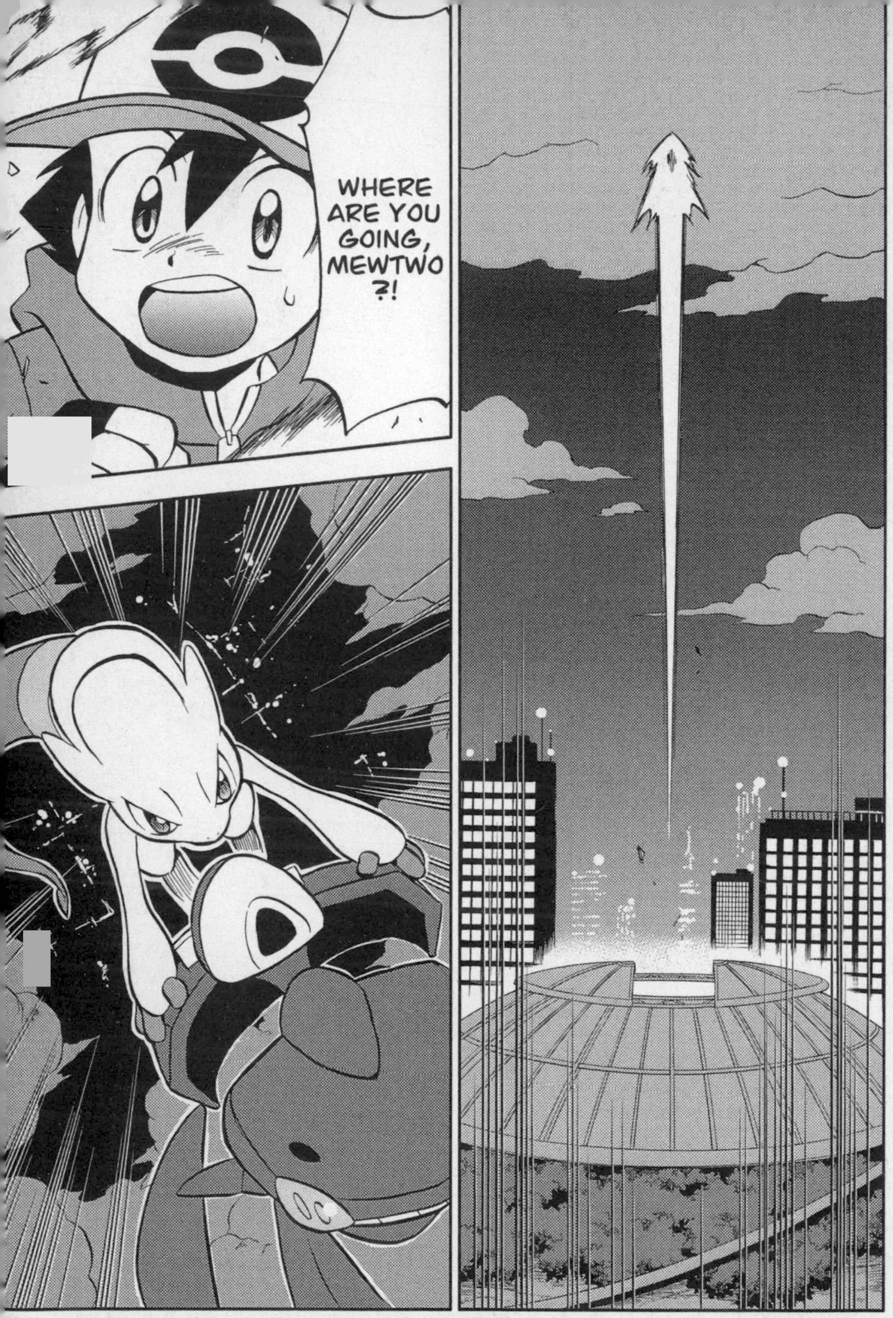
WHERE ARE YOU GOING, MEWTWO ?!

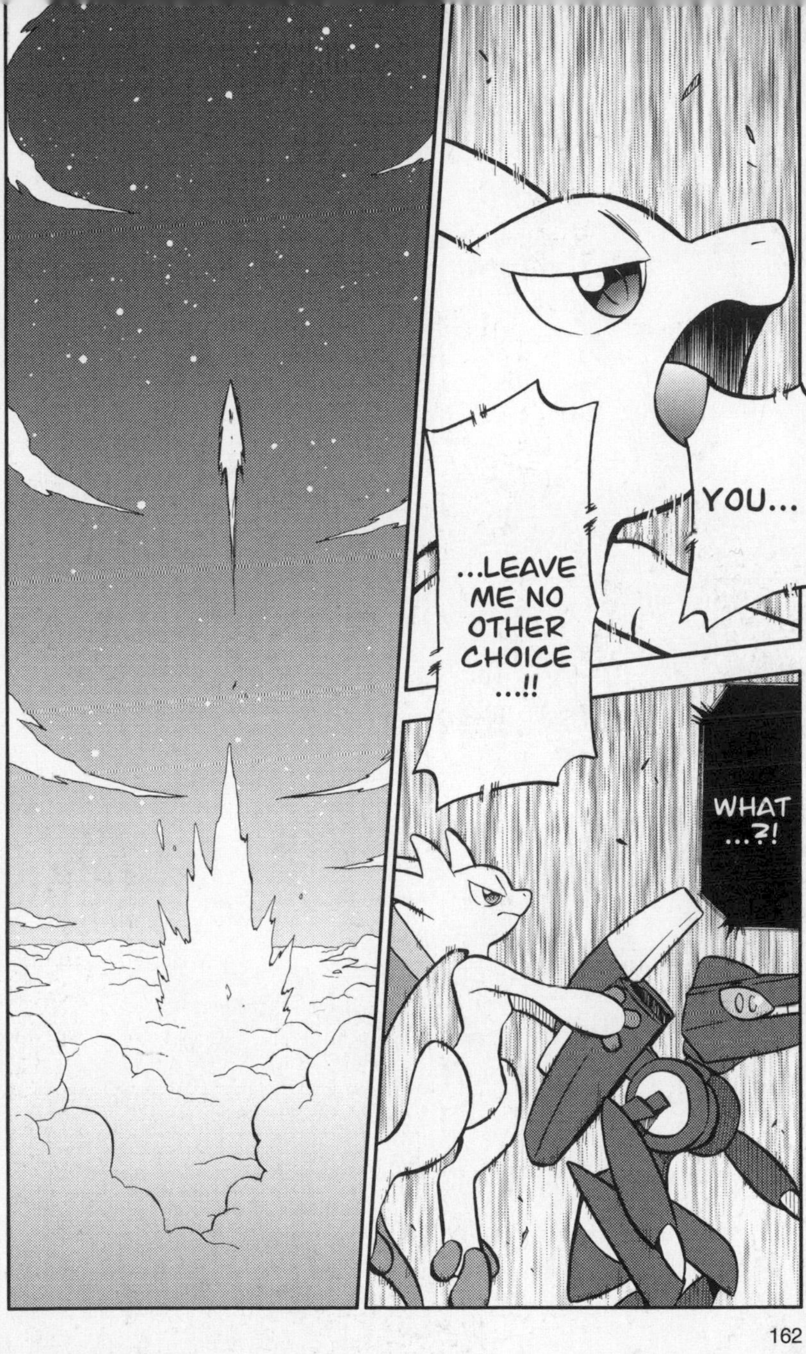
YOU...
...LEAVE ME NO OTHER CHOICE ...!!
WHAT ...?!

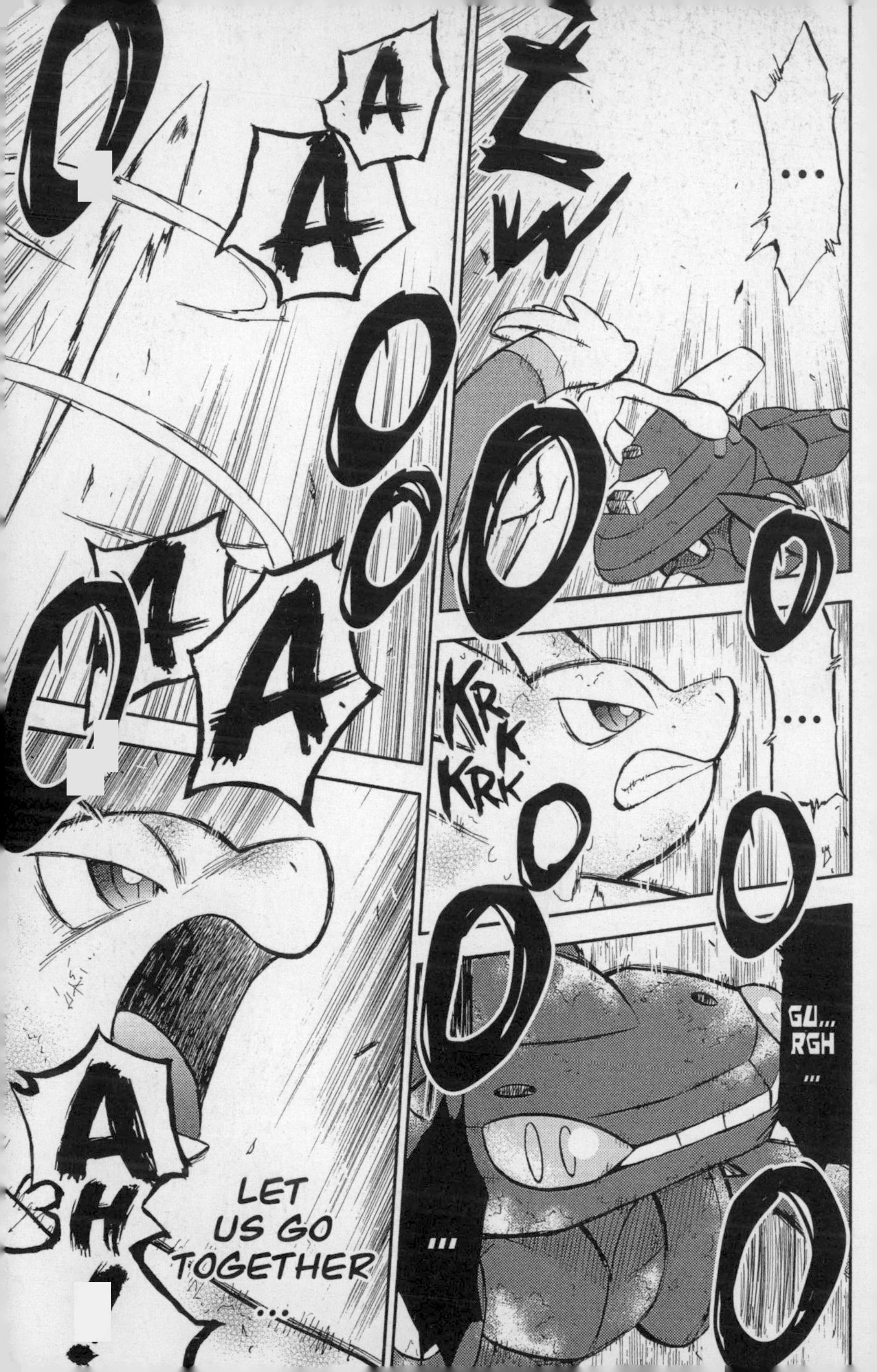
...
ZWOOOOOO
...
KRK KRK
GU... RGH ...
...
OAAAAAA
AH!
LET US GO TOGETHER ...

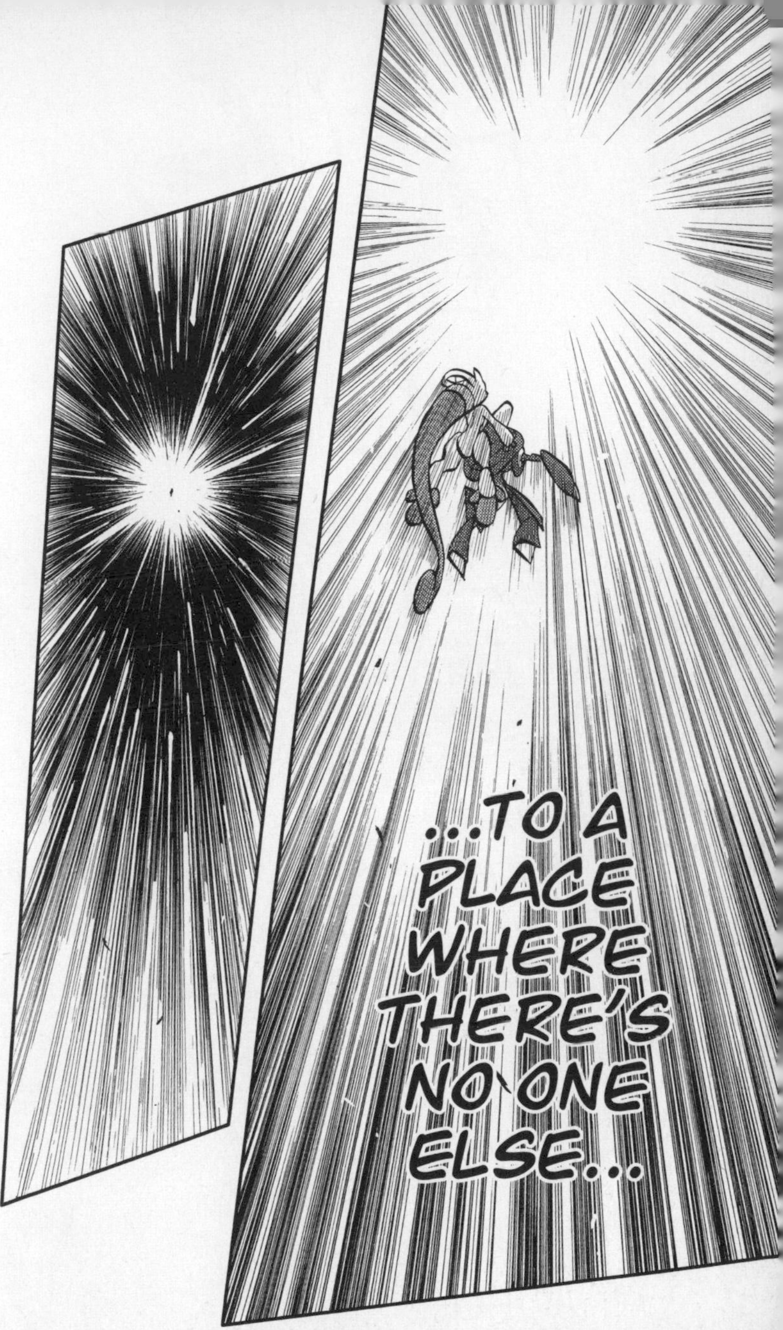
...TO A PLACE WHERE THERE'S NO ONE ELSE...

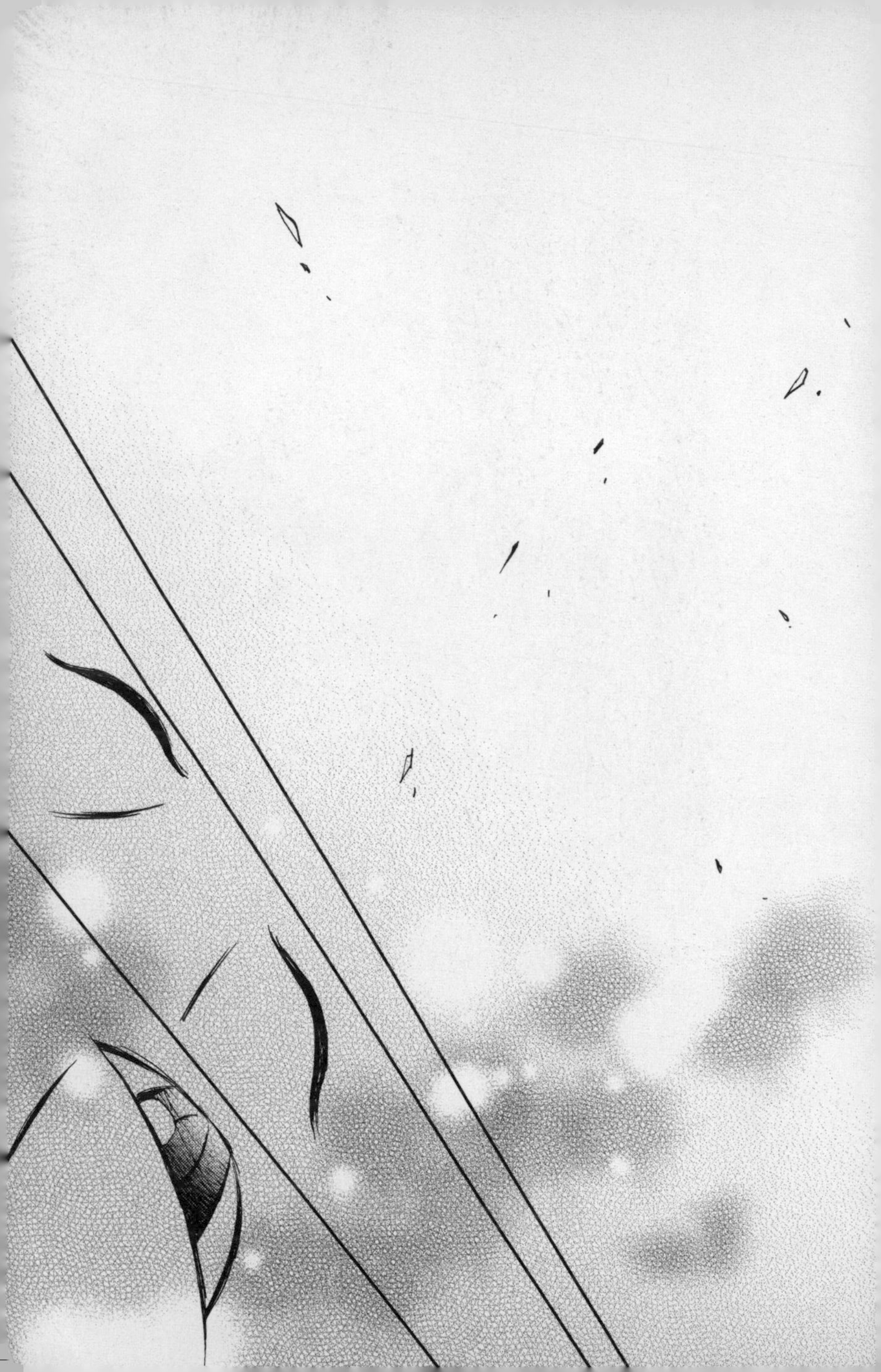

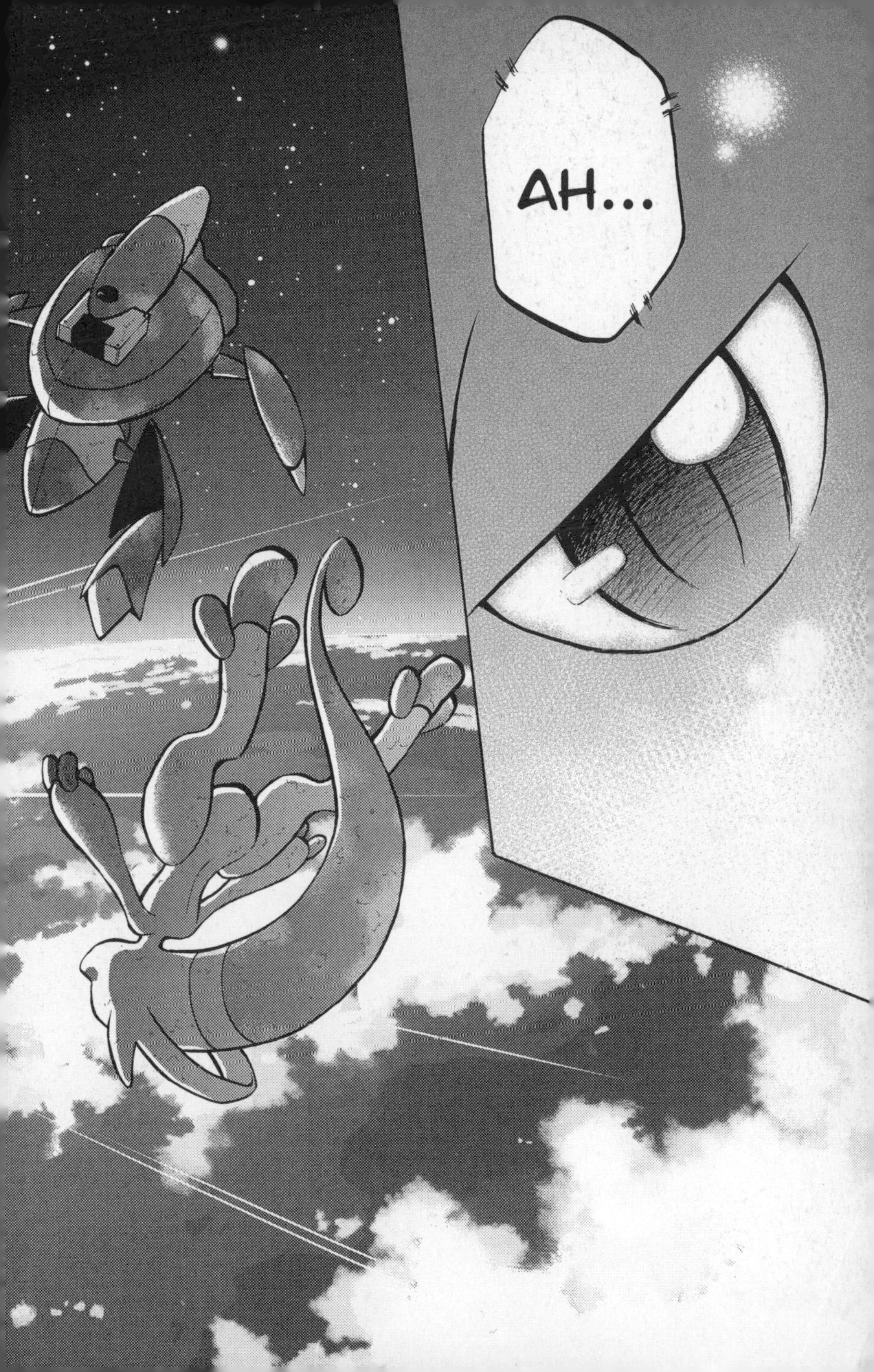
AH...

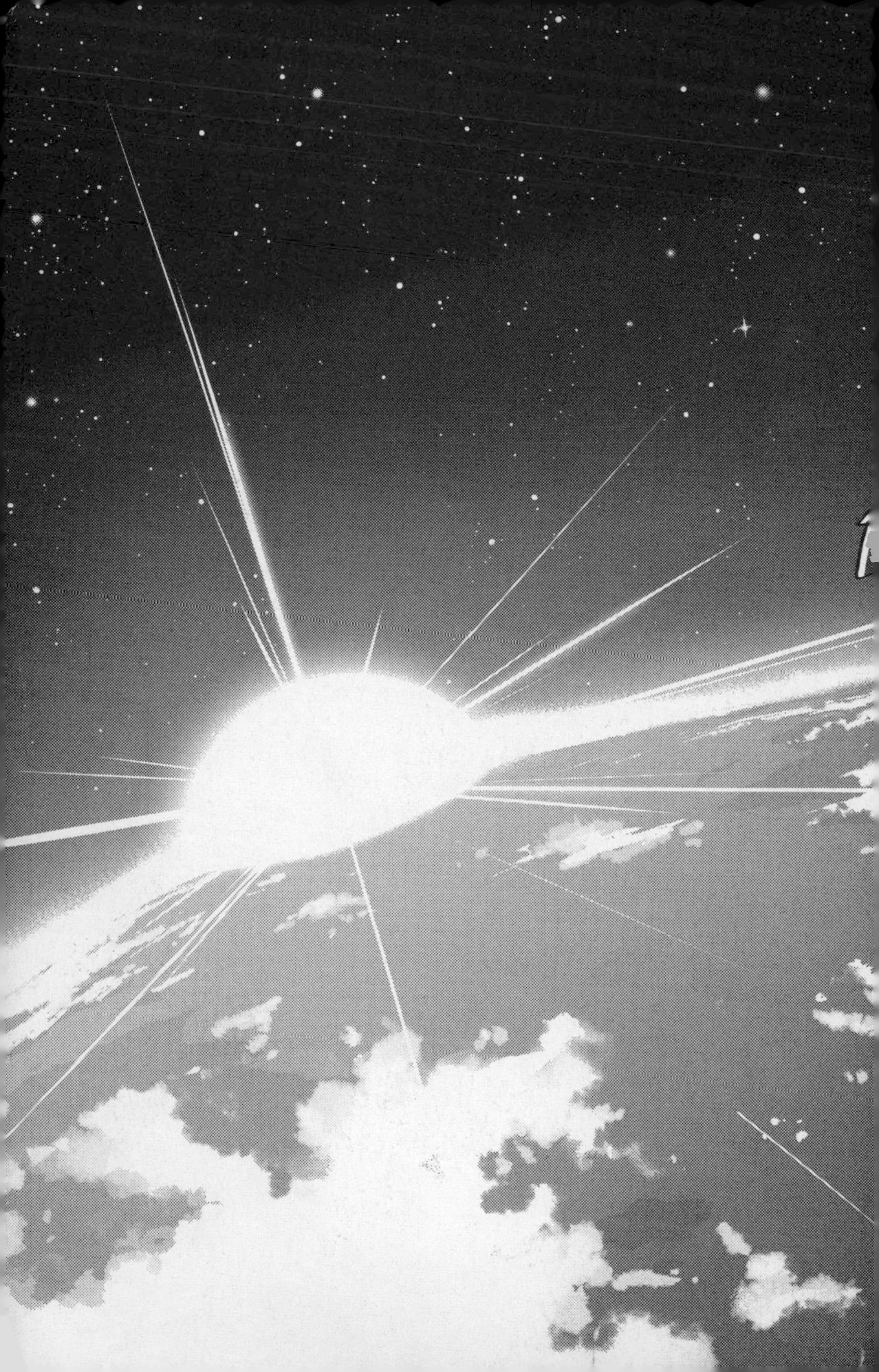

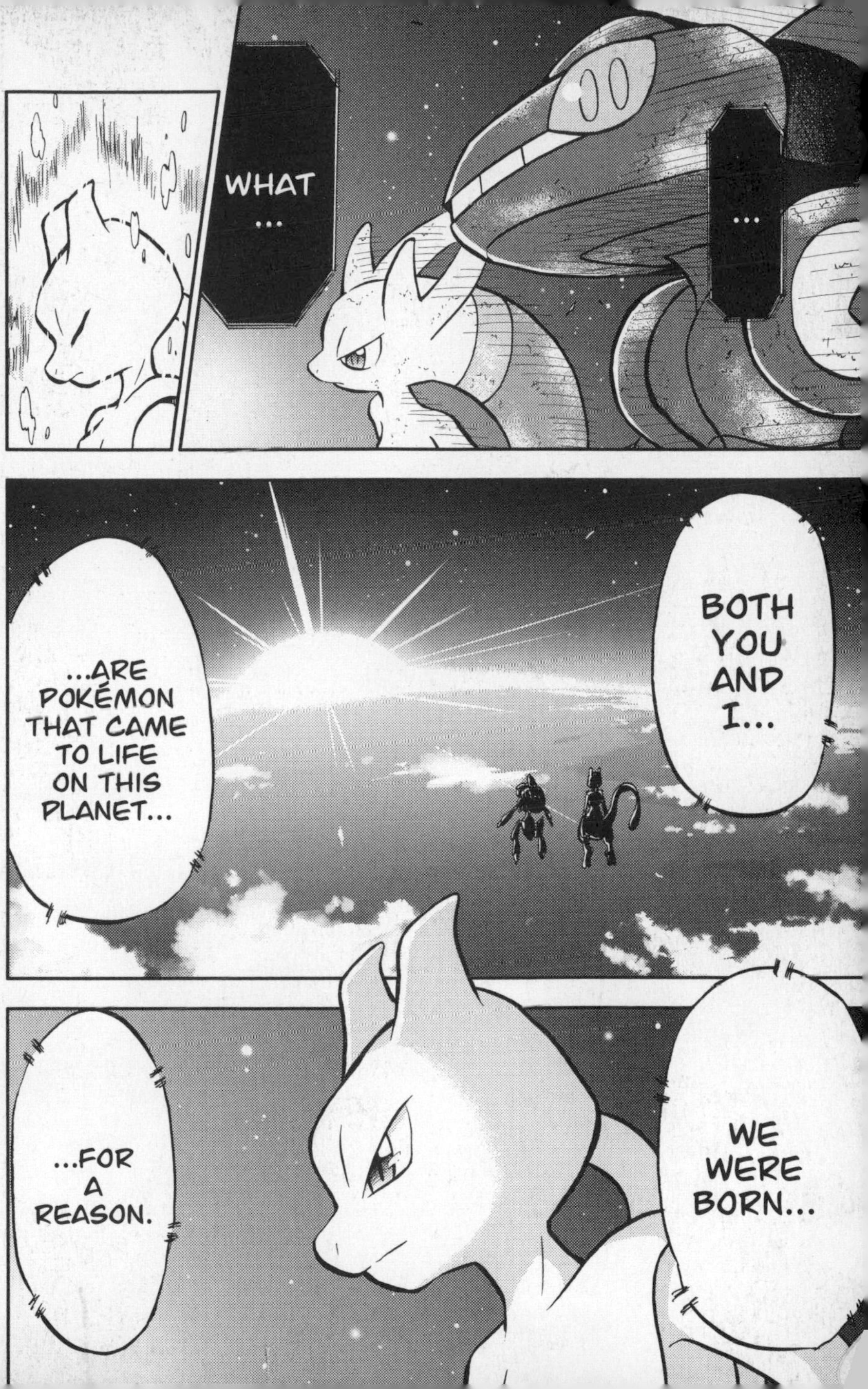
...
WHAT ...
BOTH YOU AND I...
...ARE POKÉMON THAT CAME TO LIFE ON THIS PLANET...
WE WERE BORN...
...FOR A REASON.

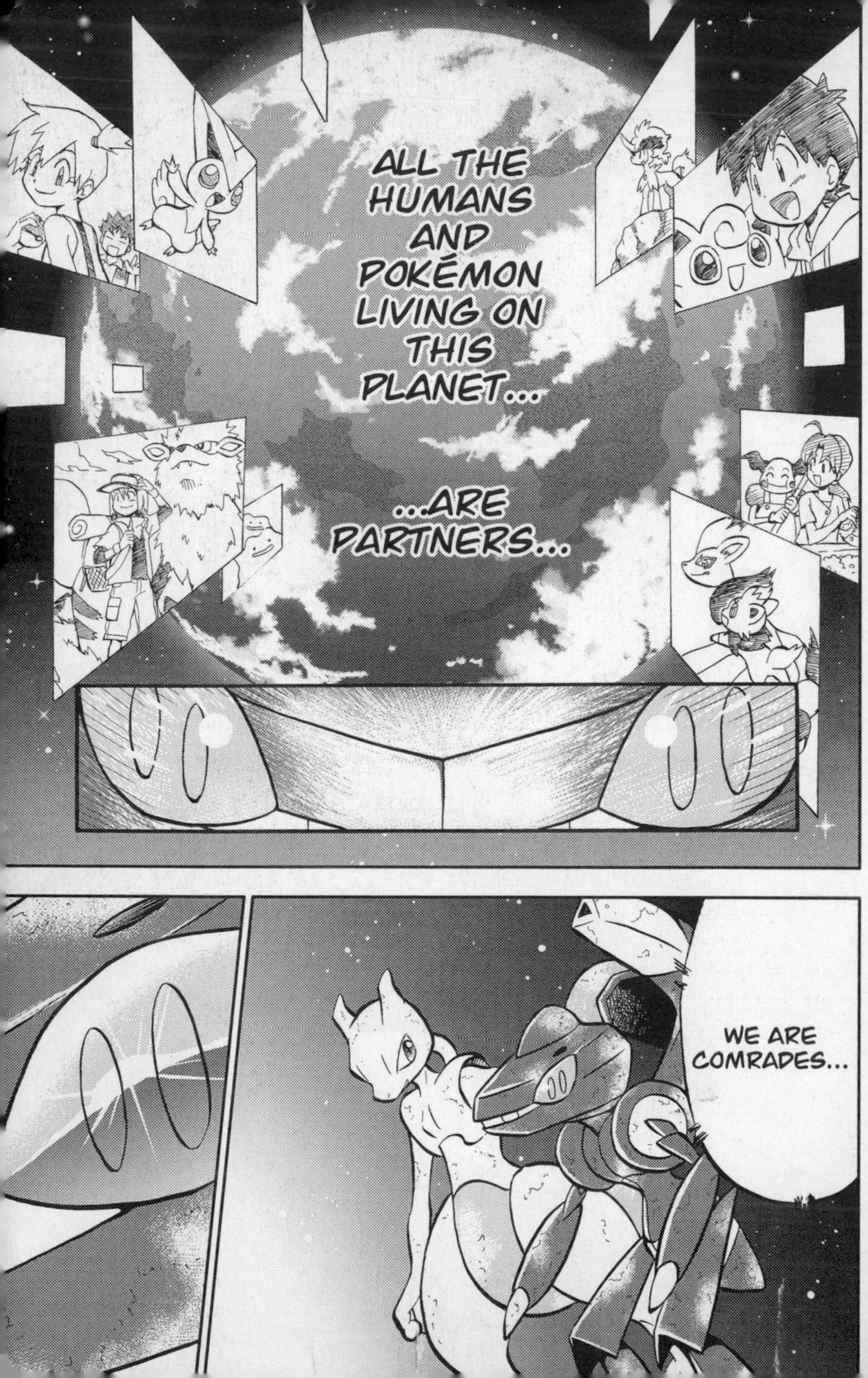
ALL THE HUMANS AND POKÉMON LIVING ON THIS PLANET...
...ARE PARTNERS...
WE ARE COMRADES...

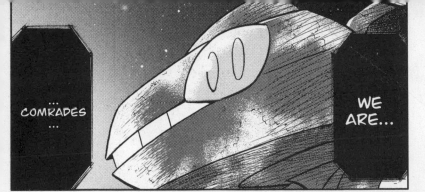

... COMRADES ...

WE ARE...

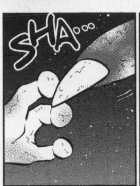

SHA...

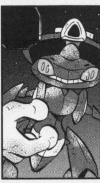

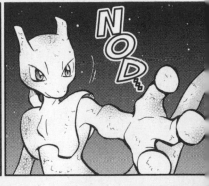

NOD...

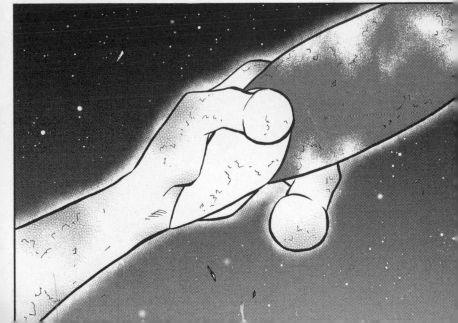

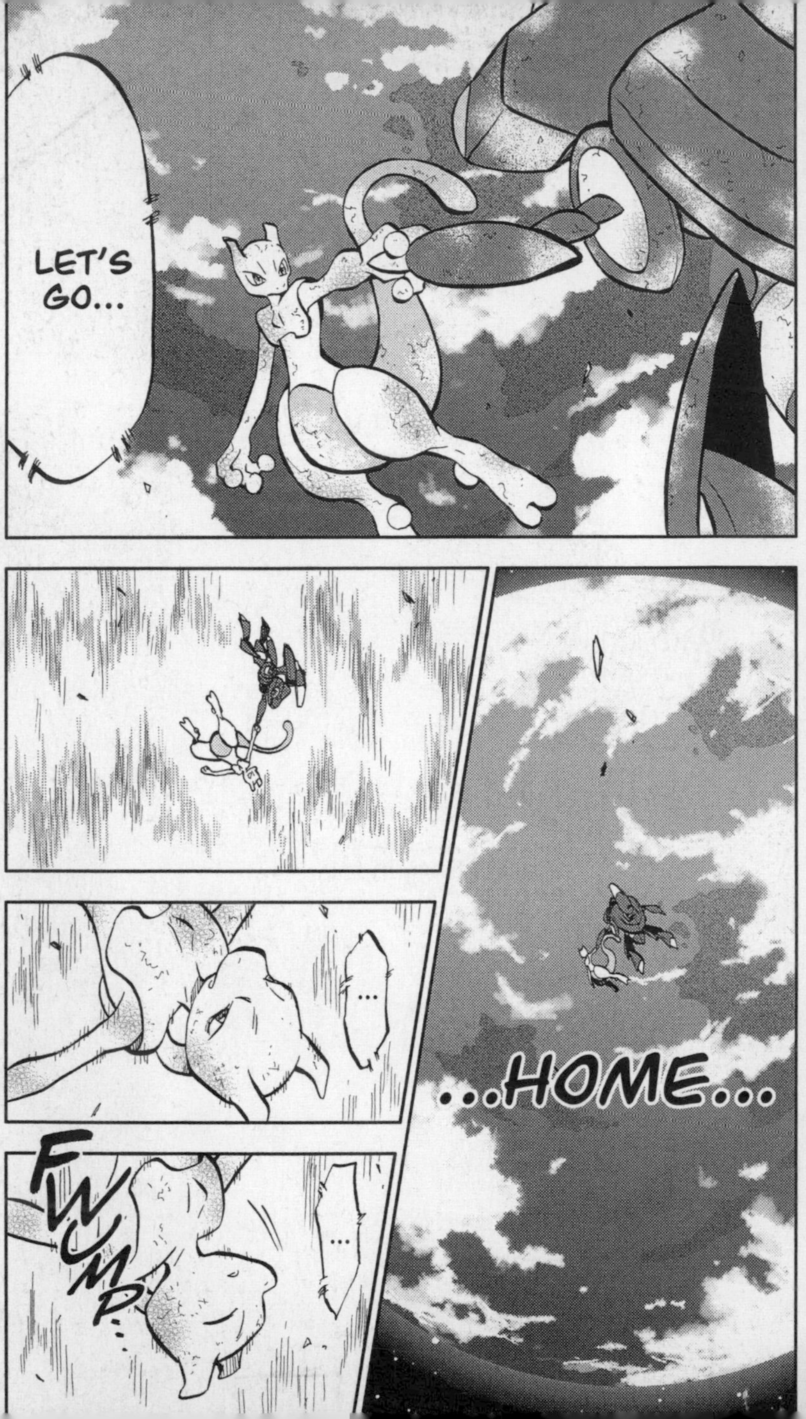
LET'S GO...
...HOME...
...
FWUMP...
...

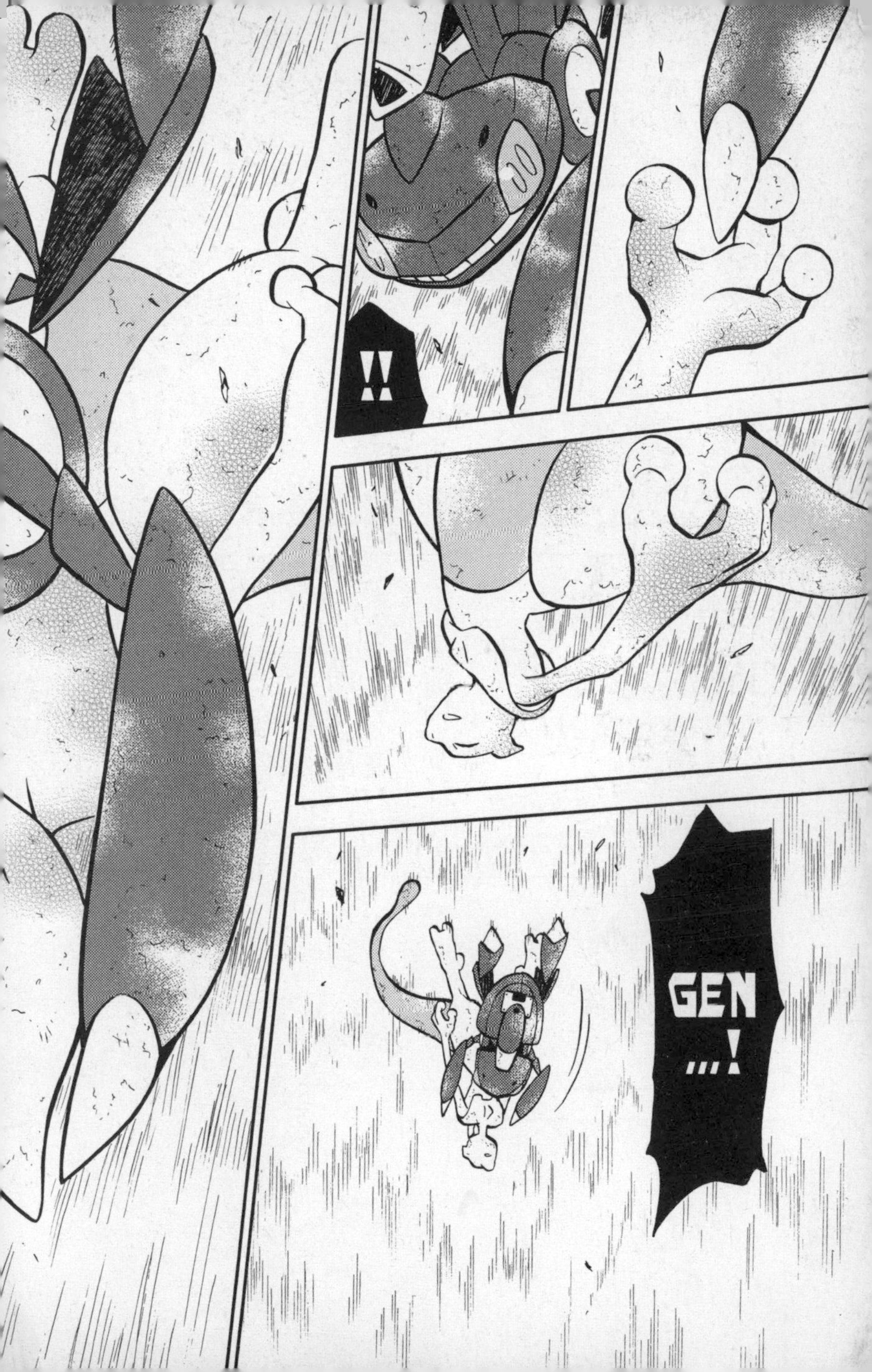
!!
GEN
...!

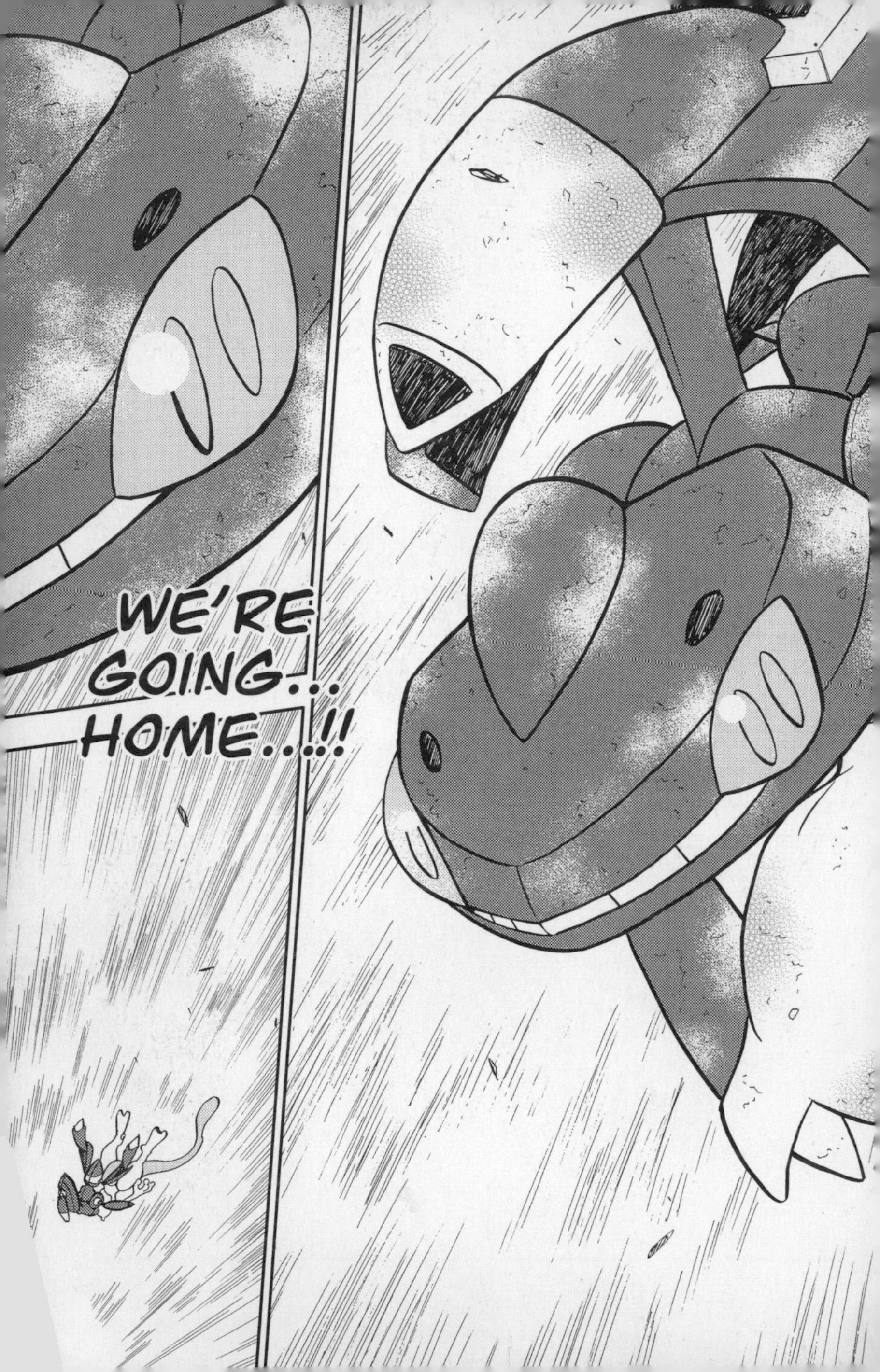
WE'RE GOING... HOME...!!

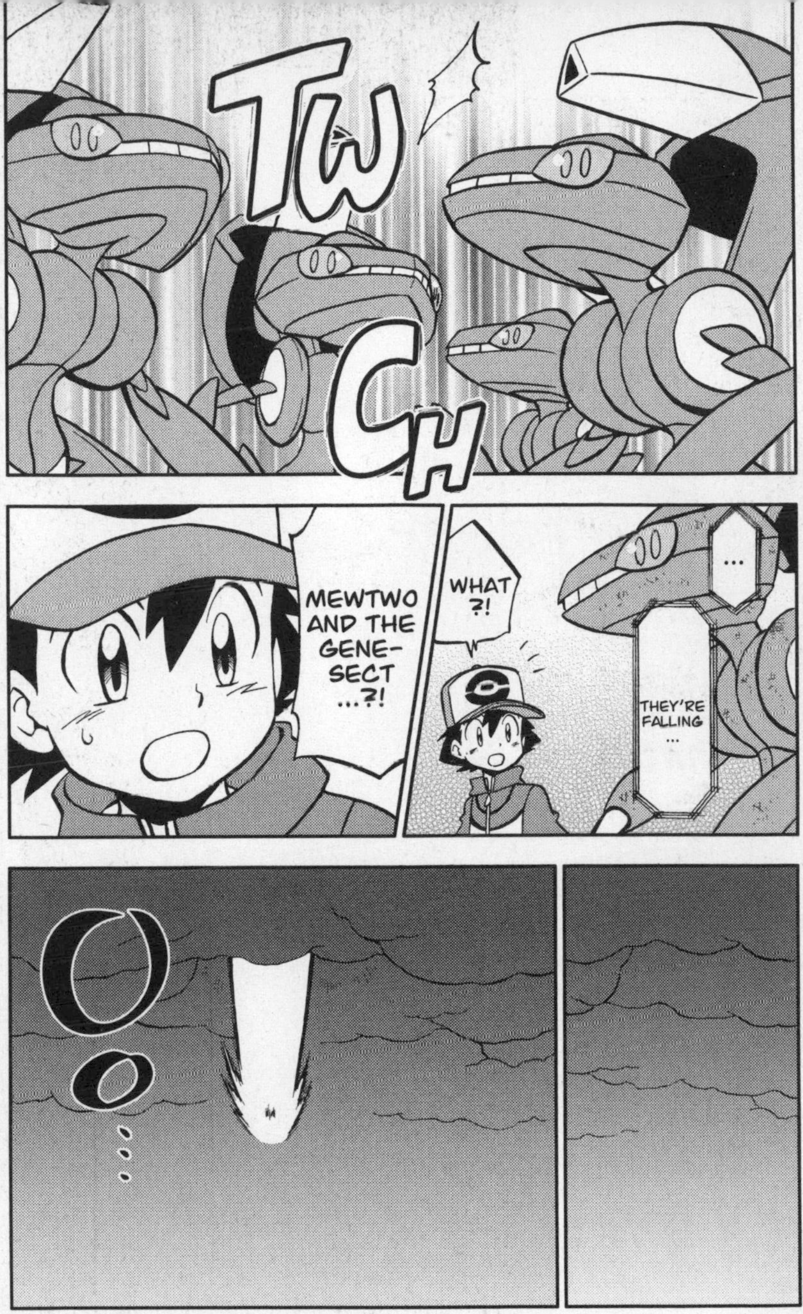

TWCH
...
THEY'RE FALLING ...
WHAT ?!
MEWTWO AND THE GENE-SECT ...?!
OO...

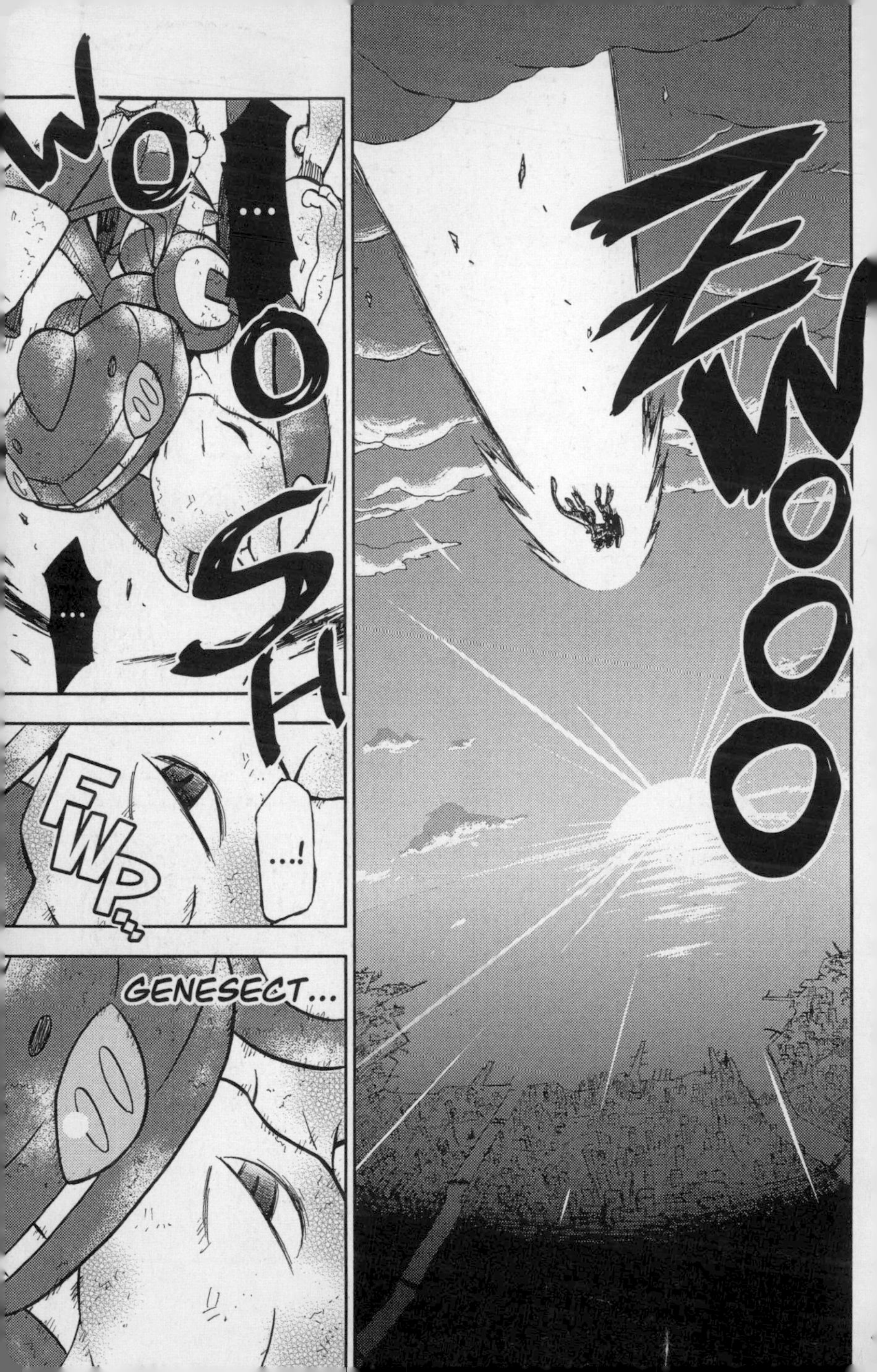
ZWOOOO
WOOOSH
...
...
FWP...
...!
GENESECT...

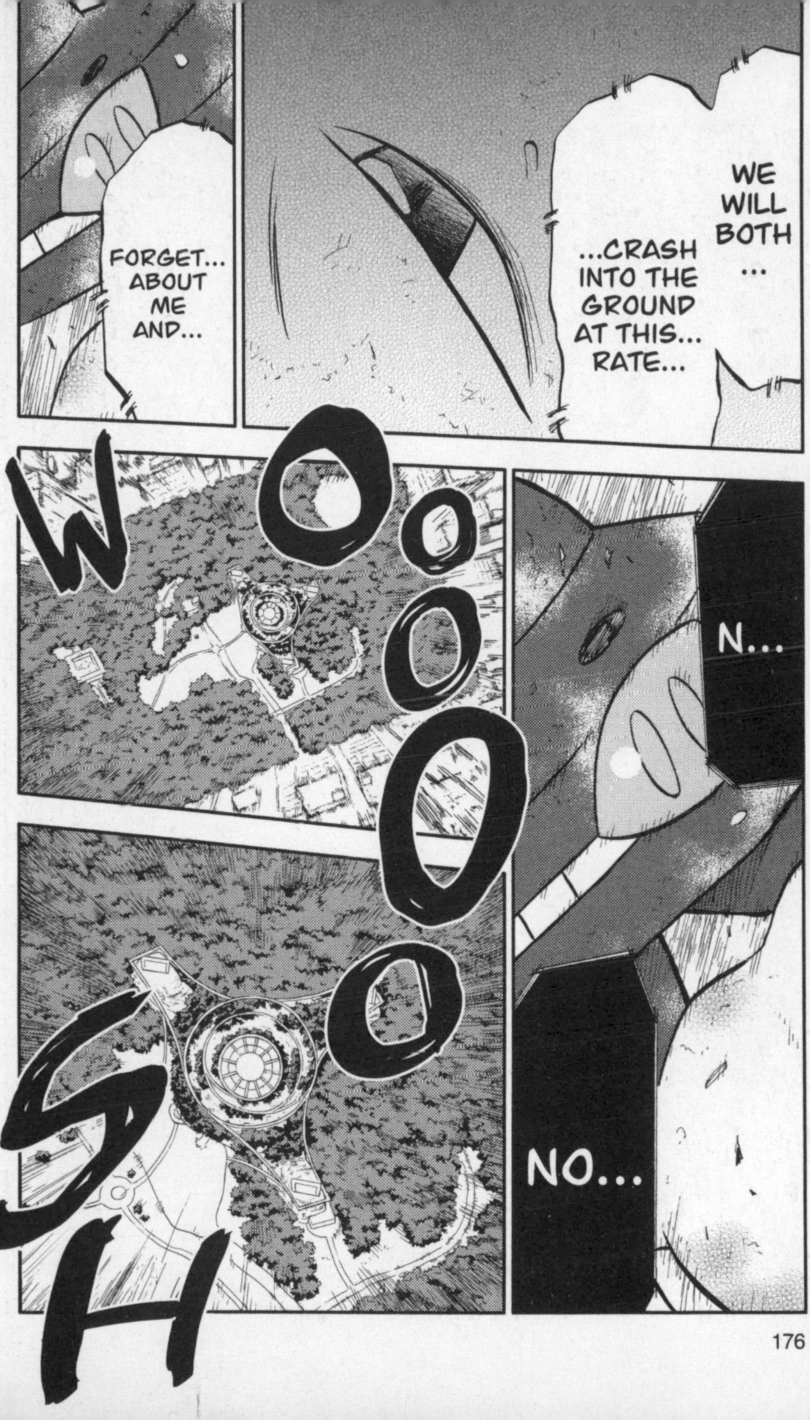
WE WILL BOTH ...
...CRASH INTO THE GROUND AT THIS... RATE...
FORGET... ABOUT ME AND...
N...
NO...
WOOOOOSH

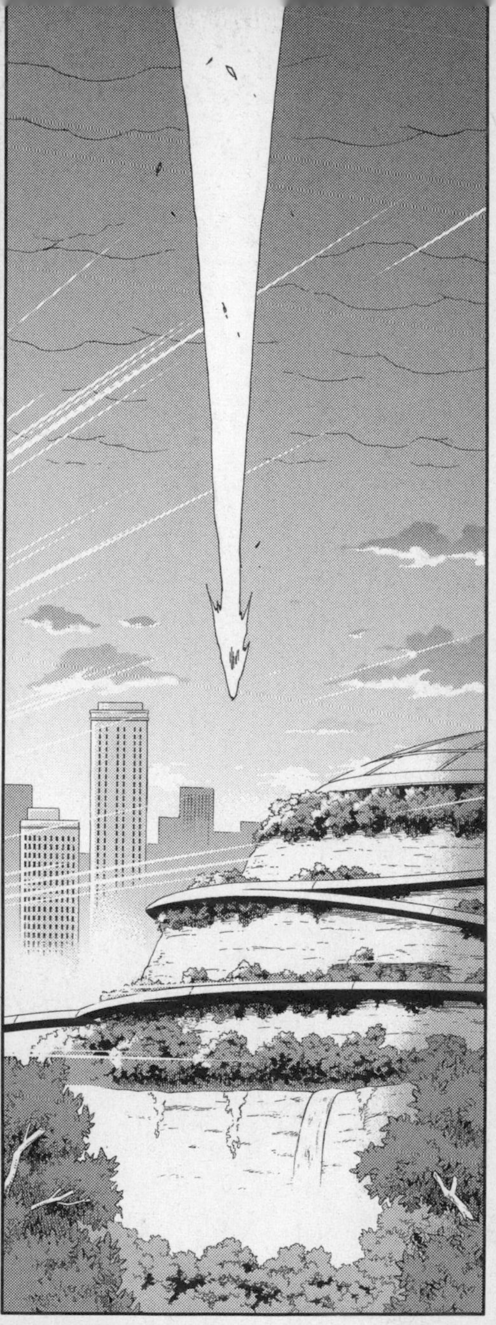

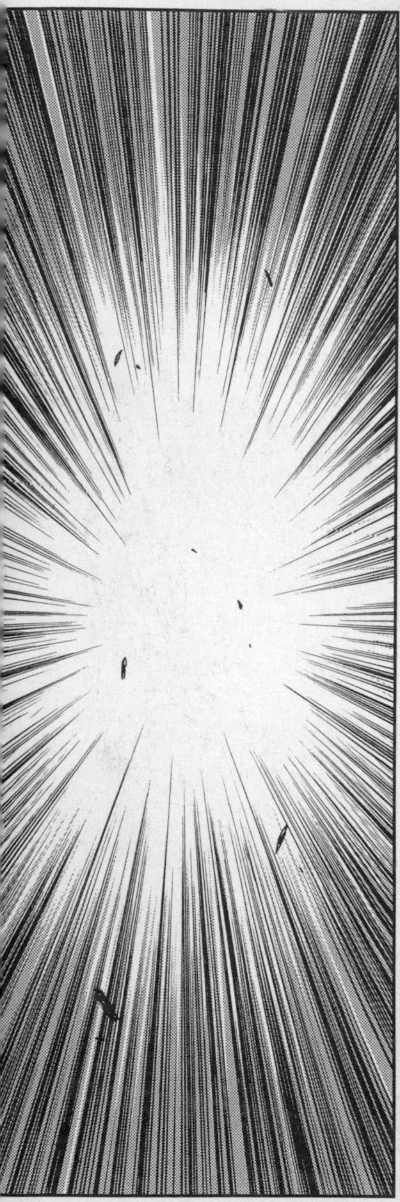

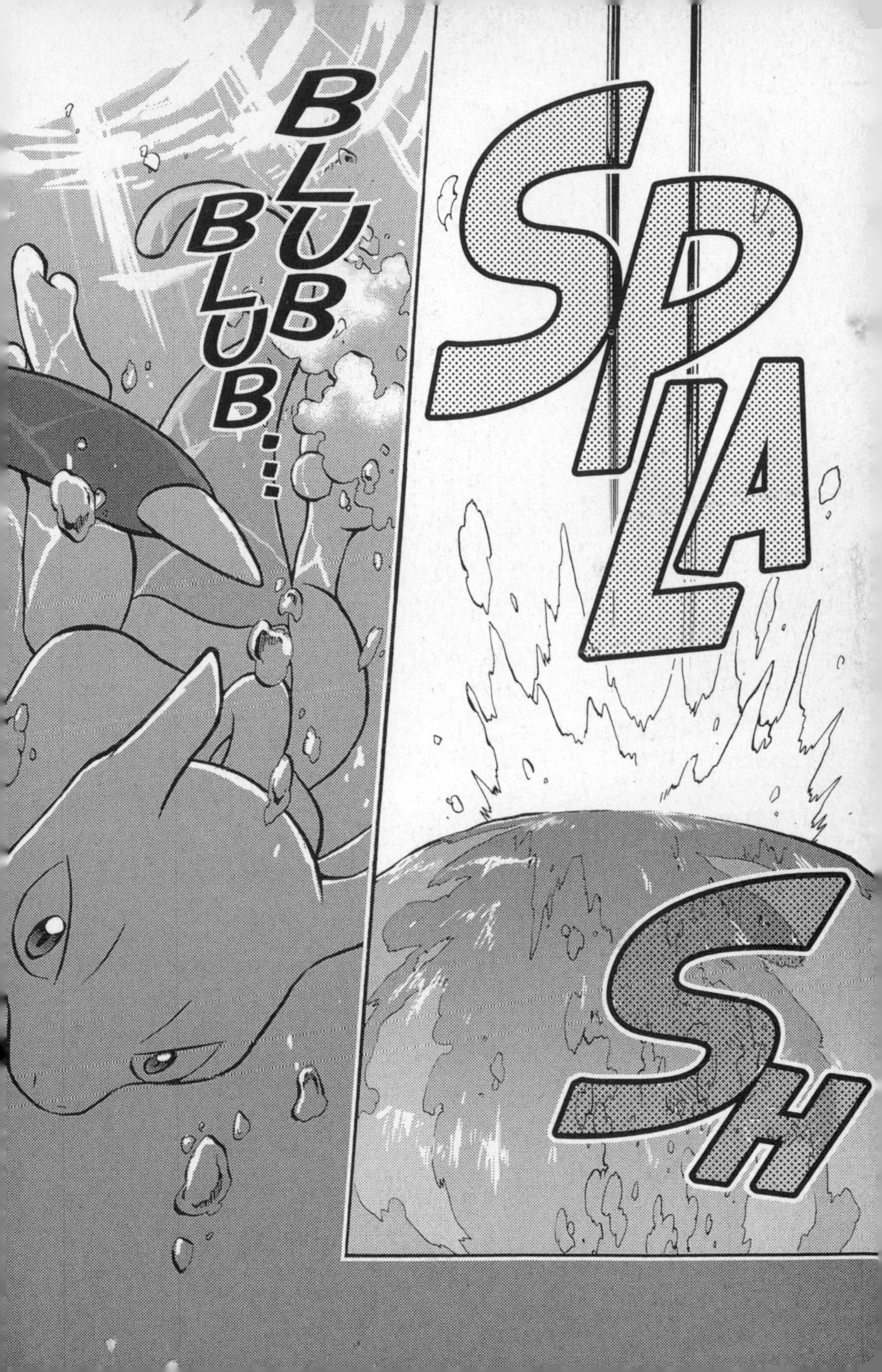
SPLASH
BLUB BLUB...

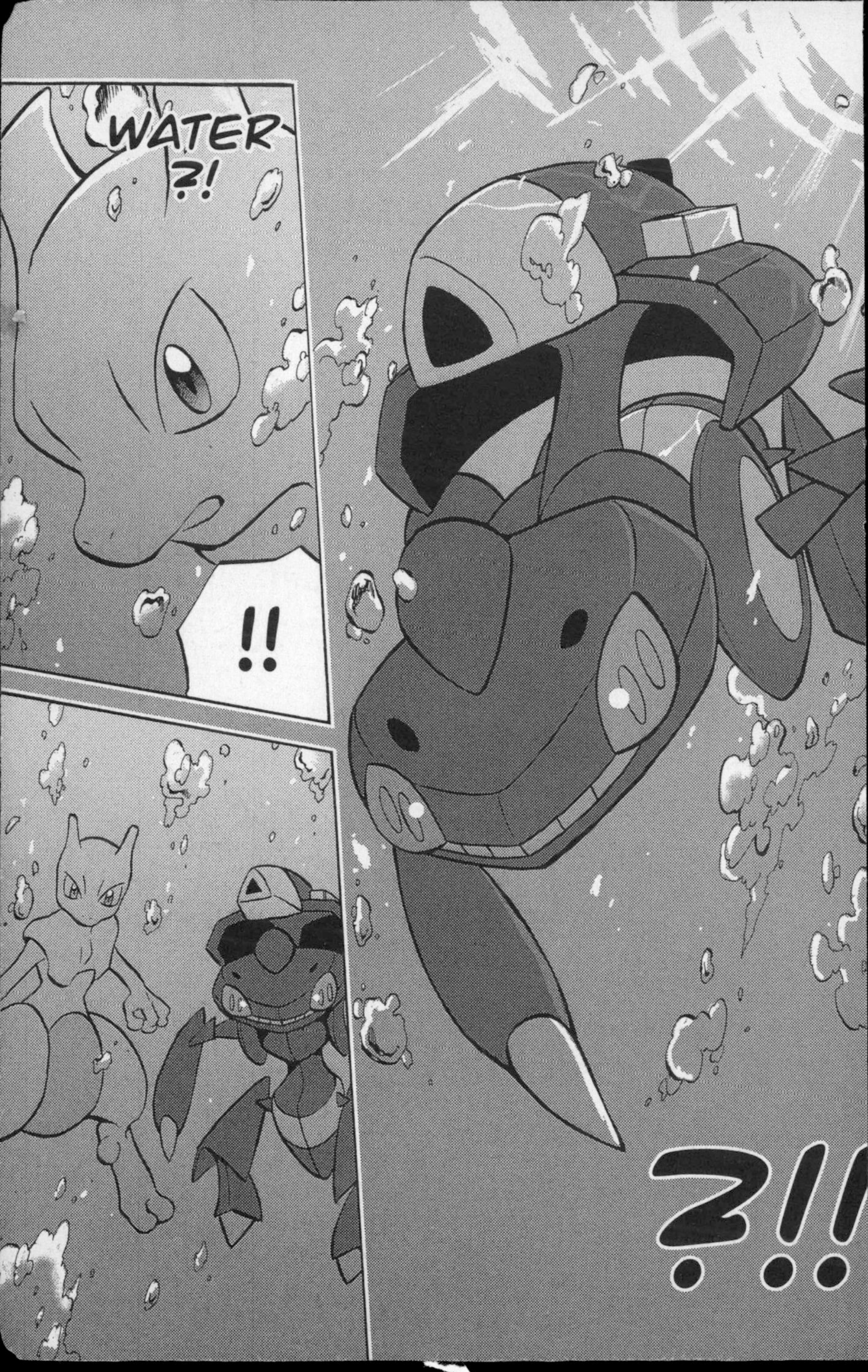
?!!
WATER ?!
!!

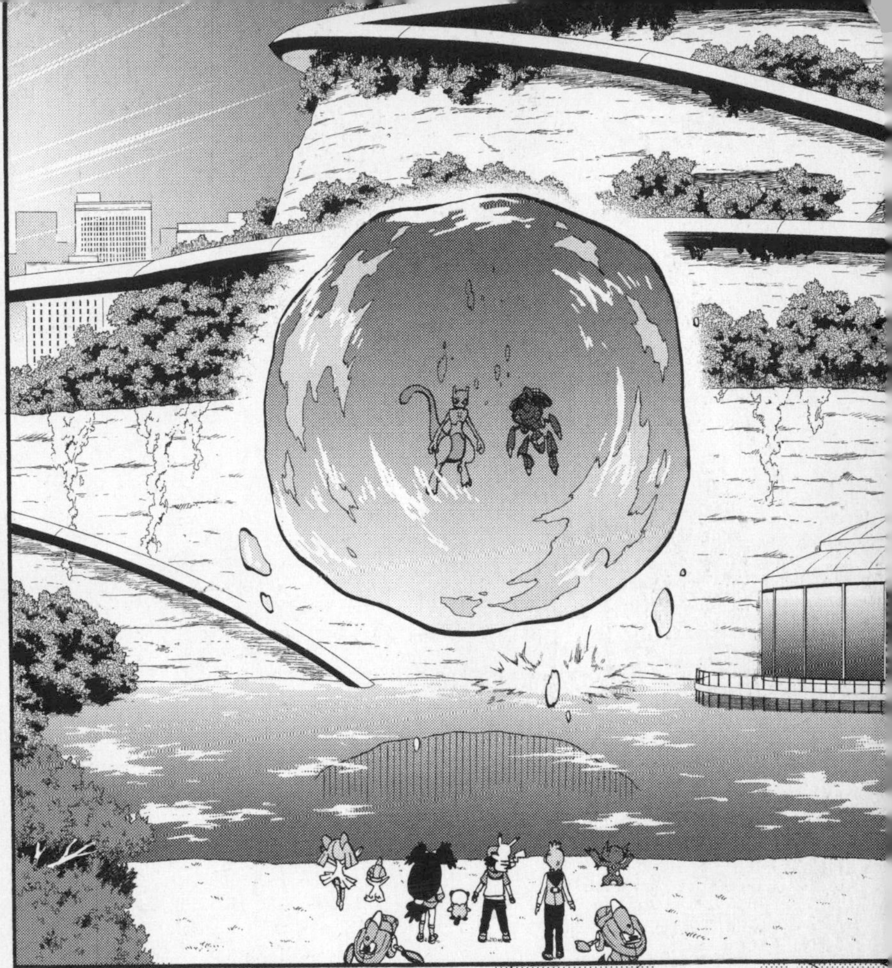

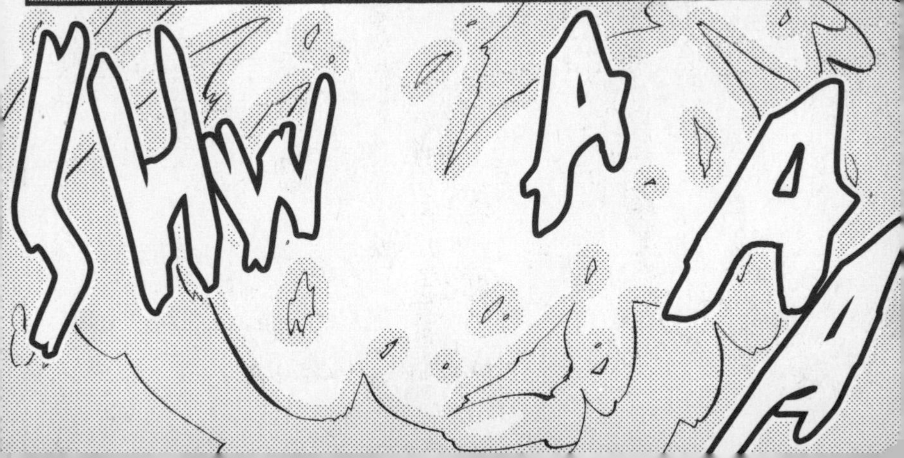
SHWAAA

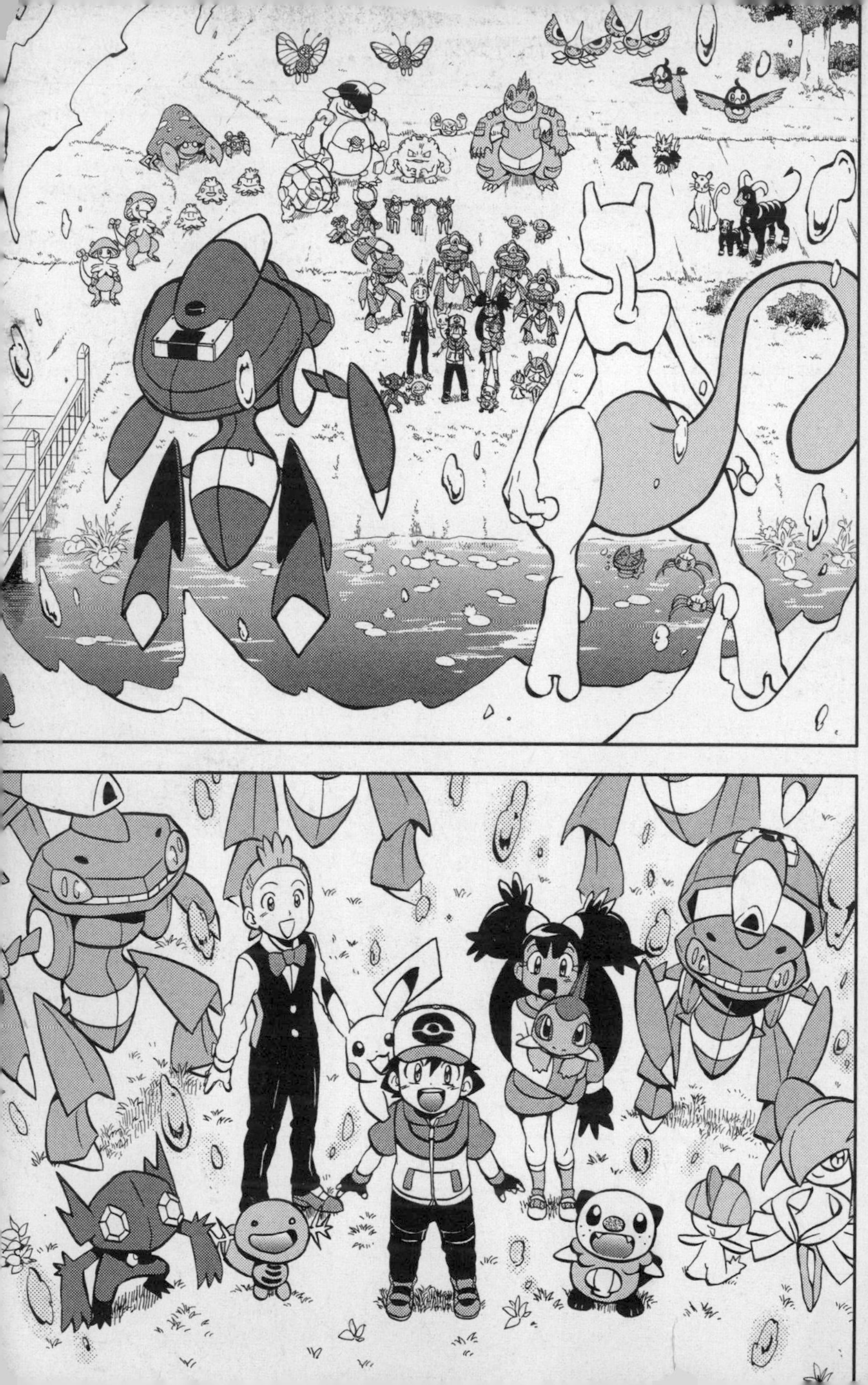

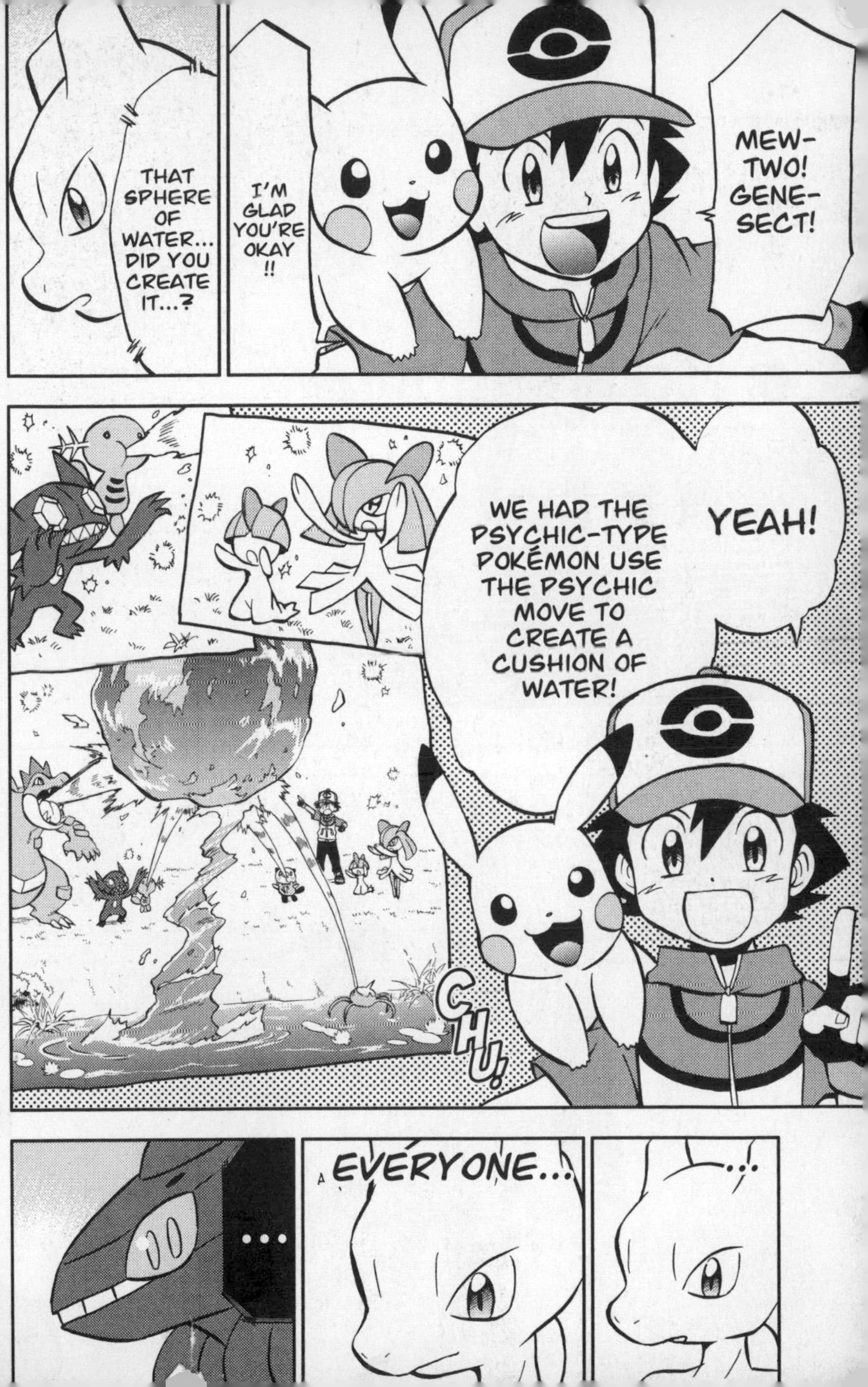
MEW-TWO! GENE-SECT!
I'M GLAD YOU'RE OKAY !!
THAT SPHERE OF WATER... DID YOU CREATE IT...?
YEAH!
WE HAD THE PSYCHIC-TYPE POKÉMON USE THE PSYCHIC MOVE TO CREATE A CUSHION OF WATER!
CHU!
...
EVERYONE...
...

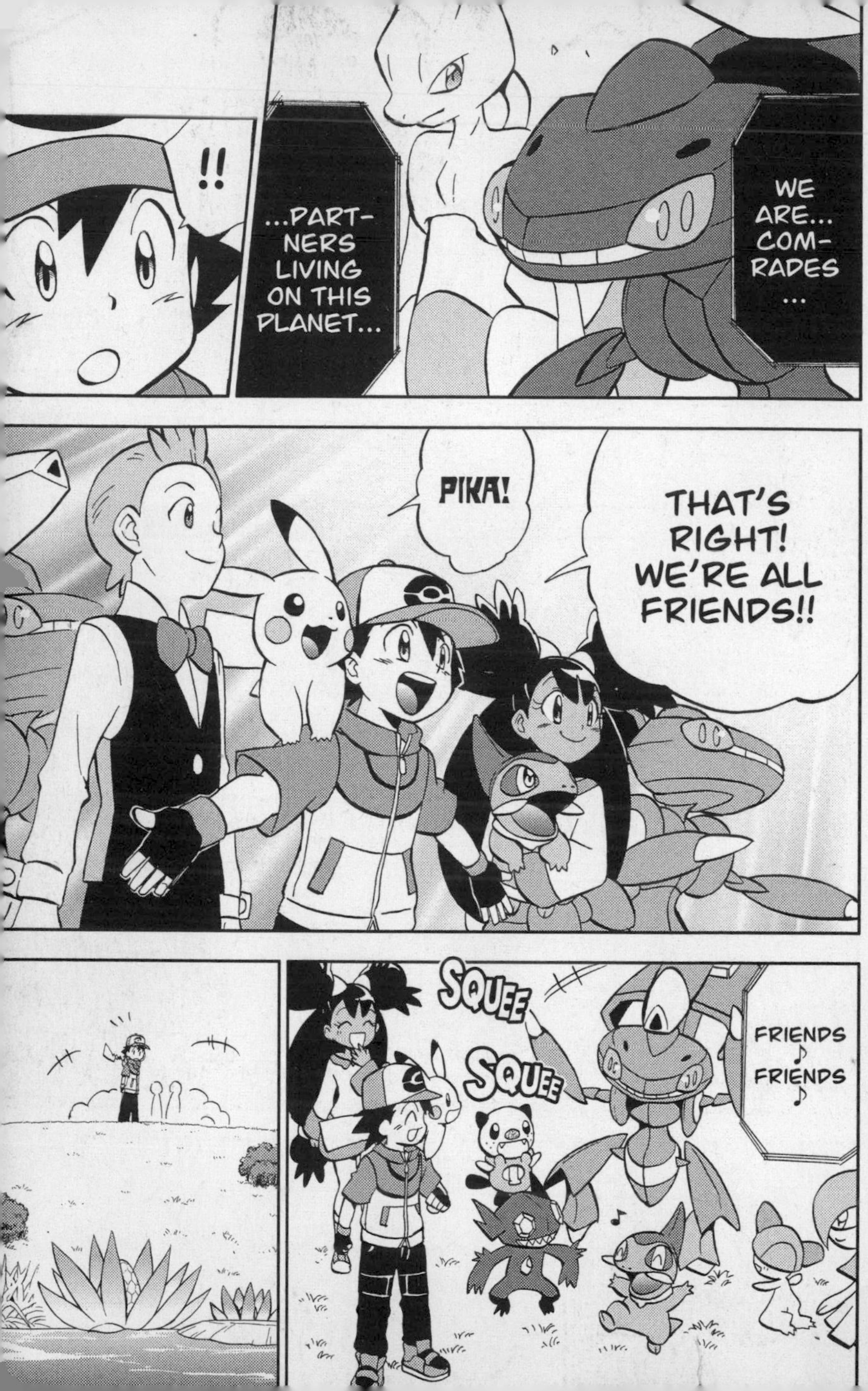
WE ARE... COM-RADES ...
...PART-NERS LIVING ON THIS PLANET...
!!
THAT'S RIGHT! WE'RE ALL FRIENDS!!
PIKA!
FRIENDS ♪ FRIENDS ♪
SQUEE
SQUEE

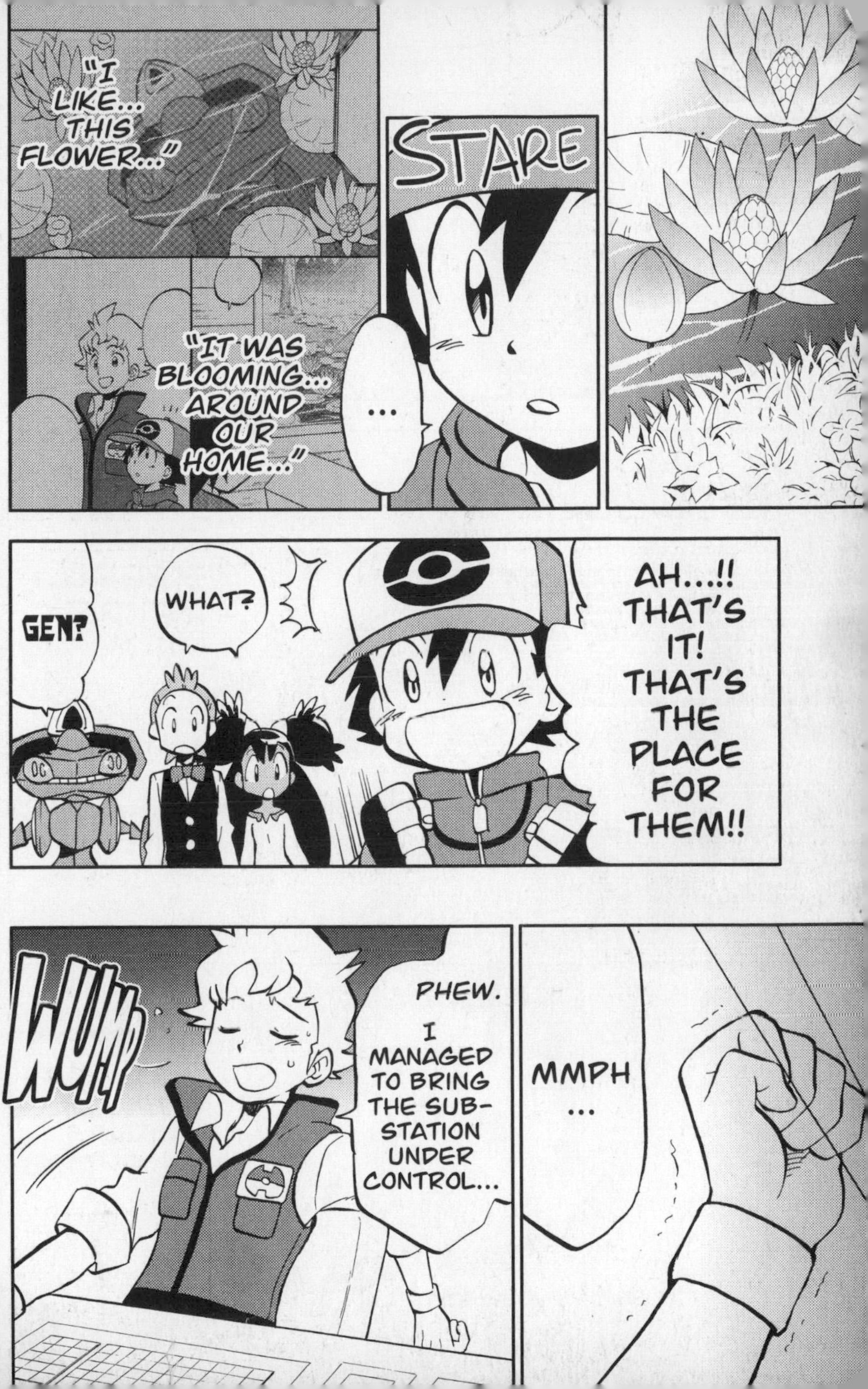
STARE
...
"I LIKE... THIS FLOWER..."
"IT WAS BLOOMING... AROUND OUR HOME..."
AH...!! THAT'S IT! THAT'S THE PLACE FOR THEM!!
WHAT?
GEN?
MMPH ...
PHEW.
I MANAGED TO BRING THE SUB-STATION UNDER CONTROL...
WUMP

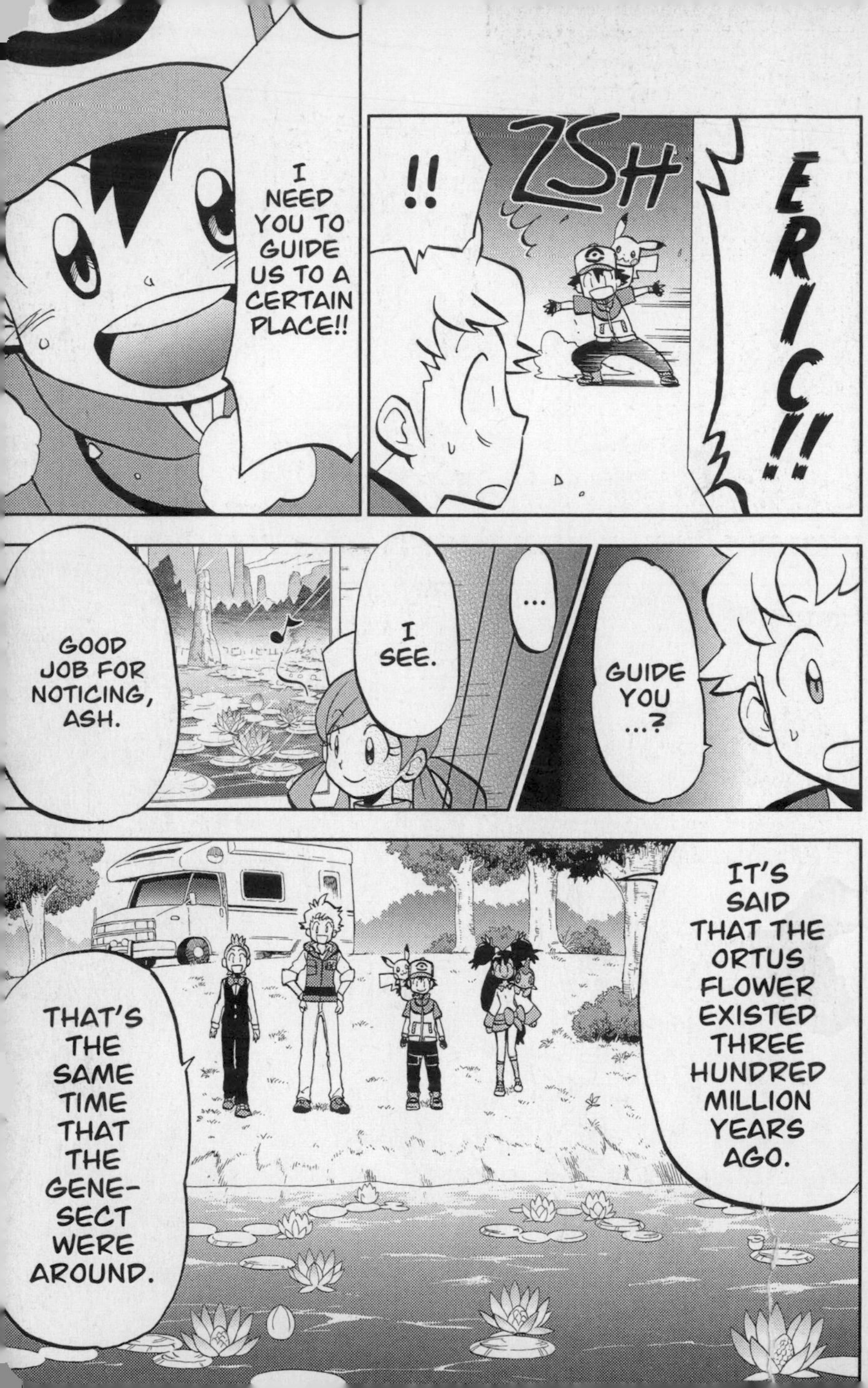
ERIC!!
ZSH
!!
I NEED YOU TO GUIDE US TO A CERTAIN PLACE!!
GUIDE YOU ...?
...
I SEE.
GOOD JOB FOR NOTICING, ASH.
IT'S SAID THAT THE ORTUS FLOWER EXISTED THREE HUNDRED MILLION YEARS AGO.
THAT'S THE SAME TIME THAT THE GENESECT WERE AROUND.

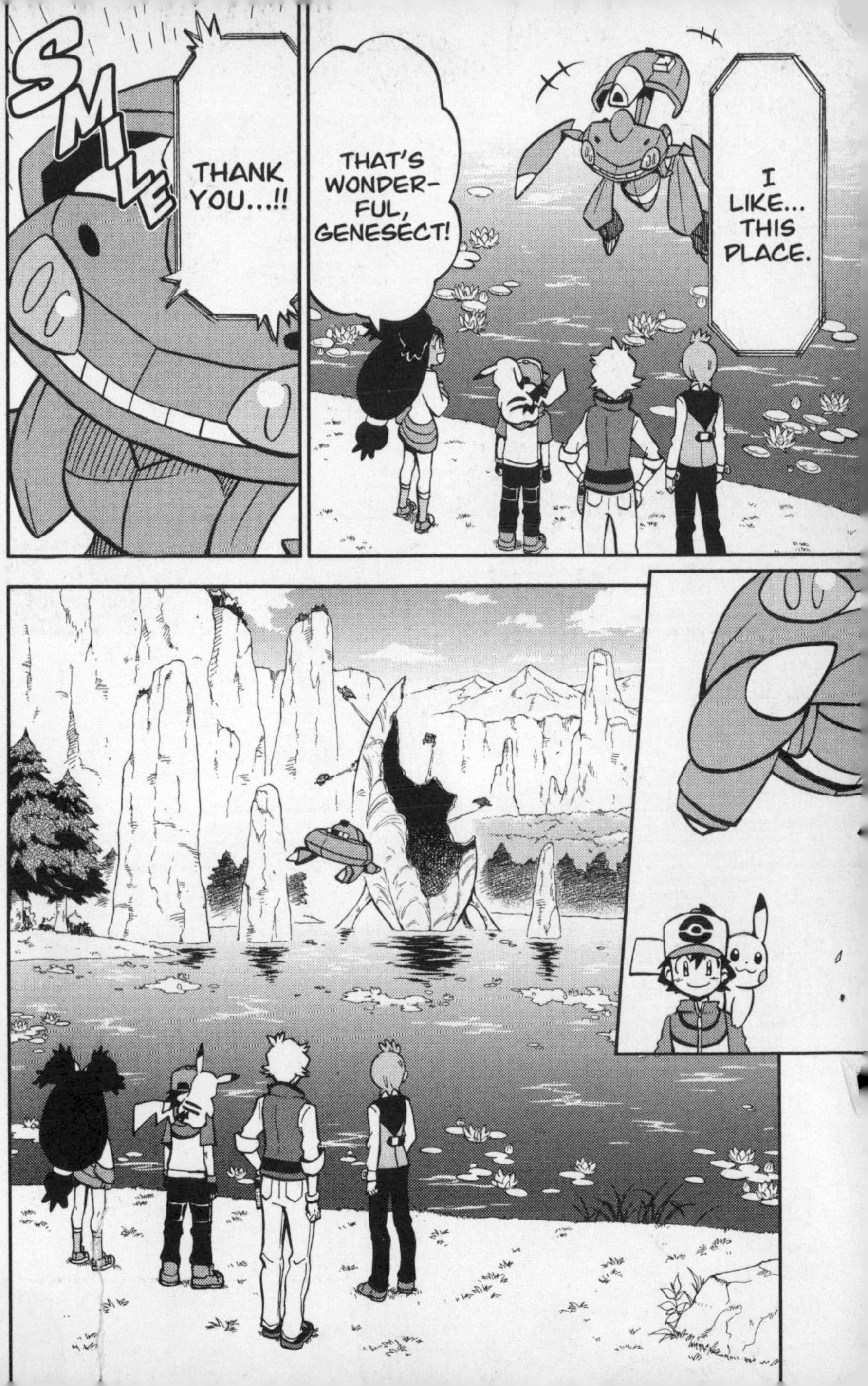
I LIKE... THIS PLACE.
THAT'S WONDER-FUL, GENESECT!
THANK YOU...!!
SMILE

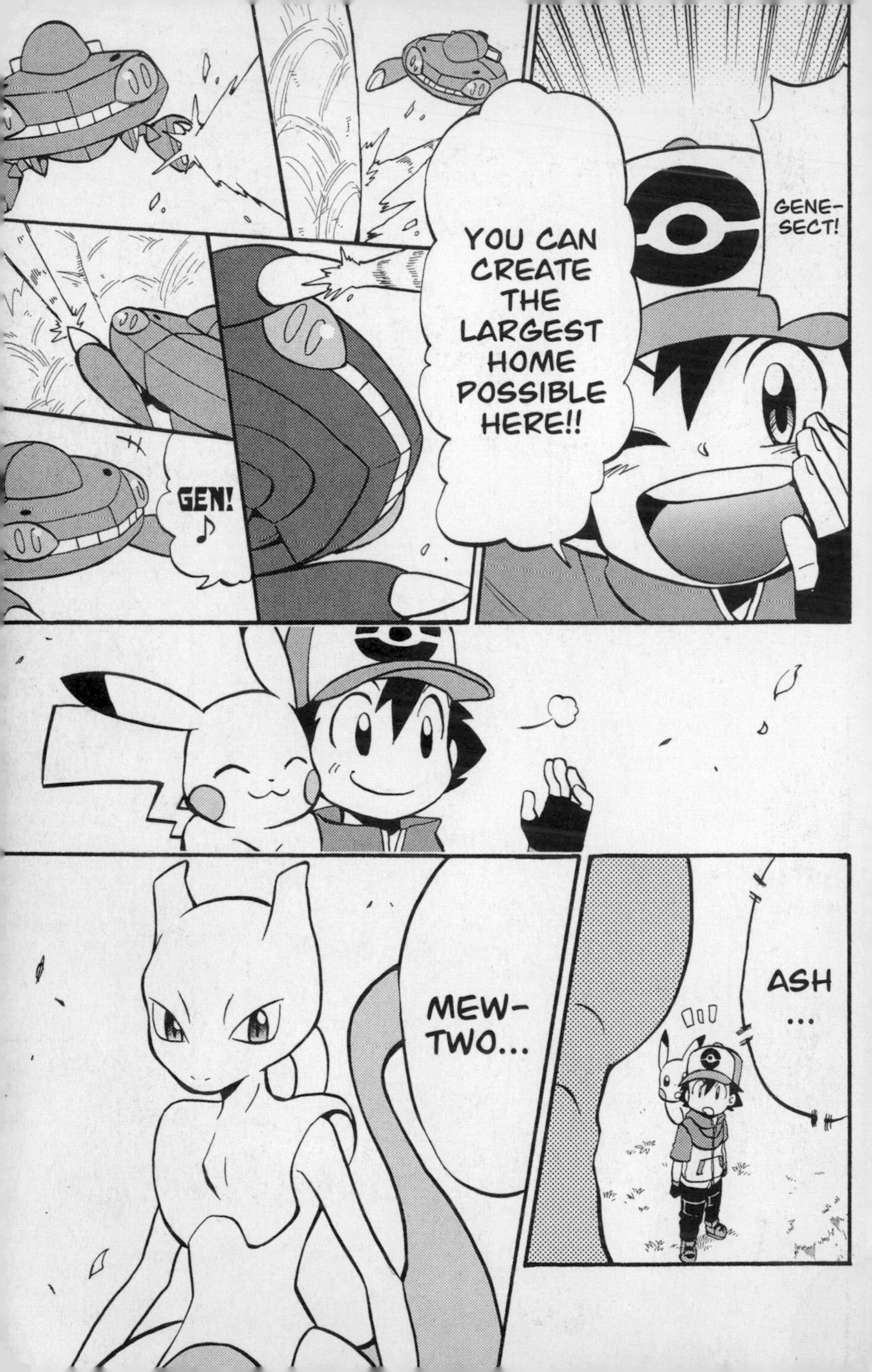
GENE-SECT!
YOU CAN CREATE THE LARGEST HOME POSSIBLE HERE!!
GEN! ♪
ASH ...
MEW-TWO...

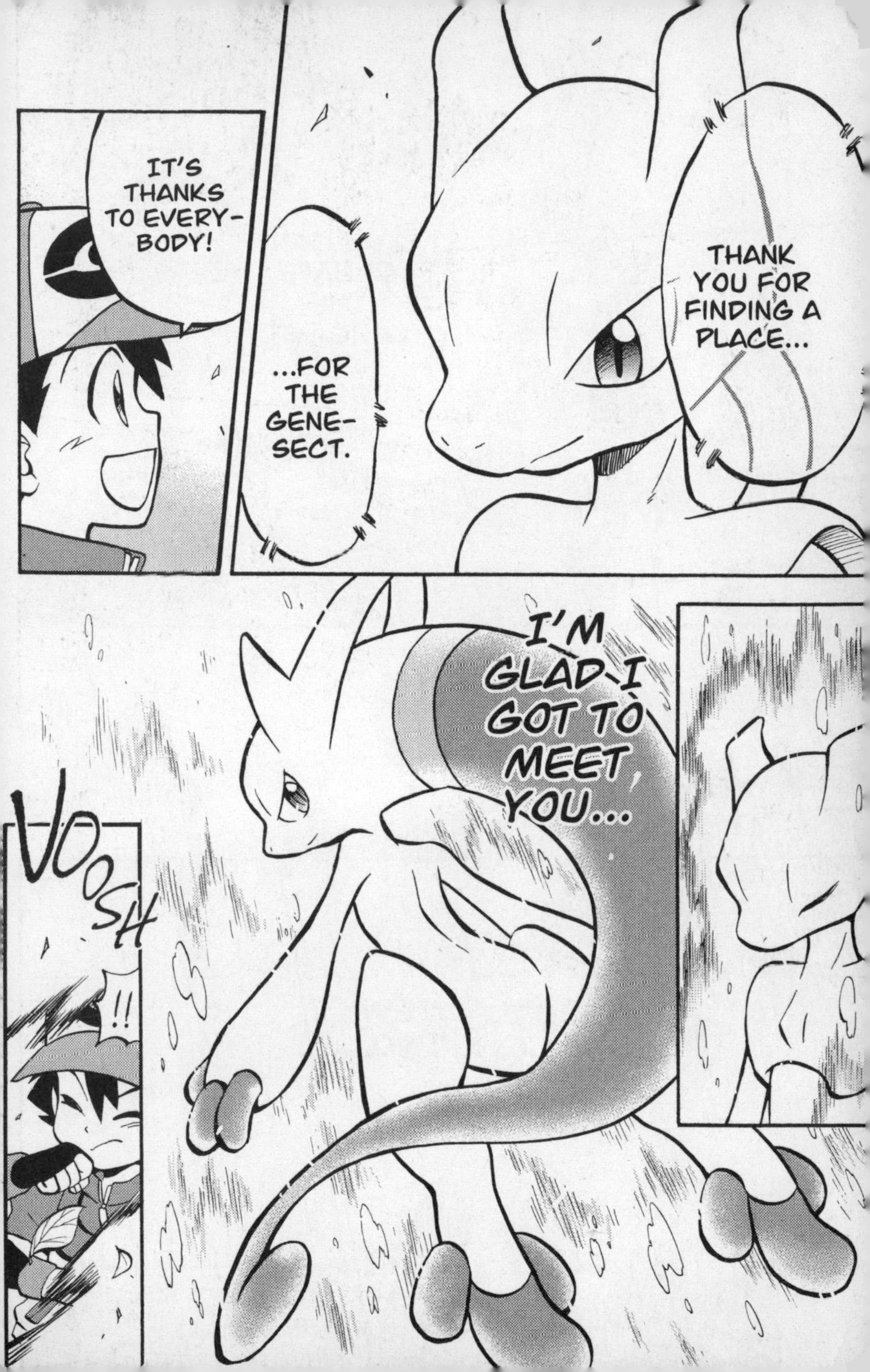
THANK YOU FOR FINDING A PLACE...
...FOR THE GENE-SECT.
IT'S THANKS TO EVERY-BODY!
I'M GLAD I GOT TO MEET YOU...
VOOSH
!!

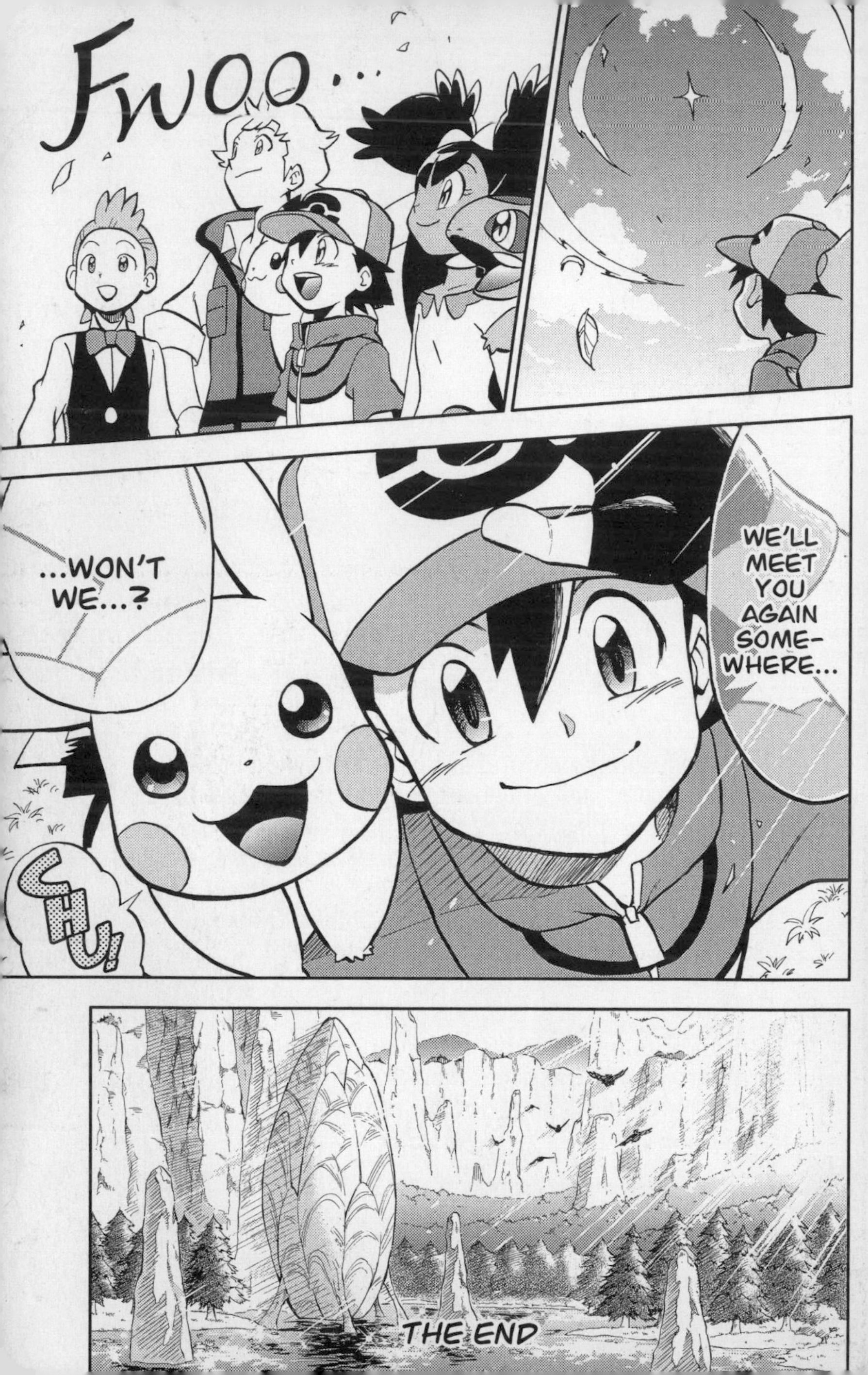
Fwoo...
WE'LL MEET YOU AGAIN SOME-WHERE...
...WON'T WE...?
CHU!
THE END

MOMOTA INOUE

ARTIST

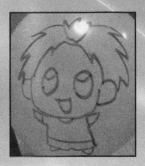

I usually lounge around at home, but when I start working, I'm suddenly overcome by the urge to go outside and play. Once I finish my work, however, I end up lounging around at home again...

The image above was drawn by Chihiro Okitsune, who debuted around the same time I did!

Born on June 19, 1985, in Saitama Prefecture, Momota Inoue received the 58th Shogakukan Rookie Comic Grand Prize for the Children's Division in 2006 for *Red Enza*.

POKÉMON THE MOVIE:
GENESECT AND THE LEGEND AWAKENED
VIZ Kids Edition

Story and Art by MOMOTA INOUE

© 2013 Pokémon.
© 1998-2013 PIKACHU PROJECT. TM, ®, and character names are trademarks of Nintendo.
GEKIJO BAN POCKET MONSTERS SHINSOKU NO GENOSEKUTO MEWTWO KAKUSEI
by Momota INOUE
© 2013 Momota INOUE
All right reserved.
Original Japanese edition published by SHOGAKUKAN.
English translation rights in the United States of America, Canada, the United Kingdom
and Ireland arranged with SHOGAKUKAN.

Translation/ Tetsuichiro Miyaki
Touch-up & Lettering/Annaliese Christman
Design/Izumi Evers
Editor/Amy Yu

Printed in the U.S.A.

Published by VIZ Media, LLC
P.O. Box 77010
San Francisco, CA 94107

10 9 8 7 6 5 4 3 2 1
First printing, December 2013

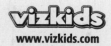
www.vizkids.com

www.viz.com

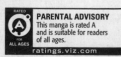
RATED
PARENTAL ADVISORY
This manga is rated A
and is suitable for readers
of all ages.
ratings.viz.com

FOLLOW US!

W9-BMY-705

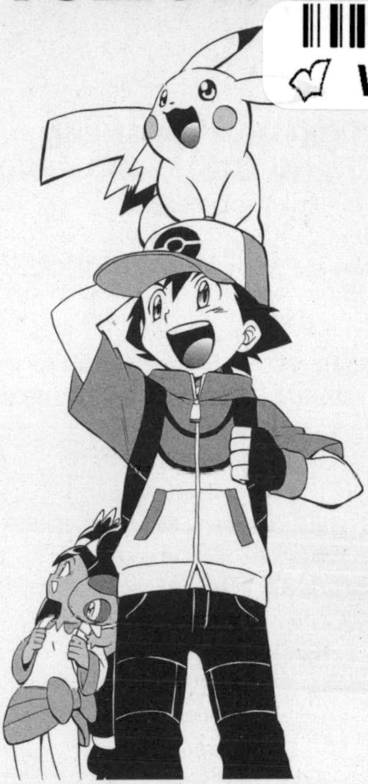

WE'LL SHOW YOU HOW TO READ
THIS GRAPHIC NOVEL!

To properly enjoy this VIZ Kids graphic novel, please turn it around and begin reading from right to left.

This book has been printed in the original Japanese format in order to keep the placement of the original artwork. Have fun with it!

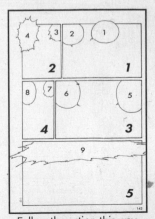

Follow the action this way.